Dear Annie,

Please accept this humble gift.

This is far from a perfectly written book but I hope the story will inspire you in your amazing journey. And in times of Darkness, look for the light!

You are a great co-worker and an amazing kind person. Don't ever forget that!
Keep Shinning,

Regina Santos
2022

A LIGHT
in the
DARKNESS

REGINA SANTOS

ISBN-978-1-66781-563-3

Copyright © 2011 by Regina Santos

All rights reserved. This book or any portion thereof may not be reproduced or used in any manner whatsoever without the express written permission of the publisher/ author except for the use of brief quotations in a book review.

This is a work of fiction. Names, characters, places, and incidents either are products of the author's imagination or are used fictitiously. Any resemblance to actual events or locales or persons, living or dead, is entirely coincidental.

ACKNOWLEDGMENTS

For my parents, Luciano Alcides dos Santos Filho, Selma Elias Dos Santos, and my son, Gregory Santos, whose compassion, patience, understanding, and love have always encouraged my writings.

A special thanks to everyone who helped me correct this book to the best of their abilities.

Without their support, I would never have made it.

This book is especially dedicated to all soldiers who fought during WWII, sacrificing their own lives for liberty.

PART ONE

CHAPTER 1

1939 arrived swiftly on the frosty fields of a picturesque northern French town, partially surrounded by dark peaky mountains and a vast emerald green lake. A walk through town wouldn't have been anything special if it weren't for the whispers of war that could be heard on every corner of every street. Tension filled the air, making it even thicker than usual, and Francine grew concerned.

She was walking slowly; her mind was somewhere far away. But who was she fooling? She was so involved in trying to fix the world's problems and planning the next moves that she often felt overwhelmed, frustrated, or perhaps just tired of dealing with all the nonsense around her. Francine thought that fighting for equality and justice would be a glorious and exciting road. However, it didn't take long for her to realize that such a road, although noble, was full of disappointments. She became exhausted with the continuous task of making people realize how hypocritical and oppressive society and their governments could be and how much still needed to be done in order to achieve concrete changes. But it was more than that. She felt trapped in the societal role that all women were expected to play. *I was never born to be inside a household, keeping my thoughts to myself and having to plan my entire life around a marriage*, she thought. No … Francine wanted more.

"Bonjour, mademoiselle," Felipe said, standing outside with his apron on.

"Bonjour, Felipe." She smiled at him. "Comment ça vas cette matin?"

"*Ça va*, Francine," he said. "Ready for some fresh bread, I assume?"

"Bien sûr," she replied.

She entered the boulangerie, heading straight to a table in the corner by the window—her favorite spot. With a cup of coffee in her hands and a warm baguette on the table, she couldn't avoid hearing the conversations around her.

"The war will happen," a man said. "I'm sure of that."

"Of course," another one replied. "Those German bastards can't wait to strike again. They'll try everything possible."

"Nobody talks about anything else besides war," Felipe whispered, passing by her table.

"Salut, Francine," Roberto said, turning around. "What do you have to say?"

Francine was already used to those questions, but she never believed they were interested in hearing her opinion. It was more a matter of amusement for the guys. They had grown accustomed to her commenting on any subject, even when no one had asked her opinion. They thought it was somewhat interesting that she, as a woman, would open her mouth and analyze anything political.

"Speculations or not, what can we do?" Francine quickly replied. "It seems there are no limits for ambition; we human beings always want more, especially in the case of Germany. I wouldn't be surprised if another war arrives. And if so, I can only hope we will be ready for it!"

"Bravo, Francine," said Roberto, along with the others, nodding in approval.

The discussion continued, growing more intense like the wind outside, crushing against the boulangerie windows in waves as Francine left the bakery.

The cold air brushed against Francine's fair skin while her trembling fingers rushed to button up her overcoat. She looked up and noticed the heavy clouds moving in, announcing an imminent storm. As she rushed home, her high-heeled shoes echoed off the cobblestones, making a distinct clicking sound as if she was the only one out walking. The atmosphere was so ominous that Francine felt as if something terrible was about to happen.

"Francine," her mother, Nicole, greeted her. "You left again without eating breakfast. What has gotten into you?"

"Oh, Mother, please," she said, placing the fresh baguette on the table. "I just wanted to go for a walk, and I ended up getting some bread."

"What are you stressing about this time?" her mother asked her in a very familiar tone of voice.

Francine knew the question that was to follow.

"Why can't you just be like the other girls?" her mother continued as expected. "You should find yourself a nice husband."

"There you go again," Francine said, already irritated. "I don't want to talk about that right now."

"When will you ever want to talk about it?" her mother said, throwing her hands up in the air.

Having no desire to continue that conversation, Francine decided to ignore the comment. She knew she wouldn't be able to change her mind. *Why was it so difficult for anyone to understand that my entire life didn't and shouldn't revolve around finding someone to marry*? She just felt so young. She still had so many other things she wanted to do and places she wanted to visit. Francine wanted to travel, get to know other cultures, and meet different people. She wanted to feel free and alive; as for love, well … she felt that could probably wait, or so she was trying to convince herself.

It was later in the day when Francine decided to go to the library and get a book. She settled down on her favorite couch, trying to make herself comfortable.

She loved that room. It was the perfect spot in the house to have privacy and silence, a place where her thoughts could flow free from outside interferences. In there, she was surrounded by knowledge and wisdom, a priceless collection of books inherited from her father's family.

The fireplace kept the room warm from the chill forming on the large windows next to where she was lying. She opened one of her favorite poetry books. Poetry had the power to make her dream, to take her thoughts away from her endless routine.

Francine had a particular preference for nostalgic poems. At first glance, that seemed to be as far as her romantic side would go. But deep inside, Francine knew she was a woman full of passion and desire. Although she had always felt she was too young to love deeply, she knew something had changed in her heart. That very thought bothered her. She closed her eyes and slowly laid her book on her chest. She knew exactly why she had picked that particular book to read.

CHAPTER 2

Three months had passed since Francine saw his face for the first time—one of those encounters that stays in one's mind forever. It happened during one of her quick trips to Switzerland. She had stopped at her favorite café, needing to kill time before meeting a few friends at a restaurant later on that day.

The pretty but simple green dress graciously hugged the contours of her body. A few black pins held part of her dark brown hair against the back of her head, leaving the remaining silky locks brushing the nape of her neck, revealing some shades of red. On her delicate face, plump and colored lips contrasted against the fair tone of her skin. Such a gentle and subtle appearance often disguised her strong personality. But if one looked closer, deep into her enigmatic green eyes, they could see the soul of a woman who was filled with passion for everything she believed in and was willing to fight for.

She held a book in her hands while a soothing French song played in the background. The place although small, had a peculiar atmosphere, due to its aged wooden furniture and the metal oil lamps scattered in all corners, revealing a rustic appearance, somewhat similar to a medieval tavern. And it was in that special setting that everything happened.

Like a mysterious instinct, Francine suddenly and without thinking turned her head toward the door. At that exact moment, their eyes met. He was a handsome, blond young man with the most stunning blue eyes she had ever seen.

It all happened in a split second, but that was all it took to capture her attention. She immediately looked back to her book, trying to pretend she hadn't seen him, but somehow, it felt like the man was still looking at her.

A group of young men sat only two tables away. Just like that, the quiet and peacefulness were over. Not only were they all talking a little loudly, but to Francine's further aggravation, she quickly realized by their conversation that they were probably Germans. The resentment from WWI never really went away, especially when there was a deep concern about another war to come.

Despite the unexpected interruption, Francine tried to resume her reading. She, of course, couldn't concentrate after that, no matter how hard she tried. Once in a while, Francine caught herself looking at him again, as if an inexplicable force was pulling her. She tried to stop herself from taking those quick looks but found that she simply couldn't. It didn't help that he also kept looking at her in a very discreet way. This did not escape Francine's attention either. She started to feel more uncomfortable and couldn't read anymore.

Francine slowly placed the book on the table, trying to coordinate her thoughts. She contemplated leaving, but she felt like she was glued to her seat for some strange reason.

"I'm sorry," a voice said suddenly, interrupting her thoughts. "I hope we are not bothering you?"

It was him, that young blonde man who was still sitting in the same spot only a few tables away. He looked right into her eyes.

Francine sat there, mute for a few seconds, as if she were hypnotized by those piercing blue eyes. They reflected a vivid and unique shade of blue. And yet, they were soft and strangely familiar, emitting calm and goodness.

The young man and his friends were still waiting for an answer. It didn't take Francine any longer to reply once she snapped out of her trance.

"Oh no, not really," Francine rushed to say in German. She stumbled on her own words, feeling somewhat awkward. She hated lying, but she was caught off guard and didn't want to be rude.

"We are probably disturbing your reading, right?" he then said in French.

"Oh, it's just a silly book," she replied, shaking her head and yet shocked by his choice of language.

Francine wanted to say more, but she hesitated. He made her feel nervous and shy.

She smiled timidly and picked up the book from the table, pretending to read it.

The young man smiled back at her, feeling something different. He noticed the surprised look on her face once he spoke French.

"I went to school here in Switzerland almost my entire life," he continued. " That's how I learned French, although I still have an accent. Then I went back home … to Germany."

"Oh, I see," Francine replied in a cold, disappointed tone. And even though that confirmed her suspicion, the mere fact that their eyes met again made her heart beat faster; her hands started sweating.

He clearly noticed the disenchanted expression on her face. But he wasn't ready to give up.

"Have you ever been there? Germany?" he asked her in German as his friends tried not to laugh.

She looked right at him, feeling a little uneasy. She couldn't tell if he was trying to have fun at her expense or if he was simply curious. Unable to figure it out, Francine didn't hesitate, and, as was customary for her, she tried to regain her composure. She put her book back down on the table and straightened herself up.

"No, I have never been there, and I probably never will," Francine spoke fluently in German, albeit with a slight accent.

All the boys looked at one another, surprised by her assertive demeanor.

"Really? And why is that?" the same man rushed to ask, feeling even more interested after her sharp reply in his native language.

Francine observed the adverse reaction she had triggered from his friends with such an answer. She actually enjoyed it. But she was still puzzled. When she looked at the young man's face, it showed no outward sign of hostility, but she still wasn't sure if he was being sarcastic or serious. She honestly didn't know how to react, which wasn't very typical for her. There was something about him that made her feel challenged, and she liked that. His interest in hearing what she had to say caught her by surprise. It made her feel alive.

"Well …" She hesitated for a moment, trying to find the right words. "I have other places I would rather go. I like places where there is peace, where people have concerns on their minds other than …."

"Other than what?" he asked with a disappointed tone in his voice.

"Do I really need to say it? Francine replied with confidence. "I guess we all know what I was referring to, don't we?"

An awkward silence filled the air. "Listen," she continued, looking straight back at him. "I think it's better if we don't talk about that. I'm sure none of us really want to have *that* conversation."

He smiled at her, or perhaps at the cute way she moved her hands while she talked.

"I'm sorry again, mademoiselle. I just enjoy hearing people's opinions, different points of view. That's all." After a short pause, he finally said, "By the way, my name is Hans."

"Francine," she replied automatically, still surprised by his answer.

All of a sudden, she saw him getting up from his chair, coming toward her.

"C'est un plaisir de vous connaitre," Hans said, offering a hand shake.

She was caught off-guard again. Her whole body trembled once she felt the touch of his hand. She had never felt so out of place in her entire life. And to make matters worse, Hans still kept talking.

"That is a nice book you're reading," Hans said, looking at the cover.

"So, you like poetry?" Francine asked, surprised again.

"Yes, some. There are a few styles of poems I like. I guess the ones that tell stories I can relate to; the ones that are a little more dramatic, perhaps nostalgic. But I do love reading all kinds of subjects in general."

Francine's lips opened slowly, staying in that position for a few seconds. Those were exactly the kind of poems she liked to read. Intrigued by the attentive way he spoke to her and his intelligent choice of words, Francine wanted to hear more of what he had to say.

Hans's friends had stopped looking at them and were engaged in their own separate conversations. Francine sensed that one of them, in particular, didn't really seem to like her at all, especially when she was talking about Germany. Of course, it was clear that they had realized she was French, and not all of them seemed to like that idea. But she didn't let it bother her much; something else was taking up all her attention and interest.

Hans was still standing right in front of her. His platinum blonde hair perfectly complemented the unique shade of his blue eyes; he was tall and relatively thin, although he had a nice body shape. There was a certain distinguished elegance about his manners and the way he spoke to her. Hans was charming without trying to be, and his strong arms and hands gave him a very masculine presence that Francine couldn't help but notice. There was a sort of energy surrounding them, an invisible line that kept them connected to one another.

She couldn't resist the desire to invite him to sit down at her table. She wanted him to come closer.

As the conversation went on, she kept trying to remind herself that Hans was a German man. But that was becoming a more difficult task by the minute. There was just something different about him that she couldn't ignore – something so genuine, intriguing, and unexpectedly fascinating. Hans spoke with his heart, full of idealism and passion for everything that he believed. He spoke truthfully. And he did it without trying too hard or trying to impress her.

Francine paid close attention to every word he said, but she couldn't stop her eyes from constantly glancing at his lips. Lips that moved perfectly by the sensual sound of his voice, making her heart slowly melt.

Hans was also very interested in hearing every word she had to say – especially opinions about controversial subjects – and she knew how hard it was to find a man like that.

The two of them managed to talk for over an hour. They had so much in common and got along so well that it seemed as if the conversation passed in only a few minutes. They talked about many things that inspired them: politics, humanity, books, music, places they had been, places they wanted to visit. They understood and comprehended exactly what the other wanted to say as if they had known each other for a long time.

The sun had already set; they didn't realize how long they had been talking until his friends were finally standing right in front of them.

"We are going to the pub, Hans," one of them said.

"Right," Hans replied, trying to think on what to say next.

"It's all right, Hans," Francine said. "I have to leave, too."

"I'll catch up with you guys later," he said sharply.

"All right," one of his friends said, giving Francine an unfriendly look. The others simply smiled at Hans, noticing his interest in the girl.

They both waited quietly until Hans's friends were gone.

"I think they might be upset with you. It's all right if you want to go with your friends. I'll understand," Francine said, without meaning a word of it. Her heart was beating fast. She did not want him to leave.

"That is all right," Hans said, feeling the same way. "They'll be just fine without me. Do you have a place you have to go to?"

"No," she quickly replied, happy with his response. "I mean, not until later."

A sweet and gentle smile spread across his face. There was nothing else that he wanted more than to be there with her.

For a brief moment, they looked at one another without exchanging a word. Strong emotions stirred deeply inside their hearts. But those were things that could only be felt and not spoken.

They smiled at one another again before resuming their conversation.

Immersed in their philosophical and engaging subjects, Francine and Hans lost track of time once more. That was until a lady working at the café informed them that they were closing.

Francine looked at Hans as if trying to figure out a way for the evening to continue. Hans looked away for a few seconds, afraid to reveal his own feelings and yet also trying to find a way not to let her go …

But at that moment, there wasn't much either one could do about it. They knew it was time to leave and what that would mean to one another.

Francine noticed how slowly they were both moving, trying to get their coats on, trying to delay the inevitable.

Outside, the dry autumn leaves swirled fast with the wind, leaving behind a brushing sound that announced changes.

Already on the sidewalk, they were trying to find a way to say goodbye. Francine didn't want to leave. She didn't want to go anywhere. Looking at Hans, she tried to find any signs that would show her he felt the same way.

"Alor, this is goodbye then," Francine said, trying to act casually as if their departure was nothing special.

"I guess so …" were the only words Hans was able to say, desperately trying to think of something to keep her by his side, even for just a moment longer.

"Bien …" Francine said, pausing for a moment. "It was really nice to meet you, Hans."

"See, Francine," Hans said, looking deep into her eyes, "not all of us are the same."

She knew exactly what he meant.

But more than that, his last words instantly impacted her emotions, bringing tears to her eyes. Overwhelmed by a feeling that she couldn't understand, she quickly looked away for a few seconds to avoid embarrassing herself.

"Well, you stay safe, Francine, wherever the wind may take you," Hans said, his voice reflecting the strange sadness that started to consume his soul.

Francine looked into his beautiful blue eyes again, eyes that reminded her of clear skies brightened by the sun. Hans's eyes worked like mirrors, reflecting light and generating sweet warmth into her heart.

"You too, Hans," Francine said, feeling the same pain.

"Perhaps … it will take you to Germany, who knows?"

Suddenly, a cold chill filled her entire body, leaving her with a strange sensation.

"We'll never know," she replied, raising her eyebrows.

He stared into her green eyes as if it was the last time he would ever see her. Then, finding it hard to continue, his voice sounded a little shaky. "Adieu," he said, offering a final hand shake.

"Au revoir, Hans," Francine said as she reached out for his hand.

She took a few steps backward, smiling at him, and then turned around. Her heart was fluttering in her chest. Confused and unsettled by a wave of sadness that took hold of her soul, she kept walking forward without noticing where she was going. She had no idea that Hans stood still for a few seconds, watching her walk away.

He wanted to say something, anything that would make her turn around and return to him. He sighed deeply. As much as it pained him to see the distance growing between them, he felt there wasn't much to be done.

Hans took one more look at her and turned around, walking in the opposite direction. In his head, thousands of thoughts came rushing in. He felt frustrated, and almost angry with himself. It was as if he was letting go of something that meant a lot to him.

Francine took a few extra steps and couldn't resist looking back. She saw that Hans was walking away. She stood there for a few seconds looking at him, not understanding what was going on with her. She hesitated for a few seconds before looking down, wondering if there was something that she could say or do.

As she resumed walking, trying to push these thoughts out of her mind, her breath caught when she heard a voice calling her from across the street.

"Francine!" Hans yelled from the other side.

Her heart nearly stopped as she looked straight back at him and smiled.

"Oui?"

"Do you need me to walk you somewhere?" Hans asked her, hopeful. "It's getting late. I'm sorry. I should have asked you before."

"It's all right, Hans," Francine said. "You don't need to worry. Merci."

"All right, then," he said, standing there on the other side of the street, extremely disappointed. "Until someday then."

"Until next time," Francine said, looking right at him and already regretting what she had just said.

He turned around and continued walking. He knew then there was nothing else he could do. He tried to push those thoughts away, pretending to ignore the power of that overwhelming feeling that took control of his heart; *what was I thinking? I just met this girl!*

Francine watched him for a few seconds more before she started moving again. She felt frustrated with herself. She did not know why she said that. The truth was that she was just trying to be polite, but of course, she was still expecting him to offer again.

She took a few extra steps forward and suddenly stopped, looking back at him. She had decided to take him up on his offer. But it was too late; Hans was already disappearing around the corner. She wanted to run after him and invite him to the restaurant where she was supposed to meet some friends, but she hesitated as she felt it wasn't appropriate. She didn't want him to get the wrong impression. *What am I thinking?* she asked herself. *I just met this guy!*

Francine turned around again, trying to convince herself that meeting Hans wasn't anything too special, but her heart said something very different. She started to feel a sense of emptiness taking hold of her soul. It was something so profound, a feeling she had never felt possible.

As Francine walked away, she realized that the distance between both of them was growing. She felt it in her heart. It could have been the last time she saw his face, and with that thought, she stopped. She looked back one more time. She passed her fingers through her hair, trying to gain some time to think, but it was hopeless, and she knew it.

She shook her head in disapproval and resumed walking toward the restaurant.

Francine tried to think about something else the entire night, pretending to pay attention to her friends and their conversations. But her thoughts stubbornly kept going back to Hans, wishing she had accepted his offer, wondering if she would ever see him again. At the same time, she was trying to make some sense out of what had just happened. She couldn't understand the sorrow that filled her heart, that strange sense of emptiness. It was as if everything in her life would never be the same again.

CHAPTER 3

Francine slowly opened her eyes and looked out the window. At that moment, she missed Hans. She missed his voice, his beautiful smile, the way he looked at her, and the way he made her feel. Hans was someone who listened to what she had to say, appreciating every word. He was the first person in a long time that made her feel understood with no need for elaborate explanations.

She took a deep breath as if she had just woken up from a dream. *How could that be possible?* She thought to herself. *First, he is German! And second, I just met him once, only for a few hours.*

Despite her logic, it was hopeless; she couldn't find a way to keep him out of her heart and mind. She wondered if he was also thinking about her. *Probably not,* she concluded, feeling silly just thinking about the possibility. But deep inside, Francine knew very well that she had fallen in love with that young German man. And, as ironic as it sounded, he was the man she could see herself with for the rest of her life.

Hans was very different from the men she had met before. He could make her believe that all her dreams were possible and her ideals something significant and profound. She could picture herself traveling with him to different parts of the world, expanding her horizons, experiencing other cultures, and doing something meaningful and exciting with her life, fighting for a good cause. No other man had ever made her feel that way. Francine's enthusiasm and passion had finally found a safe harbor within Hans's ideals and desire.

"Francine, ma chérie, you're here," a familiar voice brought her back from her dreams. It was Francine's father, Jean Dufort, a man in his late fifties.

Although he could be very strict at times, he was a good father, a good man with a big heart. Francine had definitely inherited his passion for literature, free-thinking, and debate.

"Mon père," Francine said, with a big smile on her face. "Bonjour."

"Bonjour?" Jean said, chuckling. "It's already past noon, my darling. Where have you been? Daydreaming again?"

"Yes, maybe," Francine said, still thinking about Hans. Part of her wanted to tell someone about him, share her feelings, but she knew it would be too hard to do so. Even she couldn't quite understand what was happening to her.

"Oh, I foresee trouble," Jean said, looking in her eyes.

"It's nothing, father. Really!" Francine replied, trying to push away those thoughts about Hans.

"I know you, Francine. Something is bothering you, something more than the usual."

She smiled faintly as she got up and walked toward him. "I'm just thinking about normal things," Francine said, kissing his cheek. "Don't worry."

"You never were a good liar. So, what is it that has been bothering you?" Jean asked, heading toward Francine's favorite couch. He sat there looking at her, patiently waiting for her to speak.

Francine sighed and looked away for a few seconds. She walked slowly toward the bookshelves, sliding her fingers along them.

"Father," she said, pausing and reflecting on her choice of words very carefully. "Do you think there is love strong enough to make you forget about the things you hate the most?"

Jean gave Francine a sweet smile. He knew there was a special reason for his daughter's daydreaming over the past few months.

"Francine, love is the most powerful thing in the universe," Jean told her as he gazed out the window. "If there is one thing that can cure hate, well … that has got to be it!"

She paid close attention to every word he said before she spoke again.

"So, love justifies certain things then, right?" Francine said, turning around and facing the bookshelf again.

"Who is he?" Jean said, feeling a little concerned. "Do I know him?"

"Oh, Dad, that is not it."

"Whatever it is, it has gotten into your head and doesn't appear to be leaving any time soon," Jean said, getting up to hold her small hands in his. "But my daughter, just be careful. Find out if he's really a good man. If he really loves you and he respects you, then let fate play its part."

"Love? No, Dad, it's nothing like that," Francine quickly replied, feeling embarrassed. "I was just asking a question. It is nothing special."

Jean raised her chin and looked right into his daughter's eyes. "Whoever he is, he must be special. Who else could steal your heart?"

Francine shook her head, trying to deny it to herself. She looked at her father's face and kept quiet. She didn't want to lie, but then again, she couldn't tell the truth. So, she said nothing.

Understanding that gesture, Jean decided to respect her silence. He knew she wasn't ready to tell him what he already suspected. But he believed that sooner or later, she would reveal the identity of the man who managed to do the impossible. Francine was in love.

Ten months had passed since Francine's encounter with Hans. Although she always thought and dreamed of him, she was focused on the real possibility of war after Germany had invaded Poland. It was difficult for anyone to accept the fact that, once again, war could be part of their lives. It had not been long since the end of World War I, and people still carried the scars and trauma of its horrors.

Francine would soon find her father busier than usual with his social-political agenda. Jean was a respected doctor who was also involved in political matters that could benefit society overall as well as his local community. Francine would often listen to the conversations between him and his friends when they were gathered at the library in her house to discuss politics. She would always get valuable information that she could use in the meetings she attended downtown, along with some of her friends. They were part of a small political group with a somewhat Socialist agenda, a movement that was growing stronger among the youth across France. They advocated for women's rights and many other social issues that captured Francine's interest. She was proud to participate in any gathering that stood for equality and justice for all.

Francine, like her father, was also a humanitarian. She had attended a Swiss school and became a nurse. She would often help her father and other doctors in several distant locations where people lacked the means to pay for proper health care. She loved her job. It made her feel useful, giving her a great sense of purpose and independence which she valued most.

It was early in the morning on May 10th when Francine woke up to unusual agitation on her house's bottom floor. It was the year 1940, the year that would change her life forever.

"Bonjour," Francine said, watching her mother as she moved quickly from one room to the other with Marie, their helper.

"Bonjour, Francine," Nicole said quickly before leaving the kitchen again, followed by Marie, who had a tray with several tiny coffee cups. Francine could see that something really serious had happened. When her mother came back to the kitchen, she grabbed her.

"Mother, what's going on?"

"Francine," Nicole was whispering. "Germany has invaded us. Do you understand what that means?"

Francine slowly sat down on the chair next to the kitchen table. Although everyone was expecting the war, they still had hopes that it would never reach them.

"We'll talk more later," Nicole said with a sad look on her face.

Francine rushed behind the library door, sneaking into a spot where she knew she could hear the conversation taking place without being noticed. She wanted to gather as much information as possible to pass along to her friends in the meeting that night.

The streets and restaurants were busier than usual on that late Friday afternoon, as people assembled to talk about the latest news. Francine finally made it to the small room located on the back side of the oldest building in her hometown.

"Salut, Francine," Pierre said as soon as she arrived. A man in his early thirties, Pierre was the leader of their group. He was full of idealism, a very common characteristic of the young people of that generation. His father and older brother had fought in the previous war, and Pierre never forgot the stories about death and suffering he heard from them.

"Salut," Francine replied to everyone there, noticing she wasn't the only one to arrive early that night.

"I'm going to enlist tomorrow," Pierre continued. "The mayor will go downtown to speak about the government's resolutions about the war. He has already shared the message about needing as many people as possible to enlist in the military or any other service that might be helpful."

"I'm going with you," Saul said, determined and angry. "Those bastards did it again! I knew it, that damned race."

"That is what happens when we sit around and wait for something to change," Pierre agreed. "We should have taken action a long time ago. It was obvious that sooner or later, they would invade us. They started with the campaigns in Africa, then Poland."

"This should have never happened!!" Laura said out loud. She was the only other woman besides Francine who was a member of the party. "Weren't we supposed to be in control of those pigs?"

No one was surprised by Laura's comments. She had always been very outspoken with very few reservations. She was a history teacher, a very determined woman with strong opinions, especially in matters involving politics. She also had even more personal reasons to hate the Germans, as her father and uncle had both died fighting in the First World War.

"You are right, Laura! But I don't think it matters much now what we should or should not have done," Francine said with conviction. "It's too late, and the war has arrived on our doorsteps. There's no way to go back now and try to fix it in order to prevent it."

Everyone nodded their heads in agreement.

"The question now is what each one of us can do to help!" Francine continued. "How can we stop them?"

Julian looked at Francine and smiled. He admired her enthusiasm, her courage. He was a young man in his mid-twenties. Behind his thin glasses, vivid green eyes stood out. His hair was the same color as Francine's, and they had often been mistaken for brother and sister. Living in the same neighborhood, they grew up side-by-side. But it was the strong personalities, adventurous spirits, and idealism they shared that brought them closer together, making them best friends. However, the truth was that Julian's feelings went beyond that. He had actually been in love with Francine since they were kids. He still had hope that one day she might reciprocate his feelings. *Then, I'll marry her*, he would often think.

"Those bastards will pay for having the audacity to invade us," Saul retorted, waking Julian from his daydream. "They'll be defeated fast, and I want to be there when it happens!"

"I don't know about that," replied Pierre, looking very distressed and concerned, already getting up from his chair.

Pierre knew it was his time to do something for his people and his country.

"That was what they said about the First World War," Pierre continued. "They were certain it would be over soon. But we all know things didn't happen quite like that. We should not make the same assumption, the same mistake!"

"What are you saying, Pierre?" Julian asked, a little irritated. "You think we can't defeat those bastards?"

"Are we prepared for that?" Pierre replied, very concerned. "That is the real question. Germany has been preparing itself for years and years. What about us? What have we done? Not a whole lot, I can guarantee you!!"

Everyone knew Pierre was right. But their pride couldn't accept the fact that defeating the Germans wouldn't be an easy task.

"I think we will kick them out of here much sooner than they would expect," Saul said. "Of course, we'll need a strong military presence to accomplish that. I'll enlist tomorrow."

"I can work near the war camps and help the injured," Francine said enthusiastically.

"I just want to grab a gun and shoot them all," Laura said, lighting up another cigarette.

Everyone laughed for a second, but their laughter was hollow. They were all experiencing mixed feelings. On the one hand, they wanted to be helpful. On the other, they were all somewhat frightened by the unknown of the future. They were used to hearing stories about warfare in the past tense. Now those stories were about to become a present reality.

They all had families. They all had been friends for a long time. For a brief moment, they looked at each other, maybe trying to foresee their futures or perhaps already expecting departures. Deep down, they all knew it could be the last time they might see one another alive. With those grim possibilities in mind, they all decided to go somewhere and have a drink.

The group gathered at a busy local restaurant they favored and decided to make a toast and a promise. "May we all fight for our country and be the best we can be under all circumstances!" Pierre shouted.

"Whatever happens to us, may we always find the courage to help, be useful, and never lose our souls in the process!" Francine added.

"Vive la France!" They all raised their glasses to the other people in the restaurant.

"Vive la France!" the crowd replied.

Julian always accompanied Francine home, ensuring she was safe and waiting for any opportunity to spend a few minutes alone with her.

"So, you will enlist tomorrow?" Francine asked him in a sad tone.

"I will," Julian said, looking straight into her eyes. He knew that everything would change very suddenly. He would be sent away from home. The thought of being away from her broke his heart.

"Julian," Francine continued, "take care of yourself. Be careful. I'm so proud of all of you, but at the same time … I'm scared. So please, write me as much as you can. I want to know that you're safe."

Julian smiled at her. At that very moment, he forgot about the war. He could only see Francine's beautiful face. He wanted to hold her, kiss her lips. He felt comfort in knowing how much she cared for him.

Francine took a quick step forward and hugged him. "Bonne nuit," she said before planting a gentle kiss on his cheek. She broke free from the embrace and turned around. She hated goodbyes.

"Bonne Nuit, Francine," Julian replied, his heart pounding harder and harder as he watched her walk inside her home.

He shook his head in frustration. He hoped that one day Francine could feel the same way about him. But for the moment, he knew she wasn't ready for any commitment. *I'll have to wait until after the war to see how things go, and maybe who knows ... one day ... she may marry me*, he thought sadly.

Julian walked back to his house feeling a strange sensation. He knew that on the following day, his life would take a different turn. But he was ready, ready to fight back.

Inside Francine's house, her parents were already sleeping. They weren't happy with the fact that she was part of a Socialist group. They knew it could be dangerous because of the current political climate in France. But there was nothing they could do to stop her. Deep inside, her father was proud of her, as was her mother. Although Nicole admired her daughter's independent personality, she still believed that Francine should eventually settle down, find herself a nice man, and finally, start living what she considered a normal life for a woman.

Already lying in her bed, Francine tossed and turned, unable to fall asleep. The news about the war took a heavy toll on everyone that day. But there was something else hunting her thoughts on that night. She had tried to pretend for quite some time that Hans wasn't part of her heart anymore. But she knew she was lying to herself. Hans was a constant and vivid presence in her mind. After him, no other man was able to make her heart beat faster, or make her feel so alive.

It had already been over a year since she'd seen him for the first time, but she never forgot about him. She held a secret wish that one day they would meet again. But then the war arrived, chasing her deepest desires away.

At that moment, Francine started wondering what Hans would be thinking during this time of war. *Would he agree with the oppression and cruelty of Germany and its push for power?* Francine thought. *No, not Hans ... he would never agree with any policy of invading other countries ...*

She started to remember every single subject of which they had spoken the day they met. Her memory was that Hans thought differently than most people. He was an idealist and had a clever insight into life and its challenges. Hans enjoyed other cultures – respected and valued them. He stood against injustices, participating in several political movements since his college days. He wanted to make a difference in the world. But Francine knew how fast people could change, blinded by the destructive forces of fanaticism.

In the darkness of her room, she wondered how he was reacting, knowing that Germany had started yet another war. *Would he forget about everything in which he believes? Does he think about me?* Francine asked herself, feeling foolish. *I can't care for a German man. I just can't!* She felt as if she was betraying her country, her family and friends. And she was betraying them with feelings for a man that was now considered their enemy.

CHAPTER 4

The implacable German *blitzkrieg* continued to ravage through the French territory. Focusing on the enemy's weaker line of defenses, powerful Panzers mercilessly destroyed everything in their paths. The horrifying sound of machine guns and explosions reached out to what were once peaceful green valleys. And then the earth cradled every fallen soldier. Bright and colorful flowers surrounded their unmarked graves as the soil slowly turned red.

Pierre was right, after all. In only a few weeks, France had fallen at the hands of Germany. The painful and humiliating defeat afflicted every soul in France. None of their past internal political rivalries mattered much, although status and money had become even more powerful tools. But the forceful surrender of France would impact their lives in a way that not even Pierre could have predicted.

Little by little, their town became a busy passageway that the Germans used to reach other parts of France. Some people decided to flee to other countries. Francine's father decided to stay put, as did his wife and daughter – against his advice.

Francine had been working with her father in the local hospital, helping all the wounded soldiers. At first, her father didn't want her to get involved, but he soon realized that it would be a good thing for his daughter after all. She was always keen to help, and Jean could keep a close eye on her. He feared for her safety at the hands of German soldiers scattered around town.

A Light in the Darkness

As time went on, communication was becoming more limited and dangerous. Francine started to receive fewer and fewer letters from Pierre and the other members of the group who had joined the Resistance and the army, until they stopped arriving altogether. Everyone was becoming more afraid to talk, fearful of the Nazi soldiers.

It was also getting harder to move freely as the German presence started to increase in their town. The people began to experience a shortage of food and other basic necessities. No one smiled anymore, as they were barely managing to stay alive. They had lost their freedom. They had lost their dignity.

To make matters worse, some wounded German soldiers started to arrive from several battle locations. So, Francine, her father, and their friends at the local hospital found themselves having to help those very same German soldiers that not only had invaded their country but had also taken the lives of their friends, family members and thousands of other people around the world.

Not long after, a local SS office was established in the center of town to monitor the local population and remove injured troops. They became a constant presence at the hospital.

Jean and his co-workers had a tough time receiving orders from German officials who constantly humiliated and mistreated them. But Jean's main concern was directed toward Francine. He noticed the way some of the soldiers looked at his daughter. Francine was an attractive young woman whose unique charm often captivated those around her. She was a very outspoken woman who often surprised men with her firm and elegant way of expressing her points of view. He worried that such attributes could very easily put her life in danger. There was no doubt in his mind that he had to do something about it.

Jean spotted Francine in one of the rooms at the hospital. He walked quickly toward her.

"Father, are you all right?" Francine asked him promptly as she noticed the serious look on his face.

"Follow me."

As soon as they arrived in his office, he got straight to the point.

"Francine, I don't want you working here anymore."

"Father, I will not leave you here on your own. Plus, we are so short on help, and there are so many French soldiers here who need us."

"I know," Jean said, passing his hand over his forehead. He looked exhausted. Not even in his worst nightmare could he have imagined the current situation. He feared for his wife and for his daughter, whose future was severely compromised. He tried to send Francine to England through some political connections, but she refused to leave. For that reason, they were always getting into arguments.

"The situation has changed," he added, lowering his voice as German soldiers passed by the door. "See, we can't even talk freely anymore. The Germans are taking over everything. Moreover, they brutalize, kill, and torture at their leisure. I can't and will not allow it to happen to you, do you understand?"

Francine nodded with a deep sigh. She knew her father was right. She had tried to hide from her father all the German soldiers' advances in the hospital. But she could never abandon her country or her family. She felt that by being close, she could somehow protect and take care of them. And she still had hopes that the Allies would soon come to rescue them.

"Father," Francine sighed, "I cannot leave right now. Not when so many patients need my assistance. But I promise you I will be cautious, and if things get worse, I will let you know. Then we can work on a plan for us to leave if necessary."

Looking right into Francine's eyes, Jean recognized his own stubbornness in her. He knew he wouldn't be able to convince her. *She will never leave unless I make her go by force,* Jean thought. *I need to come up with a solution ... fast!*

Amidst all the unimaginable terror and chaos caused by the war, the year 1941 had arrived. German soldiers cheerfully crowded the French cafés, celebrating the New Year in that chilly winter's night.

Not far from that spot, in one of the rooms at the hospital, something drastically different was happening; Francine held the hands of a dying French soldier. He had been placed in an isolated area to avoid the spread of infection. Francine looked at his pale face. It was late at night, and she was utterly exhausted. But she knew that those could be his final hours, and she wanted to be there for him. *He's too young to die*, she thought solemnly. His family was never located, and most of them had been presumed dead from an air attack in the Northern regions of France. So, he was alone in that cold hospital, a war hero who gave his own life for his country's freedom.

Francine held his hand tightly, looking at his face. "I wish I could do more," she said in a low tone of voice.

"You can," the young man replied with his eyes half-shut.

"André?" Francine was surprised to see him speaking.

He made a signal for her to get closer to him.

She leaned toward his head as he started to whisper.

"Francine, you can do more. Go to Arnaud's old house at midnight tomorrow night. They always meet on Tuesday and Thursday nights."

Francine just stared at him, speechless.

Understanding his own fragile situation, André didn't waste any time.

"There's a path behind it that will lead you to a location in the woods. Follow that road until …" André could barely whisper those words through his coughing. "… tell them I sent you."

Francine looked around fast, worried that someone could have heard him.

She looked at him again, trying to understand what he meant. "What exactly are you talking about?" she asked him in a calm voice.

"Shh!" André grabbed her hand with such a sudden gesture that it seemed to take all his strength away.

"It's better if you preserve your energy," Francine said sadly.

"No, I have to tell you this. Go there, Francine!" André said, trying to get his lips closer to her ears. "Promise me. But be very careful. Absolutely no one should know about it. Remember the words *votre mere*. That is the code."

Francine looked around again, finally understanding the implications related to those words. She wanted to ask more about it, but she did not want him to talk much since he was so weak.

"Merci, Francine. Merci beaucoup," André said faintly as his eyes started closing. Then, before Francine could say anything else, he took a shallow breath while his arm dropped to the side of the bed.

Still holding one of his hands between hers, she stared at him in silence. Her eyes filled with tears. Even though she was a nurse and had experienced death many times, she'd never been fully able to accept the loss of human life … especially under those circumstances.

"You are not suffering anymore," she said softly while touching his face. "This is the end of your war, and you will find peace."

She held his hand tightly again, and remembering his last words she whispered, "I will go there! Wherever it is, I will find it. I promise you!"

The next day, Francine kept busy working at the hospital. Although she couldn't stand being around the Germans, she found the strength to help French soldiers and the civilians who arrived there feeling morally and physically defeated.

It was around noon when she circled around the block and made it to her street. She soon realized, to her astonishment, that there was a group of people gathered right in front of her house. Francine's face turned suddenly pale as she saw a German military vehicle there as well. She heard loud voices coming from that direction. Without hesitating, she ran toward her house as fast as she could, breaking through the small crowd.

"You can't take him!" Francine's mother screamed out in desperation as a German soldier ruthlessly got in her way.

Francine barely had any time to react to the chaos happening right in front of her eyes when she saw her father been pushed forward by three German soldiers.

"What's going on here?" Francine asked frantically, trying to understand the situation.

Nicole reached for her daughter, terrified that Francine might say or do something that could put her own life in danger.

"They are taking your father to another place," Nicole answered through her sobs. "It seems to be another French town, but we are not sure yet."

"They can't do that." Francine broke from her mother's arms and headed toward her father. The German soldiers tried to grab her, but she broke through their line.

"Dad, they can't do this! I will not let you leave like this."

"Francine, listen to me!" her father said firmly, trying to calm her down. "It will be fine. They need a doctor at another hospital and …"

"We need to go, now!" a German soldier yelled at him, clearly impatient.

"He's not leaving!" Francine screamed back at him defiantly. "This is our house, our town! Not yours, you bastards!"

With an angry stare and a smirk on his face, one of the German soldiers took a quick step toward her. Very abruptly, he raised his hand and slapped her face hard, making her stumble to the side and hit the hall.

Her mother screamed while Jean jumped at the soldier, trying to protect his daughter. Francine stood there, reeling in shock.

The other soldier tried to grab Jean as he assaulted the German who brutally hit his daughter's face. Francine tried to get her father to stop until another German soldier held a gun to her head.

"I'll kill her right now!" he shouted at Jean.

Jean immediately spun around, looking straight at his daughter. The soldier he had assaulted took advantage of the situation by striking Jean in the head with his gun, making him fall to the ground. Francine forgot about her own injuries as she and Nicole ran toward him.

The two other German soldiers held both of them away from Jean. Francine had to gather all her strength to calm down and not react any further after one of the soldiers whispered threats in her ear. He said it in German, and she understood it perfectly. They would not hesitate to kill her father right there on the spot.

One soldier kicked Jean several times. Again, Francine tried to break free of her restraints but couldn't. The two women begged the soldiers to stop, but they only laughed in amusement.

"Enough!" one finally commanded. "Unfortunately, we have to bring him alive. For now, at least," he said teasingly as he looked at Francine.

The German soldiers abruptly pushed Nicole and Francine away. Nicole held her daughter as they both watched their beloved Jean escorted out of their house.

Jean had a quick chance to look back.

"Don't worry; I will be fine," he said, trying to console them. "I love you both."

Nicole and Francine watched Jean look back at them from inside the military jeep, trying to smile for their sake. They clung to each other as they sobbed, not knowing if they would ever see him again.

The news spread around town quickly. It didn't take long for several of Jean's friends to show up at his house to offer their support to the family. Among them, a highly decorated French general disguised in civilian clothes. His name was Gerard Moreau, a man who had become one of the most influential people in the fight against Germany. After the defeat of France, he decided to work with the Resistance helping his country and the allies.

"Jean is being transported to a location near the eastern borders for now. There's a great need for surgeons there to take care of the injured German soldiers fighting at other locations," Gerard explained. "Your father is a very respected and well-known doctor. They need him, which is a good thing … it will keep him alive."

"How long will he be there for?" Nicole rushed to ask. "Can we go visit him?"

"Madam," Gerard continued politely, "that is impossible to know. It's not safe for either of you to go there. Plus, you might not be allowed to do so. I have close friends in that area that will watch over him. We'll do the best we can to keep you informed. In the meantime, I'll do everything in my power to bring him back."

"I'll find him," Francine said. "I can go work with him. I'm a nurse."

"Have you gone insane? You can't do this to me! I'll never be able to handle worrying about you, too," Francine's mother cried.

"Your mother is right, Francine," Gerard agreed. "Your father would be even more concerned knowing you were there among the enemy and away from home. You could worsen the situation for him. Also, he gave me specific instructions to arrange for someone to watch over both of you if something happens to him. That includes having someone take you to work and bring you home every day, Francine."

"I don't need that," Francine said, standing up fast. "I want to do something else. I want to contribute to the liberation of France!"

"Francine!" Nicole couldn't take it anymore.

"No, Mom, enough is enough! I will not stand by and watch as my country, my people, and my own father fall at the hands of those monsters. I can't accept that. I have to do something else. I have to do more! I can't just work at the hospital!"

"Listen, Francine," Gerard tried to intervene. "They are used to having you at the hospital. We need you there to help our fallen soldiers and injured civilians. You have seen all the children over there. They are now orphans. They are short on help. Plus, they will not let you leave the hospital. The Germans will come here to your house and take you by force."

Gerard got up anxiously. His face reflected all his anger.

"I do understand your frustrations; trust me. We all wish we could do much more. But taking extreme measures without caution will only make matters worse. We are severely outnumbered, and too many people could be punished if we are not careful. The Germans will kill anyone at any time, just because they can. Believe me, there are people out there giving everything they have to turn this situation around. But we will prevail, Francine, I know this. Somehow, I do know it is possible. I'll give my life for the cause, if necessary."

Francine admired Gerard. She was aware that he was part of the French-English Secret Service. She had overheard their conversations one day at her house. He was a good man, and she knew he would do anything he could to help her father.

CHAPTER 5

The weeks and then months went by fast. The autumn of 1941 was already approaching, but time seemed to be moving very slowly for Francine's family. As General Gerard Moreau had promised, he got news from Jean. He had been placed in a French hospital closer to the German border. Although there were no reports of him being hurt, the news wasn't good. Jean was an excellent trauma surgeon and was in high demand. The Germans had quickly recognized his abilities and were planning to relocate him to the war zones close to Russia.

Francine was pacing in the library, rubbing her hands together in a nervous frenzy. She remembered Gerard's last words before he left her house. "I will be gone for a while," he had told her. "But don't worry ... I will try to keep you informed as much as possible."

Francine sighed, feeling frustrated. She knew communication with Jean would be even more difficult, if not impossible, in Gerard's absence. *I have to do something to help my father!* Francine thought. *I simply can't stay still and wait for news that may never come!*

It was in the middle of the night when Francine opened her eyes abruptly, waking up from another awful nightmare. She saw her father in a terrible German prison, his body contorting with pain as he was being tortured.

Covered in sweat, she sat on her bed, trying to push these thoughts away. She looked at the empty glass on top of the nightstand and decided to go downstairs to get a glass of water.

On her way down to the kitchen and still half asleep, Francine's attention was suddenly drawn to what seemed to be a shadow passing by the window of her house. She stood there, numb for a few seconds. Then, Francine remembered a gun that her father hid in the library in case of emergencies. She started to walk toward it quietly.

With her hands shaking, she carefully loaded the gun. The only sound she could hear was the thudding of her rapidly beating heart.

Frightened and alone, she stood behind the library wall, feeling as if someone could show up at any moment.

Time seemed to be standing still. She didn't hear any other noises. She knew she couldn't simply stay there waiting forever.

She took one slow step at a time toward the living room, looking around everywhere as she went forward. Finally, she carefully approached one of the windows and parted the curtain very gently, just enough so she could take a peek outside.

She was breathing heavily. Her fear deepened when she suddenly saw the shadow of a person walking around the house. Francine quickly let go of the curtain, her body froze on the spot. She started to remember that Gerard, as well as Pierre, had people watching over their house. With that thought, Francine relaxed a little … but how could she be sure?

She knew she had to find out who that person was. And she knew there was no other way but to take the extra step and confront that person directly.

It was cold and very dark outside, but Francine did not hesitate. With the gun pointed down, she took a few steps forward, looking everywhere around her. Not spotting anyone or anything suspicious, she proceeded toward the right corner of the house.

Before she could think of anything else, she was suddenly grabbed from behind. She tried to scream, but the man covered her mouth and quickly pulled her back toward the woods.

Frantic, she tried to break free from the attacker's arms. As she struggled, her gun fell to the ground.

"It's all right, Francine," a voice whispered. "It's me, Julian, shhh. If you stay quiet, I'll uncover your mouth."

Francine's body was trembling out of control. Her breathing was probably loud enough to attract attention to both of them.

"C'est moi, Julian," the voice said, trying to calm her down.

Julian slowly started to uncover her mouth, but he still held her tight.

"Julian?" Francine asked, feeling his arms around her body.

"Oui, mademoiselle," Julian whispered close to her ear. "Have you calmed down yet?"

With one sudden move, Francine broke free from his arms and turned around, looking straight at him. With her entire body still shaking, she didn't know if she should hug him or slap him across the face.

"Julian!" Francine said rather loudly. "How could you scare me like that?"

"Shhh, you're talking too loud!" Julian told her, trying his best not to laugh at the frown on her face. "Can't you just be happy it's me and that I happen to be alive?"

"Of course, I'm happy it's you, Julian," Francine said, already opening her arms to hug him.

"Francine," Julian said, worried. "Are you out of your mind? Why would you follow a stranger like that?"

"I had to know," she replied, shivering. "I saw a shadow watching over the house. How could I sleep after that? Plus, I brought a gun with me," Francine said, looking for it on the ground.

"I see! I'm glad you kept it really close to you!" Julian said sarcastically. "But knowing you, Francine, you would think a million times before shooting anyone anyway."

"Hilarious, Julian. I'm laughing so hard. You caught me by surprise!"

He looked at her, proud of her courage and determination. Those traits were among the many things that he loved about Francine, including her long brown curls, especially when they were messy. He loved her stubborn attitude and the way she pouted when she was aggravated. He couldn't help but want to hold her tightly in his arms again and protect her from any possible harm.

"Listen, Francine," Julian continued, becoming more serious. "I came here tonight to check on you and your mother. I have been doing it from time to time. I want to make sure you are safe, especially after your father's removal."

Julian could see the sadness in Francine's eyes at that moment. He came closer to her, grabbing her hand.

"Things will work out," he soothed. "Just promise me you will stay away from trouble."

She looked at him and said nothing.

"Promise me, Francine." Julian held her hands tighter.

"I'll try," Francine said, looking down again.

"Of course, you will," Julian said, smiling at her.

"When do I get to hear from you again, Julian? And everyone else? Laura, Pierre … How are they?"

"Some of them went to England for a special training," he replied, looking around. "It's a long story! However, as for Laura …"

"What happened?"

"The SS has taken her prisoner. Laura always had a hard time obeying German soldiers, just like the rest of us. But you know how she is …

she didn't think of the consequences of over-exposing herself. She was connected to the Resistance movement and got involved with some people we couldn't quite trust."

Julian paused for a brief moment, remembering everything that had happened. "She has been taken to a heavily guarded location. We've tried everything to get her out, but she has been kept under strict security in an area where …"

"Where …? What are you trying to say?" Francine rushed to ask as he hesitated to continue.

"Where people are known for being tortured and to never … well, never leave," Julian said solemnly.

"How long has she been there?"

"Too long, Francine. Too long."

Horrified to hear of her friend's fate, she closed her eyes, covering her face with her hands. She had known Laura for over seven years. Francine had always admired her bravery and the efforts she would make toward any good cause. Laura's selflessness made her feel even worse. It seemed that while Francine was trying to stay alive, everyone else seemed to be throwing themselves straight into death's path.

"We have been able to save some people, but it doesn't always work out that way," Julian continued in a sad voice.

"All of you have done so much! You risk your lives every day for us, your people, your country! Francine said, putting her hands on his shoulders.

He smiled at her sweetly. "But it's not enough! There's a lot that still needs to be done!"

Francine nodded, understanding those words very well. That war was far from being over.

"Well, I better go now," Julian said as he looked deeply into her eyes. You stay safe, out of trouble, Francine."

"Me?" she laughed. "You're the one taking all the risks. So, you, my friend, stay safe, stay alive."

"I'll keep in touch. And remember, don't follow anyone. Now go, Francine. I'll watch you until you enter your house."

"Au revoir," Francine said, squeezing Julian tightly.

"*À bientôt, mon amour*," he said in a low tone of voice as he watched her walk toward her house.

Francine got inside her bedroom but she wasn't ready to go to bed quite yet. As she sat on a comfortable chair next to the window, she could hear Julian's last words repeatedly in her head. It made her feel better to know people were watching over her and her mother. Francine thought about Laura, Julian and all her other friends. She felt she needed to take a more proactive position in the fight against Germany. The truth was that no one was safe. It was simple foolishness to think otherwise.

She knew she would have to find her own ways to learn more about her father's well-being and make a more significant contribution toward helping France and the Allies. She wasn't a coward; she wanted to do more.

As she stared out the window, she tried to think of a plan that would bring her mother safely across the border. She would have to convince her, which wouldn't be an easy task. But after that, she would be free to do other things … she would somehow find a way to join the Resistance.

At that exact moment, she remembered André, the dying soldier who told her about going to a certain address. So much had happened that she forgot about her own promise to him. She closed her eyes and tried to remember the instructions he had given her as well as the secret code. A sense of excitement coursed through her body, a feeling she hadn't experienced in a long time.

I hope they still meet on those nights, Francine prayed. *No matter what happens … I have to try!*

CHAPTER 6

It was the end days of a tumultuous December in 1941. As the war continued, food shortages, loss of freedom, and political pressure became a part of everyday life for most Germans.

Hans stood immobile by his desk, leaning idly on his chair. He deeply regretted his decision to stay in Germany.

Since the beginning of the war, he thought that his country had no right or justification for invading another one, despite the poor conditions that most Germans lived in after WWI. But even so, he could never have predicted that his own country was capable of committing such horrific atrocities against its own people and other nations.

Hans sighed in frustration, running his fingers through his hair. He was a talented mechanical engineer, but never in his wildest dreams did he think he would ever be put into such a terrible position. He had been forced to redirect his work to producing war materials. Even though he wasn't directly responsible for them, he had to inspect their production. He hated his forced cooperation, but Hans knew he had no other options. The Nazi Party and Hitler's power had grown tremendously.

Hans knew many people still hated Hitler and wanted to remove him from power, but that seemed to be an impossible task. All of those who directly opposed him were either imprisoned or executed.

Hans's face transformed as the anger he felt surged through him. He hit the table with his fist, remembering some of his friends who were killed when a group of SS soldiers invaded the place where they held secret meetings to talk and plan action against the Nazi Party and its war. Hans, alongside others, was barely able to escape. But he knew that he would have been persecuted and killed if it wasn't for his friend, Carson Beurmann. Carson found a way to camouflage Hans's actions and save his life. But that wasn't too difficult for Carson to do as he had become a very influential military Nazi officer in charge of the SS forces in his hometown.

Carson was a little older than Hans. Ironically, up until the war, he was Hans's best friend and, for all purposes, considered to be his brother. They had known each other since they were kids.

Hans leaned against the back of his chair with his hands covering his face. He couldn't understand how Carson had become so blind! But then again, he knew his friend had always been a passionate nationalist who ultimately considered Germany to be above other nations.

Carson fervently believed Hitler's policies and that he and the Nazi Party were the only ones that could drive Germany out of the pitiful condition it had found itself in since the end of WWI.

Hans had tried everything possible to persuade his friend otherwise but with very little success. *Carson is obsessed with Hitler and has become a fanatic!* he used to say to himself and his family. Then, of course, there was also the seduction of power and money. Hitler's regime offered more possibilities for people like Carson, especially those in the military, to achieve a certain status, wealth, and authority.

Nonetheless, Hans still believed that Carson had a good side to him deep inside, even if the Nazi lunacy in his head currently overshadowed it.

Hans remembered Carson as the boy who used to do anything to help his friends. He was generous, polite, and always fun to be around. That is until everything had changed.

On the other hand, even though Carson knew how much Hans disagreed with his actions, he still considered Hans, his best friend. So, Carson tried everything to convince his old friend that Germany had every right to rise against other nations, legitimizing what he considered to be the superiority of their Arian race.

Hans straightened himself back in the chair, feeling a sour taste in his mouth and sudden dizziness. He hadn't eaten much in those past few days. Actually, he hadn't eaten much at all. Food was a controlled commodity, highly manipulated by the SS forces as an important privilege, mainly available for those who were favored or in power.

Hans took a good look around his office. He knew he didn't have much choice but to stay there. He closed his eyes, remembering the events that had made him stay in that factory. He thought about his father.

It was about two weeks ago when the SS invaded Hans's house. He woke up to a scream coming from his parent's room. He rushed out the door and found soldiers in the hall. Shocked, he tried to inquire what they were doing there when suddenly something struck him on the back of the head, knocking him down.

He woke up minutes later to find himself lying on his bed, his mother sitting by his side, worried. For a brief moment, he thought it had only been a bad dream, but it didn't take too long for him to gain full consciousness and remember the preceding events. He looked into his mother's eyes and realized she'd been crying.

"Mother," Hans said, moving one hand toward the wound on his head. "What happened?"

His mother, Elga, slowly moved his hand away from the injured area. She carefully applied a warm cloth to it. Then, looking right into her son's eyes she said, "they have taken your father."

Before Hans could reply, someone was knocking at his door.

"It's Carson," Elga explained. "He has been waiting for you to wake up. I called him to come right away."

The door opened.

"Are you all right? Carson said, looking at Hans.

"Am I all right? How can you even ask that?"

"I'm doing the best I can, Hans," Carson answered, trying not to pay attention to his friend's angry tone. "Mr. Alfred has good connections. He'll soon be out of that place."

"You cannot be serious! Because from what I can recall, he has very little influence since your crazy Nazi friends took over power!"

"I don't want to see you two arguing again," Elga intervened. "It is not the time for this!"

Carson looked at Elga, faking a smile on his face. "Can I bother you for some tea?" he asked, trying to get her out of the room.

They both waited until they could hear her footsteps going downstairs.

"The Schutzstaffel has been watching us! We are like prisoners here."

"Prisoners?" Carson replied, laughing. "Hans, you have always been dramatic. You're nothing like prisoners, believe me. Plus, you have a pretty good job here, away from the war. I have always made sure you got the best treatment, even after that little incident you got yourself into."

"Incident? Friends of ours have died in there! Do you not remember?"

"Of course, I do, Hans!" Carson said, raising his voice. "How could I forget? You would be dead right now if I hadn't interfered. Do you know what it took for me to get you out of that situation? You have no idea! You know I had to find you a job that would show the SS Commanders how dedicated you are to our great Germany."

Hans looked at Carson very seriously. "Great Germany? You call this a Great Germany? You placed me in a factory that builds war machinery."

"You gave me no choice! Why can't you see what we are doing here?" "I actually see it very well! I see we are murdering people, women, and children, anyone in our way. I see our lack of freedom, our food shortages, and our forced labor. I see the madness that is everywhere, the fanatism, the cruelty."

"Talking to you is pointless," Carson said, getting even more aggravated. "You're lucky I consider you my brother. By the way, Adalie and I are having our engagement party this weekend, as you already know. You'd better attend. At least do that for me. Your father will be freed soon, and he'll be able to go anywhere he wants as long as he stays in this city, at least for now. As for you, Hans, please don't do anything stupid."

Carson got close to Hans and whispered, "they were just a little suspicious that he was participating in some sort of conspiracy. They just wanted to make sure. I know it's not the ideal situation, but Mr. Alfred has had some friends that are not too fond of our Führer. And you know that very well, don't you?"

Hans looked at him in total disbelief. He was always stunned by the casual way Carson talked about the war, about all the horrible things that were taking place.

He felt even angrier. "Not the ideal situation? You are talking about our father! Mr. Alfred, as you call him now, you used to consider your father, if you can remember that. They can invade every single home, take us as prisoners, and attack us … and we're supposed to agree with that?"

"I know! They shouldn't have come here! I've told them you're my family, and you're all clear of any activities that would compromise our country in any way. Yes, Hans, I will always have the deepest regard and respect for Mr. Alfred, who I still consider my father. But you know the dangerous affiliations you and your father have insisted on keeping could lead to some serious trouble despite my advice to stay away. So … just do me a favor and accept things have changed."

"You're unbelievable! You want me to accept this situation? My father was taken away and we got attacked in our own home!"

Carson sighed, tired of that argument. Deciding to ignore Hans' last comment, he continued, "as for now, eat something. You look terrible. Pretty soon, they will think you are a Jew walking around. Anyway, if you need anything, I'll be in the military station."

Carson turned around quickly and walked away, trying not to give Hans a chance to reply. He opened the door fast but then hesitated for a few seconds.

"By the way, have a Merry Christmas if I don't see you before that!" Carson said on his way out.

"Carson! Carson!!! Come back here!" Hans shouted furiously. He still had a lot to say to him.

But Carson kept walking, ignoring his friend's usual persistence.

Hans opened his eyes, letting out a deep sigh of frustration. He looked out the window, feeling completely powerless. They had arrested his father, and there was nothing he could do about it!

So, he stayed there in his office a while longer, watching as the first snowflakes started to fall, slowly covering the ground in a thin layer of sparkling white dust. That scene made him remember when he was younger, and he felt free, peaceful, full of idealism and dreams … just living a normal life.

And it was at that moment that his thoughts suddenly took him to a faraway place, to a foreign land, to a French girl who had stolen his heart.

Yes, he could still remember her face, every line, and every detail. It was one of the few things that brought warmth to his heart during those horrific times. He had never been able to forget her as much as he had tried. He got to know a few other women, but no one ever came close to making him feel the way Francine did. She represented everything he wanted in a woman.

He remembered quite well that day when he had gone on a trip to Switzerland with a few of his friends. They decided to enter a café to grab something to eat before going to a bar famous among the current and former college students.

As Hans entered the café, he noticed a young woman sitting by the window with a book in her hands. At that very instant, Francine looked at him. Their eyes locked for a few seconds before she quickly turned her head away. Suddenly, he felt a strange emotion run through his entire body, a feeling so strong it disturbed his thoughts.

Sitting by their table as his friends continued their conversation, Hans pretended to pay attention to them. But he knew his mind was focused on a few tables away from where a girl with brown hair and the most intriguing green eyes continued to read her book.

He noticed she kept looking at him from time to time. That simple fact made his heart beat faster, leaving him with an unexpected sensation of well-being and excitement. He remembered feeling so attracted to her that he couldn't help but take the courage to introduce himself.

And that was when everything happened. Hans felt as if an invisible and irresistible force kept pushing him to get closer to her.

He was mesmerized by the intelligent and distinguished way she expressed herself while graciously moving her hands in the air. She wasn't afraid to speak her mind. The sound of her voice made him want to hear every word she had to say. She was a person who spoke with such a passion and conviction about everything she believed in that it inspired him to think that life was even more beautiful. All those qualities made her appear even more charming.

But then, they had to leave.

He saw her walking away from him. With every step she took, his heart ached deeper. No, he couldn't understand what had happened to him. All that he knew was that he had never felt so understood by anyone else. She validated and represented all the things he felt were the most important in life. He had found himself in her.

Hans could feel all those emotions as if it had happened yesterday. He couldn't forget her. He just simply couldn't and didn't want to forget Francine. She was the first person he thought of when he heard that

Germany had invaded France. He had tried everything he could to find information about her, but he got nowhere, and the war distanced them even further.

Hans wasn't a very emotional person on the outside, but the thought of Francine being hurt brought tears to his eyes. He knew he had to do something. *I have to find her. But where? Where would she be? How can I reach out to her during this war?*

He felt often foolish for letting her walk away from him that day. But it was even worse to think she would still want to see him. *She must hate us. All of us! She must think I'm like the others. Plus, she could already be married by now. She probably doesn't even remember I exist.*

Those possibilities always bothered him, causing him profound sadness, more than he wanted to admit. So, he tried to redirect his thoughts, telling himself that Francine would never want to be with a German man. *I have to think about my parents now. I need to find a way to get them out of here.*

CHAPTER 7

The first days of 1942 were upon them. The war continued fiercely, spreading death and despair throughout the globe. Alliances were still being forged, while others started to crumble. German troops advanced further into the European territory, encountering brave but fragile resistance. And when it seemed that no one would be able to stop the German killing machine, the bombing of an American Pacific island changed everything. The United States entered the war, bringing new hope for millions of people who stood in the way of Hitler and the Axis coalition.

Francine found herself staring at the clock in the hospital. She wanted to make sure she would be out of there in time to take her mother to Switzerland. She had waited over two months to get a pass to travel there. Such a pass was only acquired after a tremendous effort from some of Jean's best friends. The SS strictly controlled all travel permits.

Francine was able to obtain a few doctors' notes that attested to her mother's urgent need for specialized care, only available in Switzerland's best hospitals. She also had to come up with a certain amount of money to be given to some German officers to guarantee their safe passage. She felt deeply outraged for having to buy their way out of the country, but they had no other choice.

A smile of joy lit up her face when she saw the clock finally marking four o'clock. On her way home, Francine couldn't help but think about the challenges of her short trip. She had to lie to Nicole, saying that she would also stay in Switzerland. She knew how upset her mother would be once she realized the truth, but that was the only way she found to convince her mother to leave France.

Francine was already packing one of her last suitcases at home when she heard a knock at her bedroom door.

"Are you ready? We need to leave now, so we don't miss the train," her mother urged.

Francine had already given instructions to Marie and her husband about her short stay in Switzerland. Reluctantly, they agreed not to say a word to her mother.

Already in the busy train station, Francine, along with Nicole and one of Jean's friends, slowly walked toward the smokey locomotive. The air was bitter and the atmosphere dreadful. It was hard to accept the brutal reality of Germany's occupation of their country.

German soldiers were everywhere, looking cold and impersonal, guarding the station with guns at the ready. *How humiliating*, Francine thought, *that we have to take orders from these bastards!*

They sat still and in silence as the train pulled out of the station. There wasn't much to say at that moment. Resting her head against the window, Francine stared at the road, already covered by a mix of fog and dust. Their hearts were filled with sorrow as they abandoned their country. Tears ran down Nicole's face. Noticing her sadness, Francine reached for one of her mother's hands, holding it tightly. They both knew this move represented yet another uncertain chapter of their lives.

Francine only stayed in Switzerland for a few days. She felt comfort knowing her mother would have companionship and support at her sister's house.

"I can't believe you are doing this to me," Nicole said one more time, not wanting Francine to leave.

"Mother, I have already explained to you why I can't stay here. Please understand. There are too many patients and not enough help. I cannot abandon our injured soldiers!"

"It is too dangerous, Francine! Things have changed! Your father is no longer there to protect you, and those German soldiers are everywhere. It is not safe for anyone, much less for a young woman like you."

Francine knew her mother was right, but that didn't mean she would hide from her duty. Quite the opposite. Francine knew she was ready to contribute toward any war efforts against the Germans.

Despite her mother's insistence, Francine could only promise that she would try to stay safe and return soon.

She arrived home to find it even more packed and heavily guarded. A long line formed on the other side of the station where people were being pushed and separated.

Francine observed everything in total disgust. Soon, she spotted Marie's husband, Frederick, who waved her over to his car. He didn't waste any time and started to tell her the terrible news. All the Jews were being removed from their homes and placed on trains to unspecified locations.

"And this is happening everywhere across the country," Frederick said, infuriated. "German authorities said that anyone hiding a Jew would be arrested or even killed. And guess who is helping them with this horrible task?"

Francine stayed quiet, afraid of what would come next.

"Some of our own people! Those traitors are working for the enemy, turning against their own!"

Francine shook her head in astonishment. More than ever, she realized she had made the right decision to go back to France. The image of that dying soldier, André, rushed into her mind as well as his last words, "Go to the address I have told you. You can do so much more, Francine!"

I have to do more than just work at the hospital! Too many people are suffering while I stand still watching this madness take place! she thought determined. She was ready to take action.

CHAPTER 8

It was past midnight, and Francine knew she wasn't supposed to be outside because of the curfew. She felt an adrenaline rush, a sense of excitement and fear, making her heart pound fast and her breathing heavier. Trying her best to stay away from the bright spots on the streets, Francine carefully moved between the light poles, hiding in the shadows. She glanced around one more time before quickly crossing the street.

The cool air filled her lungs and brought a sudden chill to her body. She tried to move as stealthily as possible.

She looked at a small house around the corner. She was supposed to find the "secret road" at this address that André had given her. The house was very old and appeared to be falling apart. She cautiously moved toward the back of the crumbling structure. There seemed to be no one there. The silence was so pervasive that she could only hear the crunching sound of her feet stepping on the rough ground. She was as alarmed as she was excited.

She turned on the flashlight while she walked toward the forest, trying to find the secret path.

It has to be this way! she thought right before she noticed a narrow road leading to the woods.

"This is the darkest road I have ever seen," Francine whispered, "and probably filled with bugs."

She laughed nervously at her own comment. *Here I am playing secret agent, and I'm concerned about bugs!* But the smile on her face quickly faded when she realized she had to keep going, and she had no idea where to find the so-called "secret place." Little by little, her body disappeared into the woods.

Francine walked for quite some time. Despite looking everywhere, she couldn't find the place. With her frustration increasing by the minute, she wondered if she had mistaken the address that André had given her. But she wasn't ready to give up quite yet.

Francine continued walking, looking closely in all directions.

When she least expected it, she heard a noise. Francine suddenly stopped. Scared, she pointed her flashlight everywhere, and her hands started to shake. She could sense someone getting closer to her. But before she could even react, a hand quickly covered her mouth, and a cap was put over her head. At first, she thought of Julian, but that thought quickly faded, given the brutal way she was being handled. Francine feared Nazi soldiers had captured her.

Her heart was beating fast, and the lack of air made everything even more terrifying. She desperately tried to break free of her captors. But two arms quickly tightened their grip around her body.

"Let me go," Francine said, struggling. "Who are you? Where are you taking me?"

Despite her insistence, no one answered her questions. She had no other choice but to continue to walk forward.

It didn't take too long for them to reach their destination. Francine heard the creaking sound of what seemed to be a door being opened and shut soon after. In vain, she kept trying to free herself.

She was harshly thrown into a chair. She could only hear some whispers. To her profound relief, the whispers were in French.

"Who are you?" a voice asked her, wasting no time.

"I can't breathe," Francine said, feeling as if she was going to pass out. "Please remove this thing from my head."

A few seconds later, the oppressive cap was removed. Still breathing heavily, Francine looked around, frightened. But the darkness of the room only allowed her to see shadows standing right in front of her.

"Who are you?" one of the men yelled at her. "You better start talking!"

"I … I will not say anything until someone tells me what is going on here," Francine replied with a shaky voice.

"Do you think you are in a position to ask for anything?" the same man asked rudely, getting very close to her.

"Do you think this is a game? Say it already!" another voice growled. "Who are you?"

"I'm not going to say my name," Francine insisted in her answer. Listening to them yell at her in perfect French gave her courage back. "I don't know who you are. But I was sent here by someone."

"Someone? Who are you talking about? You better say it fast before we kill you."

"André is his name," Francine said, guessing that she was in that secret place André had told her.

"André?" another voice asked her. "André is dead! You're lying!"

"No … I am not lying!" Francine rushed to explain. "I speak the truth. I know André is dead. I was his nurse at the hospital. I was holding his hands when he died. I don't know who you are, but maybe you will understand the words *votre mére*!"

A brief silence filled the room, and her captors looked at one another in disbelief. That was their secret code!

"Why would André send you here?" a male voice asked her curiously.

"I want to help my country!" Francine affirmed. "I want to do more."

Everyone stayed quiet for a few seconds trying to figure out what to do or ask next. They all knew they had to be very careful trusting anyone those days.

"You could have compromised everything we have built here!" someone yelled at her again. "Do you understand that? And how does a scared mouse like you help us?"

"I came down here, didn't I? My father was taken away, and so many of my friends have already died for the cause. I want and need to do something more meaningful."

There was another long silence before anyone continued.

"I'll find a way to help France, one way or the other," Francine said, taking advantage of that opportunity. "Either you guys can help me, or I'll have to do it myself."

"Great," someone said. "Now we have a hero here!"

"Listen," another voice said. "I don't know why André told you to come here. He shouldn't have. But I'll choose to trust my brother and give you a chance."

"You can't do that!" Antonio immediately replied. "Are you out of your mind?"

"We have to give her a chance," André's brother insisted. "We don't have any choice."

"We can always get rid of her instead! She could betray us. She's lying."

"I'm not lying," Francine rushed to her own defense. "You can check at the hospital. My name is Francine, Francine Dufort. I'm Doctor Jean Dufort's daughter." Francine knew she had no other choice but to say who she was. It was a matter of life or death. She thought that someone there could perhaps know who her father was.

"Jean was taken away," André's brother said. "He was a good man. I know who you are now."

"I want to find a way to help my country and my father," Francine repeated.

"I don't think your father would approve of that," the same man continued.

"Maybe not, but that doesn't matter now! And like I said … I'll find a way with or without your help."

"What do you know about us? What we do here?" someone else inquired.

"To tell the truth, nothing. Unfortunately, André didn't have the chance to say anything else. But obviously, I knew he was referring to secret activities."

"It is a dangerous road, mademoiselle," Rafael, André's brother, advised. "Sometimes, there is no way back!"

"Je sais, monsieur," Francine agreed.

"You could actually be very helpful, Francine," Rafael continued. "At the hospital, you're constantly dealing with German soldiers as well as the French ones."

"That is what I thought," Francine agreed with him. "I speak German fluently, but they don't know that. I studied in Switzerland for a long time, and I also have family there. My German is excellent."

They all looked at one another, still unsure about what to do next.

"All right, Francine," André's brother sighed. "Let's see how you can help us. But we will keep a close eye on you. Do you understand that?"

Francine was taken back to her house. She was told she would be getting instructions very soon.

She tiptoed down the hall, trying not to wake up Frederick and Marie, who stayed at the house so she wouldn't be alone. As she got into her bed, a million thoughts clouded her mind. She knew she was about to enter a new life, full of danger, distrust, and terrifying situations. Francine was about to put her own life and maybe even the lives of others at risk.

Contemplating all that, she felt a little uneasy. She wanted to make sure she wouldn't disappoint them; she didn't want to fail. More than ever, Francine knew she would have to be braver. Yes, she felt ready. Life was finally providing her with the opportunity to do some serious work.

In the following months, Francine had to learn how to write in a secret code. Sometimes, while she was working, she would hear conversations about critical matters. She would then rush to the ladies' room to write everything down on a small piece of paper, all of it encrypted.

She also had to learn how and where to hide them safely. That was always the most crucial part of her work with the Resistance. Any mistake could put everyone involved in danger, exposing many individuals and their crucial plans.

It was already late at night when Francine entered one of the rooms in the hospital. Her entire body was shaking. She had been given particular instructions about what to do once she found the papers in that office.

The entire room was dark and silent. It was usually kept locked, but she was told that it would be open, ready to get in and out quickly on that night.

Her new friends had taken care of that for her. They ensured that the German soldier guarding that post would be sound asleep after drinking his drugged coffee. Nonetheless, Francine still knew the risks. Anyone could suddenly show up and catch her. She had to be fast and efficient.

Francine took a quick look around, trying to locate the main cabinet. Once she spotted it, she walked toward it carefully. Then, reaching inside her pocket for a copy of a key, Francine started opening drawers. She was searching for any documents about the transportation of any military and hospital equipment that could benefit the Resistance.

With the assistance of a small flashlight, her cold and trembling fingers slowly sorted through all the paperwork.

She kept looking at the bottom of the door, making sure no one was passing by in the hallway.

"Here they are," Francine whispered, relieved. She had finally found some useful documents. Without wasting any time, she rushed to take photos of them with the little camera given to her.

Francine was ready to leave when she heard a noise coming from outside the office door. Her heart nearly stopped. She stood still, frozen with fear.

Outside, two German soldiers were talking. Francine noticed their voices were getting louder. *They must have caught that soldier sleeping,* she thought nervously.

Francine had already turned her flashlight off, but she was still afraid that someone might have noticed the light in the room before. The next few minutes were the longest of her life. Francine knew she could be facing certain death; this was not a game! There would be no excuses asked for or given. They would simply shoot her without hesitation.

Francine managed to stay still. She placed her hand against her mouth, trying to cover up the sound of her accelerated respiration. She felt nauseous. But after a few more seconds, to her great relief, the voices start faded, and no one attempted to enter the room.

Francine tried to organize her thoughts. She knew the soldier was now awake, and obviously, she knew she wouldn't be able to leave the room from that door. She had to find another exit, and fast.

She looked all over the dark office; there was only one other way out. Francine waited a few extra minutes. Then, she started slowly walking, taking one step at a time toward one of the windows. Taking a quick peek, she saw a light fog covering the field behind the hospital that could be useful to her.

Francine kept looking at the door while her fingers slowly moved one of the windows up. It took all her effort to prevent it from making any sound.

Several seconds later, she was able to make just enough room for her body to fit through the window.

Francine took one more look around before she jumped.

Still breathing heavily, she got up fast and fixed her uniform. She then proceeded toward the corner of the hospital building. A few more steps and she would be in a much safer place.

Suddenly, as she was turning the corner, Francine saw a German soldier walking toward her. She slowed down her steps, trying to act normal.

With her heart pounding harder and harder, it was almost impossible to remain calm. She looked down as he approached her.

"Oh, I'm so sorry," Francine rushed to say as the soldier purposely bumped into her.

"What are you doing here?" he asked her, puzzled.

"I was going home," she explained while squeezing her hands together, in an attempt to stop them from shaking. It was then that she realized that the soldier was speaking German to her and that she, without thinking, had answered in German as well.

"You speak German," the soldier said, to Francine's horror.

"Only a little," Francine tried to say, forcing a stronger accent in German. Out of her nervousness, she had made a big mistake.

The soldier, however, seemed undisturbed by her answer. He looked Francine over from head to toe without hiding his admiration.

"Why are you coming from around the building?" the soldier finally continued.

"I'm a nurse here. I just wanted to take a walk before going home," Francine said, feeling very uneasy with his intrusive stare.

"So, you like to go on walks alone … in the dark?" he asked maliciously, his eyes examining her whole body again.

"I have to go," Francine said as she tried to move past him.

"I'll see you again," the soldier said, suddenly grabbing one of her arms.

Startled, Francine stared at him, afraid he would never let her leave. "I really have to go," she insisted. "I have to be here very early tomorrow morning."

Francine slowly jerked her arm away from his tight grip. She turned around and walked away toward the hospital exit. She wanted to run, scared the soldier would come after her, but she knew that could only make things worse.

To her relief, Frederick was already waiting for her in the parking lot.

"Are you okay, Francine?" he asked, noticing her pale expression.

"Oui," she replied, still shaky. "I think so. Let's just go, Frederick. Let's get out of here, fast."

CHAPTER 9

Francine got home and waited for Frederick and Marie to go to sleep. She felt exhausted from working and from all of the stress she had experienced during the last few hours. But there was one more thing she needed to do before she could finally get some rest.

The house was quiet, and Francine knew it was the right time to move. She took a peek outside to make sure no one was there. Then, she walked toward one of the tallest trees in her backyard and proceeded with the usual steps - the notes and camera would go inside a box and then be buried by that tree.

Focusing on her task, she didn't realize someone had been watching her. All of a sudden, a familiar voice came from the woods.

"Francine?" Julian whispered her name.

Francine jumped, looking all over to find where the voice was coming from. "Who is there?"

"Julian," he said, already walking toward her.

"Julian! You scared me! Again!"

"Sorry, ma chérie," he smiled at her. "Not my intention. Trust me!!"

They hugged each other, and Francine immediately felt safer in his arms. It was a great surprise at a perfect time.

Slowly and gently, Julian moved her body away from him, looking at her with concern. "Francine, I have heard certain things about you."

"What things?" Francine asked, wondering if he already knew she had joined the Resistance.

"You'd better stop what you're doing," Julian warned in a serious tone of voice.

"Doing what?" Francine persisted, trying to pretend she didn't know what he was implying.

"Francine, you don't understand how dangerous that is. I know you're trying to contribute, trying to be helpful. But that won't bring your father back. What you're doing in the hospital is already enough. It's more than enough."

"How did you find out?" she said, unable to lie to him.

"I know the people you are working with. We often collaborate with one another. And it was during one of our meetings that I heard about a young French nurse who was helping us out with special missions inside the local hospital. I had my suspicions … So, I decided to inquire about that mysterious person. Well, it wasn't that hard to get a name. I cannot tell you I was surprised!"

"What do you want me to do, Julian? Hide? Do nothing? We have lost so many of our friends and family. I have to deal with those bastards every day at the hospital and witness their arrogance, abuse, and cruelty. I have to do something else for our people, our country!"

"I understand this, but you're already doing that by working at the hospital. You're working side by side with the enemy, as you said. That is not an easy task."

Francine shook her head in denial.

"Francine, listen to me," Julian was almost yelling at her. "You have to stop these extra activities right away. Those Nazi pigs have spies all over the place. Not to mention some of our own who have sold themselves out to the enemy. Those pieces of shit! You see … you can't expose yourself or who you're working for. Do you know what the Germans would do to you if they found out? Especially since you're a woman?"

Julian paused for a moment. "I'll tell the guys that your work has been completed and that it will stop from now on."

"No, Julian," Francine said, looking right into his eyes. "You can't do that! I am not going to stop!"

"That was your last assignment, Francine," Julian took a few steps closer to her, holding her arms gently. "Promise me."

"I can't promise you that," Francine sighed. "I don't know. I have to think about it. I don't want to give up."

"Francine, just think about it! You're working too hard at the hospital. You're already too visible because of the fact you're working with the Germans every day. That is more than anyone could have asked of you. We are proud of you, Francine. Trust me! But the other stuff has to stop! They could easily find out what you're doing. They'll torture you until you tell them everything you know. So, please understand that when I say you have to stop, it's because you will put yourself at great risk and severely compromise the Resistance. You never got any training. We really appreciate your efforts, but it is too dangerous right now. Do you understand?"

"I guess I do," Francine said, remembering everything that happened only a few hours earlier. With tears in her eyes, she looked down a brief moment. "Everything has changed, Julian. There is so much pain and uncertainty everywhere …"

"I know," he said while holding her closer to him.

Feeling the warmth and comfort of that embrace, Francine let the tears roll down her face. It had been a long time since she allowed herself to cry.

But Francine felt weak for doing so. She knew so many other people were living through circumstances much worse than her own. Too much had already happened, and they had no idea when or if it would ever be over.

"Francine," Julian said, gently wiping the tears off her cheeks. "I know things are hard for everyone. We have to keep believing; otherwise, what else do we have left? And you are not giving yourself enough credit! You work side by side with those German bastards and still have to attend to their wounded. I would not be able to do that."

Francine nodded in agreement. Deep inside, she knew he was right.

"Now, why don't you go back home and get some rest? Stay away from those other activities, all right? I'll tell your friends that the Germans have been watching your house and that it's dangerous for you and for them to continue. And you know that is the truth, Francine, it is dangerous! I'll be delivering you news as much as I can."

Francine noticed how much Julian cared for her in his eyes. She felt guilty for not loving a man who would do anything for her. But the harsh truth was that her feelings for Julian did not go beyond those of a dear friend.

"I'll stop it," Francine finally agreed. "I promise."

"That's good! That's what I want to hear!" a pleased smile spread across his face as he embraced Francine again.

"Stay safe," Julian choked up. There was a sadness in his voice that echoed all the anguish he felt inside. It was always so hard to part from her, never knowing when or if he would ever see her again.

"You, too! Take care of yourself," Francine replied tenderly.

She waved one more goodbye and entered her house. As she lay in her bed, she closed her eyes. Despite her exhaustion, her mind immediately took her to a place she didn't want to go. Francine wondered if Hans would do the same for her, the same as Julian was doing. *Of course not*, she concluded; *he's the enemy, the enemy! I'm a traitor for still thinking of him! I have to forget he exists! Even if it is the last thing I do in this life!*

But who was she trying to fool? The love she felt for him had found a permanent home in her heart. In vain, she tried to analyze it and find an explanation for such a profound feeling that even time wasn't able to erase.

Weeks went by, and Francine had not received any other secret messages or requests. Julian had fulfilled his promises. Although Francine still wondered if she had made the right decision, it didn't take her long to be sure when things at the hospital started to get more challenging for her.

The German soldier she had encountered the night when she had jumped out of the window took advantage of any opportunity to get closer to her. She pretended she didn't notice it at first, but it became harder for her to avoid his presence as the days went by.

His name was Michael Mencken, an austere German soldier who would not hesitate to punish anyone harshly who crossed his path. In his late twenties, the attractive young man would often prey on the French women, enjoying his power over them and the fear he could see on their faces. For him, seduction was an art that he had learned to master … love was simply a game.

And it was, during that state of affairs, that everything changed for Francine.

With her back facing the door and her thoughts far away, Francine didn't notice someone approaching her in that small resting room.

"How are you doing, Francine?" a voice asked her in German.

Scared, she instantly looked back. It was him, the same German soldier who constantly harassed her.

"You're not going to answer me?" Michael insisted impatiently.

As if she were frozen where she sat, she remained quiet. She had to think about a way to get out of that situation.

"I know you can understand German," Michael whispered in her ear as he got even closer. "Don't lie to me. Things could get worse for you really fast. And we don't want that to happen, do we?"

Francine's face paled.

"I don't understand what you're saying," Francine slowly replied in French, trying to look calm.

Since the night Michael had found her walking alone in the dark, he started to develop a strange and dangerous infatuation with Francine. As much as he disliked any French person, he couldn't help but feel extremely attracted to her.

Francine started to appeal to him as prey, a prize, or perhaps a fun challenge. And for that reason, he wanted to wait a little longer instead of forcing her right away, as he was used to doing with other women. He liked that game of conquest, although her strong resistance was slowly starting to drive him mad. Michael saw her as an inferior woman compared to those of the Aryan race. Nevertheless, his pride couldn't and wouldn't allow her to reject him. She would have to be his at all costs.

Looking straight at her face, Michael took a few steps closer to her, blocking her body from a potential exit. Slowly, he bent his knees to be at the same level as her.

Unable to stand up, Francine quickly moved her face away in fear and disgust.

"You will speak German and only German to me! Do you understand that?" Michael demanded, feeling angry for her rejection. "I could get you into so much trouble just by simply letting my superiors know that you've hidden the fact you speak German."

Francine knew she was in a dilemma.

"I can only speak a few things in German," she said slowly, trying to mess up on a few words. She wanted to make him think she wasn't fluent.

But Michael simply laughed at her, amused by her accent. "I think you speak just fine!"

As he looked away momentarily, Francine saw the opportunity for an escape. She got up abruptly from her chair, pushing Michael backwards.

Only losing his balance for a few seconds, he stood up quickly, and wasting no time, he grabbed her arms, pulling her close to him.

"Let me go. I have to go back to work," Francine demanded, looking right into his eyes, determined not to show fear.

Feeling a mix of anger and desire, Michael wanted to slap her across the face for what he considered to be an insult. But at the same time, he couldn't help but feel like kissing her as he continued to press his body against hers.

Before Michael could do anything else, the door behind them opened. Doctor Louis entered the room, much to Francine's relief.

"Francine! I've been looking for you everywhere!" the doctor told her, immediately recognizing Francine was in a difficult situation. "We have a lot of patients that need your attention right away. Follow me now!"

Michael stared at the doctor with anger, then he looked at Francine, releasing her abruptly.

Francine moved away from Michael and rushed to follow the doctor. She took a quick look back, noticing the fury in the soldier's eyes.

Doctor Louis headed straight to his office with Francine by his side.

"Francine," he whispered as he walked. "It's getting too dangerous for a young lady like yourself to be here."

"I know," Francine said, running her shaky fingers through her hair. "I don't know what I am going to do? He keeps harassing me."

"Why didn't you tell me that before?" Louis asked her, concerned.

"I didn't want to bother anyone. We all have more serious problems to worry about."

"Francine … I saw the way he was looking at you, and I feared for your safety. These soldiers are capable of committing the worst atrocities. They can do just about anything they want with you when we are not around."

"I understand that, Doctor Louis. I will be more careful. Don't worry!"

"You know it's not that easy," the doctor continued as they entered his office. "It seems like that soldier is going out of his way to get to you. That is dangerous. I have promised your father to watch over you. I think it's time to get you out of here fast. I have some friends and …"

"No, please, Doctor Louis. I can't run away like that. I appreciate your concern, but I'll be fine. I just need to be extra careful and pay more attention to my surroundings."

"I don't know if that will be enough, Francine. But from now on, you shouldn't stay alone anywhere in this hospital anymore. That's an order! In the meantime, I can try to talk to some of his superiors. We need to find a way to get him out of here as soon as possible. I will also ask Mother Sueli to always work by your side and watch over you."

"All right, Doctor Louis," Francine said, trying to put a smile on her face. "I won't stay alone anymore."

The doctor knew it wouldn't be an easy task to keep that soldier away from Francine. The Germans at the hospital couldn't care less for their safety. *I have to get a travel pass for her,* the doctor thought. *Then I can convince her to leave the country and join her mother in Switzerland.*

CHAPTER 10

Like so many other Germans, Hans was starting to experience more and more of the war's impact firsthand.

In his case, his struggles were primarily psychological. He felt disgusted with his country's government and everyone who supported it. The level of anger and ignorance fueled by the dangers of deep nationalism was reaching its highest point in Germany. They needed someone to blame. They needed to find justifications for what they were doing. The Nazi Party used perversive and effective propaganda based on race and ethnicity to poison the minds of those willing to accept lies, injustice, or anything that could help them to fix their own personal problems or gain a position of advantage in that new society. History was repeating itself.

When Hans saw all the Jewish people taken as prisoners to the ghettos and heard the rumors of what was happening to them inside those restricted areas, he knew he had to do something. He couldn't just stand back and watch.

Hans got out of his office and headed straight toward Carson's military station across the street. Carson's base was primarily responsible for guarding their hometown, particularly the segregated buildings arranged for the Jewish population.

He walked fast, anger and indignation heating his blood again. He was able to enter the building easily due to his friendship with the station's Commander.

"What the hell do you think you're doing?" Hans asked Carson, slamming the door behind them.

"What now, Hans?" Carson asked his so-called brother. He was already accustomed to Hans's temper over what he felt were irrelevant matters.

"What you're doing to those people is inhuman!! I can't believe this is happening here! I'm appalled, disgusted!" Hans said furiously. "I saw Mr. Elliot and his family being dragged into that awful place! What will happen to all of them?"

"Mr. Elliot and his family are Jews, Hans! When are you going to start acting more like a patriot?"

"A patriot?" Hans replied in the same tone. "Is that what you call this now? Patriotism? A bunch of brainwashed people who somehow think they are gods? Who gave us the right and power over life and death? We must have lost our sanity completely! A patriot? What has happened to you, my friend? Or can I still call you my friend? Are you going to arrest me now, too?"

Carson sighed, looking away for a moment. Hans's behavior was as expected. However, he was growing really tired of Hans's constant complaints. In Carson's young and corrupted mind, his pride and deep devotion to Nazi Germany spoke higher than any other argument. No one could convince him otherwise.

"Carson," Hans continued as if he could read his mind. "We are killing innocent people, depriving them of their family, property, and freedom. I have been hearing horrifying stories about what's happening to them."

Without looking at Hans, Carson got up and went to the window. He stopped there for a few seconds as his facial expression started to change.

"Hans … I don't understand your dangerous attachment to the Jews. They have always represented what has been wrong with our country. Such parasites should be eliminated. We have goals to meet, and we can't allow anyone to stand in our way."

Hans looked at his friend in total disbelief. He knew Carson had been brainwashed, but he never expected his friend would condone such barbaric behavior.

"Such parasites? Did I hear you right? I can't believe this. We are talking about people here! Have you gone crazy? Is that what you are doing now? Eliminating so-called parasites? No … not you, Carson. Not you, who I consider to be like my own brother. I don't know what to say except that I will not stand by and watch this happen."

"Hans!" Carson yelled as he quickly turned around, staring right into Hans's eyes. "Watch what you say and do! They still have your father. I care for your family as my own, but I can't protect you forever if you insist on behaving this way. I hope you still remember what happened the last time you tried to do something!"

"Right! Now I need protection!" Hans answered with a sarcastic laugh. "And why is that? Well … let me see … my great country, along with its great people, is turning against itself. My family and I are also prisoners of this great Germany rising before our eyes. Not to mention the millions of people that die and suffer every day with this damned war that we started!!!"

"There you go again, Hans! You have to stop with this shit!! You know very well that your father was connected to dangerous people," Carson tried to justify. "I warned him about it, but he didn't want to listen, just like you. But like I said before, he should be released any day now. I'm doing everything I can to get Mr. Alfred out of there. I like and respect him more than my own father, and you know that!"

"Yet, after everything they have done to him, our father, you still insist on defending our government and that lunatic, Hitler! You have chosen a dangerous path, Carson. I'm so disappointed and disgusted. Why is it so hard for you to see it?"

"They are simply Jews!" Carson screamed at Hans while punching his table. "They are not true Germans, and they will never be! It's you who can't see or understand what we are trying to do here. But one day, you will applaud our efforts. One day you will realize that we will finally be where we should have always been ... above everyone else, the most powerful nation in the world!"

"What are you talking about? Have you listened to yourself speaking?" Hans replied quickly in anger. "We are no better than any other race. If anything, we just fell right under everyone else ... to the lowest and most sordid level! How can you follow that man? How can you be so blind?"

"You're lucky you're considered to be my family."

"Really?" Hans said, approaching Carson. "What would you do if I wasn't? Would you just shoot me right now, like your Nazi friends have been doing to so many others, just because I disagree or stand in your way? Isn't that the new German way of doing things?"

"Stop saying all this stupid shit, Hans, before someone hears you! Like I would shoot you or let anyone else do it, for that matter. How ridiculous! You're always so dramatic, so preoccupied with others. Why can't you just be concerned with your own life? You're not only compromising yourself but our entire family and even me!"

"I don't know you anymore. You have truly become one of them, just like everyone else. You should be ashamed of yourself for following a crazy man's idea like a sheep! I hope this "Great Empire" goes under and, along with it, all this illusion of superiority!! I know things will change one day, and Germany will lose this war!"

Carson's face transformed completely, turning into a mottled red, reflecting all his indignity. Hans had finally succeeded in getting him very angry. He wanted to punch him in the face or simply arrest him for a few days to teach him a lesson.

"I could easily arrest you for that, Hans," Carson said in a shaky voice. "Be careful of what you say before you get into trouble. If anyone hears what you just said, even I won't be able to save you."

"Save me? You must be joking! The Nazis have acquired full power to save or not save people's lives whenever they wish to do so? That is wonderful! Now I have to depend on someone's mercy to save me from my own country. Look at us, my brother! Look at all the pride and glory built on the spread of misery and blood. You should be horrified by all of this! I bet your mother would be, too."

Carson's face suddenly turned pale. Hans was able to take him back in time … to a distant past. Both their families were already neighbors before they were born. From an early age, Carson and Hans had become best friends, practically inseparable. Carson was still very young when his mother unexpectedly passed away. Because his father was a businessman who often traveled out of the country, Hans's parents decided to take full care of Carson and treated him as their own son.

As time went on, his birth father's visits became scarcer. Then one day, Carson received a letter from his dad saying he got married again and was going to stay in Africa. He invited Carson to live with him and his new family, but Carson preferred to stay with the Schulzes.

Carson looked down, placing both hands against his desk. He still could feel the pain of losing his mother. He knew very well that his beloved mother, who remained vivid in his memories, would never have approved of his behavior. Until Hans mentioned it to him, he had never considered what she might have thought.

Taking advantage of the moment, Hans continued, "your mother was the personification of love, respect, and charity. I still remember her. She was always considerate and loving. She also really liked Mr. Elliot and his family, who happen to be Jews. They were really good friends. We used to play with his son at his house all the time when we were kids. Plus, he was our teacher, Carson! Damn it! Don't you remember? He was so patient with us, even when we would do something stupid in class. He's a good man. Can't you see that?"

Carson sighed. As much as he didn't want to admit it, he knew Hans was right about his mother. He missed her a lot, and Hans had the power to make him feel uncomfortable with the past.

"I'll see what I can do to get Mr. Elliot better accommodations," Carson finally said, wanting to get Hans out of his sight.

"It's not just Mr. Elliot, Carson. There are so many others …"

"Enough, Hans! I will not do more than that. And I'll only do it in memory of my mother, and that is all you are going to get. And I do not promise anything!"

Carson steeled himself.

"Now go away … let me get some work done!" Carson said, scrounging for his cigar.

Hans stood there, just staring at him.

"Auf Wiedersehen!" Carson muttered as he lit up his cigar, ignoring his friend.

Still frustrated, Hans turned around and walked away. He knew there was nothing else he could do there.

He went straight home. He wished he could just leave Germany to get away from all that insanity. But he knew he wouldn't be able to leave his friends behind, many of whom depended on him.

Immersed in his own thoughts, Hans didn't hear the voice right away calling for him from the living room.

"Hans?" Elga repeated.

"Hi, Mother," he replied with no enthusiasm.

"What's the matter?" she asked him, noticing his agitation.

"I hate this country! I hate what we have become!"

"I know, my son. A dark shadow has taken us over. We'll all have to carry it for years and years to come as a shameful mark that will forever stain our history and our people."

Hans felt very lucky to have such a loving and caring mother. Elga was very different from so many other women whose sensibility had been destroyed by the Nazi regime. Hans was proud of his family.

CHAPTER 11

Several days had passed. The sun had already set on the horizon when Hans got home from another long day at work, only to find a great surprise. He couldn't believe it when he saw his father and mother talking at the dining table. The sound of their voices filled the air, bringing a sense of happiness back to the house.

"Father?" Hans rushed over to him.

"Hans!" Alfred exclaimed, getting up from his chair.

As they hugged each other, smiles of joy and relief lit up their faces. Alfred was finally back home!

They stayed there for a long time, talking about everything that had happened during the past weeks. They had missed each other's company and conversations. Hans updated his father about the latest news and all the other atrocities being committed by the Nazis. They waited for Elga to go to bed to be able to talk more seriously.

"We need to get out of here," Alfred said, worried. "Our situation is complicated, and we basically depend on Carson to keep us safe. I don't know what would have happened to me if it weren't for his help. However, we cannot know with certainty that it will always be the case. I don't believe this war will end any time soon from everything you have told me. For now, I don't see another alternative but to leave Germany. We need to arrange documentation for us to be able to travel. I refuse to support Germany. I refuse to be part of this!"

"How about Carson? Have you talked to him? He can definitely get the travel authorizations in a faster manner."

"I spoke to him earlier today," Alfred explained. "As ironic as it may sound, we still have to be grateful to him for my release."

"I understand this, but the whole thing still infuriates me! He is a part of all of this misery. He achieved the power to release you but at what cost?"

"I know, Hans. I feel the same way. But for now, let's remember what he has risked in order to get me out of that place."

Hans decided not to continue the argument.

"Carson said he would be leaving shortly to go to Berlin," Alfred continued. "He is expecting to stay there for quite some time. He mentioned that he would try to get special authorizations to travel with some of his influential business friends to avoid suspicion. He said my case is a delicate one and might require extra effort on his part. But you see, Hans … I am not willing to wait for him. We also have other friends."

Hans nodded, fully agreeing with the plan. As for him, though, he wasn't sure if he would be able to leave Germany, no matter how much he wanted to. He had his reasons … too many people depended on him.

Hans and Alfred knew they would have to be really careful with everything they did from then on. After Alfred's arrest, they knew there would probably be someone watching them and their house.

Hans went to bed and was finally able to fall asleep easier. It had been a long time since he felt some peace of mind. The great surprise of his father's return and his supportive attitude toward the idea of leaving Germany gave Hans a new sense of enthusiasm and hope.

After that night, Hans went to work every day feeling a little more encouraged. As much as he despised working in a factory that produced war materials, he knew his presence there was vital for his Jewish friends who depended on his help. Hans was able to protect them against the fury of some Nazi officers, at least until that moment. Hans, along with his former teacher, Mr. Elliot, also found a way to provide the Jewish workers with some extra food.

In order for that to happen, they had established a careful plan. And Hans was very aware that such scheme solely depended on his authority among the soldiers who knew he was Carson's brother.

Hans wouldn't be able to trust anyone else to continue what he was doing. He felt guilty for contemplating the idea of leaving Germany. He knew he couldn't abandon them.

It was six o'clock when Hans got ready to leave work. Consumed by worries and stress weighing on his shoulders, he thought about going to a restaurant near the factory to have something to drink.

It had been over a year since he went out anywhere. He couldn't stand going to any place where people seemed to be having fun while there was so much suffering around. But that night, Hans decided to face the raw truth.

It was a warm night, lightened by the bright platinum tone of the full moon above.

Hans sat at the bar, lost in his thoughts. It was a surreal situation to be there among people whose smiles and laughter brought a creepy sense of normalcy ... as if a war wasn't happening at all.

It didn't take long for someone to recognize him and start a conversation. Hans didn't feel like talking to anyone, though. The subjects were always the same. He barely spoke, and after a few minutes, he took one last sip of his beer and excused himself, saying he had to wake up early the next day.

Walking toward his car, he passed by a dark alley. It was right at that moment when he heard screams. He stopped for a few seconds, caught by surprise. He could hear several voices, one of which was a female voice begging for help. Without hesitation, he turned around, taking a few steps back toward the alley.

As he did so, he found himself in front of a horrifying scene.

A woman was screaming and thrashing while two men were amusing themselves by ripping her clothes apart.

"No, please no!" the girl cried in desperation, trying to wiggle away from them.

Disgusted by what was happening right before him, he headed straight in their direction.

"What's going on here?" he asked loudly, trying to draw their attention away from the girl.

Surprised at seeing anyone else there, the two soldiers looked at one another.

"And who the hell are you?" one of them asked.

"Go away before you get killed!" the other shouted at him.

"Let the girl go, and then we can talk," Hans said, noticing they were both drunk.

One of the soldiers laughed at him. The other smirked, walking toward him.

Hans had no time to think of anything as the soldier was about to grab him. He reacted fast, making a fist and punching the soldier in the face so hard that he fell backward.

The other soldier looked at Hans in disbelief for a brief moment before rushing toward him. They struggled for a few seconds before Hans was finally able to push him backward until he hit the wall. Taking advantage of that situation, Hans punched his face several times as the soldier put his hands up before falling to the ground.

Hans stood there looking at both of them attempting to get to their feet – a task proving to be a lot harder due to their level of intoxication. Both soldiers looked at him, confused and surprised he could fight so well. It was only then that Hans looked at the girl. He got between the two men and the woman as she desperately tried to cover her bare chest.

"What are you going to do?" one of the men taunted him, laughing as he cleaned some of the blood off his face.

"Are you going to save the Jewish whore?" the other one added, happy to join in.

Hans understood the situation perfectly. His pulse was thundering. Even though he wasn't a violent person, he felt like beating the two beasts standing in front of him flat into the ground. He was ready to do whatever it took to teach those bastards a lesson.

The two men finally noticed that Hans wasn't kidding. They also knew they weren't in their best condition for a fight. It was then that one of them drew his gun and pointed it at Hans.

"I know the Commander of the base you both are stationed at," Hans rushed to say, recognizing the gravity of that situation. "I can get both of you into a lot of trouble very easily. I'm a rich and powerful man. And the girl is mine now. Do you understand that?"

The two soldiers looked at one another, concerned. Surprised by that revelation, they seemed to be assessing Hans's demeanor, as well as his elegant clothes.

"So, what are you and your friend, the Commander, going to do to us? We are only trying to have some fun!" one of them affirmed, still pointing the gun at Hans.

"We can find out right now! Let's go to my office where I can have access to a phone. We can wake up my brother, the Commander, and we can ask him what his thoughts are about two low-ranked soldiers pointing a gun at me!" Hans said in a serious manner. "You will regret fighting a man like me who happens to have powerful connections. How dare you question my authority, soldiers! How dare you point a gun at me!"

The soldiers looked at each other again. Their expressions sobered. They didn't want to risk their careers, much less their own lives.

Hans quickly reached for the gun that he carried around, prepared for any emergencies. He pointed it at the soldier, who had already lowered his gun a little.

"For tonight, I can show you what I can do if you would like," Hans said loudly. "You make one more move in this direction, and I'll shoot you."

They exchanged another glance. Then, the soldier reluctantly holstered his gun.

"Let's go," one of them said, getting up.

"Right," the other replied. "You can have the Jewish girl. Who needs that garbage anyway?"

They both started to walk away, stumbling into one another.

Hans followed them to the entrance of that alley, still holding his gun up, as he watched them walk away. He slowly moved his gun down. It was only then that his attention went back to that girl, who was still on the ground, sobbing and trying to cover parts of her body with her shredded clothes.

Hans looked at her with pity, noticing the terror and humiliation in her eyes.

"It's all right," Hans said, not really sure what to do at that moment. "I'm not going to hurt you."

The girl started to sob even harder. Her entire body was shaking.

Hans knew that he couldn't leave her there. He had to think of something fast. He had to get her away from there.

"Cover yourself with this and stay here, all right?" Hans said as he handed her his jacket. "I'll be back. I'll take you to a safer place."

He looked around, making sure those soldiers had really gone away. Then he ran to his car across the street and drove to the entrance of the alley.

"You have to get in the car," Hans said in a firm tone of voice. "Come on; we need to get out of here before anyone sees you! You don't need to be afraid of me. I am not going to hurt you."

She hesitated for a few seconds.

"You have to come now," Hans insisted. "People are coming this way."

She reluctantly started to walk toward his car, still very frightened.

"Come on, get in," Hans rushed her, worried about her safety.

She got in the car slowly, and Hans drove away as fast as he could.

"I'm not going to hurt you. You will be all right!" Hans repeated to her. But even he didn't know what he was going to do.

The girl simply kept her head down, weeping.

As they moved to a brighter part of the town, Hans took a better look at the girl's face. She made him immediately think of Francine. She had almost the same hair color. As he thought of her, he felt a sharp pain in his heart. He wouldn't know if the same thing was happening to Francine, whether or not she was safe. He knew she was an attractive woman with a strong personality. He could see her getting into trouble very easily. How many times he had wondered about her well-being after the German occupation of France. He looked again at the girl sitting next to him.

"Where do you live? I mean … are you at the …" Hans hesitated.

She sat there with her head down, unable to say a word to him.

He realized she must have been living in the segregated area downtown. He had heard the soldiers talking about her being Jewish.

Hans knew he had to make a decision fast. And there was only one thing to be done.

In a short while, he saw the tall gates that led to his home. He told the girl to wait in his car until his return. He went inside his house, immediately looking for his mother, who was already sleeping in her bedroom.

"Mother, I need your help. Come with me," Hans whispered in her ear as soon as she woke up.

Already in the hallway, Hans rushed to explain the situation to her, who was surprised and very concerned. She couldn't agree with his idea of bringing the Jewish girl to her home, but she knew they didn't have any other alternative at that moment. In the end, mother and son walked toward the car.

After a brief introduction, Hans took another look around, making sure there wasn't anyone watching them before taking the girl inside his home. Elga directed her to the living room while Hans went to the kitchen to get her something to eat and drink.

Elga took a good look at the girl's face. She had been beaten and hurt.

After some thought, Elga walked the girl to a guest room they had upstairs. Hans followed right after with a tray full of food.

Understanding the girl's delicate situation, Hans and his mother decided to give her some privacy.

"Try to eat something and rest. You're safe here. We can talk tomorrow," Elga promised as she left the room.

The girl looked at her with bewilderment. She was still afraid and not sure what to think of her benefactors and their hospitality.

Outside the room, Elga took a deep breath, passing her hands down her face.

"She has to go back to where she was before," Elga whispered to Hans. "Unfortunately, not one of us will be safe if she stays here."

"How can you say that?" Hans said, surprised at his mother's words. "We cannot do that to her."

"I understand, Hans. But we can't keep her here!"

"Then what do we do? Send her back to that hell? It is pretty much the same as giving her a death sentence!"

"Oh, Hans, I don't know. I don't know!" Elga replied, also wondering. "We need to talk to your father first. But, regardless of everything, we are about to leave for Switzerland soon."

"I'm not going, Mother." Hans had made his decision.

"What do you mean? You're not coming with us?"

"No, I'm not leaving with you. I can't!" Hans said adamantly. "But it's too late to talk about this now."

"Hans, you can't do this to us."

"Let's all sleep and try to get some rest," said Hans, trying to end the conversation. "We have a long day tomorrow."

"Yes, we do," Elga said, feeling more concerned. "And I hope your father can bring you back to your senses!!"

"Tomorrow, Mother," Hans said, not wanting to argue any longer.

Elga stood there watching her son as he walked away. She had a terrible feeling about all of this.

Neither mother nor son slept very well. Hans couldn't help but think about the girl. He had to do something to help her, and he couldn't imagine sending her back to that place. Hans tried to picture her face again. *She looks like Francine*, he thought. He knew that everything would drastically change for all of them. But, at that moment, he was sure he would defend that girl with whatever means he had available.

The next morning, the environment at Hans's house was very tense. Alfred was made aware of the situation. The family met behind closed doors in the library, trying to find a solution for the Jewish girl, who was still sleeping.

They knew they were facing a dangerous dilemma. It wasn't safe to keep her at the house with them, but they couldn't send her back either as they were very well aware of the atrocities committed against the Jewish people.

"We have to find a way to keep her here, safely," Hans said decisively. "We don't know of any other place or anyone that could help us! There's no other choice."

"It's too risky with the other employees. Her sudden arrival can raise suspicion," Alfred quickly replied. "Unless…"

"Unless what?" Elga asked impatiently. "I don't like where this conversation is heading."

"Unless we pretend that she's part of our family! She could be our niece that just arrived last night and will be staying with us for a few months," Alfred continued, already starting to like his own idea.

"Perfect," Hans added. "If we act naturally and explain that she'll be staying with us for a while, that should not raise any suspicions."

"At least for now. It will buy us some time to come up with another solution."

"You two must be out of your minds," Elga said, shaking her head in disbelief. "It won't work! And it will expose all of us. It is too dangerous!"

"Did anyone see you arriving with her yesterday?" Alfred asked Hans promptly.

"No, I don't believe so. I looked around several times and didn't see anyone. I also made sure I wasn't being followed when driving home. The two men were so drunk I doubt they remember anything at all."

"It's too risky," Elga lectured. "Especially after what happened to your father."

"Don't worry about me, Elga. I know it's dangerous, but what can we do?"

Elga didn't know what to say.

"We can't send her back," Hans broke the silence. "They would kill her if they thought she tried to escape!"

Alfred nodded his head in agreement, remembering his past conversations with Hans about the ghettos and concentration camps.

"I understand what you are trying to do, and I also worry about her fate, but still, it doesn't make sense keeping her here! I don't think either one of you is thinking clearly. You're putting our own safety at risk for a girl we barely know!"

"Mother, the chances of her survival if we send her back are very slim. How would you feel if she died over there? Or if she fell into the hands of the same soldiers who tried to hurt her? What if she was truly part of our family?"

"But she isn't, Hans!" Elga quickly replied. "I know what I'm saying sounds cold and heartless, but as a mother and a wife, I can't help but think about your safety and my husband's."

"Elga," Alfred said, trying to change her mind, "Hans and I understand your motives. I'm also concerned for our family. However, I couldn't live with myself knowing that we had the chance to save someone's life, and we refused."

"But what will happen to her after we leave?"

"We'll think about that later," Hans replied, not knowing the answer himself. "Besides, we are still waiting for the travel authorizations. None of our friends have been able to provide them for us yet. We might have to wait until Carson's return, and we don't know when that will happen. In the meantime, we will do what we can for her."

"And what about Carson? He will find out this is a lie."

"Well, Hans and I were talking about it before you joined us this morning. We already have a plan."

"I still don't know how this can work out."

"Hans and I have already made up our minds, Elga," Alfred told her decisively as he hugged her tightly. "Now, it is up to you!"

Elga looked up into their eyes.

"I guess I don't have much choice here," she said, defeated.

They both smiled at her.

"The question now is … will she agree with that?" Alfred asked, looking at Hans.

The three of them stayed there together a while longer, going over every single detail of their story. There wouldn't be any margin for errors. They were well aware of the implications and dangers of the lie. But none of them felt able to abandon that girl to her own luck.

CHAPTER 12

Denna woke up in that elegant but unfamiliar place, feeling very alarmed.

She tried to get up but couldn't. Her entire body felt heavy, and her head still hurt from all the bruises. The memories of the previous night slowly started to come back to her. *Whose house is this?* she thought. *Who are these people?*

A few minutes later, she heard a knock at the door. Terrified, she didn't know what to expect. She had to use all her strength to sit down, covering part of her body with the blanket.

The door started to open slowly. A friendly face appeared with a tray in her hands.

"Guten morgen," Elga said softly, seeing the fear in the girl's eyes.

The girl smiled back but didn't say a word. Denna wondered if the woman could be Jewish. *But how could that happen?* she wondered. *All Jewish families were placed in the ghettos or relocated to other places.*

Elga looked at the girl with pity and wondered about her family. *They must be worried sick!* She couldn't even think about the possibility of the same happening to her son.

Denna looked at her curiously while Elga carefully placed the breakfast tray on the nightstand near her bed.

"I am not sure if you remember me from yesterday. My name is Elga."

Denna smiled again, nodding her head. Although she still felt very confused, her fear started to subside due to Elga's friendly manner.

"You don't need to be afraid. My son was the one who brought you here yesterday."

As Denna started to remember the young man who had suddenly come to her rescue the night before, Elga picked up the tray, placing it closer to her.

"Thank you," Denna timidly said to her. "Thank you very much for helping me last night. I don't know what I would have done alone." She paused for a moment. "My name is Denna."

Elga smiled at her. "It is nice to meet you, Denna."

The young woman smiled back awkwardly, still feeling uncomfortable with that situation.

"So … it was your son who brought me here?"

"Yes, it was my son, Hans."

"I would like to thank him," Denna said with gratitude. "Are you … Jewish?"

"No, we are not. But you should not fear us. As for my son, he would like to come here to talk to you."

"I would like that," Denna looked down before continuing. "I am very grateful for everything you have done. But … I need to go back as soon as possible, before they notice my absence. My parents must be very concerned."

"I understand that," Elga gently replied. "But we fear that it will be too dangerous for you. Perhaps it would be better if you stay here for now."

Denna studied Elga, puzzled by the stranger's kindness.

The two of them continued to talk as Elga explained the situation and their plan. Denna hesitated at first. Concerned about her family, she wanted them to know she was safe. But even she wasn't sure about that. She knew she couldn't trust anyone.

Inside the library, Hans waited anxiously to speak to their new guest. His mother urged him to wait until she could talk to her first. Elga knew that the girl would need some time to think about everything that had happened.

It was only later that day when Hans finally met his new friend again.

"Come in," Denna said as soon as she heard the knock at the door.

Hans stepped into the bedroom slowly, smiling at her.

"Hello …" he said awkwardly. "My mother told me your name … Denna, right?"

"Yes … and you are Hans, I suppose," the girl replied timidly.

"So, you're my cousin now," Hans said, trying to make her feel more comfortable.

Denna smiled at him with tears in her eyes. He had saved her life.

"I want to thank you for everything you have done for me. What you did yesterday… I …"

"You don't need to remember those things," he quickly replied, not wanting her to relive the sad events of the night before.

Denna looked at Hans again, touched by the noble actions of that young man who had risked his own life to save her.

"I appreciate everything you and your family have done for me. There aren't enough words to express my deep gratitude. You have risked so much to help me!"

"It's the least we can do," Hans said with sincerity. "And I am very sorry for everything that has happened to you, to your people. I can't comprehend all the cruelty, the hatred that has taken over this country. My father, my family and so many of our friends have tried to stop the Nazi lunacy, but we got nowhere. We just couldn't stop them … So, like I said, this is the least we can do, and we are glad we can help somehow."

Little by little, Hans explained to her the details of their plan, making sure she understood there was no other way for them to deal with the situation. She would have to live there with them for a while; in doing so, she would have to play a new role and act in a certain way in front of other people. Denna would have to know about Hans's family history and be familiar with their traditions. She would have to assume a new identity and hide her own.

As Hans spoke, Denna started to think about that new reality being presented to her. Deep in her heart, she knew Hans was right. She would have to be very strong and brave.

The night arrived quickly, and in the darkness of her room, Denna felt the tears rolling down her face. Everything in her life had changed again! Even though she was in a comfortable place and being treated very well, there wasn't any guarantee that the Schulzes would be able to keep her away from the Nazi wrath. Immense guilt took hold of her soul, knowing that her family was still in a terrible place, in a dirty little room, suffering all sorts of deprivation. Her only consolation rested with Hans, who had promised to inform her family that she was alive and unharmed, and also try to help them any way he could.

Denna adjusted well to family life as time went by, making it easier for people to believe their farce. Mrs. Kaufmann, the maid that worked for Hans's family, found the girl a little strange at first. Still, not in her wildest dreams did she think the girl living in their house was Jewish. By keeping her in plain sight and not trying to hide her, the Schulzes gave the story a sense of legitimacy.

It wasn't until weeks later that Hans found a way to communicate with Denna's family. But the exchange of information only happened once through a simple note stating she was all right. Nothing more could be said as they knew how dangerous it was for everyone involved.

Hans tried to make Denna's life a little brighter. All his efforts were in vain, though, once Denna received the devastating news that her family was being moved to an unknown location. She wondered if she would ever see them again, but Hans never gave up. He kept reminding her that there was still hope that war could be over soon and the Allies could win! She would then be able to reunite with her parents.

During those times of uncertainty, they saw the days passing by, then weeks and months.

The trees slowly recovered their leaves and bright colors, announcing the beginning of one more spring. The Schulze family kept postponing their exit from Germany. Not only did they have to wait for Carson's return from his long trip to Berlin to get their authorization papers, but they also struggled to find a solution that would keep Denna safe. Should they try to take her with them out of the country? Or should they keep on hiding her there at their house until the war was over? There were no easy answers. They knew that whatever they decided to do would be of great risk.

CHAPTER 13

A gentle breeze offered some relief from that hot summer day. Francine looked out the window; her thoughts traveled far away. She remembered how much she used to enjoy those sunny days, her walks around the park, listening to the different sounds of nature all around her. Francine would be sitting by the river, watching the sun rays sparkle against the cool water running under her feet. She could feel the heat of the sun on her skin and the fresh smell of lilies in the air. There were so much beauty and pleasure in the simple things of life.

"Francine," a voice woke her up from her daydreaming.

"Oui," Francine turned around, not liking the look on Mother Sueli's face.

"I think we have a problem," the nun said, worried. "The German Commander of this establishment wants to see you."

Francine's face fell. *Would they have found out anything about my participation in the Resistance?*

"I don't have a good feeling about this, ma chérie," Mother Sueli continued. "Please tell me you haven't done anything you weren't supposed to, Francine."

"Of course not, Mother," Francine said, trying to calm her down. But inside, she was already expecting the worst. The Commander never asked to see anyone unless there was trouble.

"Doctor Louis is already there. He wanted to be there with you."

They walked together toward the Commander's office. And just like Mother Sueli had said, Doctor Louis was already waiting for Francine in the hallway. Noticing the tension on his face, she got even more nervous.

"Just try to stay calm," the doctor advised. "Let me do the talking."

"But what is going on?" she asked apprehensively.

"They didn't want to say anything," he affirmed, also worried.

Mother Sueli was ordered to stay behind as they both entered the Commander's office.

"Francine," the Commander said in a cold and serious tone. "You have been selected to be relocated to another facility." Contrary to her friend's reaction, Francine surprisingly found relief in those words. She was positive they had found out about her participation in the Resistance, so she didn't even care about being relocated at the moment.

Doctor Louis did not understand what the Commander had said in German and looked at the translator for help.

"Another location?" the doctor inquired, wondering about the absurdity of that decision.

"What did he say?" the German Commander asked the translator, a French man working for the SS in France. "Tell him not to speak unless he is told to do so."

Doctor Louis heard the reply from the translator. He felt even angrier. But he knew he had to stay calm to avoid making things even harder for Francine.

"It has come to my attention that you speak German," the Commander looked at her with contempt.

"I'm not fluent," Francine rushed to say, purposely stumbling on some of her German words.

"It doesn't matter! We should have been informed about that fact a long time ago," he added harshly, glancing at the doctor. "Anyway, we will now send you to a more appropriate location."

Francine quickly realized she would be punished for hiding her fluency in German.

"Where is she going?" Doctor Louis turned to the French translator.

"To another hospital," the man replied right after the German Commander. "Another hospital in Germany."

The two friends immediately looked at one another in desperation. The word Germany sent shivers down Francine's body.

"Francine can't be transferred there!" Doctor Louis rushed to say, followed by the translator. "We need her here. We are short-handed. Plus, we have an agreement with the German government that our people wouldn't have to be put in danger and …."

"That is enough!" the Commander said loudly, cutting off the translator. "France is under the German government's control, and its people should behave accordingly. You have no right to have an opinion on such matters!"

Doctor Louis's face turned red, revealing all his anger. It took him everything he had not to attack that arrogant and presumptuous man.

"You can go home to get some of your things," the Commander said, sitting in his chair. "Some soldiers will follow you."

"Am I leaving now?" Francine asked, still in shock.

"Yes, that was what I said! Now, leave! All of you!"

Francine looked at Doctor Louis in disbelief. He still attempted to convince the Commander to allow Francine to stay a few more days but to no avail.

The doctor looked at the Commander with hatred. He promised himself that one day, once the war was over and the Allies won, he would chase that horrendous man down and bring him to justice, no matter how far or how long it would take him.

Francine and the doctor rushed out of the office only to see German soldiers already waiting for her outside. It was then that she realized someone was staring at her from the other end of the corridor. It was Michael, standing against the wall with his arms crossed and a smirk on his face.

"They are taking her to Germany!" Doctor Louis informed the nun who anxiously waited for an explanation.

"Move!" one of the German soldiers ordered Francine, pushing her forward.

Still trying to process that information, both Mother Sueli and Doctor Louis followed Francine. As she passed by Michael, she heard him whisper, "I'll see you in Germany, Francine."

A terrible feeling took hold of her. At that moment, she knew that Michael was the one responsible for her departure. *That insolent bastard!* she thought. *It all makes sense now!*

With tears in her eyes, the nun tried to comfort the young nurse. "You will be all right, child."

"I'll find a way to get you back," Doctor Louis insisted. "It doesn't matter how long it takes. I won't give up."

Francine tried to remain calm. She knew she had to find a way out of that dreadful situation.

"You're strong, Francine," the nun said through her tears. "Trust in our Lord; he will protect you!"

Unable to say any words, Francine just nodded with a sad smile on her face.

After a quick goodbye, she was tossed inside the military vehicle. While in the car, Francine started to think about communicating to someone within the Resistance about her departure. She had hopes that perhaps they could help her escape. Her biggest fear was Michael. *Was he really going back to Germany as he had told?* She knew that if Michael were going to the same place she was, it would be the end of her life. She would be alone and with no one to help her.

Francine squeezed both of her hands together nervously as the military vehicle approached her home. Some of her neighbors came closer to her house to see what was going on. She entered the house quickly and went straight to her room. She had to find a way to leave a note in the secret location behind her house. Almost instantly, Frederick came rushing toward her. The two soldiers stayed right outside of her bedroom, watching her pack her things.

"Where are they taking you?" Frederick asked her frantically.

"Germany!"

Frederick's eyes opened widely, stunned by the news.

Francine started to whisper. "Write to my mother that I'll be relocated to another hospital. Tell her not to worry. I'll be all right. I will try to communicate as soon as possible."

Frederick looked at Francine and then at the soldiers. He knew that the situation was more serious than Francine wanted him to know.

She asked to go to the bathroom. Quickly and quietly, she grabbed a lipstick and started to write on a piece of paper she had grabbed from her desk.

She went back toward her room and found Frederick in the hallway. She carefully placed it in Frederick's hands as she hugged him goodbye. She whispered, "behind the tallest tree in the backyard, there is a box. Leave the note there. Try to find Julian and tell him everything. He might be able to help!"

"I have a gun in my coat pocket," Frederick offered Francine.

"No!" Francine exclaimed, grabbing his arm. "There are soldiers outside as well; it is too dangerous! Please tell your wife to communicate with my mother."

"Where exactly are they taking you?"

"Je ne sais pas, mon ami," Francine replied while soldiers yelled at her to hurry up. "I will be all right. Tell my mother I will find a way out of this!"

One of the soldiers pushed Francine back to her bedroom, demanding her to grab her things fast.

She took a final look around her room. *Will I ever come back?* She thought with teary eyes.

"Let's go!" the soldier shouted at her impatiently.

"Au revoir, mon ami," Francine told Frederick as she passed by him.

He looked at her, feeling powerless and angry. He felt the gun in his pocket and thought of taking action.

Francine looked back at him as if guessing what he was about to do.

"It is all right, Frederick, it is all right. Don't do anything foolish! I will be fine!"

Francine saw a trail of dust left behind as the car kept moving forward, farther and farther away from her home. As she looked back, she wondered if she would be able to return one day.

"Au revoir," Francine whispered, trying to hold the tears that stubbornly filled her eyes. She knew she would need to be even braver, no matter what lay ahead.

It didn't take long for them to arrive at the train station. Two German guards rushed Francine inside the train. She was forced to sit right next to a German soldier. She took a quick look around, desperately trying to find a familiar face, someone who could help her, to save her. She thought about her family and her friends, Julian, Pierre, and so many others. But there was no one there. She was surrounded by the enemy.

The train blew its final whistle. Slowly, the locomotive started moving forward, taking one of its passengers to an unknown location.

The night had fallen as the last rays of the sun disappeared into the horizon. Francine looked out the window, trying to find any clues to tell her exactly where she was. But all she could see were Nazi symbols spread on every wall of every building.

They relocated her to a city not far from the border between France and Switzerland. As soon as they arrived at the German train station, a military vehicle transported her to another location, stopping right before a heavy metal gate. Guards approached the vehicle and started to interrogate the driver. They soon noticed Francine in the back seat.

She looked at them with fear, not knowing what to expect.

Already inside the well-guarded military facility, Francine was ordered to follow a woman to a small building that resembled a hospital. She felt some relief in that. The same woman stopped briefly to talk to a nurse.

"Follow me," the nurse said in an unfriendly manner.

Not having any other choice but to obey, Francine followed the nurse who led her to the second floor.

Francine entered the room slowly. Before she could say anything, the nurse quickly shut the door behind her. She heard the sound of a key being turned; the woman was locking her in.

Feeling exhausted, she placed her baggage on the floor and looked around that small and cold room. There was very little furniture— a bed, a small closet, and a table.

She started walking toward the window. Outside, a few military vehicles moved in and out of the facility at a constant pace.

Her legs felt weak and her body heavy. Not having the strength to stand anymore, she walked back toward the small bed.

Soon after, the same nurse entered the bedroom again, carrying a tray with water, food, and a bag with some clothes and other hygiene products. In silence and without looking straight at Francine, she left the room in a hurry.

But at that moment, Francine didn't care about anything. There was nothing left to do but lie down on the bed and close her eyes. Francine's mind was still trying to comprehend all that had happened. She knew that anyone could enter the room. She knew that she would never be safe.

Tears ran down her tired face, and although she was feeling very scared, she fell asleep faster than she expected.

It was early in the morning when Francine awoke to a strange noise coming from outside the building. She got up slowly and went straight to the window, where she saw several soldiers forming a line. She knew they would be responsible for the deaths of thousands of innocent people.

Not long after, she heard her door being unlocked. She immediately moved away from the window and back toward the bed, trying to prepare herself for whatever was about to happen.

An older and chubby blond nurse entered the room. She resembled a Nazi man more than a woman with her cold manners and mechanical ways.

Francine tried to start a conversation, greeting her and asking a few questions about the place they were, but the woman pretended not to hear a word she said.

Frustrated, Francine stayed quiet, simply observing the nurse as she exited the room as fast as she arrived. She knew that this was only the beginning of a terrible nightmare.

Once the woman was gone, Francine hesitantly started to eat the slices of bread left for her on the tray. She had to take care of herself; she had to stay alive!

The sun was already shining brightly, allowing her to see everything that was happening outside. Leaning against the window, she noticed she was in a part of the building that went all the way around and formed a square. Right in the center was an open area filled with soldiers walking in and out. Francine had already realized that she was in a hospital inside a military facility. *But ... why?* she wondered. *Why would they bring me here?*

Francine thought about her father. She wondered if he had been taken to a similar facility close to Russia. *What is he going to do once he finds out I've been taken prisoner as well?* Francine wondered. But then again, she wasn't sure if anyone would even be able to deliver the news to her father.

The door opened again.

"Put this on and come with me," the same blond nurse finally addressed her.

Noticing it was a nurse's uniform, she inhaled and exhaled deeply. She knew there wasn't any choice but to follow orders.

CHAPTER 14

The place was busy with doctors and nurses going back and forth from room to room.

As she followed the nurse, she noticed the strange way people looked at her. *They probably know where I came from already ...* she speculated.

The woman accompanying Francine stopped before a closed door and knocked on it. A male voice responded, "Come in."

A man in his late fifties was sitting behind a desk filled with papers. He kept looking down at the papers as if he hadn't noticed the two women in front of him.

With her hands shaking, Francine tried her best not to show fear. She had no idea what she would be doing or what they would do with her. She still couldn't believe she was actually in Germany!

The man finally pushed some of the papers aside and looked straight at her face. He leaned back in his chair, placing his hands on the top of his desk.

"You were brought here to assist with our busy nursing department," the austere German doctor said. "We have been made aware of your expertise as a German-speaking nurse. We also need you to translate a few medical documents that need to go to France or are arriving from France and Switzerland."

Francine stood silently.

The doctor took another look at her and continued. "You're not allowed to leave this facility without supervision. With France's cooperation and agreement, you will be receiving proper care. That is all. You can leave now."

The doctor was as cold as the blond nurse. Francine couldn't believe that a doctor could be so insensitive and cruel. But then she reminded herself of where she was.

The days passed by slowly, constantly reminding Francine of her new reality. She started to feel even sadder and lonelier than before. It was getting hard for her to keep hoping that she would hear from her friends back in France. *Would they be able to do anything for me?* Francine thought for a moment. But she knew how close to impossible an escape was. She was in Germany, inside the enemy's territory.

She spent most of her time locked in an office translating documents. Francine made a habit of standing by the window for a few minutes and watching people outside. She started to develop a certain curiosity about the German people, trying to find any clues that would justify their radical behavior. These moments had become her only connection to the outside world.

And so, she quickly became familiar with the routines of people's lives as they crossed the street in front of the military facility. Francine noticed that a few people had a band wrapped around their arms. For everything she had seen in the occupied part of France, it didn't take long for her to recognize that they were meant to identify the Jewish population, just like in her own town in France. *I'll never be able to understand this kind of hate. How could they do this?*

With her heart full of sorrow, she missed her family, her friends and countryman. She wondered how they were, very aware that they could be going through much worse than her.

Thinking about that possibility, she knew she had to stay strong and remain hopeful that things would change one day.

Another autumn had arrived in that German city, slowly transforming its natural scenery. But Francine's life remained a dreadful and sad routine. Day after day, she was surrounded by the Germans with their coldness and fanatical behavior. She started to think the war would never be over.

It was late in the evening when Francine sat on her bed, looking up at the night sky through the window nearby. The starry night took her thoughts far away, to a place where good things happened, and peace reigned once again. It lifted her heart and made her think of happier times. She closed her eyes, clasping her hands over her heart. And just like that, Hans's image came rushing through her mind.

As much as she attempted not to, she couldn't stop thinking about him since the moment she was notified that she would be sent to Germany. But at that time, for some reason, she started to feel as if he were right there near her. She quickly remembered the last words they exchanged. *"You stay safe, Francine, wherever the wind may take you. Perhaps Germany, who knows?"*

Francine straightened herself up in the bed. She had never forgotten those words. She then understood how deeply she still cared for him. She couldn't deny it anymore ... she felt as if she truly loved him. *How is that possible? How can I love him? I don't even know him that well. And he's German;* she reminded herself. *I hate him. I hate all of them!*

Francine rolled over in her bed and cried. She sobbed as she felt her heart being shattered. She couldn't understand why she still had feelings for that German man, even after all the horror that was happening in her country and around the world. She felt like the worst traitor!

"Maybe I do deserve to be in this horrible situation," Francine said to the silent room. "I'm as sick as the Germans since I'm in love with one of them."

It was already morning when the sunlight woke her up. It took all the strength she had to get up and get ready for work. She had already lost some weight, and her face was always pale, a reflection of how she felt inside.

Francine was translating the usual papers when the sound of the door being opened caught her attention. The chubby nurse came in without saying a word. Her name was Helene. The look on her face was of pure aggravation, as she had been assigned the responsibility to watch over the French girl. She walked toward Francine and handed her a letter.

"It got here today," the German nurse said before leaving the room.

Francine stared at the return address that was written in French for a few seconds. With shaky hands she quickly opened the letter. Finally, after weeks of desperation and isolation, she was receiving some news from home.

As she read it, a big, happy smile completely transformed her face. The letter contained information about her mother and friends. Her mother's caring words made her feel not so lonely anymore.

She pressed the letter against her chest. She felt her strength return, understanding some people needed her to keep fighting and stay alive. Although the letter had no news about the war or her father, at least Francine's family knew where she was, which brought her some comfort.

A few hours later, the same nurse entered the room, asking Francine to follow her. She needed help getting supplies from a few stores in the center of the town. After weeks of imprisonment in that military station, she was finally allowed to go outside.

Francine observed the people on the streets with immense curiosity. To her surprise, they also appeared to be tense and unhappy, giving the atmosphere a somber look.

As they turned the corner, Francine noticed a large factory. People rushed in and out, right along with cars and large military trucks. It seemed to be a very busy place. As she kept looking, she felt a strange sensation. There was something about the factory that stood out to her.

She continued following the nurse, stopping at several stores to buy supplies. Francine paid close attention to her surroundings, wondering about the possibility of an escape. But as if Helene could hear her thoughts, she grabbed Francine's arms and pushed her forward.

"Hurry up! We have a lot of work to do at the hospital."

Not far from where Francine was, another girl was feeling nothing but sorrow and anguish. Denna couldn't stop thinking about her own family. Hans couldn't get any more information related to them since they got relocated. Nobody knew where they were or if they were even still alive.

It had been months since she first came into Hans's family's house. Denna felt extremely grateful for everything they were doing for her. But at the same time, she still had to deal with the constant danger of being discovered, placing everyone there at risk.

Hans always seemed to be the first to notice the girl's sadness, no matter how hard she tried to hide it. He always attempted to distract her with different conversations, games, or books.

Hans was captivated by Denna's innocence and sweet manners. She gave the house a new, lighter air. Little by little, those lies were evolving into a true part of real life. It brought a few smiles and jokes back to a household that had forgotten what it felt like to be happy.

Despite the Schulze's household changes, Elga still wanted to leave Germany as soon as possible, as she feared for her family's safety. Still unable to find anyone else who could help them, she knew they had no other choice but to wait for Carson.

It was the end of another long day of work, and Hans sat at his desk, staring out the window. He often enjoyed these rare moments of quietness.

He looked at the military base across the street and thought about Carson. *Would he be able to help us?* Hans played with the idea, still trying to find a solution to remove Denna from Germany safely. *No, of course not. She's Jewish. He would be more likely to kill her.*

Running his tired hands through his hair, he felt the same frustration that so often weighed upon his shoulders. But there was something else bothering him those days. He refocused on the military base. He couldn't understand why, but that place kept getting his attention, leaving him feeling anxious and nervous, a sensation as if something strange was happening in there.

Hans looked at the clock one more time. It was already late. Recognizing that there wasn't much he could do at that moment, he decided to head back home.

CHAPTER 15

In the meantime, in France, Julian had been informed about Francine's situation by Frederick. After a lot of effort, Julian was finally able to locate her. He knew he had to act fast as her life could be in danger.

With the help of Pierre, it took Julian only a few weeks to finally find a way to communicate with Francine. Having spies of their own located everywhere in Germany, they were informed of a person who worked in a factory near where she was staying. His name was Zachary, an Austrian mechanical engineer the SS forces had relocated to work in a German military factory. He pretended to sympathize with the Nazi regime for his own survival, even though he despised every single one of them. Before he was forced to move to Germany, he had become a member of an anti-Nazi force in Austria. His removal into the enemy territory turned him into a very important asset for the French and the British Secret Service.

Julian had stopped nearly all of his activities as soon as he received the news about Francine's relocation to Germany. Knowing what the Germans were capable of doing, he couldn't stop thinking of her alone in there. The very thought drove him mad.

Julian would do everything possible to bring her back, and on that task, he wasn't alone. His friends supported him, not only because some knew Francine but also because they thought she would probably have valuable information to share.

And so, Julian, Pierre, and some of their friends started to work on a plan to enter Germany. The goal was to free Francine and acquire any useful information that could help the Allies. And they knew exactly who was the right person for the job.

It didn't take long for Zachary to find out Francine's precise location as he had made friends with several soldiers who worked at the same military base. Some of them had already heard rumors about a French nurse who worked at the hospital. Zachary would need to use those connections to gain access to her.

It was a late afternoon when he decided to act. Zachary knew how to fake a high fever, to pretend he was very sick. As soon as the soldiers became aware of his condition, they sent him to the hospital across the street, where Francine stayed.

He waited patiently until the place finally quieted down. Then, pretending to seek out a bathroom, he looked inside different departments, trying to find a girl matching the detailed physical description he was provided with.

Aware that there were different floors, he rushed toward the staircase, when suddenly a loud noise coming from the outside got his attention. Zachary rushed to the nearest window to find out what was going on. Several ambulances were approaching the building. Not long after, he heard footsteps coming from the floor above.

He had just enough time to hide behind a wall before he saw people rushing down the stairs. There was so much activity that no one even noticed his presence.

Zachary waited until the staircase was empty to proceed to the second floor.

Suddenly, a door opened, and a young brunette woman headed in his direction. He was ready to explain his presence in there when he realized that the nurse could be Francine. She matched the description given to him.

Francine was alarmed. She had been awakened and told to get ready to go to the first floor to help the other nurses.

Still partially asleep, she noticed a strange man standing in the hallway staring at her. Francine started to walk faster.

As she passed by him, she heard a voice.

"The bathroom, where is it?" Zachary quickly asked.

Francine stopped, feeling uneasy. "There's a place there," she said, pointing it out.

Zachary clearly noticed a different accent when she replied to him. She couldn't be German. He took a chance.

"Francine?" he whispered as she resumed walking.

Francine stopped and looked back. Someone had said her name perfectly in French which she hadn't heard in a long time.

"Are you Francine?" Zachary asked her again as he took another quick look around, making sure they were alone in there.

"Yes ... I am," she replied hesitantly. "How do you ...?"

"I have something for you!" he rushed to say, taking a few steps closer to her. "Take this." He discretely gave her a letter. "I have to go now, but I will try to keep in touch."

Francine could hardly believe it. She wanted to ask him more questions, but the strange man had already started walking toward the stairs.

"Wait! Please wait!" she begged him. "Please, sir!"

As he continued to walk away, unfazed by her distress, Francine rushed toward him, "sir, please wait!" But before she could reach him, she heard the sound of footsteps coming from behind her. She slowed down, discretely placing the letter in her front pocket.

"Come fast," the German nurse ordered her.

Francine reluctantly followed the nurse while she could see Zachary moving further and further away from her. Frustrated, she watched him disappear around the corner. Francine knew there was nothing she could do about it.

Rushing back and forth between patients, Francine realized she would have to wait until she was sent back to her room to read the mysterious letter. But to her disappointment, that only happened later that night.

She entered her room in a hurry, instantly shutting the door behind her. Then, with her back against the door, she quickly grabbed the letter from her pocket.

Through several sets of secret codes mixed carefully with regular letters, Francine understood that Julian and his friends would try to rescue her. The worried and tense look on her face turned into a smile of joy and relief. At that moment, that was all she needed to know. Francine could finally hope to return home.

She lay on her bed, thinking about that day. It was the first time she saw so many casualties and injured people coming from the German side. *They are starting to feel the horrors of war closer to home,* Francine thought. But, by doing so, the image of Hans came to her mind again. *How ironic it would be to meet him here, in Germany, as a prisoner. What would he do? Would he have the same courage to help me?*

What Francine couldn't even dream of was that right across the street, a young man also wished away.

Hans leaned back in his chair, feeling tormented by memories. He looked up at the sky with great sadness. No one seemed to be able to fill the empty space Francine left inside of him after he let her get away. Then the war started. Life had lost its beauty.

He thought about Denna and his family. His parents would be leaving shortly, and he wished he could join them. He also wanted to leave Germany and find Francine, no matter how crazy the idea seemed. But he would never abandon his new cousin.

He closed his eyes and dreamed of Francine's face, holding her in his arms. "I still remember her lips, her voice. I'll never be able to find another woman like her, never."

The darkness of that night emphasized the large Frost Moon, inspiring them to think of one another even more. But for those two young lovers at heart, a life together seemed to be nothing but an impossible dream. What neither could have imagined was how close they were to one another. Only one street apart, as they admired the same starry sky.

Perhaps it was such close proximity that caused their hearts and souls to ache for yet another meeting, for one more chance to experience the taste of love.

CHAPTER 16

Leaning against the library door with his arms crossed, Hans impatiently waited for his father to finish the phone conversation with Carson, who had just arrived from his long trip to Berlin.

"He's coming tonight with the travel authorizations," Alfred said after hanging up the phone.

"How did he react when you told him about our cousin being here? And the fact I am not leaving anymore?" Hans asked his father, worrying about Denna.

"Well, he started asking a lot of questions; you know how he is. However, I made it sound as normal as possible, trying to change the conversation to other subjects of his interest, and I guess it worked."

"That's good! So, now we have to prepare for tonight."

"And he is not coming alone," Alfred added. "He is bringing his fiancée along with him!"

Elga made sure to take care of the preparations herself for a nice dinner. She knew how important that meeting was going to be. They were going to receive the traveling authorizations and at the same time introduce Denna to a Nazi Commander.

Looking at the dining table, Elga stood still for a moment. She thought about Carson and Hans when they were young, all sitting together for their daily meals. It was a very different life back then. Happiness felt as if it only belonged to their memories of a distant past. She wished everything could go back to how it was before.

Sighing with sadness, Elga took one more look around the table. Her heart ached, knowing she was being forced to leave both her sons behind.

It was later in the afternoon when the doorbell rang. The family was ready for the small reception. Carson was thrilled to go back to the residence of those he considered to be his parents. He cared for all of them as if they were his only family. He did, however, feel disappointed that they wouldn't share the same beliefs as he and his countrymen did. *One day they will understand why we are fighting this war,* Carson kept reminding himself proudly. *Then they'll see the grandeur of our nation and deeply regret not supporting us sooner!*

Elga and Alfred received them with genteel courtesy, regardless of their political differences.

Hans greeted them merely politely, not having much to say. There was still a lot of resentment that he rightfully harbored toward the man he once considered to be his best friend. But somehow, seeing Carson enter the house with a smile on his face, he was reminded of the child that used to come rushing through his living room so they could play together. Unfortunately, a lot had changed, and Hans wasn't sure if Carson represented more of an enemy than a friend. On the one hand, he protected them fiercely; on the other, he was part of the same system that threatened their lives.

"I thought I was finally going to meet your cousin, Alyse," Carson told Hans with a glass of wine already in his hand.

Alyse was the name chosen by Hans and his parents to match better with her new identity. It was all part of the plan that they had carefully developed.

"She's sick with a bad cold, that poor girl," Elga replied, trying her best to look calm. "But as soon as she gets better, I hope you can come back to meet her!"

The Schulzes quickly realized that Denna wasn't ready to meet Carson yet. She was so afraid to make a mistake that the perspective of sitting across the table from a Nazi officer made her feel ill before the evening arrived. They had no other choice but to postpone their introductions.

"Yes, unfortunately, she is not feeling well," Hans added. "She was very excited to see you."

"I am sure we will have other opportunities to meet," Carson replied full of curiosity, still finding that story about a cousin he had never heard of before very strange.

They resumed their conversation, talking about various subjects. Carson's wedding and Elga and Alfred's upcoming trip to Switzerland were the main topics of conversation.

"I hope you will be back for the wedding next summer," Carson said. "I can't get married without both of you there."

Elga smiled at the couple in front of her.

"Hopefully, we will be back, but with the war … no one knows."

"Don't worry," Carson said enthusiastically, "it will be over soon."

Looks were exchanged, but no one said anything.

Carson knew that Elga and Alfred were really running away, and he actually approved their decision. Alfred could still be seen as a possible conspirator, and Carson knew it was safer for both of them to leave Germany.

"I still don't understand why you're staying in Germany, Hans," Carson said. "You were always talking about leaving, getting away from here."

Hans looked at Carson. He was quiet for a few seconds.

"Well, you were the one who told me it would be better for me to stay here working at the military factory. Plus, now Alyse is staying with us for a while until her parents return from their trip overseas. But who knows? Perhaps we will wait until the weather warms up, and Alyse and I will consider a quick trip to Switzerland. But then again, war is everywhere; no one can escape it."

"Well, let me know when you will need more travel authorizations. And do not worry. Like I said before, the war will be over soon with our glorious victory. Then, we will all be reunited at my wedding."

Adalie looked at Carson with pride, as if she couldn't have found a better man to wed.

Elga looked at him with pity and smiled in a way that only mothers know how to do when forgiving their son's worst faults.

Alfred kept quiet for most of their meeting. He would leave Germany the next day, leaving a new member of his family and two sons behind – one who would die for Germany if necessary and another who hated it. He looked at both of them, wondering about their futures, wondering if one day they would be able to be together again in a time of peace, with the hopeful defeat of Germany.

It was only later in the dinner that Carson started to inquire about the mysterious cousin, as he still couldn't remember anything about Alyse or her family. But, already expecting those questions, the Schulzes had a perfect story to tell. 'Alyse' was presented as a distant cousin of Hans, whose privileged parents traveled a lot due to their exceptional business ventures in several countries across Europe and Asia.

They insisted on telling false stories about Carson having met Alyse and her family when he was an only child, which probably explained why he couldn't remember her.

As much as the Schulzes tried to change the subject, Carson didn't let go of it easily.

"I really don't remember," Carson repeated. "It is interesting because I usually don't forget things like that! I have no recollection of anyone talking about them at all."

Mrs. Kaufmann, upon Alfred's request, immediately poured more wine into Carson's glass.

Carson smiled at her, remembering how well she took care of him when he was a child, despite him driving her crazy running around the house.

Alfred wanted Carson to drink just enough so he could avoid searching too deeply into his memory, trying to find any real aspect of Alyse's family or its connections. With a superb wine collection, much appreciated by Carson, Alfred's plan was going well.

"I am not surprised that you can't remember her," Elga said, trying to make it sound natural. "The last time she was here, you were both small children. After that, her parents moved to China and then India, and she has never been back until now. But we always stayed in touch, and Alfred and I took the opportunity to visit them once when we went on a trip to Asia."

"Well, Carson," Alfred said, trying to change the subject. "Tell us about your trip to Berlin. I am sure you have a lot to say."

Alfred was right. Carson didn't enjoy anything more than talking about Berlin's supremacy and all of Germany's accomplishments in the war. Not that Alfred wanted to hear anything on that matter, but he knew he had to take Carson's mind away from Alyse.

Carson didn't have much else to talk about since all he knew was war-related matters. He also felt uncomfortable talking about the fun activities of military society. He knew the Schulzes never showed any interest in them. And as for his fiancée Adalie, her main concerns were fancy parties among the newly rich and powerful German officers, as well as jewels and fashion. She was a selfish and shallow woman, a person not well-liked by Hans and his parents.

To their relief, Carson and his fiancée didn't stay long.

Hans offered Carson his hand as they said goodbye. Carson ignored the hand and hugged Hans. "I miss you, brother," he said with real emotion.

Hans looked at him, touched by the gesture. "I miss our talks, too … when things were different."

Carson decided to ignore that comment like so many others. He said a warm goodbye to Elga and Alfred, as he didn't know when he would see them again.

Carson drove away with his fiancée by his side. Hans's family stayed outside watching as his car moved away from their house. Hans glanced at his parents, and they all moved closer together. They knew that they would soon be separated.

Inside the Schulze's house, Denna felt extremely guilty for being the reason Hans was staying behind. Numerous times she tried to convince him to go with his parents, but Hans would always reassure her that he didn't want to leave. Denna knew he was lying.

Denna fell asleep that night still thinking about her parents and friends. There was also Abraham, from whom she had not heard since they had been separated. She had never told anyone at Hans's house about him; she felt that it wasn't her place as a woman to expose her feelings entirely.

She still remembered his last words when he was confessing his love for her one afternoon. "I love you, Denna. I will talk to your parents next time and soon we will be married." The very next day, soldiers invaded his family's house and took all of them away. She never heard from him again. *Is he alive?* Denna wondered, hopefully. *Will I ever see him again?*

A few days after, her own family had been taken as prisoners. She was only nineteen years old and had already seen and experienced too much pain.

Eventually, Denna was able to get a job playing piano at a nearby restaurant through a friend of her family. That had helped them to get some extra food, which was very much needed. It was always a great risk for Denna when she had to walk back to the ghetto late at night. Her family worried about her every second of the day, afraid that something terrible could happen to her. But she refused to leave the job, knowing it was the only way for them not to go hungry.

On one of those nights, when Denna was walking home from her job, she was attacked. Luckily for her, Hans was passing by at the time and was able to rescue her.

Remembering the past always brought her deep distress and sadness. *Are they still alive?* Denna thought as tears streamed down her face. *Are they being hurt? Are they warm as I am now? I'll find my parents one day, and I'll find you, Abraham. I promise I'll find you. We will be together again!*

That morning arrived quickly, announcing the departure of Hans's parents. Elga still wasn't sure about leaving, but Alfred reassured her that it was the best thing to do. Alfred knew that the SS would never leave them completely alone as long as he stayed there, placing the entire family in a dangerous situation.

"Hans will be fine," Alfred soothed. "They will join us soon. My exit from Germany will make them safer."

"What if something happens to him?" Elga said inconsolably. "Our son is everything we have!"

Alfred held her, sharing the same concern. However, he also knew he had made the right decision for everyone.

After a few words of encouragement followed by warm embraces, the Schulzes prepared to leave.

"Take care of each other," Alfred said. "I know things will eventually get better, and we will reunite soon! In the meantime, I will continue trying to find a way to get you both out of here."

"You stay well, young lady," Elga said. "And take care of my Hans."

"Danke schön," Denna said with tears in her eyes. "I will never forget what you have done for me."

The house seemed empty upon Alfred and Elga's departure. Realizing that, Hans tried to put an end to that melancholy.

"So, Denna," he broke the silence, "why don't you tell me something happy about your past. I know we all have good things to remember."

Denna smiled at him. She knew she would need to find the strength to keep going. She couldn't give up.

She followed Hans toward the library, where they both could talk more freely.

Soon her face lit up as she traveled back in time, reliving happy memories that were almost forgotten.

Hans listened to her attentively, sharing his own stories, enjoying their conversation. For a few hours, they immersed themselves into a life that was once peaceful and full of beautiful moments.

The night snuck upon them. They each went to their respective rooms with lighter hearts and a renewed hope that they would reunite one day with their loved ones.

CHAPTER 17

The days were getting shorter and colder as the end of November approached. In the surrounding woods of that German city, frost started to form intricate crystal shapes on the rocks of the riverbanks. Strong wind gusts rushed through the vast streets, reaching the local hospital. Francine could feel the outside chill coming from the windows while she checked on the injured soldiers. Her presence at the infirmary become a daily routine. It was very clear that they needed extra medical personnel as the number of German casualties increased.

At that point, all of Francine's hopes were pinned to the mysterious man who had left her that letter. Unfortunately, weeks had passed, and there was still no sign of him. Francine tried to push her anxiety aside.

She walked toward the surgery room, distracted by her own thoughts, when she suddenly noticed that someone was watching her from a distance. At first, she couldn't see the face from under the military cap. But it took only a few more steps for her to realize who it was.

"Bonjour, Francine," he said out loud, his voice full of sarcasm.

She stopped abruptly. Her face turned pale; her heart nearly stopped beating. It was him ... Michael!

Without wasting any time, she turned around and started walking as fast as she could in the opposite direction. But it was already too late.

Michael quickly caught up to her, grabbing Francine from behind.

"You didn't think I forgot about you, did you?" he asked, feeling amused by the situation. "You're not going to say hi?"

"Let me go!" she said defiantly while trying to break free from his grasp.

"Let you go? But I just arrived here!" Michael replied, squeezing her tighter.

"What are you doing here?" Francine asked frantically, unable to push his arms away from her body.

"What am I doing here? What do you mean? This is my country! Don't be a fool! I came back here, and I decided to check on my French princess and see how she was doing. I wanted to make sure you have been treated well by our exceptional German manners and exemplary conduct. Perhaps you have even learned a thing or two …"

Before she could manage to say anything, Helene appeared at the end of the hallway and gave them a look of disapproval.

Knowing he had no other alternative, Michael loosened his arms, allowing Francine to escape.

"We'll see each other again. Don't be sad … I'll be back around Christmas," he teased as he watched Francine walking away. "And then no one will stop us. That's what we both wanted all along, wasn't it?"

Helene noticed the fear in the French girl's eyes but didn't say anything.

Disgusted by Michael's words, Francine kept walking fast. Once she rounded the corner, she ran. Scared and shaking, she kept checking back to make sure he wasn't following her.

She was finally able to find an isolated place where she could hide for a few minutes.

She knew she had to continue her rounds helping patients, but her mind was elsewhere. *I would rather die than have that monster touch me,* she thought solemnly. *I have to find a weapon. I will defend myself even if it is the last thing I do in this life!*

More than ever, Francine needed to talk to that mysterious man again. She needed help to escape this place, and soon.

As the days went by, she became more anxious. Michael promised to be back around Christmas. Her time was running out.

The first snowflakes of the winter season started to fall. As Francine looked out the window, she felt even more desperate. *Why is it taking that man so long to communicate with me again?* she wondered impatiently. *Did someone find out about it? Did something go wrong?*

What Francine didn't know was that a few men were already discussing a plan to save her.

"She could be more valuable for us if she stays there and keeps us informed about the German activity happening around her," said one of the men present at that meeting.

"Are you out of your mind?" Julian replied furiously. "She has already risked too much to help us. I won't allow her to stay there any longer!"

"Calm down, everyone," Pierre said, trying to keep everyone focused. "Francine needs to be taken out of Germany; her life is at risk. The Allies are finally starting to win a few battles. There is still so much to do, and the war is far from being over. But at least now we have hope."

"Exactly," the same man said. "That is why she can be very useful to us by staying there."

"I disagree," Pierre said, cutting off Julian, who was about to reply again. "Francine can't do anything for us from where she's currently placed. If anything, she could hurt our cause if they become suspicious of her. We know very well their ways of getting information from people. We need to get her out of there as fast as possible."

"Now you're talking," Julian rushed to say. "Francine's life is severely at risk, especially now with the entry of the United States into the war, as relations between France and Germany have deteriorated even further. The Germans would have no problem getting rid of everyone who is working for them overseas, like Francine and so many others."

"That is right," Pierre agreed with Julian.

"Germany is still very strong and still dominates. Let's not forget that!" the other man continued, still not agreeing with that idea. "I just think it's too risky to try to get someone out of there."

"It doesn't matter," Julian affirmed. "I'll go alone if I have to."

The conversation went on for hours as they prepared their next move with the Resistance and planned Francine's rescue.

CHAPTER 18

It was a grey Sunday afternoon, and Francine could feel the cold air cutting through her bones. She followed Helene, staying right behind her. Despite everything that was happening, she always enjoyed the few moments she could get out of that hospital and walk around the city.

Francine had a feeling that the nurse, despite her cold manner, felt a little sorry for her. The truth was that Helene had seen the uglier side of wars, and she was tired of it. She wanted the war to be over, win or lose, at that point. But of course, the nurse hid those thoughts very well, knowing how dangerous they were.

Francine looked around the streets. Once more, she contemplated the idea of an escape, but the odds were against her. The winter made that next to impossible. She still didn't know her exact location, and she had no access to a map.

Preoccupied and with a thousand thoughts going through her mind, Francine numbly followed the nurse.

"Francine," Helene said. "Go across the street over there and get us some bread. I have to go to two other places, and then I'll be back here to meet you."

Francine nodded her head.

"Wait for me!" the nurse looked right into Francine's eyes. "Don't try anything stupid. They will kill you!"

Francine waited outside the bakery for the bread to come out of the oven with her hair already covered with tiny snowflakes. She knew it was the right time to find out some information about the town where she was stationed.

"I'm new here," she told a woman who passed by her. "Perhaps you can tell me where the nearest train station is located."

The woman answered her without too many words or details.

"I need to go to Berlin," Francine continued, trying to find a sense of direction. She knew that the trip from France to Germany was too short for her to be close to Berlin. "Do you know how long it will take me to get there by train?"

"Berlin is a long way from here," the woman replied quickly, already finding all those questions a little strange.

"Danke," Francine said, feeling a little more optimistic. Since she was far from Berlin, she knew she could be closer to France/German border, perhaps closer to Switzerland.

But how do I get there? She thought, *where do I start?* She had no documents, no money, or anything of value that she could exchange for a train ticket. At that moment, she thought about Christmas coming shortly and the possible arrival of Michael.

The snow became suddenly heavier, making it hard to see ahead. Francine walked back to where she was supposed to meet Helene with a loaf of bread already in her hands. Distracted by her thoughts, Francine didn't notice she was already crossing the street.

Suddenly, the loud sound of squealing tires brought her back to reality. A car had stopped abruptly, almost hitting her.

As the driver yelled, she quickly moved back to the sidewalk. It took her a few seconds to recover from that scare. Then, looking around, she noticed the number of people who still stared at her. It made her feel quite uncomfortable.

Slowly, people went on their way, but Francine didn't realize that right across that same street, a person was standing still, looking over at her in complete disbelief.

Hans was walking back to the factory when he noticed that a woman almost got hit by a car. He sighed in relief, noticing that she seemed to be well. It was that exact moment when he could finally see the woman's face.

At first, he thought he had made a mistake. *It couldn't be her. It just couldn't be*, he argued with himself. He looked again and again. *Francine?* Hans asked himself, still doubtful.

As if she could hear his voice, Francine felt a strange sensation. Without overthinking, she automatically turned her head toward the man. Her heart nearly stopped. She couldn't believe it … only a few steps away … staring at her … there was Hans!

The snow continued falling heavily to the ground. For a brief moment, it was as if time had stopped for the two of them as if they were the only people there.

Francine stood still, overpowered by strong emotion. She stared back at him as if he were an illusion. But by doing so, she quickly recognized the same mesmerizing blue eyes. She could never have forgotten them.

It all happened too fast, in an instant. People were passing in front of them, blocking their vision of one another.

"Francine!" Helene shouted. "What are you doing standing there? I was looking for you. I knew I shouldn't have left you alone. This is the last time it will happen."

Francine gave her a confused look as if she was still trying to wake up from a dream. Helene looked at her with concern, wondering if perhaps the girl had gone mad.

"Hans!" It was the only thing she could say.

Unable to comprehend what was happening, Helene grabbed Francine's arm and started dragging her away. Francine immediately looked back, and she could still see him. She let herself be guided away but kept looking backward, trying to find him through the crowd.

It took Hans a few seconds to start moving again. He wanted to call her name out loud to get her attention. But at that moment, only a gentle whisper escaped his lips.

"Francine." He could barely say it.

With his heart beating faster, he crossed the street quickly, almost getting hit by several cars himself. He wasn't thinking clearly; he just reacted automatically to a strong feeling that kept pushing him forward. *How could this be?* he asked himself repeatedly.

He was rushing through the crowd, trying not to lose sight of her.

"Francine," he finally shouted.

As Francine saw Hans coming toward her, she stopped abruptly, freeing herself from Helene's grasp. She was able to take a few steps toward him. But the German nurse wasted no time and chased after Francine, grabbing the hood of her jacket, jerking her backwards.

"What are you doing," the nurse yelled at her. "I will never let you out again! Where do you think you are going to?"

Francine tried to break free again, but Helene was relentless.

"If you don't stop this, I will call the guards, and they will have you arrested or possibly shot dead!" Helene insisted, pointing at the guards who were already watching that scene.

Noticing the angry look on her face, Francine knew she would not hesitate to follow through with her threat. They were too close to the military base for her to continue to resist. So, she allowed herself to be pulled by the nurse.

Hans was only a few steps away from her when he saw her struggling with the nurse. Shocked, he stopped for a brief moment. He then understood the obvious, Francine couldn't be there in Germany by her own choosing.

He resumed walking, following her carefully not to cause her any more problems. Desperately, Francine kept looking back, afraid she would lose sight of him.

Hans could barely believe his eyes when he saw her entering a place that was very familiar to him, the same military station under Carson's command and right across from the factory where he worked almost every day.

Francine gave Hans one last look before she was pushed inside the hospital.

All kinds of questions and emotions came to his mind as he stopped near the gate. *What's she doing here? What are they doing to her? Is she in danger?*

Unable to take his eyes off that hospital, he tried to think what to do next.

Hans knew it was going to be tricky for him to get onto the military base. It was a Sunday, and Carson would be at home. He would have no real excuse to be there. But for Hans, nothing would get in his way of finding Francine in that hospital. He couldn't wait any longer.

"Guten Tag," Hans said in a serious tone.

"Guten tag," the young soldier replied.

"I'm here to see someone, a friend of mine," Hans said.

The soldier gave him a knowing look. He was used to seeing men wanting to enter the military facility to talk to some of the nurses.

"Your identification," the soldier asked him without hesitation.

"Here it is. I work across the street."

"And who is the person you are referring to?" the soldier asked, seemingly uneasy about the situation.

"I'm Commander Carson Beurmann's brother. I just need to talk to one of the nurses," Hans said, deliberately showing signs of irritability. He wanted to intimidate the guard.

The soldier walked away and started to talk to another guard who came back with him.

"No one is allowed to enter the building at this time unless accompanied by military personnel," the other guard replied.

Hans glared at him. He didn't have any other choice but to play the part.

"I understand. But I can guarantee you that it will be much worse for you if I have to inform my brother, Commander Beurmann, that I was denied entrance into this facility. I was given free clearance to go in and out. I need and will talk to one of the nurses inside."

The two guards looked at one another again, trying not to laugh. They were very used to that situation.

"How do we know you're the Commander's brother?" one of the soldiers replied.

Hans looked into the military base to see if he recognized anyone there that could help him.

"You just need to check with someone who can recognize me," Hans said. "Is Sergeant Franz Schmitz working today?"

The guards were still unsure.

"Go get Franz," the older soldier finally said to the other, feeling even more irritated.

Hans waited outside anxiously.

After a minute, Hans saw yet another guard approaching him. He felt relieved when he was recognized at once.

"Guten tag, Hans," the familiar voice said.

"Guten Tag," Hans replied, glad to see Franz. "I need to get inside to resolve an issue."

"We had orders to restrict civilian access to this station. But I know who you are and I don't see any problems. How long are you going to stay inside?" the sergeant asked him.

"Only a few minutes."

"Go right ahead, Hans."

"I really appreciate it, Franz. Danke!!"

Hans hadn't felt so alive since that first and only meeting with Francine. Although they had only talked for a few hours, that brief encounter was very intense. He fell in love with every aspect of her, how she spoke about life, her thoughts, ideas, and her determination. Everything about her was captivating – the way she moved, her smile, beautiful eyes, and wavy brown hair. In an instant, he immediately recognized that what he felt for her was still as strong and as alive as it had always been.

Hans took a quick look around him inside the hospital, unsure where to start searching for Francine. Then, he noticed a nurse in the nearby hallway and decided to approach her to ask questions.

"What's her name again?" the nurse asked, a little suspicious. She was used to having men claim that they wanted to see the nurse who had previously helped them recover.

"Francine," that was all he said, not wanting to give out too many details.

The nurse took a good look at Hans, noticing his fancy attire. *He's probably rich*, she thought. *Why would he be looking for that insignificant French woman?*

"I'll see if I can find her," she said in a relatively cold voice. "Please wait here."

Hans started to grow nervous, not sure what to expect.

A few minutes later, which seemed like an eternity to him, the nurse returned.

"She's already in her room upstairs."

"Can you tell her that she has a visitor?" he asked hesitantly.

"That would be impossible as she is locked inside her room," the nurse replied, trying her best not to laugh.

Hans had his confirmation. Francine was being held as a prisoner there.

"I need to speak with her right now," Hans said, feeling angry by that situation. "I have very important orders to give her."

"I understand it, but ..." she replied, not believing a word he said. "But I couldn't find the head nurse who is responsible for her either."

"Don't you have a spare key? I am sure there has to be a spare key, right?"

Hans got closer to her, looking right into her eyes.

"You seem to be an intelligent person, and of course, very beautiful," Hans said as he tried a different approach. "I am sure you can find a way. And I, well ... I would be very pleased with that."

The young nurse smiled back at him, flattered by his attention.

"I don't know where they keep the spare keys for the rooms upstairs, but I can find out tomorrow," she said, wanting to impress him. "But for now, I cannot do anything else as I was called into the surgery room."

A heavy sigh demonstrated all his frustration.

Noticing the disappointment in his eyes, she looked around, making sure no one else could hear her.

"As for now, I can show you where her room is really quick!" she said smiling. She hated the French girl. *The audacity of having her here at the same level as us*, the nurse thought vindictively. *She has to learn a lesson about her own inferiority.*

"Well, I would really like that … for now."

The nurse walked away with Hans by her side. She knew exactly where to find Francine. She was aware that she was acting against hospital policies, but she didn't care at that moment. Hans seemed to be an important man who could provide her with certain advantages in life, and that was all she cared about.

With every step he took, his heart beat faster. After so long, he was finally going to be able to have the chance to speak with Francine again.

"That is her bedroom, three doors to your right," the nurse said, with a smirk on her face.

Hans gave the nurse a serious look. He understood exactly what she was implying, and he didn't like it one bit. For a few seconds, he thought about Francine with considerable concern. He saw how easy it was to have access to her.

"Please, just don't say anything to anyone," she asked Hans, not wanting to get in trouble.

"Of course not," he replied, faking a smile. "It will be our little secret. Danke. I just need to know your name …."

"Gisele."

"Beautiful name for a beautiful woman. My name is Hans. And don't worry, I won't compromise you in any way. When do you think you will be able to get that key?"

"Hopefully, by tomorrow. I've got to go now. I am usually here in the afternoon."

Gisele walked away fast, satisfied that she had made an impression on him. *What a handsome man! I hope he will be back soon. What does he want with that stupid French girl anyway? He doesn't seem to be the type that would like someone like her.*

Hans took a quick look around, making sure there was no one else in the hallway. Knowing he didn't have much time to spare, Hans headed straight to her bedroom.

He stopped right in front of the door and hesitated for a few seconds. Then, growing more anxious, his hands started trembling. Everything had happened too fast. Hans didn't have a chance to think about what he was going to say to Francine.

He took a deep breath, and without any more delay, he knocked.

CHAPTER 19

As soon as Francine arrived at the hospital, she was sent back to her room. Helene was mad at her, thinking she had tried to escape.

"You could have gotten us into a lot of trouble!" the nurse told her furiously. "From now on, you don't leave this place!!"

At that moment, Francine didn't care about those words. Helene slammed the door in front of her. She sighed in relief for having some time alone to think about everything that had just happened.

Francine paced back and forth, still not believing she had really seen Hans.

Closing her eyes, she tried to picture his face, every detail. *The most beautiful eyes! The ones I have dreamt of for so long!* she thought, feeling her heart beating even faster. The intensity of those moments moved her so deeply; she couldn't think straight.

Hans! She repeated several times. *He recognized me! He did!!* She remembered he followed her in the streets, trying to reach her. She couldn't stop smiling. *He saw me going into the hospital!*

On that thought, she rushed to the window, hoping to be able to spot him.

And that was when she heard a knock at the door. Her entire body trembled.

Thinking it could be Hans, she walked toward the door. But how could she be sure? She knew it could also be Zachary or Michael. She didn't know what to do.

After a few seconds of an anguishing silence, she heard her name again.

"Francine? It's me … Hans! Do you remember me?" he started speaking with a shaky voice in French.

Her heart pounded harder and louder inside her chest. She couldn't believe what she was hearing. It was him … Hans.

"Francine? Did you hear me?" he insisted, worrying about her. "Are you all right?"

"Hans? From Switzerland?" she was finally able to say.

"Yes, it's me," he said, exhilarated. "I wish I could come in to talk to you, but I don't have the keys yet."

She took a deep breath and reached out to the doorknob. Not many people in that hospital were aware that Helene was keeping Francine's bedroom door unlocked in case they needed her immediate assistance as a nurse.

As she opened the door, Hans appeared right before her. She stared at him for a brief moment. A mix of deep and strong emotions started to take hold of her. Tears filled her eyes, making them sparkle a lighter tone of green.

"Hello again," were the only words he could say.

"Hi," she replied automatically.

Still in shock, she took a few steps backwards, allowing him to enter the room.

He closed the door behind him, and looking right into her eyes, he smiled. Right in front of him was the woman he had been unable to forget, the woman who symbolized everything he ever wanted.

"Francine … I can't believe you are here. I … I tried to find you before the war, but …"

The word war brought Francine back to reality. She didn't know whether to run into his arms or to be rational and hate him for everything he represented.

"What are you doing here?" Francine said coldly.

That was exactly what Hans was afraid of and yet what he had already been expecting.

"Francine … I just want you to know how happy I am to see you again finally! I tried to look for you, to find you, but this damn war …"

"Happy? This war? You say it as if it were something so natural. I don't know if you are aware that I am a prisoner here!"

"That is not what I meant," Hans said, trying to clarify things. He knew he had to choose his words carefully. "I was happy to see you today because I have been looking for you since the day we met in Switzerland. And I know you have every reason to react the way you are. I would do the same. But you have to listen to me."

As she listened to his words, part of her wanted to set her pride aside, begging for him to save her, and tell him she had been in love with him since they had first met. But things were not that simple; the reality of the situation was that Francine didn't really know Hans that well. She worried that her love for him could have been only a dream or perhaps a big mistake.

Francine noticed that Hans was very well-dressed, which seemed inappropriate given the poverty and despair of war. While so many were crying, suffering, and dying, Hans was dressed like a proud, wealthy German man.

"I'm not what you think I am," Hans said, piecing together the hurt in Francine's eyes. "I hate this war and everything that Germany is doing!"

"It doesn't look like it, Hans! You seem well! You are free! So, what is a German man in a nice suit doing visiting a war prisoner on a Sunday night?" Francine asked him sarcastically, already choking on her own words as she tried not to cry.

"Francine, I have to dress like this when I go to work, and I work almost every day," Hans rushed to explain.

Feeling confused, she didn't know what to believe.

"Why are you here?" Francine asked harshly. "Why did you follow me? Are you here to convince me of your country's reasons to kill thousands of people? Are you here to justify their actions?"

As much as Hans could understand why Francine was saying those things, they hurt him deeply. Somehow, he expected her to know who he really was, a man absolutely incapable of those atrocities.

Francine turned around, trying to hide the tears that already rolled down her face. Even she didn't quite understand why she suddenly attacked him so fiercely with her words without giving him a chance to explain himself.

Noticing she was crying, he felt even worse. He could only imagine what she had already gone through. At that moment, he just wanted to hold her and say he wouldn't let anyone cause her any more harm.

He took a few steps forward, approaching her. She would have to listen to what he had to say, even if those were his last words.

"Francine," Hans said firmly, trying to break through the wall that stood between them. "I want to help you. There are so many things we have to talk about, so many things I need to explain. I am not like them! I am not one of them. Please, let me help you."

With his heart pounding uncontrollably against his chest, he could feel tears filling his eyes. He had a hard time continuing.

"I've seen the way of the Germans," Francine replied, still unable to fully trust him. "I don't need any favors from you, any of you! What are you going to do? Use your power and influence to get me out of here?"

Feeling overwhelmed by so many emotions, she simply stared at him. It was her pride speaking.

But Hans was not ready to give up.

"I'm not like them," he insisted fervently. "I know you don't know me that well, but I beg you to believe me. Do you really think I am like those horrible people? A Nazi?"

Francine was silent.

Hans sighed, trying to choose his following words carefully.

"You have to believe me, Francine! I hate my country right now! I hate everything that is happening here. There is so much I have to tell you! But today, when I saw you on the street … I could hardly believe what was right in front of my eyes."

Hans paused, feeling all his emotions coming to the surface.

"I saw a woman who I thought I would never see again. Yet, there's no one else I would rather see."

Francine listened to every word he said very carefully.

"I could never forget our conversation that day in Switzerland … everything we spoke about! I could never forget you … never!" Hans continued, taking a couple of steps closer to her. "I tried everything in my power to try to find you. I even contacted the same café we went to in Switzerland to see if they knew you or could leave a message for you on my behalf. But then the war came, and …."

"The war came?" Francine said, looking deep into his eyes. "You and your people were the ones who started the war. Remember?"

Pausing for a brief moment, she stared at him defiantly.

"Your people have ripped apart families, friendships, people's livelihood. They have spread suffering and pain everywhere they go. You Germans have killed everything that once existed inside my heart. Do you think that I could care for any one of your despicable race?"

Francine said those last words without thinking. But, looking at Hans's reaction, she wished she could take those words back.

Hans felt as if his heart was being shattered. The fact that Francine had so much hate toward him made him realize that the dream he once had of a potential relationship with her was simply impossible. The woman who he adored couldn't love him, a German man.

Suddenly, he couldn't think straight anymore. He felt lost for words. He didn't know what to do next, as all he could feel was his heart bleeding, a pain so deep it teared his soul.

He looked at Francine one more time as if trying to find any sign of hope. But looking at her cold demeanor, Hans understood it all. There was nothing else to say or do. It was his pride then that got hurt.

Although Francine had already regretted her last words, she didn't know how to start explaining herself. There was so much to say. All the conflicting emotions she had felt for so long, all the suffering she had seen and experienced. But despite all of that, deep inside, all she wanted was to find a way to say how much she still cared for him, that she actually loved him. But she couldn't; she simply couldn't.

As Francine attempted to say a few words, Hans turned around and walked away.

He moved fast, going toward the staircase. As soon as he turned the corner, he let his entire body fall against the wall for a few seconds.

She hates me, Hans thought, feeling so naïve and embarrassed. *How could I have ever thought otherwise? I am such a fool!*

He stood straight, trying to push those thoughts away. All he wanted was to leave that place as fast as possible. He needed some time to think, alone. With his heart cut to pieces, he tried his best to look as if nothing had happened.

Hans walked slowly toward the guard station and waved goodbye to the boys.

With his thoughts disconnected, he didn't even know how he made it home.

He went straight to the library and closed the door. Then, grabbing one of his father's whiskeys and a glass, he felt deeply disturbed. The love he felt for Francine was still alive inside of him. *But, of course, she never cared for me,* Hans kept repeating. *How could I have thought of such a thing*?

CHAPTER 20

It was late in the afternoon when Denna walked around the house looking for Hans.

As she carefully opened the library door, Denna was surprised by what she saw. There, on his father's chair, Hans was sound asleep, with an almost empty bottle of whiskey next to him.

She knew Hans never drank much, which meant that something was definitely not right.

She approached him, gently placing her hand on his shoulder.

"Hans," she said softly.

Slowly, he started to wake up.

"What happened?" he asked, looking around confused. "Is everything all right?"

"Yes, everything is fine. But I am worried about you."

"Yeah, I had a rough day," Hans said as he tried to get up. "I'll feel better soon. Don't worry; I just have a headache."

"I will bring you some food. You must be hungry!"

"I am, danke."

A few minutes later, Denna showed up with a pillow, blankets, tea, and soup.

Feeling as if his head was spinning around, Hans could barely manage to eat anything.

"Are you sure you are all right?" Denna asked, still worrying.

"Yes, this is nothing. I'm feeling better already. I just need to rest some more. I shouldn't have drunk so much!"

Denna got closer to Hans, removing his shoes and placing his head back down on the pillow.

He smiled at her, feeling glad that she was there with him.

"It's cold here," she said, going toward the fireplace.

"Do you want to keep me company in the library?" Hans finally asked her, knowing she was probably anxious to hear the story.

Holding a cup of tea in her hands, Denna sat by the fire in silence, patiently waiting until he started speaking.

Little by little, she got to know about Francine, from the very moment Hans first met her in Switzerland until the events that led them to be reunited most unexpectedly in Germany.

"That's an amazing story, Hans. It is hard to believe that you found her here, of all places, and so close to the factory!"

"I know. I thought I was dreaming when I saw her there, right across the street!"

"It was as if faith brought you two together."

"I am not sure about that. She hates me! How couldn't she?" Hans said, still feeling the pain inside his heart and soul.

"I understand what you are saying. But as far as you thinking that she hates you … well … I don't think I agree! How can you be sure of that? Hans, you said that she was crying and that she said the Germans have killed everything that once existed inside of her."

"Exactly," Hans replied. "I don't know what I was thinking. Of course, the whole world hates us Germans. She should be no different, especially being held as a prisoner here!"

"Hans! I am sure she is scared, lonely … hurt. We know she has good reasons to hate the Germans. But she met you before the war. What if she feels the same as you? Based on what you told me, there is a good possibility that she could also have fallen in love with you! If that is the case, she will never be able to admit to herself that she has feelings for a German man, even though she might truly care for you. Think about it – she's being held as a prisoner. I remember that very well! I know how it feels! You are aware of what the Germans had done to their own people, like me, my family, and friends! Imagine what they have done in France?"

Denna hesitated for a few seconds. Hans could see the pain in her eyes.

"God only knows what she might have already gone through," she almost whispered.

Hans listened carefully. He knew what the Nazis were capable of doing. Denna was living proof of that.

He felt embarrassed to be a German. The thought of Denna or Francine being hurt made him feel ill and angry to a degree he never thought possible.

"You're probably right, Denna," Hans admitted. "No one knows for sure what she has already gone through. Just the fact that she was brought here against her will says a lot! I am sure you can relate to Francine's pain. And I am very sorry that both of you have to go through all of this! I wish I could do more! But as for liking me, you're mistaken to think that. She despises me. I could see that in her eyes."

"You have done more than enough, Hans! This is not your fault! You and your family have risked your own lives to help so many people! But as for Francine, she doesn't know that! She didn't meet the during-the-war Hans. She doesn't know which side you are truly on!"

Hans started to think things over.

"Did you try to explain to her what you believe in? That you're not part of this horrific regime?" Denna continued.

"I tried, but she wouldn't let me speak much," Hans said, still feeling frustrated. "I couldn't say everything I wanted to."

"Hans!" Denna said, looking at him in disbelief. "You allowed her to stop you? You, who never hesitates to say or do the right thing even if that would mean getting yourself in trouble? You must really love her!"

Almost amused by that comment, Hans smiled at her. Yes, Denna was right. He loved Francine.

Hans looked away, placing his hands on his head. Denna was starting to make him feel like he hadn't tried hard enough.

"Denna, it's not that simple."

"I know, Hans. I know those words must have been really hard to hear, especially because you love her. But think for a moment. Right now, she is probably feeling afraid, alone … vulnerable."

As Hans listened to those words, he felt sicker; his head hurt even more. He realized that regardless of how Francine felt for him, the important thing was her safety. He needed to help her in any way possible. It was his chance to do the right thing, even if she hated him. He would prove to her he wasn't and never wanted to be part of that Nazi Germany.

"I understand what you are saying. You are right! I'll do anything to help her. No matter what she thinks of me."

"Well, she will find out one way or the other that the Hans she met in the past is still the same wonderful person."

"Thank you very much! It means a lot to me. And I'm sorry, Denna. I'm selfish, I guess, just talking about myself and …"

"Selfish? No, Hans. Your story brings me hope. It's like a light in the middle of all the darkness around us. I can relate to your story in so many ways. I also miss someone special."

"And who is that special person?" Hans asked, surprised.

"Abraham. His name is Abraham."

For the rest of the night, Hans listened to Denna's story. They both shared the same feeling of being in love with someone who seemed to be impossible to reach. But most of all, they talked about courage, friendship, and staying strong for those who needed them to survive, hoping that things would change one day again!

On the other side of town, Francine also suffered deeply. She was reliving the events of that intense encounter over and over in her mind. She had seen him moving away, leaving her with the most agonizing silence. She hadn't been able to understand what brought her to say all those horrible things to him.

There was no denying that Hans seemed to care for her, but just how much she wasn't sure. But he was there. He went after her and tried to explain himself.

He didn't forget about me, she thought. *He said he wanted to help me.*

His last words still echoed in her head. She knew she made a big mistake. She hadn't given him much of a chance to explain things. She chose not to believe him.

Overwhelmed by all those emotions, she slowly dragged her body to the bed. She sobbed, feeling an excruciating pain as if it were ripping a hole in her chest. "Hans, what have I done?"

She cried until her tears started to run dry, wishing for one more chance to speak to him. *Please come back to me. Give me one more chance, and I promise I won't disappoint you again. I'm sorry, Hans. I'm so sorry!*

As the days went by, Francine grew more and more disheartened. She was starting to wonder if Hans would ever return. She kept hearing his words, again and again, words about how much he cared for her. Realizing she had made a mistake, Francine wished nothing more than to be able to have one more chance to apologize, to explain everything that had happened to her since they said goodbye in Switzerland.

As much as she tried to deny it, she loved him immensely. A love that still burned strong inside of her. She promised herself she would no longer hide it from him. No matter what happened, she needed to let him know what he meant to her, even if it were her last words!

It was Christmas Eve, and Francine's worries grew stronger. She knew Michael could be back at any moment. Determined never to let him touch her, she thought those could be her final days.

All her hopes rested with Zachary. But not having received any more letters, she worried something terrible must have happened to him.

She stayed there by the window, looking at the factory across the street. With her head leaning against the wall, she thought about what Hans could be doing at that moment. She assumed that he was probably celebrating among his friends and family, cheering for Germany, dancing with tons of women.

Feeling a bitter taste in her mouth, she passed her hand over her face, trying to dislodge those thoughts. The possibility of Hans being with another woman bothered her more than she cared to admit. She could never have imagined that Hans was doing exactly the opposite.

On Christmas night, despite Carson's insistence that he join him, Hans stayed home with Denna. They both sat by the fire, planning Hans's next moves. And even though they felt extremely sad that they weren't with their families, they were grateful they had each other's company.

Hans thought about Francine every minute of the day. He knew she was there alone. It hurt him that he couldn't do more to help her at that time. But he knew he had to be patient for his plan to work.

In the meantime, in Switzerland, Hans's parents also wondered about him and Denna alone in Germany. They shared the same sadness and worries about the future. It took a great deal of insistence from their friends and other family members to convince them not to go back.

Not far from where Hans's parents were, Nicole also worried sick about her daughter. As the months went by, she got less and less information about her. Despite her husband's influence, they couldn't manage to bring Francine back home.

And so, Nicole fell deeper into despair. She had her daughter and husband taken away from her. Both were being held as prisoners, their lives at risk.

Her sister tried to comfort her, reassuring her they would be fine. "They are so strong," she would say. "They are survivors." But nothing seemed to console her.

At the same time, thousands of miles away, Jean was worried about his family. He had no idea Francine had been relocated to Germany. On that Christmas day, he sat with some friends he made in Eastern Poland. They all cried out their concerns and their pain.

Each of them felt like they were carrying the weight of the whole world on their shoulders. Yet, they were still hoping, hoping for the end of a war that never seemed to come.

CHAPTER 21

Julian wasn't happy with the news he received. They were going to have to wait until the spring. It was too risky to get Francine out of the German hospital due to the border's heavy military presence during the winter. Their only option was to take her to Switzerland by train.

"Pierre," Julian insisted, "we have to find another way. She might not make it to the spring. We all know what the Germans can do to her. They can simply decide to kill her without any major reasons!"

"I understand what you are saying, Julian. But there will be more risks in the winter if you need to cross the border on foot. Things may not go according to plan, and we have information that Germany will move more troops toward the east in the spring. That will reduce their presence on the border to Switzerland. So, we have to wait to take advantage of that!"

Julian sighed nervously. He knew Pierre was right. But the idea of Francine being hurt or in danger was driving him insane.

Far away from that scene, another man also planned to escape from Germany alongside two women.

It has to be Switzerland, Hans thought. *We won't make it to France. We won't have a good excuse to go there. Plus, I am sure the border control to France must be extremely strict and heavily guarded. It would be too risky.*

The problem was then more related to Francine than Denna. Hans found some information about a man who could get fake identification papers for Denna. *But how the hell am I going to get Francine out of there without being noticed?* Hans continued to ask himself.

He knew he only had one way. He had to get close to Carson again. He knew how difficult it would be, but he had to do everything in his power to protect those he loved.

On the following morning, Hans woke up early and went straight to the military facility. He wanted to invite Carson for a family dinner. He knew he wouldn't be able to hide Denna from him for much longer. That would only raise suspicion toward the girl. Hans started to prepare Denna, known as Alyse, for the meeting with Carson. Carson needed to know "Alyse" to make it easier for him to ask for travel passes when they needed them.

It was extremely hard for Hans to walk by the hospital and resist the urge to see Francine. But he knew he had to wait a while longer. He didn't want to see her again without solid plans to get her out of Germany safely.

Carson greeted Hans with a smile on his face, yet concerned about what he would have to say.

"It's great to see you, Hans. I just hope you bring good news this time!"

Hans forced a smile, "well, I have promised mother I would behave better."

Carson laughed at that comment. "I miss you, Hans. I miss your humor."

The two of them did some catching up, talking about Christmas, New Year's parties, and Carson's future in-laws. But, of course, it was more of the case of Carson speaking and Hans listening, pretending to be interested.

"You had to be there, Hans. Those folks have some real money."

"I wonder where they got it from," Hans couldn't help but say.

"No, Hans. It's not what you're thinking. They are old money."

Hans raised his eyebrows in a familiar gesture.

Carson ignored the brow twitch. He was used to Hans criticizing the Nazi high society.

"You should've seen some of the girls that were there," Carson continued, leaning back in his chair, a cigar in his mouth. "You would love it, Hans. Just like the good old days."

"I thought you were getting married," Hans replied, smirking.

"You have become such a bore, my brother. I need to drag you to one of my parties."

"No, thanks," Hans replied, lighting a cigar as well. "Unless you want me to get arrested."

Carson laughed out loud. He was in a very good mood that morning. And more than that, he really missed Hans, his company, and the way they used to have fun along with their other friends. He could trust him, something that was becoming rarer those days.

Noticing that Carson seemed to be having a good day, Hans started to put his plan into action. He invited Carson and his fiancée over for dinner at his house. Carson was both surprised and happy that Hans was acting more like a brother to him.

"I'll be there," he confirmed enthusiastically. "I'll bring my fiancée with me unless you'll have other girls coming."

"No, sorry. Just what remains of our family."

"Sure. Can't wait to meet your mysterious cousin!"

The night arrived quickly. Once more, Hans went over the instructions with Denna on how to act and what to say when Carson was around. They had prepared for that moment for a long time … the inevitable was about to happen.

But Denna was nervous. Not only would she have to lie well, which she hated, but she would also have to interact with a Nazi officer, a title which symbolized evil itself.

Hans reminded her, with irony, that it would probably be Carson who would guarantee their escape from Germany without even realizing what was truly happening.

Wearing a special dress that Hans bought her for that occasion, Denna looked both elegant and beautiful. Their guests were due any minute.

As the doorbell rang, Hans looked at Denna's face and smiled. "We can do this!"

Her heart started racing when she saw a medium-height man in his prestigious military uniform proudly entering the living room. His light blue eyes reflected nothing but a piercing Nazi arrogance.

He took his military cap off, revealing his short dark blonde hair. Walking toward Denna with his fiancée by his side, he felt unusually disturbed.

Their eyes locked for a brief moment.

Carson introduced himself first. She said her name, forcing a smile.

He looked deeply into her eyes and reached out for her hand, kissing it gently.

Feeling the touch of his lips against her skin, Denna felt a sudden chill run through her entire body.

After all the introductions were made, the four of them proceeded to the dining room. Denna was quiet and reserved. She did all she could to avoid looking at that Nazi Commander. Although he was friendly, she couldn't help but feel awkward and out of place every time he set his eyes on her.

Carson was somewhat mystified by "Alyse." She didn't look at all like the other family members he had previously met. But there was more than that. She behaved very differently from most of the girls he had known. She was shy yet charming, a pretty girl with long and lustrous chocolate brown hair, naturally red lips, and long eyelashes that perfectly accentuated her smoldering brown eyes. Her almost angelic look, along with her complete lack of interest in Carson, caught his attention in a way that neither Hans nor Denna herself could have predicted.

Seemingly unable to help himself, Carson began questioning her.

"Alyse," he said, "I don't remember you at all when I was a child. Hans told me that you visited a few times."

Denna tried to stay calm. She looked at Hans, and he smiled at her reassuringly.

"I don't remember being here very often either," she said. "But I do remember you. We played a few times together. And you didn't really like to lose any games; you would get very upset. In fact, Hans went to my parent's house more than we visited here. But that was before you moved in with the Schulzes."

"It sounds like me," Carson said, laughing at that comment. "I still hate losing!"

"Apparently, she got to know you so well, even though you spent so little time together," Hans added, trying to keep the conversation light and humorous.

They all laughed.

"You don't remember her well because Alyse's parents stopped visiting us before you came to live with us permanently," Hans rushed to rescue Denna, who was clearly nervous. "My aunt and uncle went to live in England, then Asia."

"England, Asia?" Carson asked, puzzled. "Why so many trips?"

"My father was a businessman. We had to travel all the time, and I loved it! All the new places and different cultures …"

"Oh, I can imagine." Carson was intrigued. "What kind of business were they in?"

"Are you done with the interrogation, Carson?" Hans asked sarcastically.

They all laughed again.

"I'm sorry," Carson said, looking at Alyse. "It's just that Hans never really mentioned he had such an interesting family member!"

The conversation shifted to other, safer subjects. Hans made sure that Carson was distracted enough to leave Denna alone.

After dinner, Hans invited Denna to play the piano, which she excelled at. The entire time she played, something interesting was happening. Carson, who already had a few drinks, could hardly take his eyes off her. Not that he suspected anything, but rather, he was intrigued by that unique young woman whose charming ways were proving to be extremely attractive to him.

Hans noticed Carson's interest with a little concern. Although he knew that Carson wouldn't disrespect anyone from his family, he wasn't sure if his interest in Denna was a good or bad thing. Adalie, Carson's fiancée, was the one who started to feel uncomfortable with Carson's unwavering attention to that new girl.

"I think it's getting late," Adalie said politely, not liking what she was seeing.

"We can stay a little longer," Carson said. "It's not too late, is it Hans?"

"Of course not. Although, I know Alyse likes to go to sleep early."

"I think I can manage to stay awake a bit longer," Denna said, trying to be pleasant.

Hans was surprised by the assertive way that Denna responded. He was really proud of her.

Adalie and Denna couldn't be any different from one another in every aspect of their personality, looks, and attitude. But even so, the two women tried to keep the conversation flowing, talking about Adalie's upcoming wedding while Hans and Carson decided to go to the library to talk more freely.

"I'm thinking about visiting my parents in Switzerland soon," Hans said, not wasting any time.

"That would be a good idea. Our parents will be happy to see you." "Exactly. It would be great if you came with us; Alyse will be going too. Her family is always too busy with international business affairs. She's tired of moving constantly and feeling alone," Hans continued, trying to sound as natural as possible.

Carson took a moment to think.

"That sounds nice," Carson said, contemplating the idea of taking a few days off and spending more time around Hans's cousin. "But I don't think it will be possible for me, at least not now. I don't know if you've noticed, Hans, but there is a war going on. I have too many things that need to be done here. It's a crucial time for us. The Allies are starting to prolong our battles. We don't expect any major problems, but we want to make sure we defeat our enemies as quickly as possible."

For the first time in a while, Hans picked up a hint of concern in Carson's demeanor and speech. Carson tried his best not to imply anything negative about Germany, but Hans knew him too well. The war might have been finally starting to take a different turn.

"You don't see a problem for me to get out of Germany with Alyse, do you?" Hans asked, trying to show no emotion whatsoever.

"I don't think so. It's not like she's Jewish, right?" Carson asked, laughing out loud.

Hans shook his head, trying to remain calm after that comment. Although he knew Carson was joking, it was horrifying how close he had come to the truth.

"Oh, Hans. You have no sense of humor anymore."

"What kind of comment is that?" Hans said solemnly, trying not to look away. "She's part of our family. She deserves respect. And I don't like those jokes; you know that very well."

It was hard for Hans to say those last words with a straight face. But he knew he had to talk like that in order not to raise any suspicion.

"It was a joke …" Carson replied. "… a bad joke. I'm sorry. You are right. I shouldn't offend your cousin like that."

"Exactly!" Hans had no other choice but to agree.

"She's an attractive woman, Hans. Are you sure there's no possibility of a romance between the two of you?"

"Of course not," Hans said quickly, feeling even more disgusted than before. "She's my cousin, and she's like a sister to me. To us, actually."

Carson smiled and said nothing. He was pleased that Hans had no romantic interest in Alyse.

It was late before their guests finally decided to leave. Hans and Denna couldn't be more relieved.

"You did very well," Hans said to Denna as soon as he saw Carson's car driving off. "I'm proud of you."

"It was so hard," she replied, feeling sad. "I know he's considered to be your brother, but …."

"I know, I understand, and I'm very sorry you had to endure his presence. Unfortunately, Carson is a Nazi officer. I will never really accept that! But, ironically enough, he's the only one who can help us all."

CHAPTER 22

Hans focused all his energy on his plan to get Francine and Denna out of Germany. When he was at his office, he would often look out of the window and stare across the street, wondering about Francine. He feared for her life. He knew he had to act quickly.

It was a late afternoon when Hans got home and noticed they had company. Carson's car was in his driveway again. Concerned about Denna, he hurried inside the house.

"Hello, Hans," Carson rushed to say as soon as Hans showed up in the living room.

Hans looked at Denna, trying to spot any signs of trouble.

"Good afternoon," he replied, feeling better after noticing that Carson seemed to be undisturbed.

"I was on my way back home when I decided to stop by to check how you two are doing. I believe your cousin is too young to be inside the house the whole day. She should go out more, have fun. Perhaps you can convince her, Hans. We can all go out together!

"I appreciate the invitation, Carson," Denna said politely. "But at this point in my life, I prefer quiet and peaceful places. Well, I will leave you with Hans now as I need to check on how dinner is coming along. Will you stay with us?

"Unfortunately, I can't stay tonight. I have a work meeting later today. But I will definitely accept the invitation for another day. And as you don't like parties too much, I believe we can all at least go out for dinner. I know some excellent restaurants, with an elegant and calm atmosphere.

"In that case, I accept," Denna smiled, pretending to like the idea.

Ever since Carson had met Alyse, as he knew her, he had been visiting more often. And although Hans had promised to keep Carson away from her, it was becoming harder and harder by the day.

Hans knew exactly what was happening there. Carson had always been a womanizer, but still, he couldn't understand the persistent interest that Carson had in Denna, a quiet and shy girl. Carson liked outgoing and provocative women. *Perhaps he just likes the chase,* Hans thought, trying not to take his friend's actions too seriously.

"I don't know any more about the engagement," Carson finally told Hans as soon as Alyse left the room.

"What do you mean?" Hans asked him, getting a bad feeling.

"Something has changed. I don't know … I'm already bored. You know I was never the kind of man meant for marriage!"

Hans looked at him, not surprised by that comment. Carson always had trouble with fidelity. After he joined the Nazi party, things only got worse as he found himself being surrounded by more women and more parties.

But for that moment, Hans knew he had to take advantage of that situation to their own benefit as things were proving to be more difficult than he had planned. The person responsible for getting Denna's fake identity papers had suddenly disappeared. He knew of no one else who could help him with that.

"Are you sure you don't want to stay for dinner?" Hans asked, trying to be polite.

"I really want to, but I can't tonight. I have an important meeting with some of the other officers back at the base. I actually need to be leaving soon."

Denna joined them back in the living room and they talked for a few more minutes before Carson had to leave. He promised another visit soon.

The next day, at the end of his shift, Hans sat in his office awhile longer, feeling discouraged and frustrated. Like he did several times over the course of the day, he looked out the window, straight at the hospital building across the street, thinking about Francine. It had been weeks since he had spoken to her, and it was killing him. He had been hesitant to go there again without a concrete plan to offer her. But still, he wanted to see her; he needed to see her. So many things were left unspoken between them.

Without wasting another minute, he got up abruptly and rushed out of his office.

The stars shone against the darkness of that clear winter sky.

Hans stopped at a local store and bought a few items. He knew the soldiers would enjoy them.

The guards recognized him right away, opening the gate for him. It was a chilly night, and they gladly took the bag that Hans had brought them, full of whiskey, cigarettes, and a variety of snacks.

Hans didn't have a real plan. It was also the first time he didn't care. He was going to see Francine that night, no matter what, and no one would stand in his way.

Standing by the window, Francine felt a hole in her chest, a deep sense of emptiness. She felt abandoned, alienated from life.

Michael didn't fulfill his promises to be back by Christmas time; Francine hoped that he had forgotten about her and that she would never see him again. But the threat of him showing up anytime still haunted her.

Francine closed her eyes with her head leaning against the window frame, trying to fight the urge to cry. For a brief moment, she allowed herself to dream away. It was strange to think about Hans being so close to her again and yet so distant. *Would I ever be able to see him again?* she wondered, still clinging to hope.

What Francine couldn't have imagined was at that exact moment, Hans had already entered the hospital.

He decided not to approach anyone and went straight toward the staircase.

Standing behind the wall, Hans anxiously waited until there was no one else in that hallway. Finally, he fixed his clothes and slowly started to walk toward Francine's room.

The world felt as if it had stopped. The silence filled the atmosphere with all the words that still needed to be said but were never spoken.

Hans could hear his heart pounding in his chest. He knew he had to act fast before someone saw him there.

A sudden knock at the door snapped Francine out of her daydreams. A rush of excitement ran through her body. She immediately thought of Hans. She took a few steps forward but then stopped abruptly. The very thought that it could also be Michael brought her a sensation of panic, a feeling of near death.

Her bedroom door was still being kept unlocked just in case they needed her in the emergency room. Francine didn't believe Michael was the kind of man who would knock before making his way in. She knew she had to take a chance.

"Who is it?" Francine finally asked, placing her body against the door, still afraid to open it.

Hans hesitated for a few seconds.

He heard a noise coming from the stairway. He stepped forward.

"It's me, Hans. Can I come in?"

As if struck by lightning, her heart jumped instantly. A sweet and sincere smile spread across her face. Life was given her another chance. There was no one else she would rather see.

Hans saw the doorknob turning quickly, and soon Francine appeared right before his eyes.

"Come inside," she rushed to say to his surprise.

She quickly closed the door behind them.

They stood there looking at one another, hostages of all the emotions they could no longer control.

Francine felt that all the love she had held off for so long was finally coming to the surface. She didn't want to hide it anymore.

Not wanting to waste one more second, Hans started moving closer to her.

Their eyes locked.

"We need to talk," he finally said, looking deep into her eyes. "And this time, I won't leave until you listen to every word I have to say."

Francine simply nodded.

"I'm not…" he began, trying to find the right words. "… I'm not the monster you think I am."

Hans noticed the tears filling her eyes, making her look even more vulnerable. He took a few more steps forward, getting even closer to her. That time, Francine was offering no resistance.

Unable to take his eyes off her, Hans gently touched her face. "I don't want to scare you," he said softly.

Francine shook her head. She felt like she could trust him.

"What have they done to you?" Hans said as his fingers wiped the tears from her face. "I'm so sorry."

Feeling the sincerity of those words, she placed her hand on top of his, holding it tightly.

Surprised and yet deeply moved by her actions, Hans encircled her in his arms. He felt as if he was the most fortunate of all men, an emotion impossible to describe.

Feeling the warmth of his body, she leaned her head against his chest. Tears streamed down her face, washing away all the fear and sorrow from her heart.

They stayed there quietly, just holding each other.

Hans looked down at her face again. His eyes were soft, his smile tender. Placing his hands behind her neck, he slowly approached her lips, stopping right before them. Intense desire burned within him, every inch of him longed for her. Without hesitating any longer, he closed his eyes and kissed her.

Feeling his lips pressed against hers, Francine surrendered to him, kissing him passionately.

Taking Francine's face in both of his hands, he kissed her again and again, moving his wet lips toward her neck, kissing her down to her shoulders.

Francine could feel his heart beating rapidly. She could feel all his love.

He paused briefly, looking deeply into her eyes, as if asking her permission to do what would come next. She nodded, understanding that gesture. Slowly he started unbuttoning her shirt. Hans reached out for her lips again as he brought her body closer, feeling her soft skin against his chest.

One step at a time, he moved her toward the bed, placing himself on top of her gently.

Francine felt protected under the weight of his body. She closed her eyes again, allowing herself to fall into all that mystery, a new sensation, a mix of strong pleasurable emotions at every touch.

With her body steadily brushing against his, his breathing got heavier, his movements intensified. Filled with an uncontrollable desire, his hands slid all over her body, feeling every contour.

Listening to her moaning, Hans embraced Francine tightly. He could feel Francine's heart beating faster against his chest, her body shaking with every move he made, slowly, passionately, and gently inside her.

He placed his hands behind her neck as her hair tangled around his fingers. He couldn't stop kissing her.

He finally had everything he ever wanted or needed right there in his hands.

Outside, the strong wind pushed hard against the glass window. But the room didn't feel cold anymore.

In a time of war, those two young lovers started to understand the power of the sublime feeling they both shared, the one safe place where peace could still be found.

CHAPTER 23

The first specks of sunlight started to fill the room. Hans woke up with Francine still sleeping peacefully in his arms. He smiled. He had never experienced such a feeling of happiness before, nor believed it could exist. Francine loved him. He finally knew that.

Hans lay there for a few more minutes, feeling her head against his chest. He didn't want to let go of her. But he knew he had to leave before the sun completely rose.

Slowly, he moved his body away from Francine. It was one of the hardest things he had ever done. The mere thought of leaving her behind, unprotected, was breaking his heart.

He placed her head comfortably on top of the pillow, covering her body with a blanket. Hans stood there staring at her. He wanted to take her with him, but he knew it wasn't possible yet.

Putting his clothes on, he felt even more determined to get her out of there fast. He went to the table next to her bed, where he found a piece of paper and a pen.

Francine,

How dare I leave you alone? I promise I'll be back soon, and I'll get you out of here even if it's the last thing I do in this life. The happiness you brought me last night gave me the strength to overcome the impossible. And I love you. Remember that. I will be back in your arms soon.

Je t'aime

He placed the letter by Francine's side. He looked at her one more time as she still slept so peacefully. He wanted to freeze that image forever in his mind.

Hans managed to walk out of the facility before the sun was completely up. With his heart still beating fast, he got inside his car and drove back home.

Francine woke up with the sunlight shining brightly inside her room. She looked around and quickly realized Hans was already gone. She got up, noticing a note by her pillow.

With a beaming smile on her face, she read the sweet words he had left her. She remembered every detail of the special moment they spent together and their long conversation before they fell asleep in each other's arms. She knew Hans loved her.

They had talked for many hours into the night. They shared many stories about what had happened to them since their first meeting in Switzerland. He told her many things about his life and his future plans. She shared her fears and concerns, especially about Michael. He had promised to protect her and get her out of there as soon as possible, and she believed it.

Hans had only gotten a few hours of sleep before he had to go to work. He kept reliving those past moments with Francine over and over again. But he knew he had to act fast to get her out of there. There was also the urgency related to the return of Michael. He couldn't wait any longer. Hans decided to talk to Carson.

As he entered the military base, he looked at the hospital building and smiled. He knew she was there. He couldn't stop thinking about her. He wanted to go there and kiss her, hold her again. But his quest to give Francine back her freedom and ensure her safety was the most important thing at that moment.

"Hans," Carson said enthusiastically. "I'm glad to see you here. I have plans for all of us tonight."

Hans attempted a smile. He could care less about Carson's plans for the night. He had no time for chatting about irrelevant matters.

"Listen, Carson," Hans went straight to the point. "I have something really important we need to talk about."

Carson's facial expression changed completely; his smile turned into a frown. He knew that every time Hans started talking that way, he was in deep trouble.

Carson looked at the lower-ranked soldier who was in his office typing papers. The soldier understood the gesture and got up, walking toward the door. They waited until the door was shut behind him.

"What have you done now?" Carson asked him as he sat down, feeling agitated.

"It's not about what I have done but rather what I need to do."

"No, no," Carson immediately replied, already foreseeing problems. "This time, I really don't want to hear it. I really had enough."

"Just listen to me for a minute," Hans persisted, losing his patience. "It is not what you are thinking."

Carson sighed, not believing him.

"It's about a girl!"

Raising his eyebrows, Carson stared at him, surprised, not expecting to hear that at all. He chuckled. That was actually a subject that he really enjoyed talking about.

"Go on," Carson said curiously. "You scared me!"

Hans started to talk about Francine. At first, Carson was amused by Hans's description of how he had met her in Switzerland. But as he advanced deeper into the story, Carson's face and body language started to change again, demonstrating astonishment and noticeable aggravation.

In the end, for Carson's further disgust, Hans told him he needed his help to take her out of there.

"That is absurd, Hans," Carson said, getting up from his chair. "Are you willing to risk your life for a French woman who you met a long time ago at a cafe?"

"Yes," Hans said firmly. "And I'll do it with or without your help. I'll die trying if I have to."

Carson looked at Hans's transformed face. He knew Hans to be both determined and capable. Carson sat down again and lit his cigar, trying to think about what to say next. He needed to convince his friend about the foolishness of such an endeavor.

"You're going to expose yourself, your cousin, and your entire family. Do you know that? This madness could get all of you killed."

"My parents are out of reach. And Alyse supports me entirely. You seem to be the only one who's scared here."

Carson moved in his chair. He resented the implication that he was a coward. But it was the fact that Alyse supported Hans's plan that caught his attention.

"Hans," Carson continued, "this is craziness, and I will not allow you to proceed. You're betraying your own country for a stupid French woman. You can find someone else here. I know plenty of girls that would die to be with someone like you."

Hans looked at Carson with fury on his face.

"Didn't you hear anything I have said? She means everything to me, and I love her. You don't know how that feels because you have never loved anyone like this. But I do, and if my brother, my only brother, can't understand that, I'll find someone who can."

Hans turned around and started to walk away.

"Wait, Hans!" Carson yelled. "Come back here. Have a cigar, relax and let me think for a second."

Hans turned back and looked at Carson as if trying to read his mind.

"Take it!" Carson insisted, pointing the fine cigar to him.

Deep inside, Hans knew that Carson was his best option to accomplish his goals.

He walked toward him, reaching out for the cigar.

Carson looked at him for a few seconds without saying a word. Then he laughed.

"What is so funny?" Hans said, irritated.

"Calm down, Hans. It is just that, well, forget it … my point is: Have I ever denied anything to you? But this, Hans, you have to understand; this is almost impossible. Apparently, she is a prisoner here."

"You can easily have her removed back to France! You are the Commander of this station, and she's just working here as a nurse."

"A nurse?" Carson said, still puzzled. "Why was she brought here?"

"I don't know. I guess they needed someone with medical experience who spoke French. There was also the fact that a soldier was harassing her and wanted her here in Germany. Anyway, it is a long story. But it doesn't matter now. All I need is to have her back in France as fast as possible. I fear for her safety."

"That doesn't make much sense, Hans! Anyway, I will definitely figure it out one way or the other, but for now, I can't believe you are actually in love with a French woman. Are you sure this is not just a temporary infatuation? How foolish of you. Well, at least she is not a Jew. That, I couldn't help you with."

Hans immediately thought about Denna. He felt like punching Carson in the face, but he knew that he needed his help.

He took a deep breath, feeling extremely frustrated, infuriated he had to beg a Nazi man to help him out, even though that man was a person he considered to be his brother.

"Listen, I have to do some research on this woman first before I can do anything. I have so many important issues to take care of, and here you're asking me to waste my time to save a French girl. Unbelievable! Only you, Hans! You just don't understand what we are trying to do here, do you?"

"No, I don't, and I never will. But what I think doesn't matter right now, does it? All that I am asking is for you to send her back to France. Her life is in danger. She doesn't need to be here. I bet that German soldier I told you about had something to do with her transfer here for the simple pleasure of inflicting pain on her. She means everything to me. I don't know what I will do if something bad happens to her," Hans said with tears sparkling in his eyes.

Carson had never seen Hans talk about any of his past girlfriends like that. He knew he was serious, as much as he hated the idea.

"I have to say it … you're crazy, Hans," Carson laughed again, somewhat amused by all of it. "Who would have imagined? You … Hans … in love with a French prisoner. But then again, it kind of goes with your personality and …."

"That's enough, Carson! Everything is a joke to you. This is a very serious matter to me."

"So, Alyse approves it?" Carson asked him, trying to take that conversation in another direction.

Hans took advantage of the opportunity to touch Carson's heart if he still had one.

"She believes in me and what I feel for Francine. She also thinks it's very romantic. You know how women are."

"Alright. So, why don't we have dinner tonight, and we will talk more about it," Carson asked Hans, wishing to see his cousin. "Then you can tell me the whole story – how pretty she is or if you've kissed her, or perhaps …?"

Hans sighed again. He knew he had to put up with Carson's jokes, especially when it came to women. He needed Carson by his side. He had to avoid fighting with him.

"Just promise me that at least for now, you will forbid anyone from entering her room," Hans continued. "It needs to be done with urgency. Promise me! I am begging you. That German soldier could be back at any moment."

Hans walked closer to Carson, placing his hand on his shoulder. "I am begging you."

"Consider it done! Trust me; I don't want her here either. Something is not right! She is still part of a country that we considered our enemy, and I don't know who the idiot was that allowed her presence here. But I can promise you, Hans, I will find out who is behind this whole thing, and he will pay for it. I should have been notified about her. This whole facility is under my command and supervision, damn it!"

As much as Carson tried to hide it from Hans, it hurt his pride to learn he was not notified of a foreigner inside his military base.

"It has to be done right away," Hans insisted. "Also, I want to have full clearance to see her as I wish."

"Of course, you do!" Carson said with a smirk on his face. "I will take care of it!"

"No one should have access to her but me."

"Alright, alright, Hans. I got it! Just go to work now." Carson tried to get rid of him. "I have a lot to do!"

"I'll see you tonight then! I will tell Alyse you're coming. It will be a private conversation, so make sure you don't bring your fiancée."

"Of course not. Why would I? Plus, I don't believe my marriage will happen any time soon, if ever."

Hans looked at Carson and shook his head in disapproval.

"What? Come on, Hans," Carson said, leaning back on his chair. "What has gotten into you? You should be careful, Hans; love is a dangerous thing. It blinds you and weakens your strength. Look at you, risking everything for such foolishness."

"I'll see you later," Hans said, closing the door behind him.

Carson sat there, still in shock. Hans had never told him about the girl. He didn't know she was there. *So why would they send a French nurse to his military base? And why wasn't I notified about it?* Carson wondered, intrigued.

He thought it was very strange. He didn't like the fact she was there. *She could be a spy, and those idiots would never know it.*

Getting up from his chair, he started to pace around the room. *Perhaps it won't be so hard to get the girl out of here. No French person should be allowed at this military station. But first I need to know more about her. What a fool my brother is!*

Carson called for one of his subordinates and asked to speak with the head of the hospital immediately. He had to know exactly what she was doing there. That matter was far more important than her romance with Hans. Although he didn't want to hurt him, he thought he was crazy to risk everything for a mere woman.

Carson didn't mind the French much, not as much as the Jewish people, whom he had been conditioned to hate. To him, the French people were considered to be an inferior race, not worthy of any special considerations or thoughts. However, he could understand some of the interest

Hans had for that French woman in a way. *They are still women,* Carson chuckled with sarcasm.

On that same day, Francine was placed inside the office upstairs to translate documents. She actually didn't mind being isolated that time. She would rather be alone to dream about Hans more freely.

It had been the first time she'd been intimate with a man; she relived every moment, every touch. She would not have it any other way but with Hans.

Francine reached deep into her pocket and found the note he had left her. She read it over and over again. He made her feel loved. She knew he would never abandon her!

Not far away from her location, Carson spoke to the head of the hospital and found out Francine seemed to be harmless and rather useful. She was a nurse with many surgical skills, and there was a shortage of nurses like that.

"Still, I don't like the idea of any foreigner being so close to us," Carson said, full of authority.

"She's strictly secluded to the hospital area," the doctor confirmed. "She only translates informal papers for the most part."

"She could have access to other things there," Carson continued, still concerned. "She could hear full conversations, become aware of important information. I find it too dangerous. I can't really understand why someone would bring her here just because of her language and medical skills. There must be something else."

"No one really knows, Commander. It's somewhat of a mystery. All I can say is that the orders came from a German officer in France. Although we could always use extra help, I often wondered why a French nurse was brought here to our country to translate hospital papers. She could do that in France!"

"Exactly!" Carson agreed. He needed to find out the name of the officer who sent Francine and why. He couldn't discard the possibility of her working as a spy or being able to release important information without anyone being aware of it.

"Get all of the information you have on her, including the names of those who sent her here. Send it to my office when you have it. I consider this an urgent matter. Urgent and secret! Do you understand that?"

If I find something suspicious, Hans will have to get used to the idea of being without her forever, Carson thought as the doctor walked out of his office.

The sun moved down steadily into the horizon. Purple and dark blue clouds blended together, producing a beautiful spectacle in the sky. Such a work of art announced a night that was far from being over.

Carson made sure to dress really well. He was trying to take advantage of that situation. If Francine was working there simply as a translator, he knew he wouldn't have any major problems sending her back to France. *Hans will be happy, and so will Alyse*! He needed and wanted to impress her.

But by thinking of her, he once more felt uneasy. That was the first time he had to work so hard to get a woman's attention, which somehow made him feel a bit uncomfortable and weak. Little by little, those feelings started to become a struggle for him. As much as he tried to deny it, he couldn't stop thinking about her. And even though he convinced himself it was only the thrill of the pursuit, deep inside, he knew his feeling toward that uncommon German girl was much stronger.

CHAPTER 24

That night, Carson instantly engaged Hans and Alyse in a conversation about Francine's removal from Germany. He knew that it would make him look more important.

"I've started asking questions about the French girl," Carson said in a serious tone, making sure they all understood how much power he had.

Hans and Denna kept quiet, waiting for Carson to start speaking again.

"I may need a few weeks to find out if I can transfer her back to France. In the meantime, I made sure no one else would have access to her, except for you, Hans!

That was all Hans needed to hear at that moment. Carson had found a safer and better way to solve things than he had hoped for. A smooth removal of Francine from Germany to France would be ideal for all of them.

"I cannot thank you enough! You have no idea how happy that makes me feel. It is such a relief! When do you think you will have all the information you need to get her back to France?"

"Hans. There is no way I can know for sure. I'm extremely busy with endless tasks at the base. Plus, I'll be going to Berlin again soon. The war is intensifying everywhere, and I still have to supervise the removal of the Jews out of this town."

Denna almost choked on her tea. Hans knew he had to think fast.

"Can we not talk about war now?' Hans asked Carson.

"I'm sorry," Carson said, looking at Denna strangely. "I forget how much some of you ladies dislike that subject."

Denna looked at him with tears in her eyes. Hans was starting to get concerned.

"Alyse lost her best friend in the war. They were very close, a German soldier, fighting on the front lines."

"I apologize," Carson said, noticing her distress. "I was unaware of that!"

It took Denna everything she had not to cry. Then, incapable of saying anything, she timidly smiled.

"Yes. That happened recently. So, it is still a touchy subject. See Carson; everyone loses in a war," Hans continued talking, trying to fix the situation.

"Would you excuse me?" Denna said in a shaky voice.

Trying her best to avoid crying in front of Carson, Denna got up and left the living room quickly.

She arrived in her bedroom, feeling defeated. Tears poured down her face as she lay on her bed. She couldn't take all the lies, all the uncertainties anymore. Yet, there she was, having a cup of tea with a man whose ideas and views had taken away or killed everyone she loved and cared for. Denna despised Carson so much she wanted to slap him across the face, scream at him, hurt him in any way possible. And, ironically enough, she knew he was probably the only one able to give her a free pass out of Germany.

In the living room, an awkward silence made Carson feel somewhat responsible for Denna's reaction.

"I'm sorry, Hans," Carson said, feeling a little confused. "I had no idea how sensitive she was."

Hans knew he had to make up a good story.

"To be completely honest, Carson, that was the main reason why she was sent here to stay with us for a while. Her parents were really concerned about her well-being. After she lost her best friend, she grew sad and lost interest in life. For being such a personal matter, her parents asked us not to mention it to anyone. So, I couldn't quite tell you. I am sorry!"

"Oh," Carson said, feeling surprisingly jealous. "Are you sure they were just friends? It has to be more than that, right?"

"Carson … that's not really our business!" Hans objected. "Besides, you know exactly what I mean when I say friend."

"What's wrong with a simple question? You get easily irritated, Hans."

Hans sighed. At least Carson had believed his story.

"Well, I guess you are right, Carson. I apologize. I didn't mean to make you feel uncomfortable. But either way, can we not talk about anything related to the war in front of her? Is that alright?"

"Well, I guess so. But the man is dead. What can we do?"

Hans looked at him in disbelief, "How can you say that with such disregard?"

"I'm sorry. I feel bad that a German soldier has died, believe me. But there is nothing wrong in saying that a dead man is dead."

Hans shook his head in disapproval, going along with his lie.

"I'll try not to say anything else in front of her again, all right?" Carson said, still not fully understanding why anyone would be so disturbed by that subject. To him, the honor of fighting and dying for their country should overcome any other feelings or personal impressions about the war. But he still didn't want to upset the girl who, for some strange reason, wouldn't leave his thoughts.

"That is another reason why it is probably better if she goes to Switzerland, a more peaceful place. I'm just waiting to finish dealing with a few of father's business arrangements."

"I'll apologize to her another time," Carson said, already aggravated for her leaving him so soon. "Anyway, I'd better get going to that meeting. They are expecting me. You should come with me!"

"You mean … that party? I'll pass, thanks."

"Call it what you want, Hans!" Carson smiled at him, already standing up. "Are you sure you don't want to come along? You look like you can use some distractions … and tonight, I can guarantee you will find a lot of beautiful ones!"

"Maybe next time, Carson."

"Yeah, sure … I doubt it!"

"Well, I appreciate what you are doing for Francine."

"Yeah, like you gave me any other choice. Tell your cousin that I am sorry. I will make up to her next time."

As soon as Carson left, Hans rushed toward Denna's room. Hearing the knock at her door, she quickly wiped the tears off her face.

"Come in," she said.

Hans noticed the girl had been crying.

"Denna … he's gone."

"I'm sorry. I shouldn't have done that."

"Please don't apologize. I understand it. I will tell you later what happened after you left. But for now, I am the one who should be sorry. I can't imagine how hard it must be for you."

Denna attempted a smile. "But we need him," she mumbled.

"Yes, unfortunately, we do. But we'll be out of here soon. I will figure a way out. Don't lose hope!"

"And my family, Hans? My friends? Where are they? What will happen to them?"

Looking at her sobbing, Hans approached her, holding the girl gently in his arms. He didn't know how he would be able to go on without knowing his loved one's fate. He had already been informed that Denna's parents had disappeared with so many others. There were several rumors that they were already dead. Mr. Elliot had received some information from his friends. But Hans couldn't bring himself to tell her, and without any certainty, he kept hoping they could still be alive.

"We'll find them, Denna. No matter how long it takes … we'll find them."

"I don't want to ruin your day! Not after everything you told me earlier about Francine," Denna said, trying her best to stop crying.

"You should never worry about that! We are in this together, remember? And I am not going anywhere without you!"

They talked into the late hours of the night. Hans always had a way of making her feel hopeful about the future.

Back in his room, Hans lay on his bed thinking a little more positively about his plans to get Francine and Denna out of Germany. But there was something that kept bothering him, a strong feeling warning him that things wouldn't be that simple.

No matter how hard he tried, he couldn't get rid of those thoughts.

A few days had passed, and Carson had already made some progress toward sending Francine back to her homeland. Things were going his way. He had sole power at his base and a lot of influence with the higher officers.

Carson could be extremely charismatic when he wanted to be. He knew how to behave and how to speak according to the crowd he was with. His clever communication skills along with his contagious sense of humor attracted all kinds of people.

However, he wasn't the only person close to getting Francine out of Germany. Far away from his military base, a few other men carefully planned their next moves. They knew they would only have one chance. They couldn't afford to fail.

"It's now all up to you and Daniel," Pierre said, looking at both of them.

Julian looked at Daniel in agreement. They had been planning Francine's escape for months. They knew spring would be the right time to get her out of Germany.

Julian couldn't hold back his excitement. He had been on dangerous missions before, but going inside Germany was definitely going to be the greatest one of all. He knew all the risks, but he didn't care. Francine's safety was all that mattered to him.

For Julian, no other woman had filled the empty space that Francine left in his life once the war started and they were separated. Although they were never involved romantically, he still had hopes that things could change.

It ended up being quite a challenge to find the right person to go along with him. They needed someone who spoke fluent German and knew his way around. Pierre, one of the French Resistance's main leaders, was the one who helped Julian the most. Not only had he known Francine's father well, but he was also aware of all the risks she took to help their secret missions. It was neither safe nor appropriate to leave her there.

Just when they were losing hope of ever finding that right person, a young man by the name of Daniel volunteered for the task. He was an Englishman who had lost both of his parents in the war after the bombing of his entire neighborhood. He was one of the few who had survived. All his hatred against the Germans was redirected to his work with the Secret Service.

Daniel wanted to be where the action was, where he was needed the most. He knew German fluently due to some of his family ties. His parents were very wealthy and made sure Daniel had acquired as much knowledge as possible. He studied at the best schools until one day; he was sent to Austria to master one of the several languages he spoke.

Soon, Daniel became an important part of the English Secret Service. But he wanted to do more; he wanted revenge. He had asked to be sent to France or even Germany to work as a spy. *Death can come,* Daniel used to say, *but not before I kill a couple more of those Nazi Jerries.*

Pierre wouldn't be able to make the trip, but he was fully involved in the preparations. He completely trusted both Julian and Daniel's capabilities to accomplish such a mission. They would save Francine and gather all the valuable information she obtained while staying in Germany.

They all understood the dangers they would be facing soon. But they were ready for whatever would come.

CHAPTER 25

The first days of Spring had arrived, and with it, a warmer breeze that slowly melted the frozen ground.

Sitting next to her bed, Francine anxiously waited for the sound of a knock at her bedroom door. It was already Friday, and Hans always visited her after work. Her life had changed completely, she no longer felt alone or unprotected.

They both waited for Carson to get the final approval for her removal. But a new order prohibiting the transfer of foreigners outside Germany without the SS's permission placed Carson in a difficult situation. He still had enough power to figure out a way to transfer Francine independently, but he didn't want to expose himself in any way, not for a simple French girl, as he called her.

And so, for that moment, he decided to omit that fact from Hans, telling him he only needed a little more time.

Francine couldn't wait to get out of that hospital and feel free again. Dreaming about that day, she heard a noise coming from the hallway. *Hans!* She told herself.

The door opened slowly. Francine rose with a smile on her face.

But, in the blink of an eye, everything changed. That same smile completely faded away. Her face turned deathly pale. Her body jerked backward on instinct. The man who had just entered her room was not Hans. It wasn't Zachary either. Instead, it was her worst nightmare coming to life!

Michael entered the room, staring at Francine's terrified face. He slowly turned around to shut the door behind him.

"Guten abend, Francine. Or should I say bon soir?" He said with a creepy smirk. "We finally meet again. I have to apologize for the delay. I hope you didn't think I wasn't going to fulfill my promise."

In fear, Francine had already moved backward, planting herself against the wall as he walked one step at a time toward her.

"I know, I know… I am a little late," Michael continued, trying to sound more enthusiastic. "You must have waited for me every day, anxiously. So … it is understandable that you feel disappointed. But I am here now, all for you."

Francine stood there, pretending to pay attention to the words Michael spoke. But all she could think of was how she would get that knife hidden under the pillow that Hans had given her. Francine knew it could be her only way to fight him, as she was well aware of his intentions.

Enjoying every second of her discomfort, Michael started to walk around the room slowly. He stopped near Francine's small dresser, noticing her hairbrush. He picked it up in amusement.

"You are looking really good, mon amour," Michael taunted, focusing back on her. "I am glad my people have been treating you so well."

It was then that Francine saw a chance to get the knife from under her mattress. She quickly jumped on her bed, positioning her body in such a way that she would be able to reach out for the knife underneath it. She felt the cold blade in her hands, but she wasn't fast enough.

He instantly followed her sudden movement, grabbing her and forcibly turning her body around.

Francine reacted immediately, trying to free herself but found that it was useless. Michael was much stronger and quickly immobilized her.

Then, not wasting any more time, he placed himself on top of her, holding her arms violently against the bed.

"What were you trying to do, huh?" Michael said, his face reflecting his anger. "Do you think you can fight me?"

"Let go of me," Francine yelled, struggling to break free of his iron grip.

"Who do you think you are?" Michael said, already grabbing her neck and pressing it into the mattress. "You are just a stupid French whore, and that's all you are. And that's how you will be treated!"

As Francine tried to gasp for air, she used all her strength to push his face away from her.

"The harder you try, the more I will hurt you," Michael said viciously, letting go of her neck and tightening his hands around both of her wrists.

She attempted to scream for help, but Michael quickly clamped his hand over her mouth. Having one of her hands free, Francine took the opportunity to hit his face hard, scratching it with her nails, until blood started to show. Michael reacted instantly, slapping her face with all his fury.

Francine felt disoriented for a few seconds, but she wasn't ready to give up yet.

Michael tried to hold her still, and yet he tried to keep her from screaming. It was proving to be a more difficult task than he had thought.

It was a brutal struggle for survival.

At the same time, outside that room, Helene walked down the hallway, feeling glad her shift was finally over. But as she passed by Francine's bedroom, she clearly heard some strange noises. She got closer to the door and soon heard a scream. On an impulse, she opened the door. She was stunned by what she saw.

Francine was kicking and fighting a man who was on top of her trying to hold her down and rip her clothes off. The nurse stood there for a few seconds in shock. Helene had heard of so many stories like that, but watching it happen right in front of her eyes was a totally different thing.

"Get off her!" Helene snapped without thinking. "What are you doing here? This is a secluded area!"

Michael looked over and didn't hesitate. He got up very quickly and went straight to the nurse. Grabbing her hair, he pulled her in and shut the door behind them.

Taken by surprise, Helene was completely frightened.

Michael went toward her again, dragging her across the room.

Before she could scream, Michael covered her mouth, and like a mad man, he repeatedly smashed her head hard against the wall. Finally, Helene fell to the ground, unconscious.

In the meantime, Francine tried to get up. She felt light-headed. She was able to take a few steps toward the door when Michael rapidly overpowered her again, violently throwing her back on her bed. He was completely out of control. At that point, he had lost all sense of reality, and nothing else mattered to him.

Francine tried with all her might to push him away from her, but Michael was still able to rip the rest of her shirt apart. He slapped her face one more time in an attempt to quiet her down. Holding her neck again, he was able to free one of his hands and reach out to her thighs, but that time he didn't get too far. Two strong hands came out of nowhere and grabbed him, throwing him backward, away from Francine. Michael fell to the floor.

Hans could hardly believe the scene in front of his eyes. He had finally been able to go to Francine's room that night. As he got close to her door, he heard screams coming from inside. Without any delay, he opened the door fast and saw Francine desperately trying to break free from a soldier.

It all happened too fast. Michael stayed on the floor for a few seconds, in shock from being wrenched away. He looked up and saw a well-dressed man coming straight toward him. Hans grabbed him again and punched his face hard. But Michael quickly recovered from the blow and shoved Hans away, ready for a fight.

"You will regret this," Michael yelled at Hans. "I don't care who you are, but I will kill you. And then I will kill her!"

Without wasting any time, Hans quickly jumped on top of him, making them both fall to the ground. Michael hit his head against the floor, leaving him disoriented for a brief moment.

Taking advantage of that situation, Hans punched Michael's face repeatedly, blood started to come down his nose.

Francine watched the scene in horror. In the corner, Helene was slowly starting to regain consciousness.

Michael was able to recuperate his strength, and he pushed Hans to the side. It was then Hans who took several blows to the face.

Michael, now on top of Hans, held his hands against his throat, squeezing it as hard as he could.

Hans tried to push Michael off him, but without much success.

Mustering all her courage, Francine got up quickly and jumped on Michael's back. With her arms around his neck, she was able to push him away from Hans.

That was when Hans was able to spot the small knife near Francine's bed. He rushed toward it, grabbing it firmly in his hands.

As Michael tried to break free from Francine, Hans jumped on top of him. But Michael was fast enough to hold his hands before Hans could stab him. They both stayed in that position, measuring each other's strength.

They both rolled to the side, and Francine got out of the way.

Using all his strength, Michael slowly turned the knife around, pointing it toward Hans. But by doing so, Michael lost his balance, instantly making his wet hands slip through the knife's blade, splashing blood everywhere, and giving Hans the opportunity to twist back toward him, landing it deep into his chest and right through his heart. Michael screamed out loud in pain.

It all happened in a split second. Hans was still holding the knife in his trembling hands as Michael stared at him, slowly losing consciousness.

They all watched him as he closed his eyes, exhaling his last breath. Finally, Hans let go of the knife, pushing himself away from Michael. He stood up and finally looked back at Francine.

She was also standing still, stunned. She looked at him in terror and started to sob.

Hans went toward her, holding her tightly in his arms. "Are you all right?" he asked her, caressing her hair.

Francine shook her head, letting herself fall into his arms again. It was then Hans realized there was one more person in the room.

They both walked toward her, trying to help her to her feet.

Helene genuinely smiled at Francine. After all those months, it was the first time she looked at the French girl with true compassion.

They all looked at Michael's body. Hans felt a strange sensation. It was the first time he had ever killed someone.

"I have to call Carson," he said, trying to think clearly. "We have to get him out of here without anyone knowing it."

Francine nodded, still shaken up.

Hans tried to compose himself as much as he could before leaving that room. Helene recommended that he use the telephone in one of the offices at the end of the hallway. The two women waited in silence for his return.

"You did what?" Carson yelled from the other side of the line.

"I had no choice," Hans affirmed. "He was going to kill me."

"You must be joking, right? Tell me you're joking, Hans!!!"

Hans kept quiet.

"Damn it! Do you have any idea of the implications of what you have done? All for that idiotic French girl? You must have lost your mind! Do you understand the trouble you are in? I am leaving to go to Berlin tomorrow. Shit!"

There was a brief moment of silence.

"I had to kill him!!! I didn't have a choice!!!" It was Hans's turn to yell back. "It was either him or me? Which one do you prefer?"

"What do you want me to do now? What do you think I can do?" Carson yelled furiously.

"He was that soldier I told you about. He got in here against your orders!! He attacked Francine and another nurse here! He was going to kill us all. What did you expect me to do? Not fight back? Is that how you react when one of your soldiers disobeys your orders?"

Hans knew exactly how to appeal to Carson's sense of pride and honor.

"Where are you now? Shit! I don't know what I am going to do, Hans. Just give me a few minutes and stay out of sight," he continued, feeling the blood stirring in his veins. "Damn it, Hans! Do not leave that room, do you understand?"

Carson knew he had to act quickly. He had some friends, a few soldiers, who he could trust for special tasks. He usually compensated them really well and knew they would help him with whatever he needed.

Hans rushed back to the room, informing both women that Carson would help them and things would get resolved.

"He is coming," Hans confirmed. "But we have to stay here for now."

Francine agreed, approaching him. Hans revolved her in his arm, noticing all the red marks on her body.

"I am sorry I couldn't be here earlier!"

She looked at him tenderly. She could see all the love he had for her.

Hans kissed her face, pushing her body closer to him, wishing he could erase all the hurt and pain she had gone through.

CHAPTER 26

Carson entered the hospital building, drawing a lot of attention to himself. He didn't say a word to anyone as he proceeded to the upper floor. He had brought two men with him.

Hans got up as soon as he heard footsteps. He rushed outside the room.

Carson looked at Hans and sighed. He left the men outside the room as he went in.

Helene looked at the Commander with terror. She didn't want to get in trouble, but Carson's attention was primarily focused on Francine.

He threw a hateful glance at her, making sure she would see his anger. He blamed her, and only her, for that mess.

"Damn fool," Carson said, turning his face toward Michael's body.

"What are we doing now?" Hans rushed to ask him, not wanting to wait any longer.

"What are we doing now?" Carson replied sarcastically. "You mean what am I doing now? Because as far as I can see, all of you have already caused too much damage. Now, I get stuck cleaning up this mess. Or, perhaps I could just walk away and leave you to your own luck."

One could see the frustration in Hans's eyes. For a moment, Hans questioned if he had done the right thing calling Carson. *Perhaps I should have just left with Francine*, he thought. Hans hated the fact that he had to often depend on Carson for help, but the situation was far too serious for them to fix it without him. The Nazis completely dominated Germany. Hans had no other alternative but to negotiate with them!

"Get her to wear this military uniform and cap," Carson looked at Hans as if he was able to read his thoughts. "Tonight, it is Francine who has died!"

Carson walked out of the room with Hans. Francine started to change her clothes. She would never have guessed that she would have to wear a Nazi uniform one day to save her own life.

In the hallway, Carson noticed a few nurses and a doctor walking toward them. He stood up straight and looked at them with an arrogant expression on his face.

"The French nurse has been killed," Carson said, full of authority. "We are removing her body now. She was a spy, and spies die!"

They looked at him, surprised but said nothing. No one would dare to question the powerful Commander.

"Continue with your assigned duties," Carson ordered them. "Now! Move!"

Hans sighed in relief and reentered the room. Francine was able to cover her hair entirely under the hat. At that moment, she was without any doubt a Nazi soldier!

Hans and Carson took off Michael's military uniform. They grabbed Francine's bedsheets and rolled them over his dead body. Then the two guards came in and took him away.

"And those are for you!" Carson told Hans, giving him an officer's cap.

Helene received specific orders from Carson to emphasize the fact that Francine had been killed.

"You say one wrong thing or a different story to anyone, and I will have you killed so fast you won't even know where it came from," Carson rushed to threaten her. "Then I will make sure everyone knows you and your entire family were plotting against Germany. Do you understand me? From what I saw here, you are very much implicated in this bloody mess!"

"I won't say anything," Helene rushed to say. "I promise. He almost killed me."

Carson looked straight into her eyes again, wanting to make sure she would keep her mouth shut.

Helene shivered as the Commander approached her closer.

Whispering in her ear, Carson continued. "Rumors move fast, and I will know exactly who started them! It only takes one bullet." He finished his last word touching the center of her forehead.

Francine couldn't hide the disgust that had caused her. Helene froze to the spot for a few seconds.

Carson turned around and started walking away.

Francine looked at Helene one more time. "Danke," she said, full of gratitude while gently touching her arms.

Helene simply nodded.

"Let's move!" Carson said, looking back.

They left in a hurry, rushing through the hallway at a steady pace.

The three of them got into the same car. The other soldiers took a different vehicle toward another destination.

Once in the car, Hans finally started speaking again.

"Francine has to leave Germany immediately. I will go with her and …"

"Not anymore," Carson said, still furious. "You cannot go anywhere with her! She is dead, remember? For all matters, Francine was the one who died today in that room. Now keep quiet and let me think!!"

"What are you trying to say?"

"You are going to stay here, in Germany for now, Hans!!!" Carson yelled impatiently. "She is leaving all right, but she is coming with me."

"Francine is not going anywhere without me."

"Shut up, Hans! What's your problem? You are in no position to say anything here. You are lucky to know me, so lucky!"

Before Hans could reply back, Francine touched his arm as if telling him not to say anything at that moment.

Carson kept driving toward Hans's house. He kept quiet, trying to contain his anger, even though he had a lot more to say to Hans. He was placed in a dangerous situation, and he had to find a way out without raising any suspicion against him.

"I may have a plan. But we need to act quickly. She will have to leave tonight. We don't want to expose any of us. I can be killed, and so can you if anyone finds out about this."

"Leave to where?" Hans wondered.

"Switzerland! It is the only way!"

Hans took a deep breath and looked at Francine. Noticing she was scared, he held her hands tighter.

"It will be all right," he tried to reassure her.

"I know. We will find a way."

Staring at both of them for a few seconds, Carson sighed nervously. He still couldn't believe what was actually happening. Then, consumed by frustration and anger, he punched the steering wheel a few times.

As soon as they arrived at the Schulze's residence, Carson asked Hans to follow him to the library.

"I will be back shortly," he said, kissing Francine's hair. "The kitchen is over there in case you are hungry."

Already inside the library, Carson rushed to pour whiskey into two cups, *I should get rid of her myself and end this misery*, Carson thought.

Handing Hans one of the glasses, Carson got back to his own, drinking it all at once.

"I didn't mean for any of this to happen. But it was completely out of my control. I didn't want to involve you in this."

"You're risking everything for this woman?" Carson pried. "And a simple non-important French woman, to make matters worse. You have gone completely insane, Hans!"

"I am insane? Me? Look at yourself in the mirror! That uniform you are wearing is the cause of all of our problems! All this craziness. This damn war!"

"I don't have time to discuss our political disagreements now! You have no idea how much you have compromised us. I will still have to explain things after I am back from Berlin."

Hans knew he couldn't leave Denna behind. He hadn't been able to get false identity documents for her yet. He felt torn apart.

"You stay here with your cousin. I will send Francine to Switzerland. It will be easier to get her there than France. I don't want to see you with her on any train. Do you hear me? She is a foreigner, and things have changed! She needs special authorization to leave the country, one that I don't have yet. But due to our current situation, I will need to forge it! You can follow her after a few weeks if you want."

Carson paused to take another sip of his drink after refilling it again. He sighed, trying to calm down.

"Francine will be leaving Germany to Switzerland on the first train in the morning," he continued. "I will take her there myself if I have to."

"How will she cross the border?"

"I can arrange something. For now, we can type a few words on a piece of paper, and I will stamp it in my house before we go to the train station. After that, I will personally have her placed inside the train with instructions to the guards."

"What if it doesn't work out?"

"Do you see any other way? I am leaving for Berlin tomorrow! I can't have any delays!"

Hans listened to Carson very carefully. It was still too risky, but he knew he was right. There was no other way. Francine had to leave immediately for her own safety.

Hans let his body fall into his father's chair as he pressed his hands into his face. He felt exhausted and couldn't quite coordinate his thoughts. The bottom line was that he didn't want to leave Francine alone with Carson during that dangerous journey to Switzerland, where so much could go wrong.

Carson stared at him as if he could read his thoughts.

Hans got up from his chair, trying to regain control of the situation.

"How is she going to leave using a poorly produced identification once she gets to the Swiss border alone?"

"I have my ways. Don't underestimate my influence! But even so, she will need to look very presentable, and she will need to have some money with her if they go over her things. She needs to look rich, very rich!"

Looking straight at Carson's face, Hans felt tears filling his eyes.

"Please, Carson, get her out of here safely," Hans practically begged. "If something happens to her, I don't know what I will do. But I can tell you … I will hunt down everyone responsible!"

Carson looked right into Hans's eyes. He laughed, "yeah, now I can definitely see you killing someone."

Hans shook his head.

"I should just leave you alone to deal with this shit. But I can't … can I? You happen to be my family!"

Hans looked down. He wished his father was there to help him.

"I will do what I can. But I cannot take responsibility for anything that may happen to her. So, I will have her across the border into Switzerland, and she will be on her own after that. This is all I am doing."

"How do I know that she will be safe?"

"You don't," Carson said, shrugging his shoulders. "None of us really do. All I know is that she cannot stay here and she has no other place to go. There is nothing else to do except go along with my plan. It is a risk we all have to take. It is her only chance."

They stayed there looking at one another for a few seconds. Hans was trying to find any indication or assurance that Carson was telling the truth.

"We have to leave soon. Give her some nice clothes and shoes. She will have to look very presentable, not like a fugitive."

Hans went to the living room and started talking to Francine.

"That is all right, Hans," she said, determined to make it work. "I will be fine. Don't worry!"

"We have to hurry things up," Carson said, interrupting them.

Hans and Francine walked together upstairs, soon finding Denna in the hallway. After a brief introduction, Hans tried to explain Carson's plan the best way he could, considering the circumstances.

Denna took a few steps toward Francine, hugging her in support. She knew how terrifying that must be for her.

With the help of her new friend, Francine started to prepare herself for the trip. Hans had also brought her a few items from his mother's closet, including some fancy hats and other accessories.

Francine stared at herself in the mirror with Denna by her side. She looked very different wearing that formal dress and with parts of her hair tucked inside an elegant hat. Francine couldn't quite remember the last time she was able to dress up so nicely. That thought took her back to France, before the war, during happier times that she shared among friends and family.

Hans walked toward her, admiring her beauty. He carried an extra bag with him.

"Come with me," he said, pulling her hand gently.

Hans brought Francine straight to his parent's bedroom. For so long, he had hidden a few objects he could use in case of an emergency for himself and Denna. He knew they would be perfect for Francine.

"This bag has a hidden compartment in the bottom. Use them in case … something happens. There is also a gun in there."

Francine looked at him, understanding that gesture. She would still be in danger until she stepped into Swiss territory.

As if he could read her thoughts, Hans held her against his chest.

"I don't want to let you go."

"It will be all right," Francine said, trying to make him feel better. But the truth was that she was equally fearful. She didn't trust Carson.

"Listen to me, Francine. I cannot go with you because I can't leave my cousin behind. As I had mentioned before, Denna is in a very similar position as you. But no one should know about that! Absolutely no one. Do you understand? I just want you to know I am not abandoning you. I just cannot leave Denna behind. You have to trust me!"

Francine agreed, remembering a few things that Hans told her about the girl.

"I do. I trust you! And I understand perfectly."

"And there is one more thing …."

As they continued talking, Carson impatiently waited in the living room. He only calmed down when his attention was suddenly caught by the sight of Denna walking down the stairs, having her body covered by a beautiful silky robe.

For a brief moment, Carson forgot about that whole situation. He couldn't take his eyes off of her.

Denna felt a chill run through her body once she saw the look on Carson's face. She tried her best to smile at him.

"Hello, Carson, she said timidly.

"It is nice to see you again," he replied, looking deep into her eyes.

Before they could say anything else, Hans and Francine could be heard coming downstairs.

Carson immediately changed his behavior, trying to act a little friendlier toward Francine. He wanted to impress Denna with his gentlemanly manners, always available at his convenience.

Hans felt desperate. It was hard to accept they would have to part again.

Noticing his distress, Francine looked at him and smiled; her eyes were shiny with unshed tears. Yet, she also felt as if her heart was ripping apart. The anticipation of one more goodbye and all the uncertainty that came with it frightened her.

"Thank you so much for everything. Je t'aime," she said, her voice echoing all the love she had for him.

"Whatever happens, you stay alive," Hans said back to her. "You keep fighting! I know how brave you are. And I promise you … I promise we will meet again. No matter how long it takes, I will find you. I will find you!"

Looking at her lips so close to his, Hans kissed them softly.

Denna smiled as she watched the scene. Carson, on the other hand, continued to stare at her.

As if she could feel it, Denna looked back at him. Their eyes met.

There was nothing else Carson wished more than to take her in his arms and kiss her. And it was right then, that exact moment, that Denna became aware that he was attracted to her. She looked away, feeling awkward, and yet, another thought came to her mind. She knew she could take advantage of the situation to help Francine. She didn't trust Carson either.

She suddenly felt tired of always acting so scared around him. She had to be brave … brave like Francine!

Determined to act differently, she took couple of steps toward him and gently kissed his cheek.

Taken completely by surprise, Carson froze on the spot, unable to move or say anything. It was the first time he had ever felt that way. His heart beat even faster once he felt Denna's body against his and her soft lips brush his face.

"Please help her," she begged him. "I know only you can do this. Hans loves her. And I will be forever grateful."

Trying to regain his authoritative posture, he looked right into her eyes.

"I will do the best I can," Carson whispered back, staring at her lips, feeling strangely moved by her proximity.

But he wasn't the only one experiencing those strong feelings. Denna started to understand that she had a little power over him. It made her feel different, strong … courageous.

"I know you will try your best," Denna said, breaking that uncomfortable silence. "I trust you."

Listening to those words made Carson feel even more proud. But he couldn't quite understand what was happening with his emotions. How could he feel so alive by simply being next to her?

Denna looked at Hans and Francine. They were still sitting next to one another, holding each other's hands. Then, she looked back at Carson, who was still there, so close to her.

She couldn't deny it; he was indeed an attractive man. That random thought made her feel ashamed. For a brief moment, she almost forgot who he was.

Noticing something different in her demeanor, Carson touched her face. She suddenly took a step back as if his touch woke her up.

"I'm sorry," that was the only thing she could manage to say, already moving away from him.

Surprised by her reaction, Carson felt deeply offended. He wasn't used to be rejected.

"We have to go now," Carson said, feeling uneasy by what had just happened.

"Everything will work out!" Denna told Francine. "Carson always finds a way."

Both women and Hans looked at Carson for a moment.

"Thank you for all your help," Francine said, smiling at that friendly German girl.

Hans walked Francine to Carson's car. He held her for a few more seconds.

"I love you," he told her, feeling a deep pain inside his heart.

"Je t'aime, Hans." Those were the last words Francine said before getting into the car.

"We will meet again soon. Remember what I have told you."

"I do. I will communicate with you as soon as I can. I will wait for you forever!" Francine replied, trying to hold her tears.

Hans smiled at her. He admired her courage.

Francine waved goodbye as Carson started to move the vehicle forward.

Denna watched the entire scene with tears in her eyes. She knew very well what Hans was feeling. She still remembered all too painfully the goodbyes she had to say to those she loved.

She looked at Hans, who stood still in that same position, watching the car move farther and farther away from them. She placed her hand on his shoulder.

"Tell me I did the right thing," Hans asked her. "Tell me I didn't send Francine straight to her death."

"Carson knows how much she means to you. He will do the right thing. He wouldn't hurt you like that."

Hans looked at her, attempting a smile and yet unsure of what he had just done. He had a bad feeling about all of it.

He looked at his own car not too far from him.

"Hans?" Denna said as she watched him rush back into the house.

A few minutes later, with the car keys in his hands, Hans had made a decision. "I am going after her. I have to make sure she gets onto the train safely."

Denna didn't have any time to reply. Hans rushed inside his car and sped away toward the gate.

PART TWO

CHAPTER 27

After stopping by Carson's house, Hans decided to go straight to the train station. To his disappointment, they weren't there either.

His hands started shaking uncontrollably, his heart accelerated. He didn't know what else to do. *I have to find her ... I have to find her,* Hans repeated to himself all night as he kept driving frantically through the streets.

But what both Hans and Carson didn't know was that two other men had followed them from the military base all the way to Hans's house.

Julian and Daniel had confirmation from Zachary that Francine was still being held at the same location.

Both men were in complete astonishment when they watched Francine being removed from the hospital and put inside a car the same night they had come to rescue her.

Julian, disguised as an injured German soldier and Daniel as a German doctor, drove an ambulance inside the military station. It was the perfect night for the rescue! They knew the hospital would be very busy as it was getting prepared to receive many injured soldiers coming straight from the battlefields. So, it wouldn't be too difficult for them to get in and scout around without drawing too much attention to themselves.

Wearing a doctor's uniform, Daniel pretended to help Julian move around as they quickly checked each room they passed. Then, not finding Francine in any of them, they both rushed to the second floor.

Caught by surprise, Julian stopped abruptly as soon as he spotted other people at the end of the hallway that was supposed to lead to Francine's room, as described by Zachary.

Standing behind Julian, Daniel still had the chance to quickly turn around toward the staircase, pretending he was going to the third floor. However, as for Julian, it was too late. He was already inside the hallway of that second floor.

Julian knew he had to think fast. He decided to keep walking forward, playing his role as an injured soldier.

Soon after, all those people in the hallway started walking in his direction. He knew he was in deep trouble, but there was nowhere to hide.

Carson stared at Julian as he kept walking. As they all passed him, Julian looked at every one of their faces until, in total surprise, he glimpsed a very familiar face – Francine. She was dressed in a military uniform and didn't dare to look at anyone who passed by her.

Highly disturbed by what he saw, he stopped and looked back at them. *Was it really her? Francine?* he questioned. *Did I see this right?*

He took another look around that hallway and noticed that those people were originally right in front of that third door mentioned by Zachary. *It had to be her!! The same eyes! I could never mistake her!*

Following his instincts, he rushed back to the staircase, finding Daniel waiting for him. Julian made a signal for him to follow.

The hospital was crowded with people rushing back and forth. Daniel pretended to assist Julian as they walked slowly toward the back door. The ambulance was still there, to their relief.

"Drive toward the gate and follow that car," Julian quickly told Daniel as he was able to spot the same people entering a car not far from where they were.

Daniel knew something had gone wrong, but he didn't hesitate to follow Julian's instructions.

They were able to leave that military facility without any trouble and just in time to see Carson's black car turning around the corner.

"Just follow that car!" Julian yelled from the back.

"What happened there?" Daniel finally asked.

"I'm not sure. But I think I saw Francine leaving that hallway along with other people. I saw her face upstairs! But I am not sure. I am not sure."

"What are you talking about?" Daniel said, stunned. "Who are those people?"

"I have no idea what's going on. But I swear I saw Francine. We have to make sure it's her! Everything happened so fast. She was dressed in a military uniform. It seemed as if they were trying to help her out of there!"

"But how is that possible? Does she know anyone here?"

"I don't know … I don't think so. But that's what we need to find out!"

As Daniel kept following the car from a distance, Julian explained in detail the strange events that had taken place on the upper floor of the hospital. He knew then that things were about to become even more complicated.

A few minutes later, Daniel and Julian found a discreet place to park the ambulance as they saw the same vehicle entering a residence.

"Now what?" Daniel asked, looking at Julian's pale face.

"Let's get inside. There's no other way."

"But how could that be Francine?" Daniel asked him, still unsure of the situation. "That doesn't make much sense. Are you sure you didn't make a mistake?"

"I really believe I saw her. But I need to be sure! That is why we are here."

"Why would she be dressed as a Nazi soldier? Unless …"

"Unless someone else was helping her out of the facility," Julian finished the sentence, trying to figure it out himself.

"But who could that be? You know we won't be able to go back to the hospital again," Daniel tried to remind Julian.

Julian took a deep breath and tried really hard to stay calm. He knew that trying to verify his suspicions meant they wouldn't have another chance to go back to the hospital that evening.

"I'd better be right. Come on, let's go."

The two of them quietly approached the house.

Julian didn't know what to say. In his mind, Francine was either taken as a prisoner to the house or receiving help from those people. But as far as Julian knew, Francine didn't know anyone in Germany. Nevertheless, he knew something out of the ordinary was happening. Whatever it was, Julian prayed that Francine was safe.

Daniel was beginning to get more apprehensive. Their plan was taking a totally different direction. They were inside enemy territory, and time was running out.

"Look!" Julian whispered. "Some people are coming out," he said, trying to look for Francine.

They were just close enough to be able to see the faces of those in the car. Julian immediately recognized Francine.

"It's her!" he smiled, feeling as if a ton of weight had been lifted from his shoulders.

Daniel smiled back at him, tapping his friend's back. Julian had made the right call; they had found Francine!

But as Julian continued to observe that scene, he was still trying to make some sense of the situation. First, they saw another woman hugging Francine, and then a man did the same.

The entire scene was very strange to them, especially for Julian, who had noticed the warmer exchange between that strange man and Francine. It was all a big mystery that they still needed to unravel.

Daniel signaled Julian to go back to the ambulance as they saw the vehicle moving. They couldn't lose track of them!

Far away from the train station, Carson drove his car quietly. In his mind, many contradictory thoughts were taking place, disturbing him. He knew it wouldn't be too much of a problem for Francine to take the train. He was a respected and feared Nazi officer. He had enough power to have Francine sent to Switzerland. But even then, Carson knew it was risky. He would never expose himself like that. His career and ambition to gather a large fortune and more power could be dangerously compromised, and that was all that mattered to him at that moment, as he tried to come up with excuses to justify his change of plans.

Francine sat quietly in the back seat. Feeling exhausted and concerned, she couldn't think of anything to say to him. She was still shocked by all that had transpired. But it was more than that; something was telling her to be cautious. She didn't trust Carson despite Hans's explanations on how they were raised together like brothers, practically part of the same family.

Trying to find a way to protect herself, she glanced at the bag that Hans had given her on her lap. Carefully, she looked inside it, soon spotting a map and a small flashlight. Then, she slid her fingers further down and felt what seemed to be a small zipper. She opened it slowly, trying not to make any noise.

Francine could see Carson's face through the front mirror. He seemed to be lost in his own thoughts. She looked back into the bag, but she couldn't see much. Her hands shook as she recognized the object … it was the gun that Hans had told her about. Francine left the bottom of the bag open, although she wished she would never need to use the weapon.

Not far away, two men were also anxious and filled with questions. Julian was still trying to make some sense of the recent events. Daniel was equally worried. He knew things weren't going their way. As the minutes went by, they understood they were putting their lives more and more at serious risk.

"Julian, we are only a few hours away from the morning light. We have to leave soon or hide for a while."

It took a few seconds for Julian to snap back to reality.

"I know," he said, lighting a cigarette. "We'll have to approach the train station on foot. No one can see us arriving in this vehicle!"

Daniel knew that was the only way left. However, he also knew the dangers of such an undertaking.

"I can't leave without making sure she's safe. I'm sorry, Daniel. I didn't mean to get you into this big mess!"

"Well, since when do things go exactly according to plan?" Daniel smiled at his friend. "Don't worry about me! We will find a way; we always do!"

"I really appreciate you accompanying me here. At least now we know where she is. So it wasn't all a waste of time, right?"

"Not at all! And I don't know about you, but as for me … I'm having the time of my life!" Daniel continued trying to cheer him up.

"Your reputation precedes you. Now I have living proof of that."

Daniel laughed at that comment. "Now … back to the serious stuff. Francine seemed to be getting help from other people, right?"

"Right! But who can they be? As far as I know, she doesn't know anyone here."

"That's interesting, but in fact, I am not completely surprised! In this war, I already witnessed a great share of crazy things! There are still a good number of Germans who don't like Hitler! And some who still plan against his life."

They were both quiet again. Julian finished his cigarette with trembling hands as Daniel continued to drive the ambulance carefully, making sure to keep the headlights off.

In the meantime, in the car ahead, Carson was so caught up in his own thoughts that he didn't notice he was being followed at first. It was after he had driven many miles away from the city that he realized there was someone on the same road, driving far back behind him.

Carson straightened his body in the car seat. He started to feel more nervous. Being in such an isolated part of the country and that late at night, he suspected he could have been followed. He soon spotted a small dirt road in between the forest. Without thinking, he abruptly turned the car onto it.

"I think we are being followed," Carson finally said.

Frightened by that sudden move, Francine looked back, trying to see what he was talking about.

Julian and Daniel saw the car turning right onto a small road. They kept going forward. They didn't want to let the driver know they were following them.

Julian drove a little further and stopped the car, "I guess we'll have to go after them on foot."

"We don't even know where they are headed. How are we going to find them?"

"It was a small road. I don't think it could go far, right?"

"It could be, but maybe they saw us and decided to stop," Daniel wondered. "Let's hide the car somewhere around here and wait for a moment. If we don't see anything, we can follow them by foot."

Julian agreed. They waited for a few minutes.

"I'm going after them," Julian decided. "But you, my friend, you should go back to the train station and try to get out of here. You have done more than enough!"

Daniel looked at Julian's face again.

"We came here together, and we are leaving together. What the hell? We are already in so much trouble; a little extra couldn't hurt that much."

Julian smiled at his friend. He felt lucky to have him by his side.

Not far away, Carson had stopped the car as soon as he entered that road. He wanted to find out if he was being followed. He sighed in relief once he saw the other car moving forward, continuing on its way. But he still waited a few minutes just to make sure.

Francine just sat there, frozen with fear. At first, she thought Carson was trying to hide from whoever was following them. But then he proceeded to drive deeper down that narrow, dusty road. She looked around, but all she could see were trees.

"Where are we going?' Francine finally spoke to him. "It seems that no one is following us."

With no reply from him, she felt even more nervous, "Hans told me we were going to stop by your house to get the stamps for the travel authorization before heading to the train station."

"Change of plans! Don't worry," Carson said rudely.

A sudden chill ran through her body. She knew she couldn't trust him.

"Where are we going then? Why did you have to change plans?

Carson kept quiet, pretending not to have heard a word she said.

Many terrifying thoughts filled her mind. She looked at the doorknob and thought about jumping out. But it was too late!

Slamming the brakes, Carson stopped the car right before an open space in the middle of those woods. Before Francine could do anything, he got out fast and opened the back door where she was.

"Get out," Carson ordered. But Francine couldn't move. "I said get out!" He grabbed her arm.

Francine clutched the bag Hans had given her and quickly moved out of the car.

Still holding one of her arms, Carson pulled her toward the center of that open field. Then, he pushed her away from him, making her trip and almost fall to the ground. Once she regained her balance, she looked right into Carson's eyes. Carson looked back at her furiously and stood his ground.

Francine held the bag tightly against her chest. She slowly tried to reach for the gun, but Carson didn't give her much of a chance.

He reached for his own gun and quickly pointed it at her. She stood there numbly, thinking it would be the last seconds of her life.

"You and Hans got me into some serious trouble. All of this for you, a stupid French woman! Hans has definitely gone mad."

With her entire body trembling, Francine listened to every word he spoke. Her heart was pounding, her eyes wide open.

"Now, here I am, having to make a decision! And I think we both know what would be the best thing for all of us."

Francine could hardly breathe. All she could focus on was the gun aimed straight at her head. Her eyes filled with tears. She knew there was nothing she could do. She truly felt Carson would kill her right there without hesitating.

"Please don't," Francine pleaded. "Please … please, let me go. You don't have to do this! Just let me go. I won't say anything! Hans will never find out!"

Carson's cold stare was fixed on her. The image of Hans flashed through his mind. All of a sudden, he heard Alyse's voice in his head.

With shaking hands, he placed his finger on the trigger.

"Please," Francine said again, begging for her life. She looked at the gun pointed at her just a few feet away. She knew she was going to die. She closed her eyes, grasping the bag tightly against her chest.

In a split second, Carson pressed the trigger.

Francine fell on her knees to the ground. She kept her eyes shut as she heard multiple gunshots.

After a brief silence, Francine slowly opened her eyes. She could see Carson agitated, pacing around, like a mad man, cursing at her and everything else.

Still in shock, she didn't realize he had turned his gun to the side at the last moment, shooting at a nearby tree.

It took Francine a few more seconds to realize that she hadn't been shot.

"Shit!" Carson shouted, darting around like a crazy man. "Damn it!" He looked at Francine and went straight toward her.

"Damn you!" he cursed, looking straight at her face.

In a total state of fear, Francine couldn't move. She couldn't say a word.

Filled with anger, Carson quickly grabbed her hair, forcing her to stand up.

"Leave now!" Carson yelled at her, pushing her forward. "Go! Run … run before I regret this!"

Francine started to move backward, slowly at first.

"Get out of here! I said run!" Carson pointed the gun at her again.

Without hesitating any longer, Francine turned back and ran toward the woods.

Carson continued to watch her, still pointing the gun at her. He knew he wouldn't be able to look Hans in the eye ever again if he killed Francine. But he also understood that she didn't stand much of a chance in those woods still inside German territory.

He was convinced that she would die one way or another. *Not by my own hands, though,* Carson thought, trying to justify what he had just done. *Yet, somehow, I have fulfilled my promise. She was set free, alive.*

Feeling exhausted, he got in the car. Spinning around, he drove away fast.

CHAPTER 28

Julian and Daniel walked fast through that dark and narrow road. They were very close to where Carson had stopped his car when they heard the resounding echoes of gunshots.

They looked wildly around and then ran toward the direction of the shots as fast as they could. Julian felt as if his heart was being ripped apart.

As they approached the location where the gunshots had originated, they could hear a male voice. They both stepped away from the dirt road and hid behind the bushes. They could see a man screaming and ordering a woman to walk away. A few seconds later, she turned around and ran toward the woods.

Things were getting stranger by the minute. But before they could think of anything else, they saw that same man get inside his car and drive in their direction.

They both ducked into some bushes to avoid being seen. Julian tried to look in the back seat of that car as it rapidly passed them by.

"I couldn't see anyone else inside that car. Let's follow that woman! It has to be Francine!"

Daniel agreed; even though they weren't quite able to see her face before she ran away, they would need to take a chance. So, grabbing their flashlights from inside their pockets, they ran toward the other side of the woods.

Not too far from where they were, Francine ran as fast as possible with no set direction. Still afraid, she kept looking back, wondering if Carson would be following her.

Trying to catch her breath for a few seconds, Francine stopped and looked around. She could barely see anything. The light coming from the full moon above was the only thing that illuminated some parts of that dark forest. She couldn't figure out where to go next. A sensation of panic rose in her chest. She contemplated going back, but she feared Carson could still be there.

She felt both physically and mentally exhausted. Her breathing was heavy, her mind confused. It was then that she remembered there was a flashlight inside the bag she was holding. She quickly searched for it.

Julian and Daniel continued to follow the footprints they found on the cold and muddy ground.

Relying mainly on instinct, Julian felt very uneasy, growing more anxious as time went on. He wasn't completely sure if that woman they saw entering the woods was indeed Francine.

Lost in his thoughts, Julian didn't notice a light shining through the trees further ahead.

"Right there!" Daniel said as soon as he spotted that brightness.

Julian ran toward it, followed by Daniel.

With the flashlight on, Francine scanned her surroundings. But right before she started walking again, she heard a few voices. She looked everywhere, frightened. Thinking of Carson or German soldiers, she ran away fast.

Already able to see a person running ahead of him, Julian knew he had to take a chance.

"Francine!" he yelled. "Francine! C'est toi?"

She stopped the moment she heard those words in French. Surprised, yet afraid, she wasn't sure if she had heard it correctly.

"Francine, c'est moi, Julian!" he shouted.

At that time, she clearly recognized those words. Stunned, she automatically pointed her flashlight toward two people who were quickly approaching her.

Simultaneously, Julian and Daniel pointed their flashlights at her.

"Francine!" Julian said, immediately recognizing her.

As if struck by lightning, she froze to the spot, letting the flashlight fall from her shaky hands.

"Julian! Mon Dieu!"

No words could describe how they both felt as they held each other. It seemed as if they were only dreaming.

Julian took a step back to look at the face of the woman he loved so dearly. It was a miracle! He had found Francine!

Daniel stood back with his arms crossed, smiling at both of them. *We found her! In the middle of nowhere, in Germany. Unbelievable!* He thought, sighing in relief.

The first sun rays appeared in the sky as they walked toward the ambulance.

"But how did you find me?" Francine asked. "How is that possible? I thought I was going to die in those woods!!"

With their hands locked, Julian started to explain everything to her while he also asked her questions.

"Merci beaucoup," she repeated, hugging Daniel.

"We couldn't be happier to have found you! Though I have to confess, I was already losing hope. But my friend Julian here, well, he never gave up!"

Julian looked at her again with a big smile on his face.

"Now, we need to plan out our next steps," Daniel reminded them. "We have to move as fast as possible to catch the next train to the nearest town."

Resuming their journey on the road, Francine and Julian continued to talk about their own stories since she was brought to Germany. However, Francine made sure to omit her relationship with Hans, referring to him only as a friend. She knew Julian had feelings for her, and this was certainly not the right place or moment to tell him everything.

Another hour had gone by as they approached the town where they knew they could find a railroad. Daniel had found a place to hide the ambulance. The three of them went over all the details of their new plan to attempt to board the next train. Any error could prove fatal.

A thick fog covered their surroundings as they made their way toward the train station, the most dangerous part of their mission.

Julian and Daniel scanned the area with visible concern. They knew the train station was going to be heavily guarded. But what they weren't expecting was to see so many German soldiers spread out near that dense stretch of the woods. They had no idea how they would be able to approach their destination without being spotted first.

They stopped as close as possible to the other side of the train station until they could find a safer place for their next move.

"What was that?" Julian asked, taking a quick look around. He had seen something moving between the trees, not too far from where they were.

"Get down!" Daniel quickly warned. "Right there!"

Two German soldiers were walking around the area. Although the soldiers didn't notice them, they were headed in their direction. Julian and Daniel knew they had to think of something fast.

Daniel held his gun tightly in his hand, and so did Julian. They were ready for a possible confrontation. Julian signaled for Francine and Daniel to move forward. Daniel made a downward gesture to her, asking her to follow him. They started to crawl slowly on the ground, using the bushes and trees to hide.

Julian decided to stay behind to protect their backs in case the soldiers saw them. He was well aware of the severity of their situation.

Being very careful, Francine followed right after Daniel, advancing one foot at a time through the fog that helped them stay hidden.

It was time for Julian to start moving as well, but he didn't have the chance.

Suddenly, one of the German soldiers spotted Francine and Daniel. The soldiers screamed for them to stop, pointing their guns at them. Julian knew he would have no choice but to shoot them.

One of the German soldiers was instantly hit, falling to the ground. The other one turned toward Julian, and in a split second, they had both shot one another.

Daniel and Francine spun around to look back as they heard the gunshots. Daniel ran toward his friend. He saw one of the soldiers still moving on the ground, pointing his gun at Julian's body. Daniel didn't hesitate. He shot him quickly before the soldier could press the trigger.

"Take her out of here," Julian said, gravely wounded. "More soldiers will be coming soon."

"No," Daniel replied. "I will not leave you here."

Francine rushed toward Julian, grabbing one of his hands.

"We can carry you," she told him as she watched her friend already suffocating on the blood coming out of his mouth.

"Get her out of here." Julian could barely finish his words, struggling to breathe. "They are coming. Now go."

Understanding the inevitability of that situation, Daniel touched his friend's arm, smiling at him.

"Go!!" Julian screamed one more time, looking at Francine.

"No," she insisted. "We are not leaving you!"

Daniel quickly grabbed her hand, pushing her away from Julian.

"Let's go, now!" he said again, encircling his arm around her as he tried to make her move forward.

Francine looked at Julian in horror; she didn't want to abandon her friend.

Daniel heard more voices getting closer. "Keep your head down and follow me."

They walked slowly, hiding behind the trees.

As they got close to the station, Francine and Daniel heard other voices from a distance and then more gunshots. They knew Julian had tried to hold the German soldiers back.

They were practically touching the train tracks when Daniel started to hear soldiers yelling from a distance. He thought fast and threw his gun as far away as possible.

"Lay down," he told Francine. He quickly jumped on top of her and ripped part of her blouse open.

Francine looked at him, confused, while he lifted part of her skirt. Before she could say anything, Daniel kissed her, pressing his lips fiercely against hers.

Almost instantly, the other soldiers found them.

"What are you doing here?" the soldiers asked them angrily.

Daniel tried to act surprised.

"I'm sorry," he said, pretending he was zipping up his pants. "We were just … waiting for the train."

Francine quickly pulled her skirt back in place and covered her bra with her coat.

The soldiers looked around, unsure about the situation.

"Your papers?" one of them ordered both Daniel and Francine.

Francine gave them her papers, followed by Daniel. They both pretended to be embarrassed, fixing up their clothes.

A few soldiers stayed there examining their documents, while others were still walking around the woods with guard dogs, searching for more people.

Daniel and Francine stood there waiting for what seemed to be the longest minutes of their lives. Daniel moved closer to Francine, reaching out for her hand. He looked right into her eyes and placed a quick kiss on her cheek, pretending they were indeed a couple.

The soldier checking their papers looked up.

"You didn't hear the gunshots?" he asked them suspiciously.

"We did hear something," Daniel said flawlessly in German. "But we couldn't see anything. And then, we didn't hear any more noises, so we decided to … well …."

"Check them both," the soldier said, still looking unsure.

Francine's body trembled while one of the soldiers very roughly patted her down. Daniel wanted to kill him as he watched everything, trying his best to contain his anger. Daniel didn't care what would happen to himself. He would have died by Julian's side. But he had a promise to keep and a mission to get Francine out of that damned country. And for that, he knew he had no other choice but to remain calm.

"Where are you two going?" the same soldier asked.

"Switzerland," Daniel replied, straightening his body. He knew he had to look important and wealthy. "We are going back home."

"Home? What were you doing here in Germany?"

"Business matters. We just got married a few months ago, and my wife wanted to accompany me on my business trip."

"What kind of business matters are you talking about?" the soldier continued relentlessly.

"Banking business," Daniel replied sharply. "I have all the documents here and …"

"Let me see them!" the soldier rudely interrupted Daniel, grabbing the papers from his hand. He stared them down again with a stern look. "So, is fooling around with your wife behind a train station also part of your business trip?"

Daniel knew he couldn't show fear. Francine looked down.

"Well, I'm usually very busy performing important business transactions for some of your Commanders, who could care less about my personal life as long I do my job, and their bank deposits are correct and on time. But from what I can tell, I am about to miss the next train back, and they will not be happy at all."

"Sir," another soldier came rushing up to them. "The Commander wants us to check all the passengers on the next train."

The German soldier interrogating Daniel took another good look at both of them. He saw two very well-dressed people. They had the proper documents to travel, and Daniel was a financial accountant for an important bank in Switzerland.

"Get out of here. This is a very dangerous place to be fooling around. You're lucky you didn't get shot."

Daniel grabbed Francine's hand and pulled her toward the train. Luckily, they made it in just in time. They hurried aboard and never looked back.

Francine sat very close to her new friend. Traumatized by what had just taken place, her hands were shaking. Noticing it, Daniel quickly placed his hands on top of hers. She looked at him, trying to hold back tears.

"Please don't cry," Daniel whispered in her ear, placing his arms around her shoulders. "Not here."

He looked at her and smiled reassuringly, holding her hand tightly. He knew they were still far from being safe.

Francine closed her eyes and rested her head on Daniel's shoulder. It took her all the strength she had left in her body not to cry. She wanted to scream in anger and pain. She wanted to go back, plant a kiss on Julian's cheek and hold his hand; be there with him until the last minute. She never had the chance to explain how much she cared for him. He had saved her life. He had died for her.

Daniel sighed in relief as the train started to leave the station. But that didn't diminish the frustration and anguish that consumed him. He had become good friends with Julian. He appreciated all the hard work Julian had done for the Resistance in France and admired his courage.

Daniel kept his eyes focused on the window, trying to cope with all those emotions. He wanted to jump off the train and go back to kill every single one of those Germans who had taken yet another one of his friends' lives away.

But he couldn't let Julian die in vain. He had to take Francine out of Germany and keep her safe.

The entire ride, they barely spoke. There was only a cruel silence … silence in which no words could break, where even tears couldn't be shed.

CHAPTER 29

A few hours later, Francine and Daniel had finally reached the border of Switzerland. They knew they would have to go through another checkpoint.

Daniel held Francine's hands even tighter than before. They both looked at one another for a few seconds. Step by step, they walked toward the guards.

After the final check, they were both given permission to move forward. The gate was opened, and with heavy hearts, they were finally able to cross the border.

Daniel waved to a taxi cab; he already knew where he was going to take Francine. During the train ride, he'd had to rethink his previous plan. Since Julian was killed, that meant he was now the person responsible for her.

They stopped in front of a large and ostentatious house. Daniel looked at Francine and smiled.

She waited until they were out of the car to start asking questions.

"Is this it?"

"No," Daniel replied, waiting for the taxi cab to drive away. "Come this way …"

After walking a few blocks, Daniel pointed at a medium-sized house surrounded by many tall trees.

"That will be your home for a while," he said, glad to have finally arrived at their destination.

A friendly woman opened the door, smiling at both of them. After the introductions, they headed toward the basement, where a secret door led them to a channel of small rooms.

"I know it isn't a big space, but at least it will keep you safe for now," the woman said in German.

Francine thanked her.

"The bathroom is over there." The woman pointed to another area of that hallway. "I'll bring you some clean clothes and food shortly. My name is Clarice if you need anything."

"I will go up there with you, Clarice," Daniel said. "I'll be back shortly, Francine. Then we can talk. Try to get some rest."

She took some steps toward the bed nearby and lay down, feeling exhausted. Closing her eyes, she could still see Julian's face. She could still hear his last words. She allowed her tears to stream out of her weary eyes.

A few hours had gone by and Daniel gently knocked on the side of the door, trying to wake her up.

Francine looked around, trying to remember where she was.

"I'm sorry for waking you up. I don't have much time left, and I know we have a lot to talk about."

Francine nodded, agreeing with him. She noticed the food on top of the small table nearby.

"You should eat first," he said, smiling at her. "It tastes really good. I had some upstairs."

Pushing a chair up, Daniel sat next to her. "How are you feeling?"

"I feel a little rested. Thank you," she said, looking down. "I still can't believe everything that has happened! Julian … I can't accept that he is dead. He is there, in that horrible place … alone!"

"I know. I understand what you are feeling," Daniel said, also sharing the same guilt for having to leave Julian behind.

Francine looked at him, feeling immense sorrow.

"It is this terrible feeling, you know? Like you abandoned someone!" Daniel continued. "So many times I witnessed this happening ... and it never gets easier. But I can tell you that ... what Julian wanted the most was to see you far away from Germany, safe! That was our mission, and thanks to him, we were able to get you here!"

"He died because of me!" she said, wiping her tears, moved by Daniel's words. "I didn't have the chance to thank him. To say goodbye!"

"I understand, trust me. But we did what we had to do; we had no other choice. Julian didn't die in vain."

"I'm sorry, Daniel. You have also gone through a lot, and you risked your own life for me! And here I am crying, feeling sorry for myself."

"Please don't worry about that. What we are feeling is natural. You were best friends, and I am sorry for your loss. Julian was an extraordinary person as well as a great friend! That's something hard to find, making this even more difficult to accept. I have lost so many friends and my own parents in this war. Sometimes it doesn't feel real; it seems it is only a terrible nightmare! But one from which you never wake up ... you never wake up."

"I am sorry to hear that. I can't imagine how hard it must have been for you. You have already gone through so much yourself. How can we human beings be capable of committing such atrocities against one another? We repeat the same mistakes over and over again! When will it stop? When do we finally learn our lesson?

"I ask myself the same thing! I wish I had answers for you, but I fear that, collectively, we are still far from learning what it takes to stop all this repetitive madness."

Francine nodded as they looked at one another.

"And, as I don't see the world changing any time soon, you will need to stay here for a while until we can figure out what to do next. I don't know when I will be able to come back, but I will definitely keep in touch!"

Francine agreed although she felt uneasy to know that she would be locked somewhere, waiting for news to come once more. She wanted to do something else, contribute to ending this terrible war. But for the time being, she knew it was the best choice for all of them.

The days went by slowly. Clarice gave Francine some books to read. She also visited with her a few times during the day. It wasn't long before Clarice and Francine developed a friendship.

Clarice was Swiss, but her husband was French. They both hated the war and what the Germans were doing all over the world. They felt a strong need to contribute to the war effort, and so, through a network they had established, they were able to provide temporary shelter for fugitives. They quickly got used to having different people staying over at the house. Sheltering strangers had become part of their routine, part of their lives.

As time went by, Clarice noticed that Francine's health was beginning to deteriorate. Francine still felt guilty for Julian's death and worried about Hans, wondering if he would be punished for killing a German soldier.

Clarice knew she had to do something to help her new guest.

During their chats, Clarice had learned that Francine's mother was in Switzerland, in a town very close to where they were. Clarice started to think that a visit with Francine's mother might be her only way out of the permanent state of sadness.

At first, her husband, Fernand, didn't agree with that idea. He wanted to wait for Daniel's approval. But as he continued to notice the strain on Francine's face, he finally decided to help his wife come up with a plan for the girl to visit her mother safely.

Francine felt the cool breeze touching her face. She closed her eyes for a few seconds, enjoying the fresh air. It was wonderful to be able to walk outside again.

Fernand accompanied her to the corner of her aunt's house. "I'll meet you again here in three hours," he reminded her.

The plan was quite simple. Dressed in a nurse's uniform and carrying a small bag, she wore thick glasses and a blond wig. She was practically unrecognizable.

Francine walked slowly, trying to avoid drawing attention to herself. It had been over a year since she had last seen her mother. She couldn't believe she was actually there.

She knocked on the door anxiously.

"Guten morgen," said her aunt, not recognizing her but finding her strangely familiar.

"Guten morgen," Francine said with a sweet smile on her face. "I am here to visit a patient by the name Nicole."

"I didn't know she had contacted a nurse for a visit," Terese said, surprised. "But please, come in."

The door was closed behind her. She waited until her aunt walked away to start removing her disguise.

"I didn't call any nurse! It must be a mistake," Nicole said while walking toward the hallway where Francine was.

Nicole could barely contain herself when she saw Francine only a few steps away.

They both jumped into each other's arms.

"Francine!" Nicole said through her sobs. "Oh, I worried so much! Francine! It's you, ma chérie! I can't believe you are here!"

"I needed to see you," Francine said, smiling. "It's a long story."

"Someone left us a note. It said you were out of Germany and well, but that it was a secret no one could know. I thought you would be far from here. I can't believe it."

"We were so worried about you!" Terese said, hugging her niece.

"I'm staying here for a while with a friend until I can figure out where to go next!"

"Why can't you stay here with us?" Nicole rushed to ask her. "What's going on? What has happened to you?"

"I have a lot to tell you!" Francine said, holding her mother again.

"Well … let's go sit down somewhere. I want to hear everything!" Terese said enthusiastically.

Francine, her mother, and her aunt stayed talking for a long time. Francine made sure to say only the necessary things. Nicole was shocked once she learned about Francine's escape, especially the news about Julian. She had known him since he was a small child.

Those three hours went by as fast as if it had been only a few minutes.

"Remember, no one can know I am here. It can still be dangerous as we don't know what happened in Germany after I left. We don't know if they are looking for me."

"You seem to have a fever," Nicole told her daughter, feeling her forehead. "You look so pale."

"I am feeling a lot better now, Mother. No need to worry!"

"Who is taking care of you?"

"Are you eating enough?" Aunt Theresa added.

"I'm fine, trust me," Francine insisted, happy to be surrounded by so much love.

"When are we going to see each other again?" Her mother was still worried.

"I'm not sure, but I'll find a way to keep in touch. It will be alright."

"I still believe you should stay here with us!"

"I wish I could. But I need to check with Daniel first. So let's wait for his return!"

They hugged each other one more time before saying their goodbyes.

Clarice was glad to see that her plan had gone well. Francine looked fresher and happier after she visited with her mother and aunt. But, as the days went by, she also noticed a persistent paleness on Francine's face, and the fever had returned.

"We have news from Daniel," Clarice said rushing downstairs. "He said he would try to come by next week."

Francine smiled. She wanted to go to her aunt's place, but she knew she had to check with Daniel first to make sure she wouldn't place anyone in danger.

"But I'm still concerned about you, Francine. You still look so weak. You have lost some weight, and you're not eating much at all."

Francine looked down and felt dizzy. She hadn't felt hungry lately.

"I don't know. I feel strange. And everything I eat bothers my stomach."

"How are you feeling in the morning?" Clarice asked with concern.

"That is the worst time of the day. I've tried to eat more, but I can't. I feel nauseous all the time."

Clarice's suspicions grew.

"Why did you ask that?" Francine looked at Clarice's face with apprehension. "You don't think I'm…?"

Clarice raised her eyebrows. She looked at Francine with pity. She knew Francine had been in a military base in Germany. She could only imagine what the girl had to go through. In Clarice's mind, the thought of Francine having a relationship with a German man by choice was unthinkable as Francine had been taken away from her home and kept as a prisoner.

Francine sat there quietly. She had been through so many intense moments in these past few weeks that pregnancy hadn't really crossed her mind. She instinctively placed her hand on her belly and thought about Hans.

"It's all right, Francine," Clarice said, trying to comfort her. "We are here to help you. You are not alone."

Francine thanked her for caring but said nothing else.

"I'll be upstairs if you need me," Clarice said, noticing the girl needed some time alone.

Even though it was a complicated situation, Francine felt happy, as if a piece of Hans's heart was living inside of her. It was as if he was somehow closer. More than ever, Francine knew she needed to communicate with him. She couldn't wait any longer. *I need to write him a letter. I hope he and Denna can find a way to leave Germany soon!*

She rushed toward the bag Hans had given her. He had written down an address where they should meet in Switzerland once things had calmed down: his parents' vacation home.

Lying in her bed, she thought about her future and the possibility of being pregnant. Everything had changed once more. *I will always love you, Hans! And 'll wait for you forever*, she repeated to herself as she drifted off to sleep.

A week later, Daniel showed up as he had promised. After speaking to Clarice and her husband, he proceeded straight to Francine's room downstairs.

"How are you feeling?" he asked her after a warm embrace. "I heard you were ill."

"I'm feeling better now," Francine answered, feeling somewhat awkward.

"I also heard about your little trip to your mother's house," Daniel said, smiling at her.

"It was my fault. I'm so sorry, but I needed to see her."

"It's fine. Don't worry about that. Clarice has already explained it to me. As a matter of fact, I am glad you did it!"

"I am happy to hear that because I've been wondering about the possibility of staying with them at my aunt's house. What do you think?"

"Well, I actually think it makes sense. Clarice and Fernand will have other people arriving this week, and it may get very crowded here. Plus, I don't believe anyone is searching for you, which is great!"

Francine smiled, feeling great relief. She couldn't wait to be reunited with her family, especially under her new circumstances.

"I would just ask you to keep yourself out of sight for a while longer. And if you wish, I can also try to relocate you to another country. I have several contacts, and—"

"I can't leave Switzerland."

Daniel looked at her with concern, thinking that something serious had happened in his absence.

Without delaying it any longer, Francine knew she had to tell him the whole truth.

"I'm pregnant," she said all at once. "Clarice took me to a doctor far away from here, in another town, to confirm our suspicion."

Daniel couldn't hide the surprised look on his face. He was expecting to hear anything but that. He sat back in his chair. Clarice hadn't mentioned anything to him.

"It's a long story," Francine said, looking into his eyes.

Daniel obviously didn't know the circumstances surrounding Francine's pregnancy. So, he imagined the worst, like Clarice.

"Well, I certainly wasn't expecting that, but please don't feel obligated to tell me anything."

"I thank you for those words, but I would really like to share my story with you," Francine said, knowing she could trust him.

And so, Francine started telling him everything that had happened to her from the time she met Hans for the first time in Switzerland until the moment they found her in the forest. Little by little, everything started to make more sense to Daniel.

"Unexpected and improbable things often happen during war times, and love is certainly one of them!" he said, smiling at her.

Feeling understood and supported, Francine smiled back at him, glad to finally be able to share her entire story with someone special.

"He is German! But completely different than the others. He is a wonderful man who I met before the war, and he never allowed it to change who he is. He and his father have done much to help other people being persecuted by the Nazi regime."

Daniel nodded, agreeing with everything she said. He also had come to know some Germans who were against that war and all the atrocities committed by Hitler and his followers.

"You and Julian have saved my life. And Hans has done the same!"

"And you … you are expecting his child?" Daniel concluded.

"Yes," Francine confirmed it with a shy smile.

"Well, I'm glad to hear that! I see you are happy with your pregnancy. But I have to say … this is quite a story!"

Francine nodded. "Yes, I know."

"I supposed Hans must be going crazy wondering where you are. And I am sure he has no idea that his so-called brother was so close to killing you and left you there in those woods."

"Exactly. And that's why I need a favor from you!" She turned around and grabbed a letter addressed to Hans.

"And this is a letter for him, right?" Daniel said before she could explain.

"Yes, to his parents' home here in Switzerland."

Francine provided Daniel with the address, and both of them stayed talking for a while longer, planning their next moves. Daniel would deliver the letter himself. He instructed Francine not to go there for a while. It was also established that she would go to her aunt's house on that same night.

After a moving farewell from Clarice, her husband took both Daniel and Francine to her new home. Francine promised to keep in touch.

And then it was time to say goodbye to Daniel; they hugged each other tightly. Daniel had to leave for another mission right after dropping the letter at Hans's parent's house.

With a smile on his face, Daniel watched Francine as she walked toward her aunt's house. Both her mother and aunt were waiting for her patiently, right outside the door. He thought about Julian, wishing he was there to see that scene. Francine was reunited with her family!

"I guess we can leave now, Fernand," Daniel said enthusiastically. "One more mission accomplished … and we are ready for the next!"

Fernand laughed out loud. Yes, they were ready for their next guests.

Daniel kept quiet while Fernand drove them to another location to pick up the new war refugees.

He contemplated everything that Francine had told him. He was used to hearing all kinds of unbelievable stories, but Francine's was definitely a different one. He was aware of relationships that happened between Germans and French folks during the war. However, they were far from being a love story. *She was saved by a German man who she had previously met a long time ago. He put his own life at risk. He killed a German soldier for her, and he helped Jewish people escape Hitler's wrath. And, unbelievably, his brother is a Nazi Commander! That's something we definitely don't hear every day!* Daniel thought with renewed hope.

CHAPTER 30

Hans woke up abruptly with someone knocking on his car window.

"Sir?" one of Carson's guards said loudly.

Hans soon realized he was still in front of Carson's house. He had fallen asleep in his car.

"Is Carson at home?" Hans asked, pulling down the window.

"He left very early to catch the train to Berlin," the soldier answered, reaching to his pocket. "He told me to give you this!"

Hans grabbed the piece of paper and started reading it carefully as the soldier walked away. But there wasn't much of an explanation, not enough to satisfy all the questions in his mind.

Hans, everything has gone well. Don't worry. We can talk more about it once I come back from Berlin.

Even though he couldn't make much out of that message, he sighed in relief. For that moment, at least, it seemed that Francine was fine. He turned on the engine and drove away.

Denna was sleeping on the couch when a noise woke her up. It was Hans who had just entered the house.

"Hans? Where have you been?" she rushed to ask him the moment he showed up in the living room. "I was so worried."

He looked at Denna's face. He knew she probably hadn't gotten too much sleep either.

"I'm sorry. It has been a long night … I guess, for both of us! But I'll tell you everything I know."

"Are you hungry?" she asked him.

"Absolutely!"

As they prepared something to eat, Hans started to tell her about the places he went trying to find Francine and Carson's note.

"I'm sure things did go well. As a Nazi Commander, Carson has enough power to guarantee Francine's safe passage."

"I hope so. But there are a lot of things that don't make sense to me. I went all over town, and I couldn't find them. Where did he take her?"

"Maybe he used another train station, far from here."

"It makes sense, but Carson told me he would need to stop by his place first, and I didn't find them there. I want to trust him, but I won't rest until I hear from her."

"I know why you stayed here," Denna said, feeling responsible for Hans's decision to stay behind. "I'm sorry. I wish you had gone with her."

"No, please don't worry about that. I made the best decision, and I don't regret it."

Denna simply smiled at him. She knew if it weren't for her, he would have been gone a long time ago.

Days went by and then weeks; Hans still hadn't heard any news from Francine. Without any details, he had informed his parents that perhaps a friend would try to contact them, and he would need to know about it as soon as it happened. But, unfortunately, much to his dismay, no one had made any contact yet.

It was close to the end of his shift when Hans heard that Carson was back at the military base. He wasted no time and went straight to his office.

Carson couldn't hide his irritation when one of his soldiers announced Hans was there to see him. He didn't want to talk to Hans, but he knew he couldn't hide from him forever.

Trying to look calm, Carson reassured him that everything went well.

"But I can't guarantee what happened to her after I put her on the train," Carson said, not meeting Hans's eyes.

"I have to find out if she crossed the border safely," Hans said desperately.

Carson looked down, pretending to read some documents. He was also wondering the same thing. He had no idea what had happened to Francine. He just wanted to be sure she would never be seen again. Hans could never know what he had done.

"She'll be all right," Carson said, understanding Hans wouldn't leave without a better explanation. "I was the one who gave very specific instructions to the guards to make sure she crossed the border with no problems. So, what else do you want, Hans? A love letter from Switzerland stating how she made it out of here safely? I'm sure you will hear from her soon! You have to be more patient. There is a great war happening out there!"

With an angry look on his face, Hans replied. "Why the sarcasm? Don't you understand what she means to me?"

"Listen, Hans ... I did what I could. Actually, I did way more than I should have. I wouldn't have done any of it if it hadn't been for you. So, I don't want to hear anything about this anymore. It's over! I need to work now. I'm too busy helping to reorganize our troops in Northern Africa and Italy."

"Would that perhaps mean that we are starting to lose a few more battles in this war?" Hans asked, trying to obtain more information that could be translated into hope. "

Carson laughed. "How can you say that? Us ... losing battleground in the war? That's ridiculous! You can be so pathetic sometimes, Hans. You know nothing about war. You know nothing about your own country. No wonder you like the French so much. You have terrible taste, my brother."

Knowing he wouldn't get anything else out of Carson, Hans simply turned around and walked away without saying much more except for a few words of gratitude for what he had done.

Carson felt a great sense of relief when he saw Hans walk away. He wasn't comfortable with that situation either. Deep inside, Carson knew he had betrayed the friend he considered to be his own brother. But it was too late, and he could only wish Francine would disappear forever, either alive or dead!

Later that day, already at home, Hans shared his frustrations with Denna.

"I want to believe him as I have no other choice now. But I don't know, Denna. It makes no sense that she hasn't tried to communicate somehow. Her aunt lives in Switzerland. She could have dropped off a letter or something! And I still haven't been able to communicate with my few contacts that were going to get you fake identification!"

Denna looked at him, attempting a smile. She knew he wouldn't be able to get the fake identity documents for her. His contacts had disappeared long ago. Without the fake papers, he wouldn't be able to request travel authorization from Carson.

"Hans," Denna said in a serious tone of voice. "You have done so much for me … you saved my life. You and your family have taken care of me and have risked so much for doing so. I'll never be able to thank you enough. You have been separated from your family. Your parents are waiting for you, and now Francine, the woman you love, waits for you as well. I know I'm the only thing holding you here. It's time for you to leave.

I won't be able to leave Germany, at least not now or any time soon. We both know that."

"Don't say that. I'll never abandon you; you are part of our family, like the sister I never had. I'm staying until we find a way out to get out of here together. I'm not going anywhere without you."

Denna felt the tears filling her eyes.

Hans walked over to her and placed his hands on her shoulders. "Hey," he said softly. "We stay together, and that's final! We leave together, or we don't leave at all!"

As the days went by, whispers of Germany's first defeats in Italy started to spread around the world. New hope rose among the Allies as well as in the civilian Resistance movements.

In the meantime, the war intensified even more. And with that, Denna saw Hans even less, as everyone was required to work extra hours and days.

Still waiting anxiously for any news from Francine, Hans's worries and exhaustion started to take a toll on his health. Denna noticed it easily; he didn't eat or rest enough. She was growing more concerned by the day.

It was already noon when Denna decided to check on Hans in his bedroom. He didn't go downstairs for breakfast, and she worried; he hadn't been feeling well lately.

She knocked at the door several times but got no answer.

"Hans?" Denna asked softly as she slowly opened the door. "Are you all right?"

Hans was still sleeping. Alarmed, Denna walked toward him, soon noticing the sweat pouring down his face. She felt his forehead, confirming that he had a high fever.

"Hans?" Denna whispered again.

Hans sluggishly opened his eyes. It took a few seconds for him to respond.

"Denna?" Hans muttered, trying to get up.

"I was worried about you. It's past noon, and you never sleep this much."

He slowly sat up in his bed and attempted to muster the strength to stand up, but he couldn't.

"I think you should stay in bed. You are burning up!" Denna said, touching his forehead again. "I'll bring you something to eat and call your family doctor."

"I'm all right. It's probably just a mild fever. I don't think it is a good idea for anyone to come here, even the family doctor."

"I don't know, Hans. You look very sick! Well … just lie down and rest for now. I'll be back soon with some food."

Hans had no strength to argue. His head felt heavy; his entire body ached and shivered.

Denna took care of him throughout the day, but as the night fell, his condition only worsened. She then decided to inform Eugene, the Schulze's long-time driver, and gardener, about Hans's illness. Eugene agreed with her that it was time to get the family doctor.

A couple of hours later, Eugene arrived with the doctor by his side.

"His fever is really high," the doctor said, worried. "I'm afraid we might have to send him to a hospital if he doesn't get better by tomorrow."

"I'll stay here with him tonight so that I can watch him closely."

"You do that, young lady. I'll be back tomorrow morning; call me if he gets worse."

Sitting on a comfortable chair next to Han's bed, Denna checked on him several times during the night. With concern, she noticed his fever went up even higher. She knew she would have to call the doctor again. Slowly, Denna was becoming frightened. Hans was the only person she had left. She didn't know what to do if something terrible happened to him.

At the break of dawn, Denna decided to knock at Eugene's door, who resided in a small house in their backyard. Eugene had become the only person Denna had left to help her out and who truly cared for Hans.

"Eugene, Hans's condition seems to be getting worse. I don't know what to do."

Eugene rushed inside the residence, going toward Hans's room.

"You should call the doctor again," Eugene said, sharing her worries. "I would not waste any more time."

The doctor arrived at the Schulze's residence shortly after. He decided that Hans would have to go to the hospital.

Denna understood how serious the situation was. She knew she wasn't supposed to leave the house, but at the same time, she could never leave Hans alone in the hospital.

As Eugene waited for them outside the military base, Denna stayed by Hans's bedside in the same hospital Francine had been liberated from. She tried her best to cover her face with a hat, and although she was elegantly dressed, she still feared someone could recognize her.

Denna thought about writing a letter to Hans's parents informing them of his condition, but she wasn't sure. She knew that they would come back to Germany, and that was out of the question. On the other hand, she knew they would never forgive her if something happened to Hans and they weren't notified.

Hans opened his eyes halfway and looked around. He had no idea where he was.

"Good morning, Hans," Denna said, glad to see him awake. "How are you feeling?"

"Denna, where am I?" Hans asked, confused.

"We had to bring you to the hospital. Your fever was really high."

"You shouldn't be here," he whispered, still feeling really weak. "I want you to go back home."

"I'm not leaving you alone here. I was going to write your parents a letter if you didn't get better."

"No, Denna. I'm glad you didn't do that. They would come back, and I don't want that to happen."

"I know, that's what I thought at first. But you got worse, and I started to get really worried."

"I'm so sorry," Hans said, attempting a smile. "But I don't want you to worry about me. I'll be fine. I feel better already. The most important thing right now is for you to go home."

Throughout the day, Hans tried to convince Denna to leave the hospital, alleging he felt better. But Denna knew the situation was quite the opposite. His fever was still dangerously high.

"I'll go back home to get a few items for you to stay more comfortable here, but I'll be back shortly," Denna affirmed, holding his hand.

"I don't want you to come back," Hans said with a fading voice. "Stay home, Denna. I'm sure Eugene can do that!"

"I will not leave you," Denna whispered close to him. "No matter what happens, we stay together, remember?"

Unable to gather his thoughts and feeling too weak to argue with her, Hans kept quiet. But even so, he worried about the situation. The longer he stayed there, the riskier it would be for her. He knew he would have to get better fast.

CHAPTER 31

Denna tried to keep her head down as she exited the hospital. She sighed in relief once she saw Eugene waiting for her outside. She rushed inside the vehicle, glad no one seemed to have recognized her.

A few minutes later, already back at the Schulze's house, Denna gathered some of Hans's belongings when she heard a strange noise outside. She went downstairs, immediately spotting Carson, who waited in the living room.

"Good afternoon, Alyse," Carson said, glad to see her. He had waited too long to go back to the Schulze's home, trying to avoid Hans at all cost. But Carson missed her. He couldn't stay away from Alyse any longer.

Denna tried to hide her nervousness. "Good afternoon. I'm heading to the hospital to see Hans."

"Hospital?" Carson asked, surprised. "What happened to him?"

"Hans has fallen ill. Eugene and I took him to the hospital early this morning after his condition got worse," Denna said, looking down, trying to avoid making eye contact with him.

"I better go see him. I'll take you there," Carson said genuinely worried.

"Oh, I thank you, but Eugene is ready to take me back."

"Someone needs to take care of the house," Carson insisted. "I will take you there. I want to see Hans."

Denna had no other alternative but to go with him.

"What happened?" Carson asked Denna, who had been quiet the whole trip.

"He hasn't been feeling good since ... Francine left," Denna hesitated for a second. "He has been trying to find out any information about her, waiting for Francine to contact him, but so far, nothing has changed. He's been working long hours and not eating well or sleeping much."

Carson kept quiet. *She must be dead*, he thought. In Carson's mind, he had no regrets about what he had done. He was just worried about being caught. *I should have killed her. At least then, I would be sure.*

"I've been gone for so long and have been so busy," Carson said, trying to justify his prolonged absence. "I haven't been able to talk to Hans much."

Denna could barely hide the frustration those words caused her. She knew he was lying. Hans had been desperately trying to get more information from Carson, but he always had an excuse to avoid him. She also had a feeling that something terrible had happened to Francine. She didn't trust Carson ... she knew what he was capable of, like all the Nazis.

When they arrived at the hospital, Hans was surprised to see Carson by Denna's side.

"Hans, I just found out you were brought here. Someone should have contacted me about it. I had stopped by your house, and your cousin told me you were ill."

The three of them talked for a little while. Carson noticed Hans's cold manner and knew the reason why.

"Carson ... do me a favor and take Alyse back home. There are too many sick people being placed close to me here and too many soldiers. This is not a safe place for her."

Carson promptly agreed with Hans. He knew it would give him a perfect opportunity to be alone with Alyse again.

"I think it is better if I stay with you here," Denna insisted.

"I would rather have you at the house. You can make sure things are being taken care of ... please."

"But Hans –" Denna tried to argue.

"Carson will take you there. I don't want to see you here; you will end up getting sick, too."

"I will tell Eugene to stay here with you then. He has already offered his help."

"Tell him I do appreciate his concern and assistance, but it's not a good idea for you to be home alone either."

Hans paused for a few seconds as if trying to gather the little strength he had left.

"I will be all right," he continued. "For now, so I don't have to worry so much, the best thing you can do for both of us is to go home. And it's an order!"

Carson reassured Denna that Hans would have the best care at the hospital.

Denna kept quiet as Carson drove her back to the Schulze residence. As much as she told herself she hated and despised him, there was something else about Carson that troubled her mind. It seemed as he could see right through her, making her feel emotions previously unknown to her heart. She didn't know for sure what it was, and perhaps, she didn't really want to.

But those thoughts started to haunt her every day, getting worse every time he got closer to her. She didn't know why she would think of him so often. She felt as if she was again facing one more battle, a silent and secret battle, one that would further tear her soul apart. *I hate him; he represents everything evil in this world,* Denna thought, denying the possibility she would have any other feelings toward him. *I will always hate him!*

As soon as they arrived, she excused herself, saying that she was exhausted, and quickly went inside the house. Carson was disappointed, unhappy that she left him so quickly. He had expected to spend more time alone with her, taking advantage of that rare opportunity, when she was temporarily away from Hans's watchful eye. It was very clear she was running away from him.

As much as he tried, he simply couldn't understand her behavior. He was a handsome and influential man. He was the Commander of a military base in a new, powerful Germany rising right before their eyes. In his mind, he could see no reason why any woman would reject him.

But the more Alyse dodged his attention, the more he wanted her. His pride was hurt. Daring thoughts started to settle in his mind. What began as a feeling of attraction turned into a turbulent passion that grew stronger by the day. He couldn't stop thinking about her, longing to get close to her, to kiss her. Intimate dreams consumed him, leaving him incapable to fully focus at work or anything else.

Feeling frustrated, he drove home to change clothes. He had promised Denna to visit Hans later on, but before that, he would go out and have a few drinks and dinner with some of his Nazi friends. He needed to do something to take his mind off Alyse, to make him forget about her rejections.

In a fancy restaurant, Carson and so many other Nazi officers laughed, drank, and ate the best that Germany had to offer.

It was already late at night when Carson contemplated the idea of checking on Hans in the hospital. But as he got inside his car, he quickly remembered the suspicious way Hans often looked at him, insisting on knowing all the details of Francine's escape to Switzerland. Carson felt very uncomfortable. Even though he truly cared for his brother, he didn't feel like talking to him at that moment.

After having a lot to drink that night, Carson decided to go back home instead. But as he kept on driving, his thoughts were directed to someone else. He had been surrounded by dozens of beautiful women at the restaurant. He knew he could have any of them, but the entire time only one person kept crossing his mind.

The more Carson started to think about Alyse, the more agitated he became. With his inhibitions dampened by alcohol, Carson felt free to let his most inner thoughts and desires go wild. In this frame of mind, he imagined Alyse in his arms.

Suddenly, as if ignited by a powerful, mysterious force, he made a quick turn.

It was past midnight when Denna heard the doorbell ring. She had fallen asleep on the living room couch with a book by her side. She got up slowly, feeling a little woozy.

Denna took a peek out the window and saw a car.

"Who is it?" she asked cautiously.

"It's me, Carson," he replied, feeling nervous.

She stood still, feeling very uneasy.

"It's me, Alyse," Carson said again. "I need to talk to you."

Worried that something had happened to Hans, Denna opened the door quickly.

"Is everything all right? Did you go see Hans? How is he?"

"Yes, yes, he's fine. I just arrived back from the hospital, and the doctors said he was feeling better," Carson replied, not caring about lying to her.

"Oh, that is great news. I thought something bad had happened to him."

Denna kept looking at Carson, waiting for him to say something back.

"You aren't going to let me in?" Carson asked her after an awkward silence.

"I'm sorry, I just woke up. But of course, please, come in."

"Well, it's me who should say sorry," he said drunk but pretending otherwise. "I didn't mean to wake you up."

Denna was caught off guard. She wasn't expecting company, especially Carson.

"It's fine," she replied, trying to be polite.

She felt quite disturbed by Carson's intense expression. She was certain that he was drunk.

Wearing just a silky camisole under her robe, Denna felt extremely uncomfortable.

"I hope you don't mind me coming here. I needed to talk to someone. I felt horrible seeing Hans like that. I wish I had known before that he was forced to work too many hours. I could certainly have done something about it."

Denna paid close attention to every word Carson said. She knew that aside from everything that he represented, he did really care for Hans. Nonetheless, she still couldn't quite understand why he had shown up so late just to tell her that.

"Would you like some water or tea …?" Denna offered, not sure what else to say or do.

"No, thank you," Carson said, looking around the house as if he was checking to see if anyone else was there. "But I'll have some whiskey if possible."

She watched him as he poured whiskey into two cups. That situation made her feel very uneasy. No one had ever made her feel so out of place, and yet no one had ever made her feel such intense emotions. She despised him, or she completely wanted to believe she did. But her heart stubbornly told her something different, as it beat faster every time he looked at her or got closer. Scared and disgusted with her own feelings, she wanted to run away from him.

Carson was already walking toward her, holding two glasses in his hands. Denna just stood there. She was trying hard to think of a way to get out of the rapidly worsening scenario.

"Here," Carson said, getting closer to her.

"Thank you, but I don't drink whiskey," she said politely.

"Well," Carson said, getting even closer to her. "There's always a first time for everything. Just taste it … take a sip."

Denna grabbed the glass mechanically. She felt almost obligated to drink it. She knew he wouldn't leave her alone.

Carson almost laughed as he saw the grimace on her face after she took her first sip.

"It's not that bad, is it?" Carson asked her, smiling.

Denna looked deep into his blue eyes that time, trying to figure out his true intentions. They worked like magnets, making her unable to look away. She couldn't help but feel a strange sensation taking hold of her. It was chilling and yet intriguing. Something inside her made her want to prove that she wasn't that weak girl he thought of her.

"I've known Hans since we were little kids," Carson broke the silence, moving away. He knew he disturbed her. But the truth of the matter was, he didn't know what he was doing, as he had never found himself in such a position. Carson had no control over the situation as it was being played out.

Denna sighed in relief as he walked away. She decided to take a seat, preparing for the long story. Keeping one of her hands on her robe, she pressed the two sides together, afraid to expose the little bit of clothes she had on underneath.

"He and I have always been best friends," Carson continued, sitting down on another couch. "But then the war came, and a distance grew between us."

Carson took a brief pause. "I don't know. He just doesn't seem to understand our country's tremendous importance of winning the war and recovering everything the enemy took from us. We need to show the world our true potential."

Those words instantly brought Denna back to reality. She took a close look at him. She remembered all the horrible things she had witnessed in that war; she thought of her own family. She had to use all her strength to keep herself from shouting at Carson. Denna wanted to show him how much he and Hans were so different and how much she hated him and all he represented.

Carson was too drunk to recognize the immense disgust behind Denna's expression.

"What about you, Alyse? What do you think about all of this? I can't believe a woman like you doesn't have an opinion about everything that is happening out there?"

Denna opened her mouth but shut it fast. She looked away, trying to think of what to say next. As much as she hated whiskey, she decided to take another sip.

She was more than ready to explain to Carson how she really felt about the war – especially being a Jewish woman – but she knew it would be the end of her and Hans. So, she chose her words carefully.

"There's nothing to like about the war!" she said decisively. "No one really wins in a war. There's so much pain, death, despair … You need to really reflect on what you just said. Look at your own family! All separated! How many more are in worse conditions? Our country doesn't have the right to invade any other! I do have an opinion; you are right. I do believe we actually represent the worst there is in this world. And obviously, that should be something far from bringing us pride!"

Carson looked at Denna's face, completely surprised. Unable to hide the sour impression her answer had caused on him, he got up abruptly.

"I don't understand how any true German could think such a thing! But you're a woman! One who lived more outside than inside your own country. Perhaps it's to be expected."

Denna looked at him defiantly. His words were a great insult, but seeing him so disturbed about her remarks made her feel somewhat powerful.

Noticing his words didn't affect her much, Carson felt even worse and tried to fix the situation.

"I'm sorry. I didn't mean to bother you with this conversation. I'm just so tired, and maybe I drank too much …."

"I understand," Denna quickly replied, hoping he would finally leave. "Well, it's a bit late, and perhaps …."

"Tell me, Alyse," Carson looked deep into her eyes. "Why do you hate me so much? You think I haven't noticed it?"

Caught by surprise, Denna was stunned by such intrusive questions. Not knowing what to say right away, she sat there mute as she saw Carson approaching her.

"You don't have to be scared. Say whatever you're thinking."

Denna got up fast. She needed to get away from him.

"Who said I hate you?" Denna asked, feeling sick at having to say another lie and yet, trying her best to stay calm as Carson stood right next to her.

"It's written all over you," Carson said, getting very close to her.

Instantly, her heart started pounding faster against her chest. She could feel the warmth of his body. She stood there petrified as Carson's hand touched her hair. Denna's entire body trembled when she felt his breath on her neck.

"See … you're afraid of me. I just don't understand it."

"Please, Carson … I'm very tired, and it's getting late. I believe that…."

Carson didn't give her the chance to finish her sentence. He quickly placed his arms around her, pulling her closer to him.

They stood there quiet for a few seconds. Unable to think straight, she looked at his lips, guessing what would come next. But before Carson could make his move, Denna automatically pushed him away, breaking free from his grip.

Astonished by her reaction, Carson froze on the spot, silenced. He felt humiliated; no woman had ever done that to him.

"I'm sorry," Denna apologized, squeezing her hands together, feeling confused by all the contradictory emotions that ran through her mind.

"Why do you despise me so much?" he asked her, not accepting the situation.

"No, that is not what I think. It's just that, perhaps, you had too much to drink, and none of us are thinking very clearly now. We should all get some rest. We can talk about these things another day."

Carson chuckled at her comment.

Denna felt humiliated.

"I'll leave after I hear the whole truth. Who are you trying to fool?"

"Truth? What truth?" she asked, frightened.

He walked toward her, staring right into her eyes. Shaking, Denna looked down, afraid of what he was going to tell her. He touched her chin, moving it upwards. Their eyes locked.

"Something inside of me tells me that a strong feeling connects us. I can't tell you exactly what it is, but I know I am not crazy! And that's the truth that perhaps you are trying to deny."

At that moment, she almost forgot who he was. All she could see was his blue eyes fiercely staring at her, begging for the slightest sign of affection, as if they knew her most secret desires.

Carson touched her waist, bringing her a little closer to him.

Placing both her hands on his chest automatically, she didn't know what to think anymore, as she could no longer fight all those strong feelings that she tried to hide for so long.

Carson couldn't quite understand what was happening to him either. He had never felt so intensely attracted to anyone like that before. His heart ached for her in a way that made him blind, messing with his head. The passion she stirred inside his heart made him easily forget about his manners, his restraints. He didn't know how to act around her. All he knew was that he wanted her. He needed her in order to feel complete again.

In that state of mind, his lips sought hers. He kissed her passionately, moving her even closer to him.

Unable to move, Denna simply allowed him to touch her.

Noticing that she didn't seem to present any resistance, he surrendered himself to a feeling that was completely unknown to him until then. He could no longer deny it. He was deeply in love with her.

Carson pulled her toward the couch, his lips moved frantically against hers without any constraints. He laid her down quickly, positioning his body on top of hers.

"I still think we can make this work between us," he said, pausing for a moment before kissing her again.

Denna simply stared at him. She thought about asking him to stop but she couldn't, no words came out.

The intense heat generated by the friction of their bodies made him lose all control. Carson couldn't think about anything else besides satisfying all his own desires. There was no way he wasn't going to finish what he had started.

Denna struggled to admit to herself the pleasure she felt with each touch. His wet lips traveled down her neck, the weight of his body igniting a flame within her. She was scared and confused. She thought she should push him away from her, but she didn't. Instead, she felt some strange and powerful energy connecting them, preventing her from fighting back. Her mind said one thing but her heart something very different.

Carson's breathing got more labored as he removed the last pieces of clothing from her body.

"Carson," she said softly, her voice shaky. "I …"

"I am not going to hurt you," was all he could say at that moment.

Her body shivered as she felt his lips sliding over her skin.

Without even thinking, she placed her small hands on his shoulders, pressing her fingers hard against his skin. She heard him moaning again and again as he pushed his body against hers at a steady and intense pace. She found it hard to breathe, and her heart was beating faster and faster. In her innocence, she wasn't sure what to expect.

Just like that, she closed her eyes and felt things she had never experienced before.

CHAPTER 32

Denna lay there, motionless. Her mind was suddenly taken elsewhere, to a cold and lonely place.

Carson lay on top of her for a few minutes longer. He looked at Alyse and saw tears rolling down her face. He tried to say something. He wanted to apologize or simply tell her about all the intense feelings he had just experienced. But everything had happened so fast and he didn't know where to start.

He felt his head spinning and knew he had too much to drink. He quickly rose and put his clothes on.

He took a deep breath before turning around to look at Alyse's face one more time. He found her even more beautiful, with her messy hair and nude body. But remembering the imprudent way he had acted, he felt completely different, restless. He saw her there, her body still as if someone had shot her in cold blood.

Although Carson had always been intense in his relationships, he never felt anything that could come close to that. But at that moment, he was also confused, afraid of his feelings toward the girl, something as wonderful as well as frightening.

He passed his hands over his face. He wanted to say something, to fix the situation somehow. In his head, he was already trying to find excuses for his behavior, but he knew he only had himself to blame.

Along with the tears that poured down her face, her silence made him feel a terrible sensation of despair. He couldn't look at her anymore;

he couldn't face reality. He had forced his way on a woman that was part of the Schulze family, a family that took him in and treated him as their own. He had betrayed that trust.

"Alyse," he called out for her. But Denna kept looking away, feeling ashamed of herself.

Noticing the anguish on her face and not knowing what else to say or do, he grabbed his Nazi cap from the floor and quickly walked away.

Denna didn't know how long she stayed there in that same position. A mix of confusing emotions took hold of her body and soul.

Carson didn't know that her struggle had more to do with how she felt during their intimate time together rather than how things were said and done.

She punished herself with terrible thoughts as she tried hard to understand why she had given up, allowing him to touch her that way. But most of all, she couldn't accept or even comprehend the very fact that she actually felt pleasure and a strong desire once he started touching her. *How could that have happened? I hate him! I have to hate him!* She thought, trying to convince herself.

With her body aching and feeling absolutely exhausted, it took all her strength to get up and walk upstairs.

She wanted to wash her skin off her body. She wanted to remove the impression of his body on top of hers. To sweep away those memories forever from her mind.

After the shower, she lay on her bed and closed her eyes. She felt numb, lost. A flashback of everything that happened to her since Hans found her began to rush through her mind. She thought about her family, always wondering about their fate. *And Abraham?*

Tears started to pour down her face again. She felt even more ashamed. Her quest for survival had her living a lie every day. She felt trapped in the role she had to play, making her forget at times who she really was. *What have I become? Is it even worth it?*

But it was how she felt around Carson and the events of that night that further increased a hole in her heart. Suddenly, the line between lies and truth became blurry. She had to deal with all kinds of new and deep emotions. And that forced her to grow up fast and to change. No matter how hard she would try, she could never go back to be that girl she once was before the war. It was only then she realized it; the time of innocence was over.

Denna woke that Monday morning feeling discouraged and weak. Still haunted by the memories of that last night, she lay in her bed for a long time. Denna suddenly thought about Hans; *He must never find out what happened.* Worrying about his well-being and knowing he was alone in the hospital, she gathered all her strength to stand up and get ready to see him.

She arrived at the hospital later that day. She still carried the scars of the previous night on her face. She kept her eyes downward.

As she walked down the hallway, two soldiers were walking in her direction. Denna didn't notice them, but they paid close attention to her. They were the two soldiers that had attacked her the night Hans had found her.

Hans was awake and disappointed to see Denna there.

"I told you not to come here! I'm feeling a lot better, and I am sure I will be leaving this hospital soon."

Denna looked at him with tears in her eyes. She wanted to tell him what happened, but she knew she couldn't.

Hans noticed the sad look on her face. "I'm sorry," he apologized. "I'm was rude. Are you all right?" he asked, preoccupied. "You seem unwell."

Denna tried to put a smile on her face. "I'm fine," she said, looking away. "I am so glad you are feeling better. I was just so worried. Mrs. Kaufmann and Eugene were also very concerned about you. It was hard to convince them not to contact your parents. And before I forget, Mrs. Kaufmann sent those cookies for you."

"Thank you," Hans said, smiling as he reached out for one of them. "Don't worry about me, Denna. I do feel a lot better. And as for my parents, they should not know about this. There is no need for them to worry. And like I mentioned before, if they call, please tell them I am out of town on a business trip."

"Oh, Hans. I feel so guilty for leaving you here alone. I didn't mean to be away for an entire day."

"I'm glad you were away. You needed to rest. As for me, I can't wait to go back home. Please tell Eugene that I appreciate and thank him for everything he has done for us. He really is a good man. As for Mrs. Kaufmann, she is a good employee, but …" Hans hesitated to continue. He knew this was not the place for that conversation.

Denna nodded, as she was also aware she couldn't really trust her. Quite often, she noticed the suspicious way Mrs. Kaufman looked at her. She did not remember Denna as a child visiting the Schulze family.

The very next day, Hans was finally released from the hospital. But, back home, he received a message that his parents wanting him to call them right away.

Sitting at his father's desk, Hans waited anxiously for his parents to pick up the phone. He wondered if they had news from Francine.

"Hans?" his mother said gladly. "How are you? How are things going?"

"We're all alright, mother. How are you and dad?"

"We would be better if you were both here. We really miss you! But for now, we got the news you waited for so long!"

"Francine? Did she show up? Did she contact you?"

"Well, we've been gone for a while at your grandma's house in the mountains, as you know. But as soon as we came back, we found two letters addressed to you, and the name on it was Francine!"

Hans almost dropped the phone from his hands.

"Francine? What does she say? When exactly did you get those letters? What…"

"Calm down, Hans." Elga urged him. "I will tell you everything, but we need to know who this girl is."

"Let me talk to him," Alfred said, taking the phone from Elga. "Hello, Hans."

"Dad! How are things going? I heard you received letters from Francine. I need to know everything she said."

"Of course. But what your mother is trying to tell you is that those letters are rather personal …."

"I know, but it is a long story," Hans replied, understanding his parents didn't know much about her. "For now, I just need you to read me the letter. I can explain it later."

"I understand it," Alfred agreed with him. "Well, give me a minute here."

Holding his breath, Hans waited impatiently.

"The first one… she says she is doing really well and that she loves you very much and misses you. She also thanks you for everything you have done for her. She says she worries and thinks about you everyday! She mentions she has a lot to tell you and will wait anxiously for your reply."

Hans smiled, tears quickly filling his eyes. Francine was alive! She was safe! Placing his head against his hand, he sighed in relief.

"Just wait a minute," Alfred continued. "Your mother is reading the second letter."

"As I said, it's a long story, Dad," Hans said with a shaky voice, still moved by the news.

"I can see that," Alfred said, puzzled by the whole situation.

"What else does she say?"

There was silence on the other end of the phone, but Hans could hear his parents whispering.

"She says she is very worried about you and will continue to wait for your reply. She told us to leave a letter for her on our patio, and someone will pick it up, and well… this is all very strange, Hans. Who is this girl?"

"I will tell you one day, Dad. But for now, I was hoping you could write a letter to her saying everything is fine and that I am trying my best to visit Switzerland soon! She will understand what I mean."

Hans knew he couldn't say much on the phone. His father quickly realized the situation and stopped asking any more questions related to the girl. They proceeded to talk about his possible departure from Germany in a very discreet way.

"I might go there for a few days by myself," Hans continued, already thinking about meeting Francine again. "I will wait until Carson returns from Berlin to ask for a travel authorization."

Alfred knew then that Hans wasn't able to find a way to get Denna out of Germany. He wondered if he would ever be able to do it. Their situation was extremely dangerous, and he worried about them even more.

"It would be great if you could visit us for a while!" Alfred said. "For now, we will reply to that girl and will definitely contact you as soon as we hear back from her!"

Overwhelmed by joy and hope, Hans rushed to Denna's room to give her the news. Francine had made it safely out of Germany!

And so, the days went by a little brighter for Hans, who still tried every day to contact Carson, but he seemed to be always unavailable. Hans started to wonder if something serious was happening to his brother. But what he didn't know was that Carson was avoiding him. He was fearful Hans had found out about him and his cousin.

Unable to wait any longer, Hans realized he would need to go to Berlin to get what he wanted. Only Carson could provide him a travel authorization to see Francine in Switzerland.

It was the afternoon before his departure. Hans, with the help of Denna, prepared his luggage for his trip when they both heard a loud knock at the door.

They both glanced at one another at the same time. By the sound of those aggressive knocks, they both had the feeling that something serious was about to happen.

"Wait here," Hans told Denna.

Walking quickly downstairs, Hans noticed Eugene standing next to the door, looking very concerned.

"Who is it?"

"Military personnel! Perhaps, it is better if both of you …"

"Open the door now!" a voice ordered from outside as the banging became louder and louder.

The alarmed look on Hans's face expressed all the terror he felt inside. There was no doubt in his mind. He knew exactly why they were sent there.

Denna had already rushed to the window. Her face turned pale when she saw the two military units parked in front of the house. Old memories came storming through her mind. She felt as if she was taken back to her old neighborhood.

"Don't open the door, Eugene! You should go back to your house and stay there," said Hans, already rushing upstairs.

"We have to get out of here," Hans said as soon as he saw Denna in the hallway.

Grabbing her hand, Hans pushed her toward the end of the hallway, where they could access one of the windows to the back of the house.

Suddenly, they heard a loud noise echoing throughout the house.

"We have to jump!" he insisted, already opening the window.

But it was too late. SS guards were already positioned in the backyard. They wouldn't stand a chance.

Before Hans could find a place to hide Denna, they heard the sound of voices and steps moving up the stairs.

"Stay right where you are," one of them ordered, already pointing his gun at Hans.

Denna stood frozen against the corridor wall.

Hans turned around slowly, walking toward the guards with his hands in the air. "What's going on here? Who authorized you to enter my house like this?"

The Nazi soldier in charge looked straight into Hans's eyes, moving closer to him.

"We received information that a missing Jewish girl was hiding here," the soldier said in a stern voice, looking at Denna.

Hans's face turned pale, his stomach clenching. He knew they were there to take her.

"And," the soldier continued angrily, "it looks like we have found her."

Hans rushed toward her, quickly placing Denna behind him. He regretted not having a gun at the moment.

"She's my cousin! She is not Jewish! What do you think you're doing invading my house like this? I'll go to the highest authorities and have this straightened out immediately. You will regret coming here and accusing her of such a thing!"

The soldier laughed. "Who said you're in a position to say anything? Get her!" he yelled at the guards.

"You will not take her!" Hans yelled back, defiantly.

The soldier didn't hesitate, quickly pointing the gun at Hans's head.

"No," Denna shouted as she moved in front of him. "I'll go with you."

"What are you doing?" Hans asked, already pushing her to the side.

"She comes with us, or we can kill her right here!" the same man continued, then pointing his gun at the Jewish woman.

Hans' face twisted in rage. He clenched his fists, ready to fight back. But the sight of several guns pointing at Denna's head made him realize he could only make things worse. He knew he had to stay calm.

Without wasting any more time, two soldiers approached her, harshly pulling Denna away from Hans.

In an impulse, Hans tried to stop them, but he was quickly overpowered by three other guards who rushed toward him, holding his body against the wall.

"No!" Hans shouted in anger as he relentlessly tried to break free. "No!!!"

"Grab him too!" the officer said. "He'll be punished for hiding a Jew and resisting. I would love to kill him right here, but unfortunately, he has some powerful connections. As for now, throw him in jail at Commander Beurmann's military station. Take her there as well. I'll leave it up to the Commander to decide their destinies. He has already been informed."

CHAPTER 33

Hans was thrown into a cold jail cell. A terrible anguish crushed his soul. He had been unable to protect her. He felt he had failed her.

He understood the severity of his situation, but he didn't care. In his mind, it was Denna who occupied his thoughts. He needed to find out what they would do to her.

He yelled out for someone, anyone, who would speak to him. But all his efforts were in vain. No one showed up; no one cared.

As time went by, his despair only deepened. He knew what the Nazis were capable of doing. And that was the agonizing reality that ripped through his heart, filling it with hatred. He needed to get out of that prison and find a way to help her somehow. He knew he was all Denna had left.

Feeling absolutely powerless, he cried at the possibility of Denna being hurt.

Hans started to review his actions over the past few months. He blamed himself for not having found a way to get Denna out of the country. He blamed himself as if he hadn't done enough. And it was right at that moment that Hans finally heard a noise. Someone was coming.

He cleaned the tears off his face and jumped at the cell bars, trying to see who that was.

"Step away from the bars, or you will get no food," the soldier said rudely.

"I need to speak with Commander Carson Beurmann!" Hans said. "I need to –"

"I'm sure you will talk to him soon. Now, step away from the bars!"

Hans wanted to hit the soldier and kill him with his own hands. "You bastards! All of you will regret this! I promise you! If any of you do anything to her, I swear I will finish every single one of you!"

The soldier simply laughed at him, and with a smirk on his face, he threw his food on the ground.

Moving his arms through the bars, Hans tried to reach him. But the soldier quickly stepped back, laughing even harder at his failed attempt.

They stared at one another for a few seconds before the soldier turned around and walked away.

The night arrived quickly. Hans's head wound made him feel even more drowsy until exhaustion made him close his eyes.

Throughout the night, he was haunted by terrible nightmares. He saw Denna being hurt. He even dreamed of Francine, a very strange dream. He heard her screaming; he heard her crying. He ran after her but could never reach her.

Not too far from where he was, Denna was brutally pushed into a cold and dark room.

She didn't know what to think; everything had happened so suddenly. All the emotions she had experienced in the past few days came to the surface. Tears started to pour down her face. She regretted not trying to escape sooner. She regretted staying there for too long, risking the lives of everyone around her. Denna wasn't concerned about her own life. She was more worried about Hans. *It was my fault*; she kept repeating, imagining the worst that could happen to him.

She sobbed for a long time. Mentally and physically exhausted, her body started to shiver. She had no idea if it was night already as the cell had no windows. Denna knew she couldn't do anything else but wait. All she wanted to know was that Hans was all right.

Her thoughts were then redirected to Carson. She could still remember all the details of the night they spent together. She knew he would be enraged. She was sure he would confront her before ending her life.

Denna started to prepare her heart for it. But after everything that had happened between them, she was no longer afraid of him. She was tired of all those lies and having to pretend. She wanted to tell Carson the truth herself, to tell him that she was a Jewish woman and very proud of it, that she hated every single thing he stood for. And there was more ... much more to be said.

And so, the hours went by slowly as she imagined how their conversation would go. But above all, she needed to figure out how she could convince him to spare Hans!

As his vehicle moved forward, a storm was raging in Carson's head. Little by little, he started to think about the letter he got earlier that morning. As much as he would like to deny any possibility of it being true, he had a strange feeling about it deep down.

He knew somebody could have easily set him up to ruin his reputation. He would have to go back there immediately and solve the matter. *I'll kill anyone who dared to do such a thing*, he plotted.

He thought about Alyse. He started to analyze her. She had dark hair. She didn't look like anyone in Hans's family. She had shown up from nowhere. He had never heard Hans saying he had another cousin before she had appeared on the scene. And even though the Schulze's had told him they had met when they were little, Carson still couldn't recall or remember anything relating to that girl.

Carson moved in his car seat and passed his hands over his forehead as if trying to push those thoughts away. He felt his anger growing. His blood rushed through his veins. Confused, he didn't know what to think anymore. He wanted to believe that the Schulzes would never do that to him. But he couldn't be sure. *Alyse is not a Jew! She can't be one. I would never touch a Jew,* Carson continued with his inner turmoil.

Driving as fast as he could, Carson understood the perils he would be facing. The news took him by total surprise and at the worst time. He was already overwhelmed with the extra responsibility given to him after Germany's numerous battle losses that year. The upper Nazi officers were putting extra pressure on everyone. The orders were to kill any suspects, Jews, and fugitives – anyone they considered enemies of their country.

Carson thought about Hans. He didn't know what he would do if that story were true. He thought about Alyse again, feeling a terrible sensation. But the more he tried to deny the contents of the letter and Hans's probable guilt, the more he found indicators that it could be true.

Feeling pressure in his chest, he opened the collar of his uniform. He felt trapped and needed more air. He knew he could be in serious trouble if the news were to reach his Nazi officer friends. Hans was considered his brother, and they might think he was also involved in all of that mess.

Carson shook his head, not wanting to accept the reality of that situation. He would need to start making plans to free his brother and Alyse, whether or not the story was true. Most of all, he had to find a way to contain the damage the story had already produced. It could be as devastating as it was dangerous for him. He had to clear his name and his family name from that chaos. Otherwise, it could be the end of his career or his own life!

Amidst all those troubling thoughts, Carson still hoped that it could be only his political enemies plotting against him. It was easier to think of it that way. He couldn't deal with the fact that he had been fooled by his own brother and by a Jewish girl to whom he happened to feel an extreme attraction. Carson knew he had stepped on a lot of people to get what he wanted. He had dangerous enemies who could have conspired against him.

I'll kill them all, Carson thought furiously. *Every one of them will pay for this offense.*

Dominated by deep hatred, his hands started shaking. He still couldn't stop thinking about Alyse. He knew those were serious accusations for which she could be killed. Contradictory feelings caused him immense torment. If she was Jewish, he couldn't forgive such betrayal, but at the same time, he could no longer deny his love for her. He hopelessly relived every second he had spent with her that fateful night, touching her, kissing her, feeling her nude body against his. He wasn't the same man since the very moment he had laid his eyes on her.

For a long time, he thought about going back to see her, to apologize. He dreamed that she might have feelings for him, despite what he had done. He remembered her in his arms, touching his shoulders, moaning as he kissed her.

He considered asking her to marry him. He believed that would somehow make things right again. But he also knew there was a possibility she would never want to see him again.

But everything had changed so drastically; he knew none of those things mattered anymore. If she was a Jew, he could only hate her and possibly kill her for the audacity of lying to him.

Carson felt a bitter sensation, an ache in his heart. Deep inside, he felt torn between feelings of deep love and overwhelming hate.

She is not a Jew, Carson continued to repeat. *She wouldn't dare do that to me. Hans wouldn't do that! I would have to kill her myself.*

Carson arrived in town and went straight to his military station. He made sure to keep his gun in plain view. He wanted people to see the fury on his face.

"Where are they?" Carson rushed to ask one of his most trusted soldiers. "Who authorized such action? I want names, now!"

The soldiers looked at him with fear in his eyes. "I don't know what is going on here, Commander. Lieutenant Adler only told me that he would be the one handling any matters related to you. He said you would be arriving today. He is waiting for you in his office."

Carson felt relieved that it was one of his subordinates in charge of the situation. Adler was a good friend of his and owed him a lot of favors.

"Commander Beurmann," the lieutenant stood up fast as soon as Carson entered the room.

"What's going on here?" Carson shouted as the soldier closed the door behind them.

"We have a complicated situation here, Commander," the lieutenant responded, already feeling nervous. "I've tried to keep it a secret. I didn't want to expose your name."

"You did well! But now I need to know everything that happened. Who authorized their arrest?"

"I'll tell you the whole story."

As Adler began revealing the details he knew, Carson's face started to turn red as he felt his anger mounting.

"I had to arrest them," Adler said quickly. "We had to control the situation to not to raise more suspicion about it. But they are not hurt."

"Didn't anyone think it could be a plot against me?" Carson asked angrily. "Hans would never do such a thing, and Alyse is his cousin. I know that for sure. Of course, she's not Jewish! This is absurd!! Do you think I would have any dirty Jews in my own family? I know someone is trying to get me. But they will fail. I'll hunt down everyone responsible. I will kill them, every one of them! With my own hands!"

Adler took a deep breath. His entire body was shaking. He knew Carson well enough to know he meant every word he said. It was the first time he thought that story could have been a lie.

"My Commander," the lieutenant tried to explain himself. "There are two soldiers that recognized the girl, Alyse, as being Jewish. They were very certain of her identity, and she couldn't provide any papers. She has no documentation. I had to do something to contain the rumors before any High Officers found out about it. Those soldiers were instructed to keep their mouths shut. As far as I know, only a few people know about it."

"Of course, she has no papers!" Carson yelled. "Her parents are traveling overseas on very important business transactions for our country! She is on vacation. So, you hear a crazy story from two idiots, and you believe them over Hans and his cousin?"

Adler's face turned pale; he no longer could answer all those questions.

"I'm sorry, Commander," Adler rushed to say, understanding he had probably made a huge mistake. "I've told no one else. We have been waiting for you. I thought by arresting them; it would look like you weren't involved and ..."

"Enough!" Carson said, not caring to hear anything else. He knew he had to calm down. He couldn't turn Adler into his enemy.

"You have done well by writing to me immediately," Carson said in a more friendly manner. "I understand your actions. But now it's time to correct things and punish those responsible for such false accusations."

"I can bring those two men here."

"Do that now. I'll find out the truth. Say nothing to anyone else. I'll take care of the problem myself. Where are my brother and his cousin?"

"Here at the facility. I thought you might want to keep them close."

Before long, the two soldiers were already walking toward the Commander's office as Carson paced inside. He couldn't wait to find out what was really going on. He wanted to see Hans and Alyse right away, but he knew he would first have to clear their names. It could look really bad for him if anyone found out he had freed prisoners without any justification. These were dangerous times, and Carson knew that very well.

Carson took a close look at the two soldiers standing right in front of him. He could feel his blood boiling inside his veins.

"You can leave now, Adler. But wait outside for my orders."

"Of course, Commander," Adler immediately replied.

There were only the three of them in the room. Carson didn't waste any more time.

"So, tell me exactly why you accused my brother of hiding a Jew, who happens to be his cousin?"

Noticing the furious look on the Commander's face, the two soldier became frightened. They had no idea what they had gotten themselves into.

At that moment, they both regretted making the accusations. As much as they were sure that the woman was the Jewish girl they encountered in the alley, they had no idea she was related to Commander Beurmann's brother.

Each soldier waited for the other to begin speaking.

"Say something, now!" Carson shouted at them. "Who has been plotting against me at my own military base? Who are you two working for?"

Wasting no more time, Carson pulled out his handgun and pointed at them. The two men stiffened in fear.

"Commander," one of them said. "We work for no one but you. We always look out for our country's best interest, our great Germany. We didn't know she was your brother's cousin. We thought she was the Jewish girl who used to play piano at a local café. We were sure it was her when we saw her in the hospital a few weeks ago."

Carson felt his head spinning. He then understood he had no choice but to act as if it was a lie for his own sake.

"Commander," the same soldier pleaded, understanding the crucial situation they were in, "we could have made a mistake. We had a lot to drink that night when we saw that girl in the street."

"No, we didn't make a mistake," the other soldier said resentfully. "It's the Jewish girl; I'm sure of that. We both recognized her. We were simply trying to protect our country, as we are all supposed to."

The other soldier gave his friend an angry look. He knew he had just brought death closer to them.

"One is not sure; the other is," Carson said in a creepy, calm voice. "I don't like uncertainties. I don't like traitors."

Carson quickly pointed the gun at the soldier, who seemed to be sure Alyse was that Jewish girl. Without hesitating, he pressed the trigger.

A blaring sound echoed through the room.

The other soldier stood there, frozen on the spot, with blood splattered all over his face. He knew he was going to be the next one. He closed his eyes, expecting the bullet.

"I'm not going to kill you. You have done well by acknowledging your mistake. You will deny what you saw, of course. You were drunk. You couldn't remember her that well, a girl you saw only one time. So, you will say the truth, that you have made a huge mistake. I'll arrest you for a few days as punishment, and this will be the last time we will talk about this matter. If I hear any rumors, I'll personally hunt you down. I will torture you for days and days before I kill you myself. It will be an agonizingly slow death."

Still trying to recover from the terror of the last few minutes, the soldier could barely breathe.

"Yes, my Commander. I completely understand. I apologize for all the trouble we have caused. I am grateful for your mercy!"

"Tell Adler to come in. You will inform him of your decision to confess your mistake."

Adler walked in, already expecting what he saw lying on the floor.

"Send someone to pick up this body from here and clean the office," Carson said, putting his gun back in his belt.

A few minutes later, Adler had the confession on paper. He directed the soldier to an isolated cell where he would be detained for a few days.

Already back in Carson's office, Adler waited for further instructions.

"You know what to do with that soldier, right? I cannot fully trust he will keep his mouth shut. I hope you can take care of that problem for me as well."

"Of course, Commander," Adler replied, still fearing for his own life. "Should I release the prisoners right away?" he asked, feeling uneasy.

"No," Carson rushed to said. "Let me talk to them first. I have to explain what has happened. Plus, I can't release them right away. We don't know who else knows about that story. I may have to wait a few days."

"I should have known they were lying," the lieutenant said apologetically. "I've made a mistake as well. It will never happen again."

Carson looked straight at him; he knew Adler had deliberately decided to believe his story. Both Adler and Carson knew the two soldiers had told the truth. Carson was sure of that.

"It's over now. And it shall be forgotten forever."

Adler nodded in agreement.

"You have done well by keeping those rumors contained," Carson continued. "Perhaps we should start working on a good promotion. I'll personally take care of that. A monetary reward for your dedication to me and our country will be included."

Adler's eyes widened. He knew how to play the game ... he knew how to get ahead. He considered himself a smart man. He understood that the only way to get everything he wanted was by being close to those in power. He and so many others took the opportunity to achieve power and fortune at the cost of human lives. Adler didn't care much about the war anymore. He also couldn't care less if Alyse was in fact Jewish. As long as he got what he wanted out of the situation, he would believe anything.

Carson waited until Adler closed his office door before going straight to his desk. He filled up his glass with whiskey and chugged it back. He needed to think of what to do next. It was very clear to him that he had been compromised. He also knew that it would be hard to make everyone believe his story of conspiracy. But it was more than that. After listening to those two soldiers, it seemed like they were telling the truth. Everything made sense.

Carson took a few steps toward the window. Standing still, he observed all the movement happening outside. He felt numb, betrayed by his own brother and family in the worst possible way. They had committed an act of treason against their own country. Carson knew they would be killed if the truth came out. But after everything he had heard on that day, he worried more about himself than anyone else. He had to clear Alyse's and Hans's names for his own benefit.

Carson stayed alone in his office for many hours, thinking and planning his next move. He knew he needed to teach Hans a lesson. He was tired of getting in trouble because of him. *This time he went too far!!*

Although he was infuriated by the lies, he could never bring himself to do anything against his brother. The real problem was Alyse. Carson blamed her for the whole mess. It was easier for Carson to feel that way as it gave him a perfect excuse to justify his past actions. He felt disgusted by his attraction to a Jewish woman.

"She was just another woman," Carson said, thinking about the night they spent together, "She definitely deserves to be taught a lesson. She will pay for the audacity to be among the rest of us!"

The more he thought, the more Carson began to find a solution to his problem. As much as he felt killing Alyse would satisfy his pride and honor, he also knew he wanted to keep her alive and near him.

Carson drank another glass of whiskey and mulled over other disturbing thoughts. *I'll take care of Hans first. Then the Jew will learn what I'm capable of.*

He stormed out of his office, determined to put his plan into action.

CHAPTER 34

Hans lifted his head as he heard a door bouncing off of the concrete wall. He knew it had to be Carson.

He stood there listening as the footsteps got closer and closer. It didn't take long for him to confirm his suspicion. It was Carson standing outside the jail bars.

They stayed there silently, looking at one another for a few seconds. Carson was the one to break the silence.

"I should leave you there to rot until you die," he said in a cold tone of voice.

"Do whatever you want to me," Hans stood up, walking toward the metal bars. "But please, don't hurt her. It was my fault. Don't let anyone hurt her. I'm begging you."

"Ha," Carson laughed. "Save Alyse, or whatever her real name is. Of course not! How can you ask me that? There you are, not even knowing if they will kill you, and you still have the nerve to ask me to save a stupid Jew? You could have ruined me or, much worse! We could all be facing death right now! You committed an atrocious act against me and your country, Hans! You have completely lost your mind! I have always helped you, but you never change. You defended a Jew at the cost of our family's reputation and safety! And I thought you cared about me and considered me to be your brother! Can I still call you a brother after you have betrayed me?"

Hans realized then that Carson was fully aware of the truth.

"Kill me then. But don't let them hurt her. Her real name is Denna. She's Jewish … so what? What have they done to you? Nothing justifies what we are doing to them or the rest of the world."

"Shut up!" Carson replied furiously. "Keep your voice down! I should have dragged you out of Germany a long time ago! People like you no longer belong to this new great nation! Germany will be the world's supreme power. You will never understand that. Look at you! Look what you have done to yourself. All because you were trying to protect that Jewish whore!"

"Don't you ever say that!" Hans screamed, feeling anger take hold of him. "She's just an innocent girl, now alone in the world. We have taken away her family, her friends, and everything she once dreamed of or believed in! She is as good of a German as any of us!! You were blinded by vicious and dangerous propaganda, Carson! But you are right about one thing. I don't belong here in this filthy nation overtaken by fanaticism and hatred!"

"You should be killed for saying that! And you are wrong!" Carson was infuriated. "That is all that she is, Hans! A Jewish whore who has no business being alive, never mind inside our own family's house! She represents everything that is wrong with our country. She is trash. And trash needs to be disposed of!"

"If you hurt her," Hans said, looking straight at Carson's eyes, "I'll … I swear …."

"Do what?" Carson hollered at him. "You're so pathetic. There's nothing you can do now. Look at you! You're a prisoner. I'm the one who gives orders here! You don't get to decide anything! I guess all your efforts to keep her away from harm have failed."

"Don't you dare touch her, Carson! You can't do this to her!"

"Well," Carson said, straightening his uniform, "it's too late now. Nothing you can say will change the outcome. I have warned you too many times; you never listened. You would rather have yourself killed as well as your entire family, including me. You have betrayed me and your own country. You will stay here as my prisoner!"

"I don't care if you kill me! I just beg you to spare her! Whatever you need to do to satisfy your anger, do it against me. But let her live!"

"I don't think you're in the position to ask for anything right now!"

Instantly, Hans got his hands through the jail bars, grabbing Carson by his shirt.

"What are you going to do, Carson? I swear if anything happens to her …."

After a short struggle, Carson finally pushed himself away. He suddenly felt dizzy, surprised by what had just happened. They stood there staring at each other with hate in their eyes.

"She'll pay for what she has done," Carson said, trying to regain his composure. "She'll die fast, don't worry. Maybe that will be better than having her tortured to death, don't you think?"

"Don't you dare put your hands on her! Please don't do that! I'm begging you, Carson!"

Ignoring Hans's words, Carson simply turned around and walked away.

"I'll kill anyone who hurts her," Hans yelled out desperately. "I'll kill you. Don't you hurt her, Carson! Please, don't hurt her! Carson! Carson!"

Hans yelled relentlessly; his voice echoed off of the walls of the empty hallway, reflecting all the anger and fear that welled up inside him. At that point, he didn't care about anything else. He believed what Carson said; he could see the hate in his eyes. Denna was going to die. As a German man, he felt responsible for her tragic destiny. Hans hated his own people. He hated his own race. Feeling completely powerless and defeated, he started sobbing.

Not too far from there, Carson stopped in an isolated corner of the long hallway. He needed some time to recover from the emotional toll caused by his encounter with Hans. A sudden sharp pain in his heart bothered him. Hans was his best friend, and his betrayal hurt him deeply. It was the first time that he felt the weight of that war on his shoulder.

Exhausted, he breathed heavily, as he tried to compose himself. He considered those feelings a sign of weakness. He had to prepare himself to walk into Alyse's jail cell on the other side of the building. Inside his head, the word Denna echoed repeatedly. *Denna, her real name is Denna!*

Denna saw the door being opened abruptly. She held her breath in fear. It didn't take long for her to realize that the inevitable moment she dreaded had finally arrived.

Carson walked into the room with his chin held high. Right there, he wasn't Hans's brother anymore; he was a proud and fearful *Nazi Commander*, ready to do what he did best. He was trained to hurt and kill anyone who stood in his way.

Carson looked at Denna as if she was nothing. Despite his convictions, he still couldn't prevent his heart from beating fast.

Denna stood up slowly. She was ready for what she considered to be her last moments alive. But strangely, she no longer cared. She was prepared to tell the truth. It would be the end of her torment.

Carson took a quick look around that room. But in truth, he was just trying to hide his feelings. He couldn't let Denna know how much he still cared about her, something he tried to deny to himself.

"I hear we still have one last Jew walking around this facility," Carson said coldly. "I figured I could help to solve the problem."

Denna didn't take her eyes off him. She kept her head up in defiance.

"So, Denna ..." Carson continued, full of sarcasm. "That is your name, right? Your real Jewish name. Well, I hope you're happy for having destroyed my entire family."

"What happened to Hans?" she rushed to ask while trying to hold back her tears. "Where is he? What did you do to him?"

Carson laughed. "What have I done to him?" I'm tired of those useless questions. There's only one person responsible for all of this mess. You know who that is, don't you? Answer me!"

With a heavy heart, Denna just kept looking at him. She did feel all the responsibility, way more than he could ever know.

"Hans is not your problem anymore," Carson warned, trying to sound ruthless and indifferent. "But he'll surely regret covering up for a Jew. Because that is all that you are … a miserable Jew who should be eliminated!"

"So, kill me now! But don't do anything to him. It wasn't his fault. He didn't do anything. Punish me; that is what you're looking to do. Here I am! I'm ready!"

"Shut up," Carson said, infuriated, walking toward her. "You don't open your mouth until I say so. You two are pathetic! Hans has compromised our entire family because of you. And you will pay for that!"

Denna stood still, looking at him with disgust.

"Do you think death scares me after all I have been through? Look at you, you miserable creature. A man who turns against those who love him, a man whose greed and thirst for power justifies the most horrible actions. The killing of entire families, children, and innocent people – you're nothing but a monster." You're pitiful!

Denna saw his face paling as she spoke.

Acting instinctively, Carson walked quickly toward her, his hands grabbed her neck with hatred, as he violently pushed her toward the wall.

Denna put her hands on top of Carson's, trying to break free.

Carson felt the intensity of that touch. The proximity of her body confused his thoughts. He knew he would never be able to kill her. He just wanted to hurt her for all that she had meant to him.

As he felt tears filling his own eyes, he desperately fought against the deep love he still had for her.

Noticing her suffocating, he suddenly let go of her neck. He turned around, feeling embarrassed for being so weak. He didn't recognize himself anymore. He didn't understand why he couldn't simply kill her. *She is just a Jew, a filthy Jew*, Carson repeated over and over again.

Denna stood there coughing, gasping for air.

Carson looked back at her, trying to demonstrate his control over the situation.

"You will pay for your audacity of trying to be part of my family! I will make your days hell."

Denna looked right into his eyes. "Why don't you just do it now?" she said with a shaky voice, tears rolled down her face. "Let's end this, right here! You and me!"

Caught by surprise, Carson didn't know what to do next. He didn't want to appear weak before her.

He slowly grabbed the gun off his belt and pointed it at her. His hands were trembling like never before. His vision blurred by unshed tears, tears which he couldn't explain and didn't fully understand.

Denna stood still, looking at the gun. She truly believed he would shoot her. She couldn't see the emotions that churned inside of him.

"I could kill you so fast! You mean nothing to me. Do you hear me? You never meant anything to me!"

Denna wasn't expecting those words from him. Looking right into his eyes, she recognized that he was also fighting against his feelings.

"I know," she said in a low tone of voice. "How could you ever have cared for me? How could I care for you? Love you … it is impossible, isn't it?"

Carson didn't quite grasp the meaning of her words. Could she also love him?

"People like you are incapable of feeling such a thing. So, just go ahead and kill me, as you have done to so many others. Isn't that your specialty, Commander?"

Carson's face went straight from a deep red to a pale white. He felt his head spinning; his hand felt heavy. He couldn't breathe.

"Shut up!" Carson finally yelled. "I told you to keep your mouth shut! I'm the one who's deciding things here. If dying is what you want, I'm not going to kill you. That would be an easy way out for you. You will suffer slowly. You will pay for your nerve to live among us true Germans. To me, you're nothing, a nobody. Do you understand that? You don't decide your destiny anymore. From now on, you will learn how to obey orders, only my orders. Don't ever forget that! I'll make sure you are reminded of who you are every day, just another filthy worthless Jew!"

"I hate you," Denna yelled back at him, choking on her tears. "You're nothing but a murderer, a cold-hearted killer. I hate you! I'll always hate you!"

Carson froze; without even noticing, he had lowered his hand. Conflicting thoughts rushed through his tormented mind, spreading an excruciating pain throughout his heart and soul. He felt dizzy again. He couldn't think straight. And for a brief moment, Carson felt like holding her. He felt like escaping with her to a faraway place, away from the war.

Aware of his own inability to make a decision, he could only say, "I hope you enjoy the last days of your life alone." Then, he rushed toward the door and left.

Denna slowly slid down the wall. She stayed there, lying against the cold floor, sobbing.

Carson walked away. His heart was pounding faster, his hands still shaking. So much had happened and he felt even more confused. All he wanted was to be left alone to think.

As he drove home afterward, his mind wandered in different directions. He soon spotted his fiancée's car parked in the driveway, making him even angrier. That was the last thing he wanted to see at that moment.

"Where have you been?" Adalie asked as she approached him. "My friends and even my own family have been talking about you neglecting me."

Carson looked at her impatiently. "Get out of my way," he said, walking toward his home.

"You can't treat me like that," she said indignantly. "I'm not one of your whores!"

Carson turned around and walked quickly toward her. She stepped back in fear.

"What's wrong with you?"

"What's wrong with me?" Carson asked sarcastically. "You! I can't stand looking at your face anymore! I can't stand your stupid voice, your irritating presence. Get out of here!"

"Who do you think you are to treat me like this? I am not leaving until …."

Unable to control the anger growing inside him any longer, Carson got his gun from his belt and pointed it straight at her. She looked at him in horror.

"I told you to leave! Why are you standing there? Get out of here before it's too late?"

Without saying a word, she turned around and ran back to her car. Carson stood there until the dust settled around him.

The sun started its descent, slowly disappearing into the horizon. Just like Carson, millions of people suffered alone, trapped in their own nightmares. One that would continue after the morning came; one that seemed never to go away.

CHAPTER 35

It was a cool September evening when Francine suddenly woke up feeling intense pain in her belly. She kept changing positions, trying to get more comfortable. But despite her efforts, the pain grew stronger by the minute.

Noticing that her situation was getting worse, Francine understood it was time to wake up her mother. The baby seemed to be ready to be born early!

At first, it was very hard for Nicole to accept the story Francine had told her. It was quite a shock to know that the man her daughter claimed to love was German. She was aware that Hans had saved her daughter's life, but still, she didn't trust his true intentions. In her mind, Hans's feelings toward Francine could have been only a momentary attraction that would soon fade away. Nicole thought that her daughter was too innocent and naïve to see the truth.

But none of that mattered at that moment. Francine tried to focus on the baby that was about to come. It took all her strength to walk toward her mother's bedroom. A painful contraction made her scream, waking up Nicole.

"I think the baby is coming," that was all Francine could say.

"I see! Well, we need to get ready!" Nicole said, getting up quickly and helping Francine back to her room.

"Terese, could you bring us a large bowl with hot water?" Nicole asked her sister, who had just appeared on the hallway. "Grab us some clean sheets and sterilized scissors too."

Francine shut her eyes for a moment, wishing Hans was there by her side. She started to regret hiding something so significant from him.

She moved her head back as the pain increased. Strong nausea and weakness made things even harder for her.

"You have to push again, Francine!" her mother insisted. "You have to be strong! You can do this!"

She tried to push, but the baby wasn't coming out in the right position.

Nicole looked at her daughter with concern. She knew the situation was critical.

"Francine … you have to work with me to save your baby. You have to push harder!"

"Hans," Francine whispered. "Hans …"

"Francine! Listen to me! You can do this. Don't give up; you're so strong. You can do it!"

From inside the room, they could hear the rain falling. The storm had finally arrived.

Francine heard the thunder echoing inside the house. Somehow it seemed to have revived her. She knew she had to try harder.

Holding one of her aunt's hands, Francine gathered all her strength and pushed.

"You have to try again, Francine," Nicole insisted. "Come on. One more push!"

Francine screamed loudly in agony.

They all went quiet for a few seconds. Then the sound of a baby crying filled the room, and then murmurs through tears of joy accompanied the cries of the newborn.

Francine sighed in relief. A big smile covered her face when her baby boy was placed in her arms. She had never felt so close to Hans as she did at that moment. She felt the deepest and most profound love.

"He's beautiful," Terese said among tears.

Nicole smiled at her daughter and her new grandson.

"Have you picked a name yet?"

Francine nodded.

"Julian," she said proudly. "His name will be Julian!"

Amidst all that joy, they greeted the doctor, who arrived a little too late. He checked mother and child, confirming everything was fine. A few hours later, everyone was asleep in that residence.

Francine heard the creaking of the bedroom door. It was already morning, and her mother was bringing her breakfast.

"Bonjour. How are my lovely daughter and beautiful grandson doing?"

Francine smiled at her. "Bonjour. We are doing fine!"

Nicole slowly approached her, planting a kiss on her forehead.

"He's so beautiful," she said, smiling at her grandson. "Like an angel. I can't wait for him to wake up so I can hold him in my arms again."

Francine looked at her son, feeling so much love.

"You should eat, Francine. You must be really weak. You must eat really well from now on."

Francine agreed.

"What's wrong?" Nicole asked her, noticing the sad look on her daughter's face.

"I wish he could be here with me. I need to tell him as soon as possible!"

"Well, we were not expecting the baby to come so soon!"

"I know; I will write Hans's parents another letter. Would you please ask Fernand to deliver it for me?"

"Of course! Also, keep in mind that the war will end one day," Nicole continued. "It has to. Things are already starting to change."

"But even if it happens, I don't want to leave Switzerland without Hans!"

Nicole had a serious look on her face. "I understand, but let's not make any decisions now." In her mind, she feared Francine would have a huge disappointment regarding Hans. She didn't want her daughter to get hurt. But it was more than that. Nicole knew that Francine's father would never accept the situation. He would never accept that his daughter was in love with a man they still considered to be their enemy. There was still a war to be won, and the Allies had a lot of work ahead of them.

And so, Francine didn't waste any time and wrote a long letter to the Schulzes, narrating her story with Hans. She finally told them about her pregnancy and the birth of her son, their grandson. She explained to them her reasons for keeping it a secret, she didn't want anyone to worry and make rushed decisions. Francine kindly asked them to inform Hans about the arrival of his son, mentioning they were doing well. She wanted Hans to know they would wait for him there in Switzerland. And finally, she promised them a visit, so that they could meet their grandchild.

But what Francine and the Schulzes didn't know was that Hans's situation had changed completely. At that time, it was Hans who needed to be saved.

CHAPTER 36

Carson woke up early the next day. He knew he had to put his plan into action and there was a lot to be done.

He wouldn't kill her; that was the only thing he was sure of. *She'll be kept alive as a prisoner so that she can suffer more,* Carson thought, lying to himself about the true reasons that led him to make that decision. *But where will I keep her?* He knew he couldn't leave her at the military base.

Deep inside his heart, all he wanted was to keep her close to him, in a safe place where he could have full control and authority over her. As for Hans, Carson wanted to keep him locked up for a few more weeks to teach him a lesson. Hans would try to find Denna, and Carson couldn't take that chance.

He stayed in his home office for a while, finalizing the details of his sordid scheme.

A few days later, in the middle of the night, Denna suddenly woke up to the sound of footsteps entering her dark room. Carson quickly walked toward her with a cloth in his hands. He placed it over her mouth and nose. She struggled for a brief moment, recognizing his face as she slowly started closing her eyes.

Carson pretended to kill her, shooting at the wall. He wrapped her body carefully in a bedsheet. He placed the blood he had taken from the hospital all over her body and on the floor. It was the perfect idea in case anyone still had suspicions.

Carson told his most loyal soldiers to carry the body to an ambulance. "A prisoner has died," he explained. "I'll personally take care of the disposal."

The soldiers did as they were told. No one would dare to question the Commander.

Carson drove the ambulance out of the military station. He arrived at his house soon after, parking the vehicle as close to the entryway as possible.

He looked around his house, trying to make sure no one was there before bringing Denna's body inside. He then carried her upstairs to what would be her new room.

"You will learn how to respect me," Carson said, looking at her unconscious face. "You will learn one way or another."

With his arms trembling, Carson carefully placed her on a bed. He stood there staring at her for a few seconds. He still wasn't sure if he had made the right decision. Nonetheless, he knew there was no other way to keep her away from harm and under his sole control.

The sunlight shone on Denna's delicate face as she slowly opened her eyes. She looked around, trying to recognize where she was. At first, it only seemed she had woken up from a bad dream. She found herself lying on a comfortable bed in a completely different place.

There was a strange taste in her mouth. She tried to get up but she couldn't. She felt dizzy and nauseous.

It didn't take too long for her to hear a noise. Someone was approaching the room.

Having no idea where she was or who that could be, she apprehensively waited for the door to be opened. But, to her surprise, only a tray was being pushed through a small hole at the bottom of it.

"Who is there?" Denna called out.

No one answered.

"Who's there?" she asked again. The footsteps started to retreat.

She got up slowly, still feeling unwell. With unstable steps, she finally made it to the door. She hesitated for a moment before her hand reached out for the doorknob. She turned it carefully, only to realize the door was locked. She was still a prisoner.

Her attention was then directed to the tray on the floor. She hadn't eaten in over a day. She bent her knees to grab the slices of bread and the cup of water. Still feeling weak, she headed straight back to bed.

She looked around the room, wondering how she had ended up there. Slowly, she started to recollect the events of the preceding evening. *It was Carson! It had to be him*, she thought, remembering that she saw his face before falling asleep. She couldn't understand why he would spare her life when he had so much hatred inside his heart. She had no idea what to expect.

As days went by, Denna curiously listened to the footsteps as they approached the room. Food, clean clothes, books, and magazines were often pushed through the small hole at the bottom of the door. She wondered if someone was helping Carson. He wouldn't be able to stay away from his work for that long.

But what Denna didn't know was that the mysterious person who was taking care of her was someone she already knew quite well. It was Mrs. Kaufmann, Hans's family's housemaid, who was brought there by Carson himself. He had dismissed almost all his previous employees and forced Mrs. Kaufmann to work for him.

Mrs. Kaufmann also had no idea who was being kept behind those walls. She had received specific instructions to never engage in any conversation with the person being locked inside that room. She was horrified that Carson held someone captive but had no other choice but to keep quiet and follow the powerful Commander's orders.

As the weeks went by, Carson started to feel more comfortable with the situation - his plan was going well, Denna seemed to be compliant with the new arrangements and so did Mrs. Kaufmann.

But deep inside Carson's heart, things were far more complicated.

Two very contradictory feelings tore him apart: one that wanted to hold her, kiss her, and yet another that felt the need to hurt her, to cause her pain. During those moments, he felt like visiting Denna's room and committing another act of violence.

Several times he came close to it. At other times, he got his gun and thought about killing her, ending his torment. Carson was no longer the same man from months earlier. He had trouble sleeping and trouble staying awake. With the pressure of the war, things only got worse. He had to stay away for long periods of time and therefore away from Denna. Every time that happened, his anxiety increased; he felt like he was suffocating.

He feared someone would steal her from him. He feared someone would find out the truth. Quite often, he would wake up covered in sweat, feeling agitated and frightened. He would dream of her screaming at him, wishing he was dead. Other times he would dream she was dead. Slowly, Carson became delusional, taking his anger out on anyone who was close to him or dared to cross his path.

As for Denna, after putting all the pieces together, she was then sure it had to be Carson who put her in that house. She would often hear footsteps rushing back and forth by the door at night. She could see a shadow underneath the door. She could almost feel his presence. Denna would breathe in relief every time the door remained closed. Yet, she would always wonder about the reasons why he kept her alive.

But her situation was far worse than it appeared. Denna noticed something else happening to her. Something she had already suspected but couldn't confirm. She remembered one of her mother's conversations with one of her friends about pregnancy. Denna had the same symptoms. She felt desperate. With tears often running down her face, she wondered about her future and the possible child that could be growing inside of her.

On the other side of town, the autumn chill made a young man's body shiver. Hans was alone in the same jail cell.

Carson had made things a little more comfortable for him. He had been given a bed, a table, and even books. He knew Carson was the one responsible for keeping him alive. But, at that time, Hans could only feel hate toward him. He was sure something horrible had happened to Denna. He blamed himself as much as he blamed his brother.

In his loneliness, terrible thoughts of vengeance filled his mind. He kept thinking about how he was going to punish every single person responsible for hurting Denna. These thoughts, with the possibility of seeing Francine again, gave him the motivation to stay alive.

Not even in his dreams he was able to escape his torment. He could see Denna's face, as she ran away frightened, hunted by Nazi soldiers. In vain, he kept running after her, but no matter how hard he tried, he could never reach her. He would then wake up covered in sweat, his mind troubled, his body aching.

He knew he couldn't do anything to help her. Hans was convinced it was too late.

CHAPTER 37

Alfred and Elga still waited for news about Hans. Each hour that passed was another moment of agony and uncertainty.

"We have to go back! Something is not right," Elga said, worried. "It has been weeks since the last time we talked to him."

"And no one seems to be home," Alfred said, equally concerned. "Not even Mrs. Kaufmann is picking up the phone. Let's wait a few more days, and then I will go back."

"I am going with you," Elga rushed to say.

"No, you are not. We don't know how bad things are over there, and we don't need you to get involved. We also need someone here to communicate with Francine, especially now with the arrival of our grandson!"

"She is also very worried about him. It still amazes me how they reunited in Germany after so long. Now, they have a son! And Hans doesn't even know about it!"

"And we still need to meet him. She asked us to wait another month until the baby grows a little more as it was born early. And that is another reason you should stay here, Elga! We have a grandson, and we both can't leave him behind."

"Of course not. But I also don't want to leave my husband and son at the hands of those lunatics!"

"And how about Francine? Someone needs to stay here and communicate with her. I should go alone!"

"Let's write her a letter and leave it by our front door," Elga persisted. "We can ask Victoria to take care of that matter for us once we are gone. She has always taken care of our house really well. That way, we will be able to keep communicating with Francine. Something tells me that Hans is in trouble, and I don't want to stay here simply waiting!"

Alfred didn't say anything else; he also shared these feelings. Something was very wrong, and no one in Germany was replying to them.

A few more days went by without any news from Hans. Alfred prepared for his trip back home. After a lot of discussions, he was finally able to convince Elga to stay behind. It was a very sad situation for them. They used to love living in their country. But everything changed after the Nazi regime took over the government. Things started to converge down a dangerous road. Unfortunately, only a few Germans were able to recognize that.

The sky was covered with heavy clouds, promising a storm on that cold and gray October morning. Alfred said his goodbyes to Elga and headed out.

A crowd waited anxiously near the train tracks while Swiss soldiers carefully watched every movement. They knew they would be subject to German authorities on the border. That was never a pleasant encounter, even for those who were Germans.

Alfred stood among the crowd. He had a strange sensation like it could be the last time he would ever set foot in Switzerland. Like Elga, he felt that something terrible was happening to Hans. He would do anything he could to help him. He would give his own life to save his son.

The train had finally arrived, cutting its way through the fog. Alfred was about to board when he felt a hand touching his arm.

"Elga?" he asked, surprised. "What are you doing here?"

"I am going with you," she said decisively. "Hans is my son, too."

An officer right in front of them waited impatiently for the tickets, Alfred knew that was not the time for an argument.

"You shouldn't have come," he whispered.

"We will stay together. Something tells me Hans needs us both!"

Alfred sighed as he held Elga's hand in his own. She looked at him and smiled. They were there together, ready to stand up and fight for whatever lay between them and their son.

Hans's parents arrived at their residence only to find it nearly empty. Only one employee had remained there, their loyal driver and gardener Eugene.

"What has happened here? Where is my Hans? Where is everyone?"

"I don't know much, madam, but I am extremely relieved to see you both!" he replied sadly. "All I know is that some SS officers came one day and took both Alyse and Hans. They were both arrested; there was nothing I could do. I haven't heard from them since. Carson came one day and told me he was taking care of the situation but that I wasn't supposed to say a word to anyone about it, not even to you. He warned me that people were watching the house and could intercept letters and phone calls. I wanted to inform you, but I was afraid someone could find out and complicate the situation even more. Things here have been very strange. No one really knows what's going on. And then, well … Carson came one day and took Mrs. Kaufmann to his own house. I didn't understand why. She stopped by one day and told me Carson demanded her to stay there and that she was very afraid."

The more Eugene spoke, the more tears poured down Elga's troubled face.

They couldn't believe what they were hearing. Denna had been arrested, and so had Hans.

Alfred shook his head. He knew his son's life was seriously at risk. He thought Denna could already be dead.

"My son?" Elga could barely choke out the words. "What will they do to him? I knew something was wrong. This is what I have feared the most."

"Where are they now, Eugene? Where is Carson?"

"Mr. Alfred, Carson only informed me they were being held at the military station. And Mrs. Kauffmann told me Carson travels to Berlin frequently, staying there for many days at a time. I haven't seen him in weeks."

"We have to find him! He's the only one who seems to know what happened to them."

"We have to find a way to see Hans!" Elga cried. "Carson wouldn't let anything happen to him, right?"

"Of course not," Alfred said, trying to calm her down. *I really hope not!* he thought.

Alfred understood the gravity of the situation. He knew the SS were ruthless when it came to punishing people, even their own kind. He knew Hans was in deep trouble, likely more than Eugene had let on.

"Let's go to Carson's house first," Alfred said, turning around and rushing toward the car.

Two soldiers guarded Carson's house. One of them recognized Alfred and Elga.

"Good afternoon," Alfred said.

"Good afternoon, sir," one of them said.

"We came to see Carson."

"He is not here, sir. He is out of town."

Alfred wasn't convinced.

"We need to speak with Mrs. Kaufmann as well."

"No one is allowed in, sir," the soldier said hesitantly. He knew they were basically Carson's parents.

"I am Carson's father, as you know. Are you telling me that my own son has denied me entrance?"

The soldier didn't know what to do. He wasn't given any orders regarding Carson's family.

"When Carson comes back, I will make sure to report such an incident," Alfred continued. "And you know how harshly he punishes mistakes."

The soldier knew he could get into trouble for not letting them in, but he still hesitated.

"It will be a quick visit," Elga said softly. "We will just talk to Mrs. Kaufmann."

"Open the gate," he finally told the other guard.

Alfred and Elga knocked at the door, but no one answered. After a few minutes, Alfred decided to walk around to the back of the house.

"What are you doing?" Elga asked him.

"Breaking through the window. The soldiers acknowledged that Mrs. Kaufmann was in the house. We need to talk to her."

It didn't take long for Alfred to climb through the kitchen window and open the door for his wife.

They headed for the living room and then to Carson's private office. The door was locked. It was right at that moment that a noise coming from upstairs caught their attention.

They walked fast toward the staircase and immediately recognized the familiar face turning the corner. It was Mrs. Kaufmann, who was about to go downstairs with a tray in her hands.

She looked at both Alfred and Elga and screamed. The tray fell out of her hands, dropping to the ground.

"Mr. and Mrs. Schulze? I am so sorry. I didn't know you were back. You scared me. Let me clean this mess, and …."

"Hello, Mrs. Kaufmann," Elga rushed to say. "Don't worry about that. We just want to know what is going on here. Are you all right?"

"Well …" Mrs. Kaufmann hesitated to answer. "I am fine, madam. I feel better now that I see you are back. A lot of things have happened here, and I don't know much …."

"What things are you talking about?" Alfred interrupted her. "Why did Carson bring you here?"

Afraid to speak any more than she should, Mrs. Kaufmann couldn't articulate one word.

"What is going on in this house? Where is Carson? Is he here?"

"I am so sorry, madam," Mrs. Kaufmann looked down. "I don't know what is going on here. And Carson left for Berlin for a few days again."

"We need to talk to him right away!"

"I understand, sir! But I don't know when he will be back. Well, let me clean this mess quickly," Mrs. Kaufmann said, looking at the dishes spread all over the staircase.

"I wouldn't worry about that now," Elga said, continuing to move upstairs. "It is all right. We are back, and you can come with us."

"I can't," Mrs. Kaufmann replied fearfully. "He won't let me. He will be furious!"

"Carson? That is nonsense. He had no right to force you to work for him!"

"No, sir. But he has been acting very strange lately. As if … well … as if he has gone mad. I'm sorry to say that, but he isn't the same!"

"What do you mean?" Alfred asked.

"I cannot say anything." Mrs. Kaufmann started to wipe away her tears with her apron.

"He cannot do anything to you now that we are back," Elga affirmed.

"What has gotten into that boy's head?" Alfred growled. "He won't do anything against you, I promise. But now you have to tell us everything you know so we can find Hans."

"Oh, Hans! They have taken our Hans."

"Yes, we now know about it!" Elga said. "That is why we need your help!"

"But I don't know much."

"You said you couldn't say anything; what were you talking about? Why would Carson threaten you? And why did he bring you here in the first place?"

Mrs. Kaufmann stood in silence as Alfred waited for an answer. She didn't know what to do. She still feared Carson's wrath.

"If Carson is not here, to whom did you take that food?" Alfred continued.

"I don't know," she replied with a desperate look on her face.

"What do you mean you don't know? Is he here or not?"

"No, sir. It is not him."

Alfred wasn't convinced. He headed straight upstairs toward Carson's room.

"No, sir. Please, don't."

"Carson!" Alfred screamed out loud. "Carson, where are you? Come out! It is me, Alfred. We need to talk. I am not leaving."

Denna got up from her bed as if she had been struck by lightning. She had heard a noise and then some voices. She couldn't make out much of it until she heard the word Alfred. She walked fast toward the door.

"Carson?" Alfred continued, opening one of the bedroom doors. "It's me, Alfred!"

"He is not here, sir," Mrs. Kaufmann insisted as she followed him.

Ignoring every word from her, Alfred continued to move along the hallway, opening one door at a time.

"Where is he?" Alfred asked Mrs. Kaufmann, not believing a word she said.

"I told you, Mr. Alfred, he is in Berlin."

"So, to whom were you taking that food?" Elga asked her, repeating her husband's words.

"I don't know. I just follow orders, and I am not sure who …."

Before she could finish her sentence, a faint voice came from behind one of the doors.

"Mr. Alfred?" Denna said.

"Who is that?" Elga said, rushing to the door.

"I don't know. I never get to see who is behind that door."

"Mrs. Schulze?" Denna repeated.

"Denna?" Elga finally recognized the voice. "Denna! Is it you?"

"Yes, it is me!"

Elga tried to open the door.

"Why is she locked in?"

"Who is Denna?" Mrs. Kaufmann questioned him, not used to the name, as everyone else knew Denna by the name Alyse.

"Where is the key?" Elga asked her impatiently.

"Only Carson has it," Mrs. Kaufmann said, feeling very confused. She had never understood why Carson was keeping a prisoner in his own house.

"Please help me," Denna said.

"We will," Elga rushed to say. "What have they done to you?"

"I will break into the room," Alfred said. "Move away from the door, Denna."

"Please don't, sir. Carson will kill us all!"

"I do not fear him!"

"Wait, Alfred," Elga said, thinking. "Wait for a moment."

"What do you mean? She is being held as a prisoner."

"But she is also …" Elga hesitated to say.

Alfred sighed, trying to calm down. He knew Elga was right.

He looked at Mrs. Kaufmann again.

"Why didn't you say anything?"

"I don't know who this Denna girl is," Mrs. Kaufmann said, even more confused. "Plus, Carson has threatened to kill me if I tell anyone that he is keeping someone here. It makes me feel awful to be part of this, but there was no other way. I don't know who she is or why she is being kept here. I am so sorry."

Alfred looked at Elga. He understood that Mrs. Kaufmann didn't know that Alyse was actually the same person as Denna, and that was a good thing.

"Mrs. Kaufmann," Elga continued. "Could you make us some tea, please? We could use some for our nerves."

She hesitated for a few seconds, but she knew she couldn't do anything else but follow orders.

They waited until she walked downstairs to continue.

"What should we do?" Elga asked her husband. "We cannot take her home. It's not safe anymore."

"I don't know," Alfred said, shaking his head, still trying to make sense of that situation.

"I can't believe this! Why did he bring her here?"

"Listen, Denna," Alfred said. "We will find a way to get you out of here."

"How are you?" Elga asked her. "Are you hurt?"

"I am all right now," Denna said through her tears. "But how did you find me here? And, where am I?"

A million thoughts crossed Elga and Alfred's minds.

"Has anyone heard about Hans?" Denna rushed to ask.

"We don't know much. We just got here today," Alfred explained. "We have to wait for Carson to come back. But I will find a way out of this mess."

There was silence for a few seconds.

"What is happening here?" Denna asked them again.

"Well, it's a long story," Elga replied. "But believe it or not, you are actually at Carson's house. And it is Mrs. Kaufmann who has been taking care of you. But she doesn't know it is you, Denna. Apparently, no one knows you are here!"

Denna had confirmed her suspicion. Carson was the one who had brought her there *but to his own house?* She thought, astonished.

"It's so hard to believe this! All of this!" Alfred said.

"I know. And that's why you have to be very careful," Denna said, concerned. "Actually, you should just save Hans and run away from here. As for me, there isn't much hope. All of you have already overexposed yourselves for me. And I don't know what Carson has in mind!"

"Don't say such things, Denna," Elga said. "We will find a way to get you both out."

"How long have you been here?" Alfred asked.

"I don't know for sure. Maybe two months?"

"Dear God! I wish we could take you right now!" Elga said.

"Me too. But I don't think it is possible or safe for any of us. You have to think about Hans now and nothing else! I feel so terrible for everything that has happened to him. It was my fault."

They could hear her sobbing through the door.

"Don't say that, Denna. It is not your fault for wanting to live."

"You did nothing wrong! Do not blame yourself for all the horrendous crimes being committed by our people," Alfred added. "And trust me, this time, we won't leave without you two! But for now, you will need to stay here in his house a while longer. I will think of a plan!"

"I understand. But what about Hans?" Denna asked.

"No one knows for sure. We think he's still being held at Carson's military station," Alfred continued. "At least that is what Eugene heard from Carson himself. And that's why we need to talk to him as soon as possible. Carson has a lot of explaining to do. I will get all the answers from him one way or the other. And I don't care what I have to do to get both of you out of this situation."

"I just don't understand why he is keeping you here!" Elga said. "There is so much we still don't know."

"I have been wondering the same thing myself," Denna replied.

But before they could continue their conversation, they heard Mrs. Kaufmann announce that the tea was ready downstairs.

"We have to go to avoid suspicion. Do not communicate with Mrs. Kaufmann!" Alfred requested. "She doesn't know who you are, and it's safer this way. We will come back to see you as soon as possible."

"All right, I understand. I am so happy to hear your voices."

"At least we know you are here, hidden from everyone else! Take care of yourself. We will be back soon!"

"Be brave, Denna," Elga soothed. "We will be back. You are not alone anymore."

Alfred and Elga walked away slowly. They knew they had to talk to Mrs. Kaufmann and give her instructions on how to proceed.

"You should not say anything to anybody," Alfred advised her. "This has to be a secret. No one should know about it, or our lives will be at risk! Do you understand?" Mrs. Kaufmann nodded in agreement.

"You must continue to take care of this girl the best you can. We will come to visit often. But as soon as Carson returns, we have to be informed. Find an excuse to leave the house and come to us!"

"Sure, I can do that, sir! But that could be weeks from now."

"We don't know that. As for now, we can only hope it won't take that long!"

Despite the severity of that whole situation, Alfred and Elga returned home feeling more hopeful. Denna was alive, and for some mysterious reason, Carson had spared her life. That meant only one thing: Carson could still help them!

CHAPTER 38

The first snowflakes already covered the ground, but time went by very slowly for Alfred and Elga as they waited for Carson's return. They had no confirmation that Hans was still locked inside the military base. They tried everything in their power to enter the prisoner detention area to try to find him, but no one was allowed there without Carson's approval.

Carson had arrived home during the last week of November. He had been gone for too long and was concerned about his new guest. But not much had changed inside him. That same love and hate struggle haunted his mind.

He was talking to Mrs. Kaufmann when they heard the doorbell ring. He wasn't expecting any visitors.

"Who could that be?" Carson wondered.

Mrs. Kaufmann avoided looking at him. She walked quickly toward the door.

"Mr. and Mrs. Schulze?" she said, pretending to be surprised to see them.

Carson felt all the color drain from his face.

"Where is Carson?" Mr. Alfred didn't waste any time. "We saw his car outside."

Mrs. Kaufmann couldn't say a word; her entire body was shaking.

Carson stood there in shock. They were the last two people he expected to see.

"Well, we need to talk to … you!" Alfred said, pushing his way in before seeing Carson standing a few steps in front of him. "What are you two doing here?" Carson asked coldly. "I cannot believe you came back!"

"Is that how you talk to your second mother and father?" Elga replied in a sad voice.

"I am sorry. But in the current state of affairs, you must know it's very dangerous for you two to be here."

"We have come to see Hans," Elga insisted. "He is still imprisoned, isn't he?"

Carson took a deep breath. He still felt deeply hurt by all their lies and deceit.

"What is happening here?" Alfred asked impatiently.

"So, you dare to ask me what is happening here?" Carson asked, chuckling.

They all looked at Mrs. Kaufmann, who was still standing there, not knowing where to go or what to do.

"You can leave now," Carson ordered.

They waited in silence as she walked out of the house.

"I hope you don't mind me bringing Mrs. Kaufmann here," Carson added, noticing the angry look on Alfred's face. "There was no one else in your house besides Eugene. I thought it would be good for her."

"You can stop that right now, Carson. We already know that's a lie!"

"A lie? You want to talk now about lies?" Carson replied furiously.

"We should go to the library! I don't want anyone to hear us," Elga intervened.

The three of them walked to the library quietly, already anticipating the seriousness of that talk.

"We found it very strange that you brought Mrs. Kauffmann here," Elga started.

"She can definitely go back with you now that you two are here," Carson said, feeling very uncomfortable with the situation. "Although, I hope you change your minds and go back to Switzerland as soon as possible. Things have changed, as you probably know by now."

"And that was the reason why we came back! Are you asking us to leave Hans behind in a jail cell?" Alfred said with authority. "I am not leaving without my son, your brother. If you still can remember that!"

"Where is he? Is he still at the military base?" Elga rushed to ask.

"Oh, so you want to talk about that? You come in here and act like you have done nothing wrong! And you still expect me to explain things to you?"

"It is not like that, Carson!" Elga tried to calm him down. "You have to understand that what we did …."

"Understand? What is there to understand besides betrayal?"

"Don't talk to her like that!" Alfred demanded.

They stared at one another defiantly.

"Let's all calm down, please! But, of course, you already know what we have done. But that's not why we came here! What was done is already in the past, and we can't change it. We had our reasons …."

"You talk as if you haven't committed a crime!" Carson replied to her, shaking his head. "The situation is far more complicated than you think."

"Germany is committing the crimes! Not me, not your mother, and much less Hans and that innocent girl!" Alfred shouted, already tired of that useless argument.

Carson looked at him, making sure Alfred could see all the anger he was hiding inside.

But before he could reply, Elga approached him, reaching out for one of his hands.

"We need your help to get Hans out of that prison! That's all we ask. Please, Carson! We all know our opinions won't change, so there is no need to argue any further."

Carson removed his hands from hers before walking toward his desk.

"You have all gone mad!"

"What's happening to Hans?" Elga asked as tears already rolled down her face.

Noticing the distress he caused her, Carson tried his best to calm down.

"Some people became aware of what was happening in your house while I was in Berlin. Unfortunately, when I found out, it was already too late! I still think some of them could be watching us! All of us! I tried my best to contain that situation, but there were no guarantees. And that was the reason I had to keep Hans away from everyone … hidden in a jail cell."

"But you could …."

"What you all have done was too dangerous! Too serious!" Carson yelled. "Hans would have been killed if it wasn't for my intervention … again! Now he is paying for what he has done. Even so, after your betrayal and lies, I wouldn't let him rot in there or have anyone harm him. You should know that! I just want to wait a while longer until that story is forgotten."

Elga looked at Alfred, feeling a little more relieved.

"You are our son as well! Hans's brother! So why are you doing this to you family? Alfred asked him.

"Things wouldn't have been this way if all of you had stayed away from certain matters. The only people to blame are yourselves! You never bothered to care what could have happened to us. And all because of a simple Jew! A piece of trash, worthless! For her, you all lied to me! You are lucky I considered you my family!"

"Considered?" Elga repeated, disappointed.

"Now ... look at us!! There isn't much that can be done now!"

Alfred looked down and tried to control his anger. He knew Carson would not understand his outrage.

"We trust you to do the right thing," Elga said, looking right into his eyes.

"Too bad I cannot say the same about you!"

"And talking about mistrust and lies," Alfred said with disgust, "where is she?"

Carson looked at them, astonished. *Have they found out about Denna?* he thought in fear.

"We consider her to be a part of our family!" Elga added.

"That's absurd! A dirty Jew will never be part of our family. Never! Do you hear me?"

"You owe us some respect!" Finally, it was Alfred's turn to yell back. "We haven't raised you to act like this!"

"You have done a poor job then! You don't know the meaning of respect. You betrayed me and your country!"

"How could you say such a thing?" Elga said through her tears. "We love you. You are our son, too! You gave us no choice but to hide the truth from you. As a Nazi man, you hate all of them! Why? What have they done to you?"

Carson stood there quiet. Deep inside, even he didn't know exactly why or how he could grow such hatred inside of him.

"I don't want to argue anymore. We didn't come here for that," Alfred tried to regain his focus. "We just want to know where she is. We can take care of her. We need to talk to Hans, too."

"Take care of her? That's impossible as she is dead! And why do you still care for a Jew?"

"You lie!" Alfred shouted back. "I demand respect from you. You are still just a boy!"

Carson hesitated for a few seconds, breathing heavily.

"Respect? Do you really want to talk to me about respect? You are the ones who disrespected me, our country, and our so-called family!" Carson said, furious. "And who are you to call me a liar? You would defend a Jew over me!"

"You don't know what you are saying! You have lost your mind. You are blinded by fanaticism!"

"Stop it, both of you," Elga yelled at them. "I cannot see you two like this. Enough! Enough anger and hate!"

"It is better if you both leave right now," Carson said, still staring at Alfred.

"Carson," Elga pleaded, "please, don't do this. I still see the good in you. You are still that little blond boy that always made us laugh. The one we learned how to love and care for as a son. Don't do this to our family!"

"You were the ones who compromised our unity when you decided to help that girl. Now Hans is arrested, and soon it could be all of us!"

"Just let me see Hans," Elga begged. "I have already seen you. I need to see him. Please."

Carson sighed. He looked away, trying to gain some time to think. But at the moment, he just wanted to get rid of these two.

"I will see what I can do," Carson said, feeling exhausted.

"And the girl?"

"It's enough for now!" Carson replied, still unsure if they knew about Denna staying in his house.

"I will make sure you have permission to see Hans sometimes. But that's all I will do. I don't want to see you here anymore."

Elga looked at Alfred, signaling they should leave. For them, there was a mystery surrounding Carson's decision to hide Denna there. Ironically, she was safer there than any other place in Germany.

"Let's go, Elga."

"When can we see him?" Elga asked one last question before walking out of the room.

"Soon," Carson said, turning around.

He stood there for a few more seconds, trying to calm down. It actually pained him to treat them like that. He loved Alfred and Elga, but he still felt the sour taste of their lies and deceit.

"Mrs. Kaufmann!" he yelled out loud as he headed to the living room. "Come here, now! We need to talk!"

Hearing his screams from outside the house, she rushed back in.

"What have you told them about the girl?" Carson asked her furiously.

"Nothing!" Mrs. Kaufmann swore. "Absolutely nothing!"

"You'd better keep your mouth shut. You'd better never say a word, or I will kill you. You and your entire family. Do you hear me?"

It took Carson everything he had not to take his anger out on her.

"I won't, sir. I won't say anything. I promise!"

"Now, get out of here!" Carson said, still staring at her. "And remember, no one is allowed in this house! No one! Not even them!"

"I understand, sir!"

"And you will continue working here until I say otherwise!"

As Carson watched her walk away, he thought about Denna. He rushed upstairs to check on her.

He quickly turned the doorknob, realizing it was still locked just as he had left it. *Good, that's good!* He thought, feeling better. He stood there for a few seconds, debating whether or not to go in. It had been months since he had seen her.

He reached for the key inside his pocket, holding it tight in his hands. But he still didn't know what to do or what to say once he went in. For him, it was humiliating to show any emotion, especially toward her. *She is just a Jew, nothing more than a filthy Jew,* he repeated over and over again in his head. *Why should I hesitate? She is my prisoner now, and I can do whatever I want with her.*

With his hand shaking, Carson turned the key. He grabbed the doorknob and pushed it forward in one swift movement.

Denna was in her bed, sitting against the wall with a book on her hands.

She scurried backward instantly as soon as she saw the door suddenly open.

It had been a long time since she had seen his face. But not one day had gone by without her thinking about him, always fearing this moment would come.

Carson gave her a stern look. But all that he saw was a scared and beautiful girl trying to hide from a monster. For a brief moment, he forgot about who she was. Conflicting emotions stirred inside him.

They stayed there staring at one another as if trying to guess each other's next move. But all the love that Carson tried so hard to hide from her was stubbornly and fiercely coming to surface, winning the battle.

Carson looked away, unsettled by his own feelings. He started to walk around the room.

"Don't think I am doing this for you," he said, trying to appear cold and uninterested.

Denna stayed there quiet. She couldn't care less about what he had to say. But that was another lie she told herself. Deep inside her heart, things had already started to change. It had been only a few months since the day she got pregnant, but she could already feel the baby moving inside her.

Her maternal instincts were stronger than her disgust. Little by little, she started to feel love for the small creature innocently growing inside her.

"What happened to Hans?" Denna asked him, taking advantage of that moment.

"Hans?" Carson laughed. "Do you really think I would let anyone hurt him over a Jew like yourself?"

Despite his hurtful words, Denna couldn't be more relieved to know that Carson had protected his friend.

"He is just receiving a little punishment … well deserved!" Carson continued. "He is lucky that I consider him my brother, although I am not too sure anymore. But no matter what happens to him, you should not waste your time worrying about it. You will never see each other again!"

The emotional impact caused by those words could be felt deep inside her heart. Tears quickly filled her eyes. There was so much she had to say to him. But she didn't know where to start.

"You feel so powerful, don't you?" Carson asked, irritated by her silence.

"Powerful?" Denna chuckled. "Look at me. I am your prisoner, and you have already given me a death sentence. I am in your hands. This is nothing even close to power."

Denna looked down, trying to fight her tears. She felt so lonely, so tired. But it was worse than that. The baby growing inside of her started to make her feel stronger emotions toward Carson. As if there were an invisible and powerful string connecting the two of them together.

Carson couldn't take his eyes off of her. He also felt the weight of the world on his shoulders, more than anyone else could imagine. He fought against an intense urge to keep talking to her, to be near her.

"If you weren't …" Carson blurted out without thinking. "Maybe …."

Denna looked at him, surprised. It was the first time she didn't see the superiority act in his demeanor. There was such sincerity in his last words;

she started to wonder if Carson did have some feelings for her. And like him, that very thought stirred up the same conflicting emotions inside her.

Carson sat on the chair by the small table he had set up for her. He passed his fingers through his hair. He had never felt so weak.

Denna looked at him for the first time in a very different way. Perhaps the prolonged period of suffering started to make her change. She saw a lost and vulnerable man. A handsome man who, by his own will, had chosen hate over love. *If he weren't a Nazi ...* Denna whispered without fully realizing the extension of her own words.

Carson looked straight at her face.

"Why did you decide to take this path?" Denna finally asked him.

"What do you mean? We true Germans were chosen to live a life of greatness. That's something you would never be able to understand."

The response didn't surprise her. She thought about the irony of her expecting his child.

Carson got up abruptly and started walking around the room.

"I'm still thinking about the right punishment for you," he said, trying to look in control again.

Denna said nothing. Still, her silence bothered him.

He looked straight into her eyes. He couldn't resist any longer. He slowly approached her. She coiled against the wall near her bed, trying to hide her belly.

"Look at you! Such a frightened little creature."

He sat on her bed, and with a sudden gesture, he grabbed her blanket and pulled it away from her. He wanted to expose her body, making her feel uncomfortable. But he got much more than that.

His face suddenly changed. Instinctively, Denna placed her hands on her belly.

He wasn't sure what he had seen until she made that move.

Carson got up at once, feeling completely shocked. That was the last thing he was expecting to find once he entered that room.

Scared, Denna could feel her heartbeat throughout her body. Carson looked at her as if trying to confirm it; she was pregnant.

He turned around, passing his hand down his face.

Denna knew she had to be brave. She had to find a way to defend her unborn child.

Pushing her fears aside, she got up slowly and walked toward him. She stood there for a brief moment.

"Feel it," she said softly. "It is moving already."

Unable to coordinate his thoughts, he looked at her in disbelief as she stood right there in front of him. It was as if her sudden proximity had hypnotized him.

She reached out for his hand, carefully placing it on her belly.

Not knowing how to act, he just let her guide his shaky hand. His entire body trembled as he touched her skin again.

He stood still; her hands remained on his.

She finally let go. But Carson kept caressing her belly, sliding his fingers towards her hips.

A strange and irresistible sensation took complete hold of her, making her feel light headed. She wasn't sure if she had done the right thing, but it was more than that. It was her heart that slowly melted with his touch, fiercely reminding her of how much she still desired him.

Carson looked straight into her eyes. Then, at her mouth. He approached her lips, but he hesitated to go any further.

Denna stood there, unable to take her eyes off of him.

Noticing she didn't move away, Carson came a little closer. She was breathing fast; her body was shaking. He felt he was losing control to the same intense attraction that made it impossible for him to resist.

Slowly, Denna also felt her resistance crumbling. She wanted him there. She wanted him near her.

She closed her eyes the moment she felt the touch of his lips against hers. She felt her guard coming down, and her feelings started to take over.

Placing both his hands behind her neck, Carson brought her closer to him. He moved his lips against hers with passion. All he wanted to do was to hold her tightly in his arms, touch every inch of her skin, caress her entire body.

Noticing that she responded to his kisses, he felt an intoxicating feeling of happiness, one that completely took hold of him. Nothing else mattered!

He placed her on the bed slowly. With every move, he made sure to look at her face. He made sure he wasn't hurting her.

Denna noticed the difference in Carson's actions … they were gentle, caring. And with that, her most inner feelings came to surface, she felt at ease, she felt loved. She was ready to give herself completely to him.

Holding her hair gently between his fingers, Carson kissed her with all the love he had hidden inside his heart. He enjoyed every touch, every move. Only he knew how much he had missed her. How many times he drove himself mad trying to fight his thoughts, dreams, and desire to be near her, making love to her again.

He had never allowed himself to feel such sensations with such a lack of constraint. Ironically enough, he felt as if he had finally found true happiness by loving the one he was supposed to hate.

With her eyes still shut, Denna felt all the intensity of that moment. She knew she would never be able to understand why she allowed herself to forget who Carson was, who he represented. She felt a warm sensation in her body, her soul. In between the arms of that German Nazi man, she felt surprisingly, disturbingly happy.

CHAPTER 39

Carson woke up a few hours later and looked at Denna's face. He thought she was sleeping, but Denna just had her eyes closed.

At first, he still felt the sensation of joy. But as the minutes went by, his prejudice started to take hold of him again. He didn't know what was happening to him.

He looked at her one more time. He wanted to touch her face, pull her closer, but he caught himself and hesitated. *What am I doing?* Carson thought. *I cannot do this! I can't allow her to do this to me.*

Feeling stifled and ashamed of the love he had for her, he got up and left the room fast, without looking back.

Laying down on his bed, Carson tried to get some sleep. He didn't want to face reality; he simply couldn't accept that he was in love with a Jewish girl who had the power to make him forget about all things he valued most. He wasn't ready for any of that. He felt weak, like he was a fool, a traitor.

However, things had changed again. She was expecting his child.

Many thoughts crossed his mind. He contemplated the idea of running away from Germany with her, away from the war. A place where they could live their romance without fear. But that idea quickly vanished as he reminded himself who she was.

He tossed and turned in his bed, unable to make a decision. But one thing he knew for sure. *It has to be kept a secret!* he repeated, both ashamed and afraid to lose her.

Still lying on her bed, Denna opened her eyes as soon as she heard Carson closing the door. She couldn't accept that she had allowed him to touch her again. She couldn't understand why she didn't resist or try to fight back. *Have I simply given up my life?* Denna thought. *That must be it; it has to be it!* But she knew that couldn't be farther from the truth. She couldn't help but relive all the intense emotions she had felt when she was in his arms.

She closed her eyes again, trying to push those thoughts away. She figured she had lost her mind. Nothing else made sense anymore; everything was out of place. She held her pillow tightly, feeling disgusted with herself. She had fallen in love with a Nazi officer, and by finally acknowledging the truth, she saw her whole world falling apart.

Carson woke up late in the day. He knew he had to present himself at his station. He had a lot of work to do.

He passed by Denna's room and stood there for a few seconds. *This is foolishness,* he thought, trying to deny again his feelings. *She is simply an amusement.*

He straightened his spine and continued down the stairs.

Carson arrived at the military station and immediately asked to speak to some of the guards. He carefully instructed them to allow Hans's parents to visit him a few times a week. As for Carson himself, he had no desire to see Hans again. It had been months since he last spoke to him. Still angry and hurt by what he considered to be a great betrayal, he had decided to keep him a while longer in that prison to teach Hans a lesson and keep him away from Denna.

Carson then found out he had to leave the following day again. A very important meeting among most officers was going to take place in a town near the capital. Germany was starting to lose ground in Leningrad, and they needed as many men as possible.

It was already late at night when Carson finally arrived home. He had tried everything he could to forget about the moments he had spent with Denna that day, but it wasn't that easy. He could still feel his body melded to hers. Denna was a regular part of his thoughts, a permanent presence in his mind.

Carson stood still in the hallway for a few seconds. He looked at her bedroom door. *I will not see her again. I can't keep doing this!* But his heart said something very different, constantly reminding him of what he couldn't fight against. *Maybe when I come back, I will talk to her. I need some time to plan this thing! I will take her away from here … maybe to Switzerland or even Africa if necessary!*

He walked faster toward his room. He lay on his bed trying to fall asleep, but somehow the very idea of Denna being right next door made him feel agitated and restless. *I know how to get fake papers for her,* he continued planning. *She can stay in Switzerland with the Schulzes for a while until I can meet her again. Maybe Africa will be the safest place for her once we win this war.*

That idea put him more at ease, and he was finally able to fall asleep. But even then, he dreamed of her in a terrible nightmare; he desperately tried to find her but couldn't … until he saw a casket. And to his horror, it was she, Denna, right there, her body lying motionless inside; she was dead.

Alfred and Elga received a letter from Mrs. Kaufmann regarding Carson's departure that morning. The words on the letter were very clear … they would finally be able to see their son.

They arrived at the military station bringing Hans some of his favorite food, clean clothes, and several books. They knew anything would help relieve his suffering.

After the strict formalities, Elga and Alfred followed one of Carson's trusted guards toward Hans's room. He had been removed from the prisoner's cell to a cleaner and better place.

Hans lay on his bed, numb. It had been several weeks since he had a conversation with anyone. He had received a note from Carson stating that he would have to wait a while longer to be set free. The only thing keeping his sanity was his desire for revenge.

He heard the door in the hallway open and sat up very quickly. He wondered who it could be. He immediately thought of Carson.

As the sound of voices approached his room, Hans saw shadows from under his door.

The soldier opened the door abruptly and announced a two-hour visit only. He could hardly believe who was standing right there in front of him.

"Hans!" Elga ran into her son's arms and sobbed.

"Mother! Dad!" He said with disbelief while embracing them.

"Look at you," Elga finally said, threading her fingers through his hair. "You look so thin! Are you all right? We have worried so much!"

Hans smiled at her, struggling to hold back his tears. "I'm fine, Mom! I'm so happy to see you two, but you shouldn't have come. It's too dangerous!"

"We couldn't wait any longer! No one was giving us any information about you. We had to come back."

"You still shouldn't have come! There is nothing that can be done, at least not for now."

"There is always something we can do. We are not leaving without you this time. Without both of you!"

Hans looked at his father, puzzled. "What are you saying?" He whispered. "Is she …?"

"It is a long story. There are still complications."

"But, Dad?" Hans tried to say. "So, she is alive …?"

Elga nodded. "We still have a few problems, but we are trying our best to resolve them. But we will, Hans!"

Alfred got close to his son and whispered, "We should not talk about it here. But, as your mother mentioned, we are working on it. She is all right for now, far from this place."

She is alive! She is alive! Hans thought as he cried. Elga brought him closer to her, hugging him tightly.

He allowed the tears to stream down his face, enjoying the comfort of his mother's embrace. He wanted to ask more, but he knew it wasn't the place for that. At least he had the most important information; Denna was alive!

"Germany has started to lose ground all over the world," Alfred continued to whisper. "We have to be patient."

Hans nodded. "It's so good to know that! I have been here unaware of what is happening on the outside."

"We have so much to tell you!" Elga continued.

"I am sure. So … how have you been? And Francine? Any other letters from her? I have been so worried and frustrated. I am angry for being here, unable to communicate with anyone or do anything!"

"It has been a nightmare to stay away from you. But as for this Francine … we have a lot of news."

"What happened? Is she all right?"

"Yes, yes she is," Elga said, trying to find the right words to continue. "Well, we were communicating with her regularly. She was also very worried about you and asked us to say that … that she and your son are waiting for you!"

Hans stood there speechless while both of his parents waited to hear an explanation.

"Son? What? What do you mean?"

"What kind of relationship did you have with her?" Elga couldn't help but ask. "We left, and the next thing we know, we are grandparents and …"

"Let him think, Elga," Alfred said, trying to give Hans a moment to absorb such news.

"I am a father? So … I guess …" Hans said, smiling. "Why didn't she say anything before? Why didn't she tell me she was pregnant back then?"

"Well, I am sure she had her reasons. She sent us several letters. We wish we could have brought them with us, but we figured it wouldn't be a good thing in case we got searched at the border!"

"Just tell him everything she said," Alfred requested, smiling at his son.

Little by little, Hans was becoming aware of what had taken place with Francine while they were apart. She found out she was pregnant soon after she arrived in Switzerland and decided to keep that from him because she didn't want him to worry even more or make a rash decision that could place him and Denna in danger.

"So, I am a father!" Hans said enthusiastically. "I wish I could have been there! I need to get out of here fast. I have to meet them! How is he? My son? What's his name? I have so many questions."

"I can imagine!" Elga said, smiling at him. "Francine told us how you two met again here. It is an incredible story!"

"Yes, Hans. We finally understand why you didn't want to tell us much about Francine over the phone," his father added.

"We didn't have the chance to meet our grandson yet, as he was born prematurely. But don't worry, Francine said he is doing very well. She wanted us to wait a while longer so that he could grow a little stronger. It seems she really loves you, Hans!"

Resting his head in his hands, Hans could think of nothing else but his child. He couldn't stop smiling, thrilled by the great news. Francine was the love of his life, and they had a son together! Suddenly, he felt his hope completely revived, his strength fortified.

They continued talking as Hans tried to explain a few things. But the two hours went by really fast, and they soon heard footsteps getting closer.

"I don't want to leave you!"

"It's alright, Mother. I'll be fine. You gave me a lot to think about. The best news!"

"Carson said you would only need to wait a few more weeks! We will come to see you as much as we can."

"I can't wait! And in the meantime, don't forget to tell Victoria to explain to Francine that everything is going well and that I am very happy to know I now have a son! She also has to know I am trying my best to go to Switzerland, to see them! But I don't want her to worry. I should be out of here soon, and there is no need for her to be aware of my current situation."

"That makes sense!" his father replied.

"I have been writing some letters to all of you as I didn't know what would happen to me. Here ... take some of those with you and please send these ones to Francine. I will have more to give you next time you come to see me."

Elga and Alfred rushed to hug their son.

After saying goodbye, Hans stood there trying to make some sense of all he had heard. He couldn't believe how things had completely turned around. Just when he had lost all hope, he got to see his parents again and received the most wonderful news about Denna, his beloved Francine, and the unexpected arrival of his son.

He lay down on the bed, remembering all the moments he spent with Francine, the most amazing nights of his life.

Although Hans didn't know exactly when he would leave the military base, he felt hopeful that his situation would change soon. *After what I have found out today, anything is possible*, he thought. He knew that another day would come, and he would have to be ready to do whatever it took to keep the ones he loved away from harm.

CHAPTER 40

The turbulent year of 1944 had finally arrived. Gigantic war machines turned what were once quiet, simple places into valleys of despair. The silence was often broken by the sound of bullets. Explosions lit the dark nights while tears and blood soaked the ground.

The Germans started to see their casualties increase. But it wasn't until the fall of Leningrad that, for the first time, Germany suffered a major loss in that terrible war. The new year had finally brought the Allies a taste of victory.

Francine and her family also shared that joy in Switzerland. They couldn't wait for Germany to be completely defeated. It was their only hope to see Jean again.

Francine felt encouraged by the few letters she had received from Victoria, explaining that Hans couldn't be happier to find out about his son and that he was doing everything in his power to reunite with them. He said he had to stay there a while longer to finish some unresolved business, making sure to omit the fact that he was arrested.

In the meantime, in Germany, the Schulzes kept themselves busy between Hans and Denna's visits. Mrs. Kaufmann, although terrified of disobeying Carson's orders, had no choice but to allow her former employers to enter the house.

Denna still kept her pregnancy a secret. Feeling ashamed, she didn't know how to start explaining what had happened. She also waited for Carson's return amidst feelings of sadness for loving him and guilt for the same. Her only consolation was the few moments she spent talking with both Elga and Alfred when they came to visit her, always bringing news from Hans and encouraging her to hold onto hope.

But everything moved very slowly as they still waited once more for Carson's return. At times, they wondered whether or not Carson had forgotten about Denna and Hans.

Little did they know, there was nothing Carson wished for more than to go back home. He needed to see Denna again. He also worried about Hans being isolated for so long. But Carson was far away, deeply immersed in warfare. He knew those were dangerous times; nothing could be done without him being present, as he could no longer trust even his most loyal soldiers.

The temperature had dropped into the single digits on that quiet winter night. Without warning, bombs fell from the sky like rain, blowing apart houses, businesses, and anything standing above the ground. The terrifying sound of explosions awoke that entire city.

It was the first time that Germany had suffered a massive air strike. It was their turn to experience the consequences of their own actions.

Trapped inside his room, Hans rushed to the window, desperately watching the utter chaos outside. He knew there was no way out of that place.

It didn't take long for him to hear yet another loud explosion. He was thrown to the ground from the force of the impact. The bomb had hit the opposite side of the building where he was being kept.

When Hans was able to open his eyes again, he was covered in debris and dust. He took a look around, noticing that one of the walls had been completely blown off. He could barely hear or see anything.

Getting up slowly, he walked carefully toward the broken wall, taking the opportunity to escape. People rushed in every direction, panicking.

But he didn't get far, as a much closer explosion shook the entire floor he was in, making part of the remaining ceiling fall on top of his body.

A dreadful silence filled the air for a few seconds, followed by screams soon replacing it.

As the minutes passed, the surviving inhabitants started to leave their shelters, one by one, still trying to understand what had happened.

Carson's military station, as well as the factory across the street, had been mostly destroyed. The remains of both buildings were all coated in a thick layer of dust and smoke.

Everyone was astonished when they saw the degree of destruction. No one could ever have predicted it. Lost in their false confidence and pride, the German Nazis never thought they could be attacked and destroyed in their own country.

The sun slowly broke through the horizon, revealing even more of the destruction caused by the airstrike.

Hans was woken up by the noise outside. He opened his eyes, but that time he couldn't see anything. It was still too dark for him, too foggy.

He heard sirens and loud voices coming from all directions. Slowly, he started to remember what had happened before he blacked out. He couldn't believe he was still alive.

His vision was blurry, although he could still see some flashes of light and some shadows. He tried to move, but he felt a strong pain coming from his legs. He screamed in agony.

"Another one here," a voice said, coming closer to him. A few minutes later, medical personnel placed him in a vehicle.

On the other side of town, a neighborhood was also brutally devastated. Carson's house was among many residences that were destroyed by the bombing, leaving very little behind.

Between the debris, Denna's body lay still. She was asleep when the explosions started. Then she had heard a loud noise, and everything collapsed around her. But she wasn't the only one there. Mrs. Kaufmann had been sleeping at Carson's residence for months at his forceful request.

At the Schulze residence, things looked very different. Eugene had rushed to the basement once the explosions began. As the sun came out, he went upstairs to check things out. The Schulze's property was miraculously intact.

Eugene walked outside quickly, noticing that Alfred and Elga's car wasn't there. Concerned, he remembered they had decided to go to Carson's house right before the airstrike started.

He checked inside the house one more time, calling out for them. But no one answered. Eugene knew there was only one thing to do. He got inside Hans's car and drove fast through their devastated neighborhood.

As soon as he turned the corner, he was shocked by what he saw. Most of Carson's house had been destroyed. He spotted what was left of Alfred's car and rushed toward the falling structure.

He walked through the debris and smoke looking for them. It didn't take him long to spot the two bodies that lay side by side. He had to prepare himself for the worst.

He approached them carefully, leaning toward Elga's body. He checked her pulse and then Alfred's. But it was too late.

"Help!" a voice was heard from a distance, snapping him back to reality. "Help!"

Eugene looked around quickly. But he couldn't see anybody.

"Here," Denna called out. "Help me, please."

Eugene could track her voice that time. He followed it until he found a body under a pile of bricks.

"I will get you out of there!" he said.

It took all of Eugene's strength to remove Denna's body from the debris and rubble.

Eugene looked at her familiar face. She was covered in dust and blood, but he soon recognized her. To his surprise, it was the girl he knew as Hans's cousin, Alyse.

"I will take you to the hospital," Eugene said, noticing she was pregnant.

"No," Denna rushed to say. "I can't go there."

Eugene remembered the rumors about the girl being Jewish and understood; he couldn't take her anywhere public. Ironically, she would have a better chance to live if she stayed away from the hospital.

He carried Denna in his arms, placing her carefully inside the car. Looking back at the house, Eugene thought about Carson and Mrs. Kaufmann. He knew they could still be there under the wreckage.

Eugene walked back toward what was left of Carson's house. He yelled out their names. He searched for their bodies. After a few minutes, he realized there was no one else there, or at least no one who was alive. He decided to drive Denna back to the Schulze's house. He would still have to go to the military station. He had to check on Hans.

Eugene took Denna to her old bedroom. "It will be all right," he said, trying to soothe her. He still couldn't believe she was alive and with only a few cuts and bruises. As for the baby, it was impossible to tell. There was nothing else he could do for them at that moment.

"I will be back. I have to look for Hans!"

Denna nodded, still feeling disoriented. "Bring him back to us," she was able to whisper.

After what seemed like a long time, Eugene arrived at the military station. Dozens of bodies lay around while other people screamed out for help. Military personnel and medical staff traded information. Family members waited in agony to hear news about their loved ones.

Eugene knew then that Germany was in trouble. Having been born in Russia, he was brought to Germany when he was only eight years old. Although he had lived in Germany most of his life, he hated the Nazi regime.

As he walked around the debris, Eugene grew more concerned. He deeply cared for Alfred and Elga, but Hans was very special to him. He had known him since he was a baby. Eugene had seen his first steps; he had watched him grow up, turning into a kind and dignified man, just like his father.

Still hoping he could be alive, Eugene continued to search for Hans; he wouldn't give up!

"Most of the seriously injured were taken to the hospitals at the nearby towns," a nurse informed. "Others have been taken to an improvised medical center right over there." The nurse pointed across the street.

He rushed through the medical tents, one by one.

Eugene was about to exit the last tent when a nurse treating a patient on a nearby bed caught his attention.

Eugene got a little closer, and although the man's face was partially covered in blood, he recognized him.

"Hans!" he exclaimed, rushing toward him.

The nurse looked back to see who was speaking.

"Do you know who this man is?"

"Yes! I work at his house."

"He is part of the military personnel, right?" the nurse asked, continuing to treat Hans's injuries.

Eugene thought carefully for a second.

"Yes," he replied. "He is an engineer and was visiting his brother there."

"Very well then. We will need his information to be filled out."

Eugene nodded. "How is he?"

"He is sleeping now; his condition is stabilized. It is a miracle he has survived. He has a head injury, but it doesn't seem to be anything too alarming. He also has a broken leg. We have to wait until he wakes up. There is nothing else to do until them."

"I could still take him to a hospital in another city," Eugene insisted.

"Well, you can try it. But I can tell you right now all the hospitals nearby are completely full. Actually, in his case, it won't really matter where he is. Someone just needs to watch over him constantly, making sure he doesn't get worse. And as for his broken leg, it just needs to be set. We can do it here, but you will have to wait."

"Is he in any condition to travel today? I can take him home later."

"A short trip, perhaps," the nurse said.

Eugene waited impatiently until Hans's leg was finally put in a cast. He knew he had to get Hans out of there before more questions could be asked. He also had to rush back home to Denna, who was there all by herself.

Hans was carefully placed in the back of his vehicle. Eugene drove off, relieved that he was able to take Hans away from that place.

As he arrived home, he heard a noise coming from the back seat.

"Hans," Eugene said softly. "It's me, Eugene. I brought you back home! You are finally home!"

Hans slowly opened his eyes, moving his head up, looking around him.

"Eugene, is that you? Where am I? I cannot see anything!" Hans asked desperately, trying to get up from the car seat. "My leg!" Hans fell backward, feeling the pain.

"You broke your leg, Hans."

"Eugene?" Hans said, panicking. "I can't see you well. I cannot see much at all."

Eugene took a closer look at his face.

"It's all right, Hans," he said, trying to keep him calm. "The nurse said they found you under a broken wall. Something hit your head and must have affected your eyesight. I'm sure it will get better. Let's get inside the house."

They moved carefully, step by step. Eugene sighed in relief once they reached the couch. Hans was alive and at home.

"And my parents, Eugene? Where are they?"

Eugene hesitated for a few seconds.

"Hans, they are not here. But I will explain things later. You need to eat something and rest for now."

"Where did they go? Are they all right?"

"Yes," Eugene responded, knowing he had to lie. "But for now, you should rest."

Hans struggled to keep himself awake. The medication he had received made him very tired.

"And Denna? Have you heard from her?" Hans could barely finish saying those words before he felt his eyes closing again. "Denna. We need to find her."

Eugene wondered who that could be. He had no idea it was Alyse that Hans was referring to. But before he could ask, he noticed Hans was already asleep.

Upstairs, Denna also slept in her bedroom. Eugene spent the entire night going back and forth between Denna and Hans. He understood these were going to be difficult days, but he wouldn't get discouraged. He knew he was the only person there that could help them.

CHAPTER 41

Denna opened her eyes and looked around. Her head still hurt. She immediately placed her hands on her belly. The baby was moving. She smiled thankfully.

It took her a few seconds to recognize the room. *This can't be true!* she thought. But it was the sight of Eugene sleeping on a chair by her side that confirmed where she was, bringing back foggy memories of her journey there the day before. She couldn't be happier to be back at that house.

Denna got up cautiously as her whole body still ached.

"Miss?" Eugene woke up once he heard Denna moving.

"Hi, Eugene. It's so nice to see you!" Denna said, smiling at him.

"How are you feeling?" Eugene asked, standing up almost instantly.

"I still feel some pain in my head and arms, but I feel better already. What happened? How did I end up here?"

"I'm glad to know you are feeling better. You are very lucky to be alive! I found you in the middle of debris. The airstrike destroyed Carson's house."

"I don't remember much. I heard the sound of explosions, and then everything seemed to collapse around me. But tell me, Eugene, where is everyone? Elga, Alfred? And Hans? Did you hear anything about Hans?"

"Miss, Hans is alive! I brought him back here yesterday. But, as for his parents…"

"What happened to them? And Hans? You said he was here?"

"Yes, he is here. I found him inside a medical tent, set up near the military base. But unfortunately, his parents didn't survive."

Denna looked down, covering her face with her hands. "What happened?"

"The bombing," Eugene said, also feeling her pain. "They left the house as soon as the bombing started."

Denna stared at him quietly as tears filled her eyes. "This is all so horrible. Where… where were they going?"

"They were going to Carson's house. I found their bodies lying there," Eugene paused for a brief moment. "As for Hans, he is downstairs. He broke his leg, and his head is badly hurt."

Denna could hardly believe everything she was hearing. "I need to see him."

"He should be sleeping in the living room; I haven't said anything about his parents."

"You did well, Eugene. I want to go see him now. Can you help me downstairs?"

"Of course, Miss. Alyse."

"And by the way… my name is Denna. You probably know my story by now."

Eugene looked straight into her eyes, as if trying to piece everything together. Things were finally starting to make more sense to him. Denna and Alyse were the same person.

"I heard a few things. But none of that matters to me besides your well-being and Hans's."

Denna smiled at him with profound gratitude. "I cannot thank you enough!"

They both walked downstairs together.

The sight of Hans peacefully sleeping touched her deeply. A faint smile appeared on her face. They were there, at his house, together! She once thought they would never see each other again.

"I have to take care of his parents' bodies," Eugene whispered.

"Are you going to bring them here?"

"Yes. They will have to be buried in our backyard, perhaps near their favorite garden."

Denna agreed, feeling immense guilt. She knew they had gone there to see her. She felt responsible for their death.

She looked at Hans, with her heart shred to pieces. She grasped his hands, ready to stay by his side while Eugene left.

"I am here," she said softly. "We are together again." She smiled at him, caressing his hair gently.

Her sudden touch made his body jerk awake. Hans slowly opened his eyes.

"Hans!" said Denna, getting closer to him.

Hans moved his head, trying to follow the familiar voice, but he still couldn't see much.

"Hans! It's me … Denna!"

"Denna? Denna? Is that really you?" said Hans, moving his hands toward where she was.

"Yes! It is me," she repeated in tears, embracing him.

They held each other and cried, moved by what they both considered to be an impossible reunion.

Hans saw nothing besides dark, blurry figures in front of him. But at the moment, all that mattered was that Denna was there with him again.

"Denna! I can't believe you are here! I thought I would never see you again! Carson told me … he said he would …."

"I know. I felt the same way! But we are here together! Somehow, we made it, alive! We have so much to talk about, Hans."

"I almost lost my mind wondering what they would do to you. But then, my parents arrived and told me that you were all right, safe. They couldn't say anything else at that time."

Hearing Hans talking about his parents, Denna knew she would have to tell him the unbearable truth.

"I still can't see anything," Hans said, completely frustrated and fearful he had lost his eyesight indefinitely. "There was this explosion, and then suddenly everything was dark."

"Your head got injured last night," Denna replied, remembering what Eugene had told her. "I am sure you will recover well. Give it some time. And I will be here with you, right by your side, always. I will help you to get better."

Hans smiled; his heart filled with joy.

"You should lie down again, Hans," Denna said, placing a kiss on his cheek.

"I'm fine, don't worry. I feel a lot better now hearing your voice. And my parents? Where are they?"

"Hans, they … something terrible happened!"

"What are you saying? Where are they?"

"They didn't make it. I am so sorry, Hans!" Denna stood in silence for a few seconds. "They were killed during the bombing last night. Eugene found them outside Carson's house."

The emotional impact of those words made Hans close his eyes. "No! No, not them! Not them, Denna! NO!"

Denna knew exactly how he felt. For everything she had heard and seen, she already knew that the chances of her own parents being alive were very low.

Unable to find the right words to say at that moment, she helplessly watched Hans crying.

"Please tell me it is not true," he begged her, feeling an excruciating pain inside his heart.

"I'm so sorry, Hans. I wish I could change everything!" Denna said, embracing him tenderly.

"What happened to them? You said they were at Carson's house. What were they doing there? Where are they now?"

"Eugene is bringing them here," Denna stated, gently wiping some tears off his face. "He is bringing them home! He set up a place in the backyard. Near your mother's favorite garden."

"I never had the chance to thank them. To say how much I loved them."

"I am sure they knew how much you loved, respected, and admired them!" Denna replied, touching his arm gently.

Hans nodded, wiping the tears still streaming down his face.

"And Carson? Has anyone seen him?"

"No. Eugene said he looked around but couldn't find anyone else at his destroyed house."

"No one else? What are you talking about?"

"It was my fault!" Denna blurted it out. "They had gone to Carson's house to see me yesterday when everything happened. They were trying to get me out of there."

"From where? You said … Carson's house?"

"Yes," Denna confirmed. She knew it was time to tell him the whole truth. "Carson was keeping me there! At his own house."

"At his own house?" repeated Hans in disbelief. "How is that possible?"

They both stayed quiet for a brief moment.

"My parents never told me where you were staying. Now I know why!" Hans continued with a shaky voice. "They said you were fine but never told me any details. But I still can't believe he brought you there! Why? I don't understand it. I saw so much hatred in his eyes when he went to see me in that jail cell. He told me he would make you pay for lying to him. I would never expect he would get you out of that prison, much less bring you to his own house!"

Denna looked away. She still had a vivid memory of those days as well.

"It is a long story, Hans," she said, feeling the whole weight of the world on her shoulders.

"So … Carson was keeping you … as a prisoner?" Hans wondered, trying to make some sense of it. "My parents obviously knew about that. But why was Carson keeping you there?"

Denna got up fast and turned around.

"Yes, they knew I was there, and they would visit me often when he was out of town. And that's why … that's why they were there last night! They died because of me!"

"That is not your fault! Don't say that! It is this damn war! This damn country! Carson could have taken you out of Germany if he wanted. He, Hitler, and all his supporters are the only ones to blame."

Denna stayed silent. She still had so much to explain to him.

"Denna, what happened while I was in jail? I feel like you are not telling me everything."

She knew she couldn't hide her biggest secret from Hans forever. Grabbing one of his hands, she slowly placed it on her belly.

"You … you're …"

"Yes! I am pregnant." Denna finished the words he couldn't bring himself to say.

Hans never expected anything like that. He stayed quiet, feeling overwhelmed by everything he had heard from her. So much had happened while he was detained.

"I am all right, Hans," Denna affirmed, trying to calm him down.

"It is not all right!" Hans replied, still in shock. "Who…? Who did this? I mean … I …"

"It is not what you are thinking! I'll explain it to you …."

As Denna started speaking about the events that followed after he was brought to the hospital, the look on his face completely changed. Hans started to remember all those times he had caught Carson looking at Denna with desire. But even so, he knew Carson really well. He would not have hesitated to kill Denna unless he felt strongly toward her.

It was right at that moment when Hans put the pieces together. "Denna … is it …? Is it Carson's baby that you are expecting?"

With her heart beating faster, she confirmed what Hans suspected. "Yes, it is his baby."

Hans sighed. He couldn't accept that. Everything seemed to be falling apart.

"I can't believe he … I don't know what to say. That bastard! I …. I am sorry!"

"Please, Hans," Denna stopped him. "Don't worry about that now. You have gone through so much already. I am all right. Trust me! I just hope the baby is all right, too."

"Does he know about this? Does anyone else know?" Hans didn't want to let it go.

"Yes. He knows and only him. I couldn't tell your parents. I didn't want to cause any more problems!"

Hans didn't say anything else. He didn't want to upset her any further. But inside his heart and mind, rage was starting to replace sorrow.

He blamed Carson for his parents' death. He hated him. He would never forgive what he did to Denna, to all of them.

"He didn't really hurt me," Denna continued as if she could read his mind.

"What did that bastard have to say about it? What was he thinking?"

"I don't know, Hans. All I can say is that he started to treat me well after bringing me to his house. It was so strange … as if he was trying to …."

"Protect you? He was hiding you there! He was protecting you!" said Hans unable to deny the truth. "He … a Nazi man … protecting you!"

"I think he … maybe …." Denna hesitated for a few seconds. "There is so much more to this story, Hans!"

"He likes you! He must be in love with you! That's the only explanation."

"I guess," Denna wondered herself. "But do you really believe that? How is that possible?"

"I don't see another reason. What he feels for you has to be much stronger than his hatred for what you represent! But you said there was more to the story? What happened between you two? Did he force you to …?" Hans couldn't quite say what he was thinking.

"I don't know how to explain it to you," Denna said, feeling still conflicted. "He didn't necessarily force me. It wasn't like that. I … I started to feel different around him. I don't know how to say this to you …."

Completely shocked by her answer, Hans was lost for words. He noticed she didn't refer to Carson with any animosity. He started to understand that perhaps Denna, somehow, had also developed feelings for Carson, as impossible as it may seem.

"You don't need to feel obligated to tell me anything else, Denna," Hans said, understanding her situation. "I apologize if I made you feel that way. For now, we need to prepare for the baby that will come. We have to keep you both safe!"

With his heart deeply aching, Hans still tried to grasp the fact that his parents were no longer part of that world. He thought about everything he had just heard and recognized that huge irony. His parents died trying to save Denna from Carson, not knowing that he had fallen in love with her, a Jewish girl. And by doing so, Carson saved her from certain death.

Days went by since they had been reunited. Denna stayed right by Hans's side as he mourned the loss of his parents.

While she had already fully recuperated from her wounds, Hans's vision hadn't returned. She tried her best to console him, telling him not to lose hope. Little by little, Hans started to learn how to deal with his new physical condition.

They would spend most of their time together, talking for hours. Hans told Denna about his son and everything else that had happened since they were separated. He tried to keep her spirits up, often telling her how happy he was to become an uncle soon. But their situation was still very complicated. Carson was nowhere to be found; they were far from being safe.

Hans waited apprehensively for both the telephone and mail services to be restored. Since the bombing, he had no way to communicate with Victoria in Switzerland. He wanted to make sure Francine knew he was alive and doing everything possible to leave Germany.

As the war got closer to their doorsteps, they understood Germany was in deep trouble. Their nightmare could finally be over soon.

CHAPTER 42

Another spring had arrived. As the war progressed, the Allies advanced forward, breaking further through the German lines.

Francine communicated with Victoria, who still didn't have any information from the Schulzes. The postal services had been compromised, and she knew there was no guarantee that her letters would reach their destination in Germany. Even Daniel hadn't communicated in the last few weeks.

On the other side of the border, in Germany, Denna's footsteps could be heard rushing through the Schulze's residence toward Hans. She had a letter in her hands.

"Hans!" she said excitedly. "It's a letter from Switzerland!"

That was exactly what he had been waiting so long for. Hans got up from the couch at once. "Francine! It has to be her! Come on, Denna, please read it to me!"

"There are two letters inside the envelope, both from Victoria," Denna said, already opening the first one.

"Victoria says she is very worried as she hasn't received any news from your parents in a while."

"They probably didn't receive our letters with all the explanations," Hans said, still feeling the pain from his parent's death.

"Yes, it seems like it. She also says here that Francine sent them several letters wondering about you, me, and your parents!"

As Denna started to read the letter aloud, his heart felt more at ease. He finally had news from her.

"Victoria says that Francine and your son are doing really well. She says Francine often communicates with her, mentioning details about Julian's growth and physical characteristics similar to you, Hans! But she says Francine still worries very much about all of us, wondering if there is anything she could do to help."

"Maybe the phone lines will be restored soon! I need to talk to Victoria over the phone. It is clear that she hasn't received any of the letters we have sent her, which doesn't surprise me, the way the war has turned against us. Victoria needs to know about my parents. She will have to be the one to write a letter to Francine, explaining some of the things happening here. But we should continue to send them letters. Maybe one of them will make it there!"

Denna knew she was again the only reason why Hans decided to stay in Germany. But with her pregnancy, she couldn't tell him to leave. She couldn't go through that alone. Hans was the only person she had left.

Those letters from Francine brought them new hope, making them realize there could still be a brighter future, where the war would be over, and they will all be free to live their lives again in peace. Hans and Denna got what they needed to keep believing, fighting, and waiting.

And so ... time went by very quickly.

It was a warm night when the sound of a scream awoke Hans. He feared someone had found Denna.

He got up fast and walked forward, feeling his way toward the door. Hans had lost most of his vision, but he could still see some dark images.

He made it to the hallway when Eugene arrived, calling for him.

"Hans!" he said urgently. "Denna is having the baby!"

Eugene helped Hans as they both walked across the yard to the small house behind the Schulze's residence where Denna lived, hiding from the world.

"Hans!" Denna cried, relieved to see him there.

Hans reached out for her hand.

"It will be all right," he said, holding her hand tightly.

As the minutes went by, Denna's situation got worse.

"We need to find some help," Eugene said desperately.

"We need a doctor," Hans agreed.

"No! Please don't!" Denna insisted. "If anyone finds out I am here, they will come and take us away again! I have to protect my baby!"

Hans was not sure what to do. He knew that getting a doctor would help Denna but that it could very well get her killed.

"Don't get the doctor! Promise me, Hans! No matter what happens…." Denna said faintly, panting from weakness and immense pain. "They will kill us all. No one can know about this!"

Denna screamed loudly again, squeezing Hans's hand between hers.

"We can do this! Just us!" Denna said courageously.

Understanding her concerns, Hans nodded, grasping her hand firmly.

"We are going to do this together! Eugene, could you please get us some clean towels?"

Denna started to push hard, but she was running out of strength. She shrieked and sobbed; the pain was just unbearable.

"You can do this," Hans assured her, feeling frustrated he couldn't help her more. "Don't give up!"

Eugene looked at Hans, concerned. Denna had lost too much blood. Her situation was critical.

"One more time!" were the only words Denna heard.

She opened her eyes again and gathered all the strength she had left. Screaming, she gave one last push, and Eugene received the baby in his arms.

Everyone was silent. It took a few seconds for the baby to start crying.

"It's a boy!" Eugene announced cheerfully, placing the baby in a towel. "We need to cut the umbilical cord."

"I can hold him," said Hans with joy.

It was at that moment that Eugene looked at Denna's face.

Denna had heard the first sound of her baby crying before smiling and closing her eyes.

"Denna?" said Eugene. "Denna!"

"What's happening?" Hans asked, concerned.

"She has lost a lot of blood," Eugene stated, checking her pulse.

"We need a doctor! Eugene, call the doctor and tell him it is an emergency, he has to come right away! Please, you have to do it right now! Denna? Denna, answer me!" Hans tried to wake her up. But Denna's heart had already stopped beating.

Eugene shook his head. Placing his hand on Hans's shoulder, he continued. "I think it is too late, Hans. She is no longer breathing…."

"No!" Hans screamed. "It can't be too late. Get a doctor, Eugene! We need a doctor here!"

The little boy started crying as if he could sense all the sadness around him. "Let me hold him," Eugene said already grabbing the baby from Hans's arms.

"Wake up, Denna! Wake up!" Hans yelled, touching her face. "Your baby is fine. It is a boy! He is fine. He needs you!"

Eugene stood there quietly, the baby in his arms. There was nothing he could do to console Hans.

"*Come on, Denna!*" Hans begged, resting his head against her chest, desperately trying to hear a heartbeat. "Wake up! Please … just wake up. Don't do this to me. I can't lose you! I cannot do this alone!"

But Denna's body remained motionless.

"Get a doctor, Eugene! Please! We need a doctor right now!"

"Hans," Eugene said gently. "She lost too much blood. She is no longer breathing."

"No! No! We still can do this! Wake up, Denna! Answer me! Please just answer me …" Hans yelled repeatedly. "Don't leave me alone …

Eugene placed the baby in the small crib near Denna's bed. He Approached Hans, touching his arm.

"I can take care of her," Eugene told him. "But first, we need to look after the baby."

Hans stood stunned for a few seconds.

"Why? Why did she have to leave us? She deserved to be happy. After everything she went through … she can't die! She deserves to live free, away from here! I promised her!"

"She is free now, Hans! Her suffering is over.…" .

Hans leaned toward her, trying to hear any sound that could give him hope she was still alive. But her heart and lungs remained silent. Realizing she was indeed no longer with them, he embraced her motionlessly body. He sobbed. Once more, he felt the deep pain of losing one more person he cared so much for and loved.

"Denna, I'm sorry. I'm so sorry!" Hans repeated, still holding her in his arms.

It was only when the baby started crying again that he found some consolation.

Hans caressed Denna's face one more time, placing a long and tender kiss on her cheek. His soul ached with a profound and corrosive sense of loss. With tears streaming down his face, he slowly got up and moved his hands toward the crib.

"She wanted his name to be Abraham," Hans said with his heart consumed by sadness. "I promised to take her away from here. I promised her, Eugene. I made a promise to take her out of Germany. I promised her … and I failed!"

"You did not fail, Hans! Part of her now lives in this child," Eugene comforted him. "You can still take her out of here through Abraham. It is her child who needs you the most now. He needs you to be strong. He has no one else."

Those words produced the desired effect on Hans. He started to compose himself. He leaned toward Abraham's face, placing a gentle kiss on his rosy cheeks.

"I want her to be buried in our backyard, close to my parents," Hans said as tears streamed down his face. "Can you help me with that, Eugene?"

CHAPTER 43

Early the next morning, they buried Denna's body. A beautiful arrangement of flowers done by Eugene was placed above the ground where she lay. The following days went by sadly and slowly in that nearly empty house.

Mourning the death of his loved ones, Hans spent most of his time by Abraham's side. He hired a nurse to take care of the child, saying it was his son and that the mother had died.

There was nothing keeping him in Germany anymore. All his friends and family had either been killed or taken away at that point. Hans knew it was time for him to leave. And for that, he would need travel authorizations. He thought about Carson. He still hated him. He couldn't bring himself to ask him for any favor. How could he? He despised everything he had done to Denna. He blamed him for his parents' death.

He tried to gather whatever monetary resources he had left in Germany to find another way out. But he quickly realized what he already knew. Only Nazi officers had the power and authority to provide travel passes.

Holding Abraham in his arms, he knew he had to put his anger and pride aside to do what was the best for the little child he considered to be his own nephew. He also had Francine and his son, who waited for him. If having to beg for Carson to give him authorizations to travel was his only choice, he would not hesitate.

With the phone lines never restored to the civilian population and the intense battles fought closer and closer to Germany, Hans had stopped receiving any letters from Victoria. As he impatiently watched the months passing by, he wondered if the war would ever be over … if one day he would be finally able to walk out of Germany.

It was late at night when Eugene rushed toward Hans to deliver the most awaited news. He was able to confirm that Carson was indeed alive and back in Berlin. Hans knew it was only a matter of time for Carson to show up at his house.

The clock marked a little past 5 pm on that warm July afternoon when Carson finally walked onto the Schulzes' property. After the bombing, Carson was not authorized to go back home, and among many other officers, he was sent to the eastern borders of Germany.

He was completely shocked when he heard about the degree of destruction in his hometown and his own house. He thought about all of those he left behind, but especially Denna. He anxiously waited to find out what had happened to them, until one day, he finally got the news. It seemed everyone had been killed at his house and that nothing was spared. He felt as if his whole world had collapsed around him. Believing that Denna had died during the air attack, he thought about nothing else, as his heart seemed to have died along with her.

As the days went by, Carson immersed himself into work matters, trying to forget his pain and the devastating sorrow that had completely taken over his body and soul.

He found out that Alfred and Elga had also died but that Hans was alive. As much as Carson wanted to go back, he also didn't want to face his brother. Even though he knew that sooner or later, he would have to confront him.

Carson looked very different after Denna's death. His face was thinner, his mind even more troubled, and his body debilitated by the continuous battles he had fought. He no longer seemed to care about the war or anything else.

He was surprised when he was sent back to his hometown. The Allies were getting closer, and he was ordered to organize its defense.

Eugene opened the door, his eyes widened when he saw the familiar face right in front of him.

"Hello, Eugene," Carson said in a cold, indifferent tone.

"Mr. Beurmann, I'm glad to see you back."

"Hans? Is he here?"

"Yes, sir. He is upstairs."

"Tell him I'll wait for him in the library."

With a heavy heart, Carson took a few steps onto the room. A family photo standing right on top of Alfred's desk got his attention. He walked toward it and grabbed it with his shaky hands. On that photo, Elga, Alfred, Hans and Carson himself smiled happy for the camera. It was taken right before Carson had decided to join the Nazi Party.

His eyes teared up as he remembered that those who he considered his own parents were no longer there.

Hans entered the library, catching his attention. They both stayed quiet for a few seconds. The moment they waited for so long had arrived.

Looking at Hans's face, Carson noticed he had a vague look in his eyes. He realized something was wrong with him.

"What happened to you, Hans?" Carson asked him without hesitation.

"During that same airstrike that killed our parents, I got injured. But I am sure you know that already," Hans said, still feeling the pain of their loss inside his heart. "Remember? I was still your prisoner at that military station."

Carson looked down for a brief moment before he replied, "I wanted to come back! But I wasn't allowed."

"Of course not!" Hans said after a chuckle.

Trying to find the right words to explain things better, Carson stayed quiet for a moment.

"I guess I lost my eyesight forever," Hans continued, still trying to accept that fact himself. He paused for a few seconds. "They found Mrs. Kaufmann's body a few days later."

Unable to take his eyes off of Hans, Carson anxiously waited to hear the name Denna. He thought Hans already knew he was hiding her in his house.

"Carson... we have a lot to talk about," Hans finally said in a mournful tone of voice. "I'm going to tell you a very sad story. I just ask that you listen to everything I have to say before you speak."

And so, Hans started to tell him about the first time he saw Denna in that dark corner downtown. He mentioned the conversation he had with his parents about keeping the girl there with them. He told him about the airstrike that took his parents' life and finally about Denna's death and the baby.

As he heard her story, Carson's face turned completely pale. All kinds of different emotions went through his body and mind. Denna didn't die during the bombing. *She was alive that entire time until ... until she had my child,* he thought, feeling overwhelming sadness. He regretted deeply not having returned sooner.

Understanding the impact that those words would cause him, Hans stood quiet, giving him some time to think.

Carson tried his best not to let all those emotions take hold of him. But it was hard, really hard. He suffered more than he would like to admit. He had lost his parents. And then Denna, the first woman who made him experience the taste of love. But there was much more! She was able to carry on with her pregnancy, and he was now a father!

"Hans. I'm so sorry for your parents' death, our parents!" Carson finally broke his silence, not knowing what else to say. "I loved them, too."

"I know that. They felt that they were truly your parents. And as for Denna… she is outside, alongside them, in the backyard," Hans said, tears rolling down his face. "We did all we could. But now, she is free."

Looking into Hans's eyes, Carson could tell he already knew the entire truth. He felt a sudden chill run through his body. For a brief moment, he couldn't move.

Hearing about Denna's death during childbirth made him feel as if he had lost her twice. The same sharp pain inside his chest reminded him of the love he had tried so hard to deny.

They stood quietly again, a heavy silence that meant so much.

Carson could no longer hold his tears. There was only one thing he wished to do at that moment. He rushed out of the library without saying anything else.

He could see the cross and flowers in the backyard. With every step he took, the pain intensified inside his heart, pain so deep that it crushed his soul. Tears flooded his eyes. No, he had never cried for anyone since his mother died.

But being there, right before where her body lay, he knew there was no more hope for them. Suddenly, nothing else mattered to him … no war, no race supremacy, and no blind prejudice. It was a very new and strange sensation for him. He felt like an empty space had taken the place of his once cold heart — a heart Carson believed he had full control of before Denna appeared in his life. Somehow, she found a way to slowly cure his hate by teaching him the true meaning of love. But it was too late; he finally understood it. Not being able to hold his emotions anymore, he fell to his knees and cried.

Hans waited patiently in the library. He knew exactly where his brother had gone. He had no more doubt that Carson loved Denna in his own twisted way. Love was the only thing powerful enough to convince Carson to keep her alive, risking everything he valued the most.

As more time went by, Hans started to worry. He asked Eugene to take him outside.

"Carson," Hans said, placing his hand on his brother's shoulder. "Come inside."

"No! I just want to be left alone." Carson said, pulling away from Hans.

"Your son …." Hans insisted.

"I cannot do this now, Hans!" Carson replied, trying to wipe the tears off his face.

"It was her last wish. She wanted us to save his life, to protect him."

"It doesn't matter now," Carson answered bitterly. "Nothing matters now!"

Understanding his pain, Hans knew there was nothing else he could say that would change his state of mind.

"I will be inside when you feel ready to talk," he said, already walking away.

The sun had completely disappeared on the horizon when Carson finally went into the house. He went straight to the library to find something to drink.

Hans heard ice clinking and started to move in that direction.

"Carson?" he asked. "I will bring you some food."

"Leave me alone, Hans," Carson said, brushing him off. "I don't want to eat anything now!"

"But you will, brother!" Hans yelled to him. "You will eat and take care of yourself because I cannot stand losing anyone else!"

Carson watched Hans struggling to walk on his own. A few tears slowly rolled down his face. It pained him to see Hans like that. He felt completely exhausted. All the control he thought he once had was gone. Pouring more whiskey into his glass, he wanted to forget about everything that happened in the past few years. He wanted to disappear and erase all those memories.

Hans went back to the library, bringing back a tray with some food and water. Carson looked at him and sighed. He knew he had to tell him everything.

"You don't know what I have done," Carson started.

"Maybe I do ... more than you think!" Hans replied sharply.

"No ... it is not about Denna. You will hate me forever."

"What are you talking about?" Hans asked him hesitantly, without really wanting to know. "Did you do anything to Francine?"

"Not really," Carson answered, feeling some regret. "I was going to, but I couldn't. I let her go ... but I don't know if she has survived."

"She is alive!" Hans affirmed, realizing that Carson had no idea.

"Alive? So ... she made it?" Carson replied, surprised.

"I thought you told me you put her inside the train?" Hans asked, suspecting something wasn't right.

"Yes ... well ... I just didn't know if she made it through!"

Hans always knew there was more to that story, but he decided not to question Carson any further. All that mattered to him was that Francine was well and safe. He also had to think about Abraham.

"I guess I need to thank you!" Hans continued, changing the tone of that conversation. "Aside from everything that happened, you still have done a lot for us! And for that, I am very grateful."

"Have you heard from her ... Francine?" Carson asked, surprised by Hans's reaction.

"I got a letter saying she is all right," Hans told him without wanting to disclose too much. "I have no idea where she is, but I do hope that one day I will find her. But now, we can only change our future choices. I need to fulfill my promises to Denna. We have to get your son out of here!"

Deep inside, Hans still wanted to confront him for everything that Carson had done to her. But in the end, he also realized that it was Carson himself who had saved them so many times!

"I need papers that can get the baby out of here with me," Hans requested.

Carson looked directly into Hans's eyes. He knew that was the right thing to do.

"I will get them for you as fast as possible! It doesn't matter what I have to do. I will get them for you!"

Hans was pleased to hear that. "I know it also has been very hard for you. I perhaps never thanked you enough. You have sacrificed and risked a lot for us! You have also lost the ones you loved the most. So many things have changed! But if it is all right with you … I will take care of your son. I will love him as my own!"

Carson kept silent for a moment. He still had mixed feelings about being a father, about his son.

They talked some more in the library. Carson ended up falling asleep right there. Part of him really wanted to see his son. But he never did. The brave, proud Nazi Commander didn't have the courage to face that new reality.

A few weeks had gone by, and Carson knew he would have to leave town soon. With their defenses ready in that area, some of his troops were diverted to the French-occupied regions.

Carson was able to request papers for his son, Hans, and Eugene to get out of Germany. However, the authorizations had to come from Berlin, and it was impossible to know when they would arrive.

"Someone I trust will bring you the papers," Carson said. "It may take a while, but it will happen!"

"We can wait! Thank you so much!" Hans said with great relief. "But before you leave, I think you should see him."

"Hans," Carson said, afraid of how he would feel. "It is better if I don't. I don't think I can …."

"Just go upstairs," Hans cut him off. "You never know when you will be able to see him again."

Carson sighed. He was nervous. He had never taken the initiative to see his son for a reason. He didn't feel ready.

"He is still sleeping," Hans insisted. "Just go see him."

As Carson walked upstairs, Denna's face came rushing to his mind. He tried to push those thoughts away, but it was simply impossible. Every step he took made him feel closer to her.

He hesitated for a few seconds before opening the door. *I have to do this!*

At a distance, he could see Abraham's tiny body. A wave of strange and deep emotions took hold of him as he walked slowly toward the crib.

Standing right before his son, Carson watched him as he slept peacefully. *He looks so much like me!* he thought.

Suddenly, the baby woke up, catching him by surprise.

Abraham looked straight at him and giggled, moving his little hands up in the air. Carson smiled back at him automatically.

He wanted to hold his son in his arms, telling him he would keep him safe. And yet … he said nothing.

Feeling what he would often call a weakness, Carson turned around fast and left the room.

"Take care of him for me, Hans," Carson approached his brother. "Perhaps one day I can …."

Carson couldn't finish his sentence. Too many conflicting feelings still existed in his mind and soul.

Hans nodded. "Don't worry; I will protect him. I will take care of him as my own son until one day you may want to … see him again."

"I don't know, Hans. I don't know how to feel about this! Everything seems so out of place. Who knows what the future holds now?"

For a brief moment, nothing else was said. They both understood the significance of that those words. It could be the last time they may see each other.

"Carson," Hans said, breaking the silence. "Thank you for the papers. For everything! I know that … it was you … you who always saved us!"

"You don't have to thank me for anything," Carson replied in a caring way. Hans had always been his best friend, and even with the war, those feelings never changed.

"Well … I understand you will be leaving to other war zones soon. So, I want you to know … you will always be my brother! Always!" Hans said emotionally.

Carson hesitated before saying his next words as he fought the tears that instantly filled his eyes.

"I can say the same about you! Although sometimes you drive me crazy! But in the end … I should be the one thanking you!"

Hans smiled. In a split second, he remembered the happy times they had together in that house. It was a long time ago. But despite everything that happened, deep inside his heart, he still considered Carson to be his brother.

"I have to go." Carson picked up his coat and started moving toward the door.

"You saved Denna's life, in a way," Hans called to him. "I am not sure if you knew or were aware that she … I believe she felt the same for you!" Hans finished his last words remembering everything Denna had told him. And even though she never completely admitted to him, he could tell, she also fell in love with Carson.

Carson looked at Hans, surprised. His heart exploded against his chest once he heard her name again. He often had wondered if she could ever love him back.

"You saved our father's life when he was arrested. And my own a few times and the life of the woman I love! Now you have done the right thing one more time! I knew you were not that bad after all!"

Carson smiled at him, at his brother! He stood still, simply looking at Hans. He would never forget those words!

"Take care of yourself!"

"You too, Hans!"

And so, nothing else was said. Carson turned around and walked away.

Hans heard the sound of the door being shut, and with that, another chapter of his life had been closed. *Will I ever see him again?* he thought, feeling so many different emotions.

Eugene watched Carson's vehicle driving away. He felt relieved, knowing he was gone.

Carson left that very morning for France. He was responsible for holding the last German line against the Allies, who had occupied most of the French territory months after D-Day.

CHAPTER 44

The wet leaves of the Autumn of 1944 were still falling when Hans finally received the travel passes to leave Germany alongside Abraham and Eugene.

Fully dressed in one of Carson's military uniforms, Hans looked almost unrecognizable. He knew they had a better chance of crossing the border if they followed every detail of Carson's instructions.

They sat in silence as the taxi driver made his way toward the train station.

Without any warning, several airplanes flew by the city, launching bombs to the ground. The loud sound of explosions caught everyone's attention, reminding them of the previous airstrike. Screams and gunshots could be heard from far away.

The taxi driver stopped the car abruptly and tried to get some information from a man who was running by them.

"You better get out of here!" the man said. "They have arrived! They are here!"

Eugene looked around franticly. Military tanks and jeeps rushed toward the outer side of the city. It was happening everywhere. People ran for cover, but it seemed there was no safe place to hide.

"We have to get out of this street!" yelled the taxi driver.

"Rush to the station!" Hans urged. "We must be near!"

But it was too late. They were already downtown, and the driver went as far as he could amidst the hundreds of people running around the streets, trying to escape. Further ahead, cars piled up on the road, trying to make their way out of town in one way or another.

"I cannot go any further," the taxi driver yelled at them. "You have to get out!"

"Please, sir, we cannot leave!" Eugene appealed. "We have an injured man and a child."

But the driver heard nothing but another sound of an explosion nearby.

"Leave now! I'm turning around!" he demanded, frightened.

"We will have to walk," Hans said. "We will miss the train!"

Eugene helped Hans and the baby out of the car. Amidst all the chaos, they sprinted toward the station.

People were pushing each other around, fighting for any possible spot on the train. The Nazi soldiers could barely keep people away from the tracks.

"Move away, or we will shoot!" the soldiers screamed. "No one will be allowed to leave!"

"Wait here, Hans," Eugene told him. "I will be right back."

Eugene pushed his way through the crowd and did not stop until he finally reached one of the soldiers.

"Move back!" the soldier yelled at him.

"I have to get onto that train," Eugene quickly said. "I am responsible for Commander Carson's brother and son's journey to Switzerland. I have special authorizations for that."

"Commander Carson?" the soldier immediately replied curiously. "The Führer has ordered everyone to stay here and fight. He wants us to destroy all railroads leading to Berlin and the bordering lines of Germany!"

"But we are going to Switzerland," Eugene said loudly, trying to make himself heard.

"The train will not leave!" the soldier shouted. "The railroads are already being destroyed!"

Eugene looked back at Hans, who stood on the other side, holding Abraham.

"I said leave, now! Move away!" the soldier continued aggressively.

Hans held the baby tightly. He could feel the mayhem developing around him as Abraham began to cry.

"We will have to go back, Hans," Eugene said, returning to grab Hans's arms. "No one will be able to leave town. They have blocked all the roads and train tracks!"

"We need to find a way, Eugene!" Hans insisted, not wanting to wait any longer.

"I tried everything, Hans! I explained who you were, and still … he said the Führer is ordering everyone to stay and fight!"

Hans could barely move through the crowd. It was Eugene who had to make room for them to walk away.

They all heard another explosion that sounded much closer than the previous one. Hans knew they had no other choice but to make it home.

"We will have to walk back, sir," said Eugene concerned.

They started to move carefully through all the debris and destruction. People were still outside, desperately trying to find their loved ones and evaluate what they still had left. It took them over an hour to make it home.

"Just another block, sir!" Eugene affirmed, already able to see the Schulze's residence from a short distance.

Soon after they made it home, they started hearing more explosions, more gunshots from a distance. The Allies had finally broken through to German territory.

They stayed in the basement throughout the night. Once more, Hans would have to wait to leave Germany.

It was morning before they finally decided to check things outside the house. Eugene left the basement first. Crouching to look out the window on the ground floor, he was stunned to see non-German troops approaching. He rushed back to the basement.

With Abraham still in his arms, Hans tried to decide what they would do next. But he didn't have much of a chance to think as loud voices could already be heard coming from the upper floor. Soldiers had entered the Schulzes' house.

"The uniform!" Eugene whispered to Hans, who hadn't had a chance to change out of Carson's clothes.

"Is there anyone in there?" a soldier asked, opening the basement door.

Trying not to make any noise, Eugene helped Hans get rid of the Nazi military coat.

"Right here!" a soldier yelled out loud in English.

Eugene placed his hands on Hans's shoulder.

"There are some people inside this house, too!" the English man yelled to the other soldiers.

Hans heard the footsteps rushing down to the basement. It was too late for him to get rid of the rest of the uniform.

"Put your hands up!" an English soldier yelled in German.

"Look what we have here," one of the soldiers said. "Another Nazi coward!"

"I am not a soldier," Hans rushed to say. "I am …."

"Shut up!" one of the American soldiers shouted at him.

"None of you are Nazis anymore, right?" the other English soldier added. "Now, you are all angels!"

Hans and Eugene couldn't understand a word. The same English soldier approached Hans and spat on his face.

"I am not one of them!" Hans replied in French, thinking he would have a better chance to be understood.

"Oh," the English soldier laughed sarcastically along with the others. "*Parle Français* now.…"

"I had to wear the uniform so I could escape," Hans said in French again.

"Let the other man keep the child for the moment," the English soldier ordered. "I want someone to interrogate this soldier. I want to know everything about those people. Something tells me we will find out a lot of good information here!"

"Move!" another soldier said, pushing Hans forward.

"And Abraham? What will happen to the child?" Hans asked worriedly.

"I can take care of him until you are back, Hans," Eugene said, trying to comfort him. "Do not worry. I will wait here for you with Abraham!"

"Keep him safe, Eugene! I should be back soon! But if not, take the baby to Switzerland, to my parents' house!" Hans called back loudly to Eugene as he was being pushed up the stairs. "Find Francine! You need to find Francine! She will help you with the baby."

Hans stumbled on the steps, falling to the ground. "I am blind. I can't see!"

"Get up!" the soldier yelled, grabbing Hans by his shirt and pushing him forward.

"Find Francine, Eugene! Victoria knows where she is. Go to Switzerland!" Hans kept shouting.

Two soldiers held his arms as they made their way out of the house. Hans tried in vain to convince them he was a civilian and hated the Nazi party. He told them he was attempting to flee Germany with a Jewish baby and Eugene.

An English sergeant had arrived at the house and heard some of the words Hans had said. One of the soldiers explained the situation in detail.

"I am not a German soldier," Hans kept repeating.

The sergeant also took a good look at him and his uniform.

"Well," the sergeant told the others, "take him to our camp for now."

Hans could hear people shouting everywhere around him, along with the sounds of heavy military vehicles moving. Machine guns and tanks were fired against German soldiers who were still resisting. Hans understood then that the German empire was finally crumbling.

They were all speaking English, and Hans wasn't familiar with the language. The Allies had started the process of finding the Nazi military officers, who they knew to be hiding among the civilian population. They thought Hans was one of them.

He was placed in a separate corner from the other prisoners. They were inside a building, an improvised base camp for the Allies.

Hans waited anxiously for an opportunity to explain things. But it wasn't until later in the evening that he heard a few voices in a foreign language.

"Get him," someone said.

Hans felt his body being pulled up.

"Take him to the sergeant's office," another soldier said.

Hans heard the sound of a door being closed behind him. The interrogation quickly started.

"Who are you?" the sergeant asked him, followed by the translator.

"My name is Hans Schulze," Hans rushed to say. "I am a civilian, not a soldier. It is a long story, but I can explain everything."

The English officer took a close look at him. He was already aware that Hans was blind.

"Well, Hans Schulze," the sergeant replied. "I am Sergeant Miller, the person responsible for you from now on. So, my question is, if you are a civilian, what were you doing in a military uniform then? It doesn't make sense, does it?"

Hans thought about the irony of that situation. He was being mistaken for a Nazi officer. He knew it would be hard to convince them otherwise. He was once again trapped, stuck in Germany.

"I have been trying to get out of the country for years. I knew that if I dressed as a soldier, I would have a better chance to do so," Hans started. "I stole one of the uniforms from someone I knew so I could escape."

"Oh, so you were actually trying to get out of Germany wearing a Nazi military uniform. That's interesting! We usually hear the opposite," the sergeant laughed sarcastically.

"But that is the truth!" affirmed Hans.

The English officer looked at the young German, not sure what to believe. He knew Hans couldn't be an active military soldier or an officer being blind. But it was more than that. The sergeant also noticed that Hans didn't behave like the other German soldiers they had captured. There was something different about him.

"Why do you want to leave your own country?" Sergeant Miller continued. "This is your country, right?"

"I am German. That is right. But I was never part of the Nazi regime, nor did I ever sympathize with it. I despise everything they have been doing. I hate Hitler! That is why I wanted to leave."

The sergeant was intrigued. He knew some officers would say just about anything to be set free, but then again, Hans didn't come across as insincere.

"Listen, I don't have much time to waste. We are not going to hurt you. At least not now, not if you tell us everything you know. We just want information."

Hans took a deep breath, trying to think about his next words.

"I don't know anything else. I know it is hard for you to believe me. I understand! But I have been trying to get out of here for a long time, and I couldn't. My parents have died as well as my Jewish friend, Denna. I am the one who is responsible for her child; she died in childbirth, and I need to take him to Switzerland."

"I am a little confused. That baby found in the basement was actually from a Jewish woman?" the officer asked, already aware of some things that Eugene told the other English soldiers when he was interrogated.

"Yes," Hans said. "She was Jewish. We were hiding her there, in my parent's house. I promised I would … save her …."

"You and your family hid a Jewish girl inside your own house?" the officer asked him curiously.

"We did hide her," confirmed Hans. "They were going to kill her. And as we couldn't get her documents to leave the country, I stayed behind with her."

"Interesting. So, you decided to stay and watch the horror your people started to spread around the world! Very convenient, don't you think?"

"Not all Germans were Nazis, sir!" Hans stated, feeling extremely frustrated. "I understand you cannot simply believe me. But I ask you to consider the fact that my family, and my friends, have died trying to stop them. My own parents died trying to save a Jewish girl. I was arrested by the SS, and so was my father. I know this might not be much for you. But for me, I have lost almost everything I once knew and loved."

That answer took Sergeant Miller by surprise. But he wasn't convinced yet.

"And that makes up for everything your people have done?" he asked Hans.

"Of course not! Nothing we can do will ever make up for it. But my family and I were never like them or ever even involved. But I know what has been done. And believe me … I am both ashamed and appalled. I know there will never be an excuse for all the atrocities that Germany has committed."

The sergeant kept looking at Hans. For some strange reason, he had a feeling that Hans spoke the truth.

"I was trying to escape with Denna's baby," Hans continued. "Only certain military personnel had full clearance to leave the country, as I have said before. But it was exactly on that same day that the attack happened. The German military forces would not allow us to board the train. We had to go back home. I didn't have the chance to change clothes. Do you think I would still be wearing the uniform if I was a true soldier?"

The sergeant thought it made sense.

"Where did you get the uniform?" Sergeant Miller continued his interrogation.

Hans sighed. He knew he couldn't lie. Sooner or later, the truth would come out anyway.

"I used to have a friend, a longtime friend. He is an officer now against all common sense. I tried to persuade him not to join the Nazi party, but he didn't listen to us!"

"You mean, a Nazi officer?"

"Yes," said Hans. "But …."

"So," the English officer interrupted him, "on the one hand, you save some Jewish people, and on the other, you befriend Nazi officers. That makes it a very interesting situation, don't you think?"

"I don't befriend Nazi soldiers," Hans rushed to say angrily. "I hate them! Carson was raised by my parents. He has been like a brother to me. He has always been treated as part of my family. Then the war came, and we grew apart. We tried to make him change his ways, but he was too blinded by propaganda to see the truth. And although he has done horrible things, he has helped me save my friend Denna's life, even knowing she was Jewish. He was actually the one who gave me the authorizations to leave the country with the baby."

The sergeant was astonished by the story. Hans didn't seem to be lying. But the sergeant still wasn't completely sure. He had been trained to deal with all kinds of good liars, especially secret agents.

Sergeant Miller looked at the other English soldier who was transcribing the conversation.

"All right, here is what we are going to do. I will get some information about you and your family. Then, we will talk again. Perhaps by then, you will remember more things, things that could be helpful to us. So, I just need your so-called brother's full name, and we will try to find out some information about him. Do you know where he is?"

"His name is Carson Beurmann. But I don't know where he is. We haven't heard from him in weeks, not since he was sent to France after the Normandy invasion."

"You said his name was Carson, right?" the sergeant asked him again. "We found a few documents with his name on them at your house. Are you sure he isn't really you?"

Hans couldn't believe what he was hearing. He couldn't believe all the accusations being brought against him. But then again, he knew it made sense. He had been caught wearing a German military uniform, and Carson had left a few of his documents inside the house during his last visit.

"His house got destroyed in a bombing a few months ago," Hans rushed to explain. "I can give you the address. I told him he could leave the few things that remained in my house. Some of his documents were there. But I am not Carson. I am not a Nazi soldier!"

"We have already checked a few things," the officer said. "We know there are two people in this story: Hans and Carson, but what we can't figure out is which one of them you are."

Hans sighed in frustration. "There are some documents and pictures in my house here in Germany as well as the one in Switzerland," Hans said, knowing he had to provide some proof. "There are also some family members who live there and other employees. And also …."

Hans hesitated for a few seconds. His eyes filled with tears.

"There is Francine, the French woman that I love and my son! They are waiting for me in Switzerland. We also helped her to escape from Germany."

The English officer leaned back in his chair. He had heard many stories but nothing quite as elaborate as this one.

"So, you and this French woman …." the sergeant prompted.

"We met before the war … we love each other! We have a son, and I haven't even met him yet," Hans explained in a sad voice. "She is waiting for me. She has been waiting for too long."

"What was she doing here in Germany?" the officer wondered. "Was she perhaps a spy?"

"No. She was being held as a prisoner. She is a French nurse."

The English sergeant looked at the other two soldiers standing next to him, not knowing what to think. For some strange reason, he believed that maybe Hans was telling the truth. But he still needed proof.

"I don't know if you are a good German man as you say, or if there even is such a thing," the sergeant said sarcastically. "Or perhaps you may just be the most creative bastard I have ever met. I will have to check on your story. You better not have wasted my time."

"I am telling the truth, sir! I can provide addresses, names of people who can confirm who I am and what I have done. But in the meantime, I would like to know if Eugene and the baby are all right?"

"They are fine. The baby stayed with him at your house."

"Eugene is a good man! I would like to talk to him if possible. He can go to Switzerland and get all the proof you need! He can reach out to all the people that can testify on my behalf, especially Francine."

"We will see … I'll think about it!"

Despite his persistent requests to speak with Eugene, Hans was sent straight back to the place where they were keeping the prisoners. He tried to remain hopeful that they would find out the truth and let him go eventually. It was a terrifying feeling, not knowing what was going to happen. Once more, his life was in someone else's hands. He thought about Francine, his son, and Abraham. He knew they were all waiting for him. He had to find a way to communicate with Eugene. He was the only person that could help him at that moment!

Sergeant Miller stayed in his office, thinking about the story he had just heard. He always felt very confident in his ability to tell who was lying and who was telling the truth. But with that young man, he just couldn't be sure.

The English officer gave directions for the other soldiers to find more information about Hans.

"Send a letter to our contacts in Switzerland," he said. "Try to find someone at his residence or someone by the name of Francine, anyone who could know anything about that man. Even if he tells the truth, I still want to know about his brother, Carson, the Nazi officer. He might try to make contact with them, and I want to know when that happens. His brother is the kind of man we are looking for. In the meantime, leave him here in this building. Make sure he doesn't get sent anywhere else without my permission."

The Allies continued their advances through German territory. Sergeant Miller had to leave in a hurry for yet another German town that had just been seized. In the meantime, Hans had to stay in that improvised prison, among other German captives, and without any access to visitors.

Eugene wasn't sure what to do next. He was unable to communicate with Hans. *You have to go to Switzerland and find Francine!* Eugene remembered Hans's last words before he was taken away. He certainly did not want to leave Hans alone in Germany, but he knew he had no other alternative. *I can always take the baby to Hans's house in Switzerland, find that woman Francine, and then return to Germany to help him!*

Not being considered a threat by the Allies, Eugene started to inquire around, searching for any information about the possibility of leaving Germany.

After a lot of effort, he finally got authorization to leave the country with Abraham. He had enough documentation to prove he wasn't born in Germany.

A few days later, holding Abraham tightly in his arms, he was able to board a train at a nearby town, one of the few that were still operating.

Eugene understood very well the importance of that task. Both Abraham and Hans depended on him. Not only would he have to make sure Abraham would be delivered safely to Hans's house in Switzerland, but he would also have to find a woman named Francine.

"Sir," a voice woke Eugene up. "We have arrived at the border."

Eugene thanked the man and proceeded toward the guard station.

A few minutes later, he entered the Swiss territory. "We have finally made it," Eugene said, smiling down at little Abraham.

CHAPTER 45

Since the Normandy invasion, things had completely turned around for the Allies. But the war continued with intense German resistance.

After receiving an urgent letter from Victoria requesting her presence, Francine prepared to go to the Schulzes' house in Switzerland for the first time.

"I will go tomorrow, first thing in the morning," Francine said anxiously. "Victoria told me there was something really important she needed to tell me. She mentioned she had finally received some news from all of them. I have that same sensation again that something horrible has happened to Hans."

"You cannot go there alone!" Nicole replied, concerned. "They are Germans!"

"Mother, things have changed! It is much safer here in Switzerland now."

"I will go with you, then," affirmed Nicole.

"I would rather go there alone," Francine insisted.

"Let's wait for Daniel or at least take someone else with you!"

"I haven't heard from Daniel for months," Francine said. "I cannot wait anymore!"

"Please, Francine," Nicole said, not giving up easily. "You have a son now!"

Francine sighed.

"I can go with Fernand," Francine compromised.

Nicole still worried about her daughter. She wasn't completely convinced that Hans was indeed a good man, as Francine described.

It was very early in the morning when Francine rang the doorbell. Her body was shivering more out of nervousness than from the cold air outside.

Victoria rushed to the door.

"Bonjour," Francine said, looking at the young girl.

"Bonjour," replied Victoria awkwardly. She was used to speaking German.

"Je suis …." Francine contained herself, realizing she should be speaking in German. "My name is Francine. You must be Victoria?"

"Yes, it is me! Please come in," Victoria rushed to say. "I will get Eugene."

"I will wait for you here in the garden," said Fernand.

Francine walked inside Hans's parents' house, observing everything with curiosity. In an instant, Francine spotted an older gentleman looking at her from the hallway.

"So, you are Francine?" Eugene said, walking slowly toward her.

"Yes," she replied, shaking his hand.

"My name is Eugene. I am Hans's family's long-time employee in Germany," he continued. "But please, let's sit down somewhere and talk."

Francine nodded, smiling at him.

"I will bring you some tea," Victoria said enthusiastically. She was thrilled to have finally met the mysterious girl she communicated with in those letters.

They both sat quietly for a moment. Francine's attention had been directed to a beautiful family picture inside the library.

"Those are his parents," said Eugene.

"It's a beautiful picture!" said Francine, missing Hans even more. "Are they still there with him? What is happening?"

"We have a lot to talk about," affirmed Eugene. "Hans told me to find you!"

Francine could feel tears filling her eyes. She was so happy to hear something from Hans again.

"Is he all right? Just, please … tell me he is all right! I haven't heard from him in so long! Victoria told me in her last letter that you would need my help!"

"I will tell you everything," Eugene promised.

As Eugene started speaking, Francine's face reflected all her emotions.

Although Eugene didn't know the entire story, he talked about the events after the airstrike. From the moment he found Denna in the middle of the debris to Hans's arrest.

"Hans's last words before he was taken away were for me to bring Denna's baby to Switzerland and find you," Eugene finally concluded. "I think he wants you to take care of the baby until he comes back."

Surprised and astonished by all she had heard, Francine got up at once, pacing around nervously. At that moment, she fully understood why she had stopped receiving any news from him.

"Mon Dieu! So much has happened!! And there I was completely unaware that Hans was arrested and … all that tragedy! I need to help him! We need to help him right away!"

Eugene promptly agreed. "He is there alone! I need to go back as soon as possible with proof that he is not his brother, Carson."

"Exactly! And I will help you with that! I will do everything and anything to prove his innocence!"

"I am so glad to hear that, miss!"

"It will be an honor to take care of her child, Eugene! I can't believe she died … that poor girl! And his parents? Hans must be suffering so much! And after all he has done … they still arrested him?"

"He will be very happy to know you will be taking care of Abraham. Now that you are here, I can leave right away and bring proof that Hans is not a Nazi officer."

"We need to help him fast! I can go back with you, Eugene. I can tell them my own story. They can't keep him there!" Francine tried to organize her thoughts. "I can have baby Abraham brought to my aunt's house. They can watch him while I am gone. I also have powerful friends that can help us!"

"Unfortunately, I don't know much about his situation after the arrest, as I was denied access to him," Eugene said, remembering all the events. "We will need all the help we can get! He is being held by the Allies. Maybe your friends could help!"

"I will try to contact them as soon as I get home. But I need to know everything that happened until the moment he was taken as a prisoner, all the details. I will write a letter to the officers responsible for his arrest and also a personal letter for Hans." Francine tried to think of a plan. "You can take them with you; maybe they will help him right away! As for now, perhaps it is better if I stay here a while longer in order to reach some of my friends. They work with the Allies and will definitely attend to my request! We will keep communicating until I return to Germany."

"I will keep sending you all the information I get," Eugene said, agreeing with her plan.

"I will come back tomorrow with all the letters, Eugene!" Francine stated, getting ready to leave. "I have so much to do before you leave again! Thank you so much, Eugene. For everything. We will be forever grateful!"

Francine held Abraham gently in her arms as Fernand drove her back home. She remembered Denna really well. She thought about the Jewish girl's tragic fate.

Francine entered her aunt's house with her mind racing. She needed to act fast. She would move to Hans's house in Switzerland, as instructed by Eugene. She would have to find a way to contact some of her friends, especially Daniel. Hans was in danger, he was alone, and it was her turn to help him out.

Two weeks had passed, and Francine had already moved to Hans's house despite her mother's insistence for her to stay. Francine wrote several letters to her friends in France, asking for help in Hans's case.

As she waited impatiently for any news, her mother finally received a letter from Daniel informing them about Jean. But the English spy wasn't aware that the Allies had taken Hans.

"Your father was sent to Italy! But he is doing well," Nicole happily told Francine during one of her daily visits.

Among tears and smiles, they hugged each other, hoping to be reunited with Jean soon.

As the days went by, Francine grew more concerned. She still hadn't received any letters back from her friends. Only Eugene communicated with her, but the news wasn't good. Hans was still kept as a prisoner, and the officer responsible for him was away. No one could have access to Hans without his approval.

Ever since the liberation of France, Nicole insisted on her daughter going back home with her. But Francine refused to go anywhere without Hans.

"I will go back to Germany as soon as I talk to Daniel," she told her mother.

"Francine … how can anyone help him after all the Germans have done? There is still a war out there!"

"I don't care what people think! He is not like the rest of them! How many times do I have to say this?" Francine replied, frustrated. "I will try everything to get him out of there. I will never give up! He saved my life and so many others. Now, it is our turn to help him. I hope that there are still people out there that can see beyond his nationality. There were Germans who risked everything they had to fight against Hitler! They deserve to be recognized! Hans is that speck of light in the middle of that chaos!"

CHAPTER 46

As the Allies advanced further through German territory, Hans still waited for news. It didn't matter how many times he had tried to explain things; no one listened to him. No one wanted to believe him. Sergeant Miller, the officer responsible for his case, was still out of town, and nothing could be done until his return.

For Hans, the worst part was to be perceived as a Nazi officer. It pained him that anyone would think him to be capable of the atrocities for which he was being accused. But Hans didn't really blame them. He knew the indescribable terror that the Nazis had spread within Germany alone. He could only imagine the degree of devastation wreaked throughout the rest of the world.

In his loneliness, Hans wondered if Eugene was able to leave the country finally. He would dream that Eugene found Francine and Abraham and was now safe.

Weeks had gone by when Sergeant Miller finally requested Hans's presence again.

"I have been able to get more information about you," the English officer said. "I received several letters from your friend Eugene, and I did have some people come here to identify you from that factory you used to work at. They confirmed the fact that you were not a Nazi officer. But they also said your so-called brother, Carson Beurmann, was."

"Just as I have told you," Hans rushed to say. "Am I free to go then?"

"Not yet. We will need to know as much information about your brother as you can provide. He could be very important to our future operations here in your country."

"But I don't know where he is! I don't know much about his work because I was never involved and didn't want to know about his military matters."

"But like I have said before, I still need you around just in case he decides to come by this area."

"He would never come back here!" Hans frustratingly tried to explain.

"And why are you so sure?" the sergeant asked him.

"Why would a Nazi officer dare to go back to an area occupied by his enemies? I have two children that need me and are waiting for me. I still have to meet my own son! I just want to get out of here. I am tired, so tired of this war!"

"We are not the ones who started the war, are we?" the sergeant said angrily. He took a deep breath. The truth was that he also felt very tired. But he knew they still had a long way to go before the war was over.

"Look, you're just going to have to wait a little longer. You may be a good man, as you say, but you have to understand that you are still a German, one that is connected to an important Nazi officer. And just like your people, we are also not quite ready to show any sort of compassion. We still have a war to win, and it is too early to start releasing prisoners, wouldn't you agree?"

"Please!" Hans begged before being removed from the room. "Let me at least have a letter sent to Francine in Switzerland and Eugene. They need to know where I am and about my situation here."

"I will see what I can do."

Sergeant Miller thought for a minute. He didn't want to be unfair to a man that seemed to be innocent. *A French woman and a German man in love? In a time of war? That is quite a story.*

"Soldier," he started saying, having made up his mind. "Take this man to a separate section and help him write a letter, then bring it back to me afterward."

"So," another soldier asked once Hans was out of the room, "what do you make of that?"

"According to all the information we have, it seems he is telling the truth," The sergeant said. "But how can we be sure there is not more to that story? In the end, his so-called brother was a powerful Commander in this area. However, if he really did all those things he has stated, I have to say it's one of the most fascinating stories I have ever heard so far—and believe me, I've heard plenty!"

As much as the English officer tried to look indifferent to Hans's situation, he made sure to help him write two letters. One would go to Switzerland and another to his house in Germany, as he wasn't sure where Eugene was.

A few more days passed. Hans woke up to someone calling out his name.

"You have a letter," the soldier said rudely, tossing the letter at him.

Hans felt the envelope hit his legs. "I cannot read it!"

The English soldier laughed at him as he understood what he said in German. "And why the hell do you think that is my problem, you German piece of shit?"

"Bitte," Hans begged desperately. "Is there anyone here? Please, someone, help me! Please!

Despite his persistence, no one answered him; no one was around. Most prisoners had been relocated to another place. Hans was the only one in that jail cell.

CHAPTER 47

The news that Francine had so long waited for had finally arrived. Daniel contacted her as soon as he got her urgent message from one of his friends in France. He had promised to help her with Hans's case right away but asked her to stay patient in Switzerland.

Meanwhile, Francine also received a letter from Eugene about Hans, stating he was still held as a prisoner in their city. He said he had tried everything he could to get him out of there, but it was not working.

Francine wanted to go to Germany and talk to someone directly. She needed to prove Hans wasn't a Nazi officer. But she knew things didn't work that way. The war still went on fiercely inside the German territory. No one would listen to her. So she had no other choice but to wait a while longer for Daniel.

Later that month, both Francine and Nicole found out that Jean had finally been freed and was on his way back to France. Nicole could hardly wait to see him again. After all they had been through, his release was a miracle.

"Francine, it's time for us to go back home!" Nicole persisted.

"Don't waste your time on that subject again, Mother," said Francine. "You would never abandon dad, would you? So, please don't ask me to leave the man I love behind."

Nicole knew Francine too well to think she would ever give up fighting for Hans.

"Tell dad I love him, and I am really sorry for not being able to see him now. But I am sure it will happen soon! I know things will work out!"

The warmth of the sunlight slowly melted the remaining snow on the ground. The trees started to recover some of their greener tones while tiny purple flowers shyly blossomed near the water streams. Another spring was right around the corner.

News about Germany being surrounded circulated fast across the globe. The Allies were finally breaking through the last German lines.

Amid those victories, Francine received the most awaited letter.

Dear Francine,

I apologize for the delay, but I can finally say that I have found Hans. He has been moved to another location away from his hometown, that is why it took me so long to find him. The officer responsible for him is nowhere to be found, and his situation seems to be the same as the other German prisoners. Unfortunately, I am afraid that very little can be done until we can find the officer I mentioned. However, no one has any proof that he has been affiliated with the Nazi regime, which is good. The problem is that his brother, Carson, is a Nazi officer.

I believe they are trying to use Hans to get to his brother. I don't see the point in that, as Carson will probably never go back there. So, I do believe they will eventually understand that and let Hans go free. I have contacted Eugene as you have instructed. He has provided me with some valuable information proving that Hans was indeed a good man whose family has helped some Jewish populations. I have also been told that Hans and his father were part of a political party who strongly opposed the Nazi regime. His father was once arrested for that, and Hans narrowly escaped death due to his "brother's" influence. I also heard about his parents' death as well as the Jewish girl he tried to protect. He seems to be exactly as you have told me.

I know the situation is not easy, but I somehow find myself very involved in this matter. No innocent man should be held in prison. I also have some work to do here in Germany related to what you already know I do best. However, I have decided to take care of Hans's case personally. I will not leave Germany until I can solve this issue. But I beg you to be patient and not come here. I have also spoken to our old friend Pierre and am still trying to talk to Gerard. I am sure they will be able to help.

We all have been helped by a few Germans who kept sending us some valuable information during this war, proving a few of them do not deserve to be imprisoned or treated as enemies. But we also have to agree that not everyone follows the same character, making it very difficult to convince anyone of what we know. Therefore, we have to wait until Germany is ultimately defeated. It won't take much longer, believe me!

I will keep in touch. In the meantime, I will try to talk to Hans directly. I will try to find out how he is doing and, of course, give him some news about you and his son as you have instructed.

Votre ami,

Daniel

Francine placed the letter against her chest as she took a deep breath. Her eyes filled with tears of joy. "He found Hans!" Francine said. "He found Hans!"

As much as Francine wanted to go to Germany right away and help Daniel, she knew she had to follow his advice and stay in Switzerland for the moment.

Although that letter from Daniel brought her a great sense of relief, she was still deeply concerned about Hans's health and state of mind, and rightfully so. He had been kept a prisoner for months, alone and away from those he loved. And much worse, he was being treated like he was the enemy.

Hans had finally found someone who read Eugene's letters to him. He cried once he heard about Eugene and Abraham's departure from Germany and their safe arrival in Switzerland. He could hardly believe it. His prayers were answered. Eugene had found Francine and Abraham. They were all working together to get him out of there.

But Hans's enthusiasm didn't last long. Someone entered the jail cell and grabbed his arms, pushing him forward until he was thrown into a military vehicle.

Hans was relocated to a prison camp, along with many German soldiers, miles away from the city. He tried to ask questions. He asked to speak with someone in charge. But nothing worked.

In the beginning, Hans was still hopeful that Eugene would find him. But as days and weeks passed, he started to feel like he could be lost forever, alone, and unaware of his surroundings. Slowly, Hans started losing his sense of reality. His health deteriorated.

"There are probably hundreds of us here," a German soldier once told him. "But I know we can defeat them all again!" the soldier said deliriously.

A few times, amid his frustrations and severe mental exhaustion, Hans started to shout about his innocence.

"I am not one of them!" he would say loudly, trying to walk as he stumbled on other people's legs. "I am not one of them! Do you hear me?"

Some soldiers looked at him as if he had gone mad. But a few others whose pride was severely hurt started to direct their anger and hate toward Hans.

It didn't take long for three of them to surround him one afternoon.

"So," one of them said, "we have a traitor here."

"It's too bad that he is already blind," another said sarcastically.

"You bastards," Hans said, trying to focus in the direction of those voices. "You are the reason why we are here. You are the reason why she died, Denna, and my parents. Do you think I fear you, cowards?"

"You should," one said. "Traitors like you were the ones responsible for our fall."

"And you should be punished accordingly," the other German soldier retorted. "No mercy for the weak ones!"

They all raised their hands in a Nazi salute. Then Hans felt the first set of hands punching his face. And then another.

Hans tried to block the punches with his arms and elbows, guessing where his attackers were. But that only brought on more laughs among those who were hitting him.

"The blind man looks like a clown," one said. "He is not a true German. He must have been adopted."

"By a Jewish whore," another added.

Hans felt the anger grow inside him. He instantly reacted and hit one of them straight in his face, breaking the soldier's nose.

"You piece of shit! I'm going to kill you!"

The three soldiers jumped on Hans mercilessly. They hit him harshly, kicking and punching with fury.

The Allied soldiers guarding the prison camp did nothing but watch. They were amused as they watched them hurting one another and thus sparing them the work.

"Kill yourselves out, you Nazi pigs," one soldier encouraged them outside the barbwire gates.

The other prisoners didn't help him either. They all had been there in that prison for months on end. All of them were mentally and physically exhausted. They were hungry and cold and too weak to fight for anything else. Not caring about the war anymore, they just wanted to go back to whatever they would find left of their homes. They, too, had lost many friends and family members.

The three soldiers stopped hitting Hans only when they got too tired to continue.

"He is probably dead," said one of them.

"No," the other added. "He still breathes. Let him live his last days in agonizing pain."

"Let's go," the third one said, walking back to their usual corner.

Hans lay there, unable to move. Several of his bones had been broken. He started to lose consciousness due to the amount of pain and injuries to his head. Hans had no idea how close to death he was. The morning came fast as he laid in the same spot. Blood marks and bruises were covering his entire body. He was barely recognizable.

Anyone who looked at him would think of an immortalized statue, one that could easily symbolize all the suffering and brutality of that long war.

Hans started to wake up very slowly, but his mind wasn't clear. A high fever had struck him, further debilitating his weakened condition. His body shivered. Once in a while, amid his hallucinations, he opened his mouth halfway and started to say random words—words that were lost in the air, words no one could fully understand.

"Francine," he could barely whisper. "I can see you. I can still see you, Francine …."

Soon after, a fellow prisoner moved carefully through the crowd to reach him. It was a Nazi soldier who had watched the brutality of the past night. He wanted to take action, but he knew he didn't have any strength left. He felt ashamed.

The soldier approached Hans, placing his hand on his forehead. He quickly recognized the seriousness of his condition. Hans needed medical assistance.

He approached one of the guards trying to get their attention toward the injured soldier, but they did nothing but scream at him to move back.

"This man is dying!" the soldier shouted back.

"Move back, or we will shoot!" one of the guards threatened.

The German soldier went back to where Hans was. He grabbed his coat and placed it on top of his body. He believed Hans was still one of his people, still a German who needed assistance.

The Nazi soldier stayed by his side the entire day. He wanted to make sure no one else would dare to attack the man again. But it was too late … the condition of Hans's health was reaching its limit.

It was late afternoon when the prisoners saw a military Jeep bringing a few Allied soldiers. Every time that happened, they knew something was about to change. New orders would probably be given, and people would probably be removed.

Jumping off the Jeep fast, Daniel went straight to the gate. He talked to the head of the guards at that prison camp, showing all the papers he had in his hand.

"Where is he?" Daniel asked promptly.

"How would we know?" one of the soldiers replied. "They're all in there, hundreds of them. Most of them have name tags. Good luck!"

Daniel was already used to that kind of reciprocity toward anything German. "It's payback time," was a common attitude. And Daniel shared the same feeling. It had been a long and cruel war. They had seen the most inhumane acts take place and had lived through Hell. And right there, right in that camp, lay the ones solely responsible for the start of this insane war.

Two other soldiers accompanied him when they entered the prisoner's camp. They were mostly sitting in the muddy fields, some with their heads down, others looking nowhere. Daniel saw the humiliation, defeat, and anger in their faces.

There were so many of them that Daniel had no choice but to start calling for Hans out loud.

"Hans! I am looking for Hans Schulze," he shouted in German.

They all looked in his direction, but no one spoke a word.

As he continued walking, Daniel paid close attention to every one of them.

"Hans!" Daniel continued. "Hans Schulze!"

It didn't take him long to reach the place where the Nazi soldier sat beside Hans. The soldier first heard what seemed to be merely a whisper. But then, as Daniel got closer, he clearly heard the name Hans.

The soldier looked around and noticed that no one answered. That was when he realized that there was one man who could not speak for himself, even if he wanted to.

He quickly looked at Hans and moved his body slowly to the side, trying to find any reference to his name.

Daniel had already passed by them. He kept walking, slowly increasing his distance.

The soldier wiped the blood off Hans' name tag. There wasn't any doubt; it was Hans!

"Hey!" the soldier got up, screaming. "Hier!" he yelled to get Daniel's attention.

CHAPTER 48

Daniel heard something and immediately turned back to see a man waving his hands in the air. Not wasting any time, he walked quickly toward him.

"You said the name Hans?" the German soldier asked without hesitation.

"Yes," Daniel nodded. "Are you him?"

"No … but I believe this man is," he said, pointing at Hans, who was on the ground looking as if he were dead.

Daniel stared at the man on the ground for a few seconds. He could barely see the man's face underneath all the bruises and the blood.

Daniel glanced at that German soldier, waiting for an explanation.

"Some of the soldiers here never liked him," the man told him. "They called him a traitor because he kept saying that he wasn't one of us. Last night, they took it out on him."

Daniel knelt closer to Hans, reaching out for his name tag. There he read the name - Hans Schulze.

He took a closer look at him. Although he was severely injured, the description given by Francine seemed to be a match. All the facts pointed to be Hans! Daniel knew he had indeed found him.

"Let's get him out of here," Daniel spoke to the other guards.

They both looked at one another.

"What are you two waiting for?" Daniel pried. "Help me get him out of here! These are orders coming from a French general. It is in that letter I have given you! Unless you two want to take the responsibility of explaining why this man has died here, you'd better start helping me right now. He has important information to give us. The general is waiting for it. It is an urgent matter."

Daniel knew exactly what he was doing. He had no official letter allowing the removal of Hans from the prison besides a letter written by Pierre. He had no other choice but to lie; he knew Hans would die if left in there.

As Daniel began to cradle Hans's head, he turned to the German soldier who had helped Hans.

"You, soldier," Daniel said, looking at him. "What is your name?"

"Jan," the soldier replied. "Jan Becker."

"You have done a good thing today," Daniel told him. "I won't forget your name."

The two English soldiers and Daniel carefully carried Hans to the Jeep and rushed him to the nearest hospital. Daniel wasn't sure if Hans was going to make it. The image of Julian dying appeared in his mind. So many of his friends and family members had suffered the same fate. But it was during those moments when he tried to save a life that he could finally find some peace. That was what made him keep moving forward, continuing his work no matter how hard it could get.

The hospital was located in a nearby German town seized by the Allies. A few days went by until the doctor finally gave Daniel some news.

"He seems to be recovering steadily, but his life is still at risk," stated the doctor.

Daniel had already written to Francine as well as some of his friends in France and Switzerland. He knew he would not be able to get Hans out of there without proper authorization.

With unshakable determination, Daniel made sure to stay by Hans's side, waiting for any good news from his friends. Unfortunately, it didn't take long for him to receive an unpleasant surprise—one of the English officers wanted to speak to him privately. Daniel knew exactly what it was going to be about.

"Who has given you orders to take a German prisoner out of that camp?" Lieutenant Joseph Carter questioned him.

"I have orders from France requesting his removal from Germany to Switzerland, sir," Daniel replied politely.

"And who are you?" the lieutenant continued curiously.

"My name is Daniel Haswell, sir. I work for the English Secret Services."

"All right! But that doesn't mean you can take him away! Does it?"

"Sir, he is not a soldier," Daniel argued. "He has been placed there in error. Hans has helped save several lives— both French and Jewish— and he was taken to prison in his own country for doing so. He also fought against the Nazi party. His parents died a few months ago trying to save a Jewish girl. Should I go on, sir?"

The English lieutenant felt somewhat awkward. He wasn't expecting such a passionate defense.

"Still," he said authoritatively, "I am responsible for the camp, and no one can leave without my consent! You can tell your French friends that."

"I will have them to come here personally, if necessary, sir. Perhaps they can explain the situation to you better," Daniel warned. "That man has been beaten severely within an inch of his life by German soldiers inside that prison camp who consider him a traitor."

Lieutenant Carter sighed. The truth was that he could care less about any German person getting hurt, but he didn't want to get into bad terms with any French or English authorities.

"Perhaps you can explain a little why he was placed in my prison camp?" the officer continued in a more friendly manner.

"It is a long story, sir," said Daniel. "I'll be glad to go over all the details. But for now, we are just trying to make things right."

"Well, Mr. Haswell," said the lieutenant. "He can stay in this hospital until I get the right information and proper papers for his release. But as soon as he recovers, he'll go back to the camp until you bring me proof of what you are saying."

"Sir," Daniel continued in a serious tone, "I am an Englishman. I have been working with the special unit services all over this continent throughout this war. And as so many others have done, I have risked my own life to try and defeat Germany. I would never defend or lie about saving a German life if I didn't truly believe that he or she was indeed a noble person. Hans went against his own country, saved the lives of others, and risked his own life only to end up in the position you see him in right now, sir!"

Lieutenant Carter took another look at Hans and saw his condition. As much as he hated to admit it, he knew Daniel wasn't lying.

"He can stay here, for now," the officer repeated one more time. "But if I were you, I would rush to get me some documentation on this 'noble man' as you call him. Honestly, I would have no problem releasing him under your care, but I also have to answer to my superiors, who have given me specific orders not to let anyone out of that camp without their consent. Strange things have already been happening. It turns out that some other countries have been taking special interest in some German scientists that are being held in that field. We need to be careful. We don't want to free the monsters, do we?"

"I understand, sir! And I will do as you told me," Daniel replied, already thinking about his next move.

"Who did you say you work for again?"

"Well, I was placed in France mainly under Pierre and General Gerard's command."

"All right, then bring me an official document allowing his removal from here, with a signature from the general and another English officer. That should do it!"

"Yes, sir," Daniel agreed, thankful to have gained some time.

As the lieutenant exited the hospital building, Daniel understood the urgency of the matter. He had to act fast before Hans would be thrown back into the prison camp again. The same soldiers who hurt him would probably want to finish the job if he was sent back.

The doctors informed Daniel that Hans's recovery was going to be very slow. He took it as an opportunity to go back to France and try to contact the general - his good friend who certainly would not have any trouble getting a signature from any English officer.

Daniel asked Eugene to stay with Hans in the hospital during his absence. Having a plan in place, Daniel wasted no time and headed straight to the train station.

The rumors about the death of the Führer brought tears of joy all over the world. The Allies knew that victory was right around the corner.

Already back in her beloved town in France, Nicole tried again to persuade her husband to change his mind.

"I don't want to hear anymore," Jean repeated angrily to his wife. "If I see him, I will kill him."

"You don't understand, Jean," said Nicole. "She loves him."

"He is German! German, Nicole! And he got her pregnant!" Jean reminded her. "Is that the deed of an honorable man? She must have gone mad!"

"Does that even matter now, Jean?" Nicole argued. "Look around us! Look at all the lives lost, all the suffering. We are so fortunate to still be alive. Your daughter could have been raped, hurt, or killed. You should be grateful that she is alive. We should be thankful to Hans for saving her life! And now we have a beautiful grandson …."

"As far as I'm concerned, Julian and Daniel saved her life!" stated Jean. "Julian died trying! I can't believe Francine is doing this to us."

"Haven't you heard anything I said? Hans killed a German soldier to protect Francine. Our daughter was taken as a prisoner as well, and she has survived. She fought for France and risked her own life. She is a brave and courageous woman. You are just saying these things because you're upset that she fell in love with a German man!"

"And you say that as if it's such a normal thing!" Jean yelled at her.

"I know," Nicole agreed, trying to calm him down. "I know how hard that is. I also felt the same way at first. But once you hear about what that man has done for some many people, you will …."

"Oh, now every German man is a saint! My daughter can't be with one of them. I will never accept that. And I will not see her again if she insists on this madness. She has made her choice, and so have I."

Nicole knew how stubborn her husband and daughter were. She would need some time and a lot of patience to convince him otherwise.

Eager to see her daughter and grandson again, Nicole went back to Switzerland for a quick visit. Jean would not see Francine, and Francine would not leave Switzerland without Hans. Nicole had no choice but to travel back and forth between the two countries.

But with her mother's arrival, Francine knew she could finally put her plan into action.

Francine had received Daniel's letter explaining that he had finally been able to gather enough documents and signatures to get Hans out of Germany and into Switzerland. But she didn't want to wait any longer once she found out Hans had been seriously injured. She feared for his life.

Nicole begged her daughter not to go back, but Francine had already made her decision. She took the train the very next day, leaving her children under her mother's care. She would go straight to Hans's residence, where Eugene already waited for her.

On the way back to Germany, Francine thought about everything that had happened since the beginning of that terrible war. *So much has changed in our lives… in the world!* She thought. Amidst all the misery and terror of that war, Francine and Denna somehow found some peace alongside Hans, sharing their love and pain. Those equally powerful memories would often collide with one another. It was up to Francine to decide which one would prevail. She often had relied on her son and Abraham to brighten her days.

Not being able to get much sleep the night before, she slowly closed her eyes. In her dreams, she relived talking to Hans in the coffee shop where they had first met. She saw his face when they were saying goodbye and watched him turning around the corner. She ran after him, but he vanished. She looked around desperately. She screamed out his name.

"Mademoiselle," someone gently touched Francine's shoulder, waking her up.

Francine opened her eyes, feeling alarmed. She looked around and saw some people staring at her.

"I am sorry, miss," an older lady said calmly. "You seemed to be having a bad dream."

Francine nodded, remembering the nightmare.

"I just …" she tried to say. "I feel like I have lost someone really important in my life."

"It was probably just a bad dream," the kind woman replied. "I am sure the person is all right."

Francine looked at her and smiled meekly. Then she looked out the window.

"I haven't seen him in over a year …" Francine whispered. "I know he is hurt. I don't even know if he is still …."

Francine couldn't finish her sentence.

"Well, you seem to be a brave girl. I can see that in your eyes. Look around us. All of us are carrying the scars of a war that has deeply marked us forever. But there is still one thing that can cure the pain and minimize the horrible memories which hurt us every day. And it seems to me that you have already found it."

Francine was enthralled.

"It is love that keeps us alive," the lady continued. "Love keeps us moving forward despite the absence of hope. It is love that illuminates the way, like a small light guiding us through the darkness."

Francine peeled away from the woman's face to look around. On that train, every person was somehow living their own drama. Francine wondered if they would be able to recover one day, if they would be able to feel happiness again and finally find peace.

"You are right, madam," she finally said. "It is love that can cure the hate. It is only love that can make us believe again, that gives us the strength to get up every morning, no matter how close to the impossible things can get."

"Self-love, love for another, love for life," continued the lady. "All forms of love, but love indeed."

Francine took a deep breath, looking down. "What if … what if you happen to love the one who is considered to be the enemy?"

The lady looked right at her and thought for a few seconds.

"Then you have done the hardest thing of all. You have seen through the layers, gone under the skin, deep into the heart and soul. You have understood the meaning of sublime love."

Francine truly smiled for the first time in a long while. The woman's words deeply touched her.

"It is easier when the enemy happens to be a good man," said Francine with a smile still on her face.

The lady grinned back at her and touched her hand.

"People make their own choices," the lady added. "We are so different and yet so alike. But it will always be hard for others to understand that. But it doesn't matter, as long as you know the truth."

They continued their trip in silence. Yet, ironically, on that train to Germany, Francine had heard everything she needed.

CHAPTER 49

Francine made it to Hans's house after a few inquiries. She stood in front of the door for a brief moment before knocking. Her hands were shaking. Scenes of her imprisonment, Julian's death, and her escape came rushing into her mind.

Eugene opened the door with a big smile on his face, feeling extremely happy to see her finally there.

"Francine! I'm so glad you have arrived!"

"How are you, Eugene?"

"Well, a lot better seeing you here," he admitted.

"That's good. But you look concerned. Did something else happen to Hans? Is he still at that hospital?"

As soon as Francine stepped inside, Eugene started filling her in.

"Hans recovered faster than they expected. Then, one day, I went back there, and he was gone! A nurse told me he was sent back to the prisoner's camp."

"When did that happen? I can't believe they took him back!"

"A few days ago."

"And Daniel?" she inquired. "I thought he had all the documents needed to get Hans out of that hospital."

"I haven't seen him since he left Germany," Eugene replied. "He did tell me he would be back soon, though. I guess no one was expecting Hans to be released from the hospital so fast!"

"And now he is back there alone!" said Francine, standing up and pacing the room. "They will kill him. We need to go there! Can you take me there, Eugene? Please take me to him."

"I know where the place may be. But I doubt they will let any of us in."

"We will see about that!" Francine said with conviction. "I will get in there one way or another!"

On that gray late afternoon, a heavy fog slowly covered the road and the fields around it. Francine and Eugene kept quiet the entire trip. So many different emotions passed through her mind. She had waited too long to be able to see Hans again. Her heart and soul exuberated at the anticipation of that meeting. And yet, the idea of him being hurt and alone in that awful place was horrifying.

The camp was located on the outskirts of a nearby town, in the middle of an open field. Inside its barbed wire fence, prisoners of war waited for a verdict to decide their fate. The desolation was clearly stamped on each one of their faces, making the entire place look dreadful and sinister, enough to make anyone shiver.

Once they approached, Francine's heart nearly stopped beating. That very thought of Hans being there among those soldiers made her panic.

She and Eugene walked fast toward the guard station.

"I am looking for Daniel Haswell," Francine announced bravely in French, hoping they knew who Daniel was. "We came to see Hans Schulze."

The guard looked puzzled. He had already seen too much fuss about that man named Hans.

"No one can see him without authorization," the guard said in English, as he understood very little of the French that Francine spoke.

"Daniel Haswell?" Francine asked again.

"I don't know anything about him," the guard said, shaking his head.

Francine couldn't understand English, but she understood that Daniel wasn't there.

Another guard who could speak some French heard the conversation and came over to help.

"The man you are looking for, Daniel, is not here," the guard informed her.

"Who else can I speak to?" Francine asked desperately.

"The lieutenant, Lieutenant Carter," the guard continued. "But he is not here either."

"Where can I find him?" Francine insisted, pushing for an answer.

"Possibly at the military station we set up in town."

Francine sighed, feeling frustrated.

"Merci," Francine continued with a fake smile. "I came all the way here from Switzerland to see one of your prisoners. Could you let me in? I need to find him! His life is at serious risk!"

"I am sorry, miss," said the guard. "I cannot do that. We have specific orders not to let anyone in without authorization."

"But it will be a short visit. I promise. I am French, and I was once a prisoner, too. There is a man inside those gates that helped me escape Germany. I need to see him."

"I understand it, and I am so sorry miss," the guard repeated. "C'est ne pas possible."

Francine tried telling the guards of her relationship with Hans, but they still wouldn't let her in. She insisted on his innocence.

"No one is allowed in without authorization from the lieutenant," the soldier said in his broken French.

"Francine," said Eugene. "We will have to wait for Daniel."

"But we don't know where he is right now," Francine replied, not ready to give up. "My God, how much longer do I have to wait? Hans is in there!"

Eugene understood her reaction as he felt the same way. However, he knew there was nothing else they could do. The guards were not going to let them in.

Francine took a good look at the prison camp. She felt a chill run through her body. Her hands were cold, and her heart was beating fast.

"Are you all right?" Eugene asked, concerned.

"I can't leave him here!" Francine cried. "I can't just walk away! I have to see him!"

Eugene nodded in agreement.

Suddenly, Francine spun around and headed back toward the fence, trying to find Hans.

"Hans!" she started to yell.

Eugene was about to follow her when he saw a car approaching the front gate. He saw three men quickly walking in his direction.

"Sir," the guards quickly corrected their posture upon seeing Lieutenant Carter. He had decided to accompany Daniel once they had provided all the information necessary to justify Hans's release.

"Open the gates," Lieutenant Carter commanded, noticing Eugene standing just outside of it. "And who are you?"

Eugene was about to answer when Daniel suddenly spotted Francine a few feet away.

"Is that–?" Daniel hesitated for a moment. "Francine?" Francine heard their voices and turned around, recognizing him right away. She rushed toward him.

"Daniel! I can't believe you are here!" Francine said, literally jumping into his arms.

"I could say the same about you!" he joked.

"I couldn't wait any longer!"

"So it seems!" Daniel smiled. "So, were you trying to break through the wired fence with your own bare hands?"

Francine chuckled and hugged him again.

"I am so glad you are here," she said enthusiastically. "We need to get in there and find him!"

"Come with me," said Daniel, already grabbing her hand. "We got everything we need to get him out of here!"

"So," the lieutenant spoke up, "I am assuming you are the famous Francine. And, of course, you are here to see Hans as well. All this trouble for a German man! Unbelievable!"

Francine didn't understand his words and relied on Daniel to translate them.

They all stared at the English officer as they awaited his verdict.

"It's not safe for her to come with us," Carter said to Daniel.

"Sir," Francine said in French, guessing what he was saying. "I do not fear anyone at this point."

"She really wants to get in, sir," Daniel said. "Believe me… she knows how to take care of herself!"

"I am not going to be responsible for anything that might happen here," the lieutenant threatened, clearly aggravated.

"You can come with us," Daniel confirmed, looking at her. "But, you will stay close to me. Understood?"

Francine nodded, almost in tears.

"You two soldiers, come with us!" the English lieutenant ordered, pointing at two of the guards. "Let's find Hans!"

CHAPTER 50

The sun was setting fast, cutting through the dark clouds. The heavy fog had already spread through the entire field. Francine, Daniel, Lieutenant Carter, and two other soldiers entered the secluded area.

"Stay close," Carter whispered.

All the soldiers and Daniel had their guns ready in case any incidents arose.

"Stay by my side, Francine," Daniel told her.

"Hans Schulze!" the lieutenant called. "I am looking for Hans!" he said in the little German he knew.

Their presence caught the attention of all the surrounding soldiers. Most of them remained still, simply observing the commotion. Others moved slowly with their heads down. And a few stared at them defiantly.

"Translate for me, please," the officer muttered to Daniel. "If any of you bastards attempt to do anything against us … one wrong move, and I will blow your heads off!" he screamed at the prisoners, followed by Daniel's translation.

As they furthered entered the camp, darkness had settled entirely around them. A drizzle started to fall, followed by the sounds of thunder breaking through the sky. The environment could cause chills in even the bravest of all men.

Francine looked carefully at all those soldiers, desperately trying to spot Hans.

"Hans!" Francine shouted. "C'est moi, Francine! HANS!"

There was no answer.

"Francine, stay close!" cautioned Daniel.

The rain started to fall harder against the ground, slowly turning it into the mud.

Out of desperation, Francine started to move faster among all the soldiers, calling out for Hans, inciting their curiosity as she spoke French. "Hans! Où êtes-vous?"

Trying her best to see through the fog, Francine continued to scream his name, stumbling in the thick mud. With her entire body shaking and her heart pounding uncontrollably, she had a hard time focusing. Tears started to roll down her face. She could barely see anything in front of her.

"Hans!" she kept screaming, but there was no sign of him. Instead, Francine could only find sadness and anger on the faces of those soldiers as they sat there, motionlessly.

"Francine, wait," Daniel tried to rush toward her.

On the other side of the field, Hans sat side by side with hundreds of German prisoners. Lost in his own distant thoughts, he felt and shared the desolation and hopelessness around him. His head and legs still showed signs of the serious injuries he had sustained, aggravated by his blindness.

Luckily, the soldiers who had hurt him had been removed from the camp before he was returned. But the Nazi soldier who had helped him had also been relocated. He was alone in there with no one to speak on his behalf.

Daniel and the English officer also shouted for him. "Hans Schulze! We are looking for Hans Schulze!"

It took Hans a while to recognize the sound of his own name. He slowly lifted his head as if awakening from a nightmare. He still felt very weak.

"Hans!" he heard a voice again from far away. He wondered if he was hallucinating.

Hans tried to get up, but he couldn't. He tried again and fell back down, feeling the cold mud on his hands. He simply didn't have enough strength.

"Hans!" Francine yelled desperately. "C'est moi, Francine! Please, Hans … please answer me!"

It was then that he recognized the most beautiful voice, a voice he hadn't heard in a long time but had never forgotten. *Is that … is it Francine?* he thought. The voice came closer and closer.

"Francine?" he finally whispered, trying desperately to get up again. "Francine!" Hans hollered with all the strength he could muster. He kept falling back to the ground, splashing mud all over his face. Frustrated and unable to see anything, he started crying.

Suddenly, Daniel heard a voice.

"Quiet, everyone!" he rushed to say. "I heard something. From that direction, I think." He pointed toward the West side of that camp. Francine rushed in that direction, as did everyone else. With their clothes soaking wet and shoes covered in mud, they relentlessly looked for Hans.

The rain continued to fall hard upon them as if it was trying to wash out all the sorrow and blood off that German soil. Strikes of lightning briefly illuminated that night. One could almost think that it was the end of everything they once knew right there in that field.

"Hans!" they all yelled at the same time, trying to see through the fog.

Hans could finally hear his name clearly.

Still feeling disoriented, Hans desperately moved his head toward all directions, trying to find out where those voices came from.

"Hier!" Hans was finally able to yell.

"Hans?" Francine instantly stopped. She recognized his voice.

"Stay close, Francine," Daniel insisted. "It is too dark and hard to see."

"Hier!" Hans repeated, still questioning whether he was dead or alive. It had been too long, too much waiting.

At that moment, he remembered that the Nazi soldier who helped him had given him a flashlight right before he was removed from the camp. He had told him to use it to get one of the guards' attention if someone decided to attack him again.

Hans placed his shaky hands in his pocket and reached for the flashlight. He took a good grip of it, trying to find the switch.

"Hans!" they all continued to scream out his name, trying to spot him.

Hans felt the switch at the tip of his fingers. He turned the light on.

"What is that?" Francine spotted a speck of light cutting through the fog.

Hans started to blink the light on and off. "Ich bin da!!"

"Over there!" the lieutenant said.

Francine was already running toward the light.

"Wait, Francine," called Daniel.

But Francine didn't hear a word. She started to run toward Hans.

"Hans!" she shouted.

"Francine!" Hans said, hearing her voice.

As tears rolled down his face, he placed his hands against the ground, trying to push his body up.

Gathering all the strength he had left, Hans pushed his body upward, screaming out in pain.

He breathlessly stood. He tried to take a few wobbly steps forward but stumbled on another soldier's legs.

"Get out of here." One of them pushed him away, making him fall to the ground. The flashlight rolled away from his hands.

"There he is!" Daniel exclaimed, pointing his own light at Hans.

Francine could finally see him. She frantically moved through the crowd.

"*HANS!*" Francine cried, sprinting as fast as she could. The others hurried behind her. Hans was only a few steps away from her.

Without hesitating, she let her body fall to the ground and reached out for him.

Suddenly, Hans gasped as he felt the warm touch of her body, her arms encircling him.

"Francine?" he said, holding her tightly. "Is it really you?"

"C'est moi," she said, sobbing. "C'est moi."

Unable to speak, they held each other close and cried.

Hans slowly pulled away from Francine, his hands moved toward her face, caressing it gently. He remembered its shape and every line. He felt her hair in between his fingers as tears continued to pour down his face. There had been many times when he'd been sure he would never see her again.

The others had also arrived. They were all moved, touched by the scene in front of them.

Francine reached up for his hands and kissed them repeatedly. Then, looking right at Hans's face, she smiled, "we will get you out of here."

"Francine," Hans said, choking out the words. "I …."

"I am here," she said, placing her head against his. "I am here, Hans!"

Hans smiled as he brought her closer to him, resting her head on his shoulder, promising himself he would never let her get away from him ever again.

The rain continued to fall upon them, but Hans and Francine could hear nothing else but the sound of their hearts beating fast against one another. At that moment, the world wasn't such a cruel and cold place anymore. Their love had survived through the depths of ignorance and hate.

"Help me get him out of here," the English officer finally said, feeling regret for keeping the man at the camp for so long.

Daniel, the lieutenant, and Francine helped Hans get up and walk toward the gate.

All the German soldiers stared at them as they walked away. They simply couldn't understand why those they considered to be their enemy had gone there to save a German soldier, which was what they thought Hans was.

Despite their cold hearts, they wished they were in Hans's position. They wished to be out of that hell. But they couldn't understand that most of them had never shown any compassion to anyone who wasn't part of their selective group. So, aside from their compatriots, they didn't have anyone who would speak on their behalf. They were there alone. They were receiving what they had given – absolutely nothing.

Eugene couldn't believe it when he saw Hans's face. It had been many months since that fateful morning when the Allies took him away.

"Hans!" Eugene rushed toward him. "It's me, Eugene!"

They embraced each other tightly.

"You are free, sir!" Eugene said as a few tears ran down his face.

"I can't thank you enough, Eugene! You have always been a great friend! You've never abandoned me or my family! I actually feel as if my parents are here now."

"I am sure they have been watching over you," Eugene replied.

Francine held Hans's hands. "You are safe now," she whispered in his ears. "Je t'aime!"

He held her against his chest, placing a gentle kiss on her wet hair.

"Je t'aime, Francine," he said, feeling as if he were living a dream. "And I will always love you."

Daniel and Eugene helped Hans inside their vehicle.

"Thank you, sir," Francine genuinely said as she told the lieutenant goodbye.

"Take care, miss," Lieutenant Carter said, feeling a lot better now that it was all over and everything had worked out.

As the officer watched their cars drive away, he couldn't help but shake his head. "Well, that's something you don't see every day," the officer commented.

"And what's that, sir?" the guard asked.

"Friendship and love that goes beyond hate," he said. "That man, that German man, is still our enemy."

Francine sighed in relief and rested her head on Hans's shoulder as the car finally pulled away. It was hard to believe they were finally together!

They stopped at Hans's house to get a few of his things before departing to Switzerland.

"Do you think we will ever come back one day?" Eugene asked Hans.

"I don't think Francine would be happy here," Hans replied, shaking his head.

"Are you going back to France after Switzerland?" Daniel asked them.

It was Francine's turn to reply. "No, probably not. I don't think it would be a good place for Hans."

"I will send someone to take care of the house until we decide what to do," Hans said. "My parents and Denna will always be a part of it."

"I could always stay here, sir," replied Eugene.

"Of course not, Eugene! You are part of our family!"

As they were preparing to leave the house, Hans knew he had to do one more thing. He held Francine's hand as they walked together to the backyard. They stood there in silence for a few minutes.

"Denna," Hans said tearfully after saying goodbye to his parents, "I will leave Germany now …" Hans stopped briefly, trying to hold off his tears. "I know I promised you … I promised we would always be together. I will not break that promise. I will take you with me in my memory and my heart. I love you, cousin, and I will take care of your son as if he were my own."

Hans leaned forward and placed his hands on the ground. Francine placed a flower on her grave.

"I'm so sorry," Hans said, still feeling the pain of her death in his heart. "I am so sorry!"

Francine held his hand tightly.

Above them, a few stars shone in between the dark clouds. So much had happened through those last years. They carried the weight of everything that had been lost in their hearts and souls, sad memories that will never be erased.

A few minutes later, they all walked out of the Schulzes' house together, ready to leave Germany. Their vehicles headed straight to the train station.

"How could I ever thank all of you?" Hans asked emotionally.

"There is no need for that, Hans," Daniel said, shaking his hand. "The way I see it, we also have to thank you for all you have done here. You saved Francine's life. And you have done a lot more than meets the eye from what we were told!"

Hans smiled.

"Take care of Francine," Daniel continued. "But be careful; she can be extremely stubborn!"

They all laughed.

"I know you are in good hands," Daniel said to Francine as they embraced.

"We will see each other again soon!" she replied, feeling immensely grateful. "Merci, merci beaucoup mon ami!"

They said their goodbyes. Daniel would stay in Germany, as he still had a lot of work there. The war in Europe was over, but he had a new assignment to identify and locate all Nazi officers!

A few hours later, holding each other's hands, Francine and Hans, along with Eugene, walked across the border; they had finally made it into Switzerland … together!

CHAPTER 51

Hans woke up after sleeping for almost an entire day. Francine had been there by his side the whole time.

"Hans?" she called his name softly.

Hans smiled once he heard Francine's voice. He still couldn't believe he was at his home in Switzerland with Francine by his side.

"Are we dreaming?" he asked her. "Is this real?"

Francine kissed him deeply before placing her head on his chest.

"I can hear your heart beating," she said. "If this is a dream, then it is the most beautiful dream, and I don't want to wake up!"

They heard a knock at the door.

"Come in," said Francine.

The door opened swiftly, and a child entered the room, running toward his mother.

"Julian," Francine said, full of love, as she grabbed him up into her arms.

Hans sat up, speechless.

Nicole stood in the doorway, watching the scene with tears in her eyes.

"Julian," Francine started, trying not to cry, "this is your father … Hans."

Julian looked at Hans and smiled shyly.

"Why don't you go give your daddy a kiss?" Francine could barely say it through joyful tears.

Julian jumped out of his mother's lap and walked over to Hans. He placed a small kiss on his cheek and waited.

Hans smiled and tried very hard not to cry. He placed his hands in the air, searching for Julian's face. He touched his little face and his arms.

"Can I have a hug now?" Hans asked him gently.

Before Francine could help him, Julian jumped onto the bed and into Hans's arms.

Hans held his son to his chest. He couldn't hold back the tears anymore.

Julian looked at him curiously as his little fingers tried to catch Hans's tears.

Hans wiped his face quickly, trying not to scare his son.

"Daddy is very happy," Hans replied reassuringly, messing with Julian's hair. "Daddy couldn't be any happier! I waited a long time for this moment."

The child giggled at him, nodding in agreement without fully understanding what he said and very amused with Hans's slight accent when speaking French.

"What is that?" the child asked, pointing at the bruises on Hans's face.

"Well, daddy …" Hans wasn't sure what to say. "It was too dark, and …" Hans didn't want to lie. "Daddy fell down and got hurt."

Julian placed his little hands on Hans's bruises. Hans took his son's hands in his own and kissed them.

"So," Hans changed the subject, shaking the tears away, "I've heard you are a very clever boy!"

Julian nodded. "Oui!" the child said, making them all laugh.

"Grandma," Julian said. "Cookies!"

They laughed again, happy to be all together.

"Salut, Hans," Nicole said, looking at Hans's deep resemblance to her grandson. "He is clearly your son, I see! The same hair, the same smile … everything!"

Hans smiled, still not quite believing what was actually happening.

"It is a pleasure to meet you, Madame."

"I bet you love cookies, too?" Nicole said, trying to make everyone stop crying. Julian had already jumped back into her arms.

"All cookies," Hans agreed, smiling. "My mother had to hide them really well when I was a child."

"That sounds familiar," Nicole said, tickling her grandson.

Francine laughed, placing her hands on Hans's arm.

"Welcome home!" said Nicole genuinely to her future son-in-law.

"Merci!" Hans responded gratefully. "And where's Abraham? Can I hold him?"

"I will bring him," Nicole said.

Once Hans felt Abraham in his arms, a big smiled stretched across his face. He was safe there, just as Denna would have wanted.

"He is doing very well," said Francine. "Julian loves him already."

"Your mother was an amazing woman and friend," Hans told him with a sad tone in his voice. "Just like her, you are now part of our family. I will watch over you, always."

The sunset displayed a bright orange-pink glow in the sky, making that cool September afternoon even more beautiful. The soft breeze carried the sounds of violins announcing the bride had arrived.

Francine walked carefully through the backyard, wearing a long, off-the-shoulder pearl-colored lace gown with her hair held up by an ornated shiny beaded pin.

She stood before the improvised white carpet that would lead her toward Hans while the sunrays shone against her teary eyes. Francine looked straight at her beloved soon-to-be husband. Suddenly, she felt as if the two of them were transported to that café in Switzerland, a long time ago, when they first met. Hans's blue eyes still worked as a mirror, reflecting the warmth and all his love straight into Francine's heart. Flashbacks of those past years rushed through her mind. So much had happened, and yet, right there in the Schulze's backyard, Francine was living her dream.

Sharing the same emotions, on the other side of the yard, Hans tried to stand still. He could sense Francine's presence.

"She is here!" Daniel whispered to him.

Hans smiled. With his heart beating faster and faster, he could feel the tears filling up his eyes. Yes, he could see her through the eyes of his soul. He remembered the first time he saw her at that café years ago. He remembered every detail, the perfect shape of her lips, her mesmerizing green eyes, and the sweet sound of her voice. How could he ever forget that very moment when he first saw her?

Nicole held Abraham in her arms as little Julian followed right behind Francine, holding their wedding rings. Francine looked back at her son and smiled. Dressed up in a tiny tuxedo, Julian looked like an angel.

As she slowly walked down the aisle, red rose petals were thrown at her. She looked at every one of their friends' faces who came for the small wedding. She knew that each one of them represented an essential part of her story with Hans. Daniel, along with his fiancée Angela, Pierre, Marie, Frederick, Clarice, Fernand, Eugene, Victoria, and her aunt, all shared their happiness.

At last, Hans held Francine's hands between his.

The sunset projected its last rays of light against the soon-to-be-married couple.

After the priest pronounced the last words, Hans reached out for her. He caressed her face gently, feeling her tears on his fingertips. Francine closed her eyes the very moment his lips touched hers. There were no words to describe what they meant to one another, the profound love they shared.

Among claps of joy, the couple prepared for a family photo. Hans held Abraham, while Francine held Julian, and Nicole stood next to them. They smiled sincerely, and with a quick click of the camera, their happiness was immortalized.

A few days later, Nicole was ready to go back to France to be with Jean, who decided against being part of their wedding. But, as for Nicole, she was happy to know that Hans was finally there for her daughter.

"My father," Francine told Nicole before she left, "I know he will never accept …"

"The war is over in Europe now," Nicole reassured her daughter. "Just give it some time. I'm sure he will come around."

Francine smiled weakly and shrugged. But she knew her father too well to know that wouldn't be the case.

"I will see you in France on Christmas!" confirmed Nicole.

"Mother," Francine replied, still worrying. "As much as I want to see Father, my friends, and my country … I can't leave Hans."

"Who said Hans couldn't come along? He is your husband now."

"But people there …" Francine hesitated. "It is still too soon. I don't want him to be mistreated."

"He is part of our family now," Nicole affirmed, kissing her daughter on the forehead. "No matter what anyone says."

"They might not allow him to enter France," Francine pointed out.

"We will see about that!" Nicole promised.

Christmas soon arrived. All over the world, people wondered how they could pick up the pieces of their shattered lives and make something out of nothing after the war. Many of them had lost everything they had. Many of them had no one left in their family. They wondered how they would be able to go on, haunted by all those horrible memories. There was still a lot of pain, a lot to grieve over.

Francine, Hans, Eugene, and the kids finally arrived in France. Francine's heartbeat accelerated as soon as she stepped foot on French soil. "It has been years!" she said, looking everywhere around with joy.

Once Francine and Hans got out of the car, Francine stood silently and stared at her house. She could hardly believe she was back.

Julian ran toward a man on the corner, taking care of the garden.

Jean looked at the little boy approaching him. He knew he had to be his grandson. He breathed in deeply, pretending he wasn't moved.

"What is that?" Julian asked him in French, catching his attention.

"A very special plant. I am removing it from this spot and placing it over there!" Jean said, pointing at the other side of the garden.

Francine held Abraham in her arms with Hans by her side. They both stood back, listening to the conversation. Hans knew Jean didn't want to see his daughter because of him.

"Are you my Grandpa?" the child asked, catching Jean off guard.

Jean looked over at his daughter, and then, he took a good look at Hans. A smile spread across his face as he looked back at Julian, "well, I guess I am."

"Grandpa!" Julian continued. "I want to help you with the plants."

Jean crouched down to be at the same height as the child.

"It is hard work," he said, staring at his grandson.

"I like that," Julian quickly replied, smiling and already grabbing his grandfather's tools from the ground.

Jean looked over at Francine and Hans one more time. Nicole was already watching from the window.

"Your eyes," Jean said, looking back at his grandson. "They are the same shape as your mother's."

"Grandma said that, too," Julian said, making Jean chuckle.

Nicole opened the door slowly.

"Grandma!" Julian said, running toward her.

Jean looked at that scene and felt remorse for not seeing his grandchild before.

"Well," Jean continued, "it is getting too cold out here. Why don't we all get inside?"

Julian came rushing back toward him.

"What about the plants, Grandpa?" he said impatiently. "I want to play now."

"And the same attitude as your mother, too!" Jean affirmed, making everyone laugh again.

"Let me hold Abraham," Hans said, making sure he spoke French.

"Why don't we get some chocolat chaud, and then we can come back outside?" Nicole asked, wiping off the tears from her face.

Julian nodded happily.

"Father …" Francine said as she walked toward him. "I am sorry. I am so sorry!"

"It is all right, my girl," Jean soothed, pulling her close in an embrace. "It is all right."

"I love you, dad!" Francine said, holding him tenderly.

Jean quickly wiped off the tears that stubbornly rolled down his face. He looked back at Hans for a few seconds, still stunned he was standing so close to a man he still considered to be his enemy.

"Grandpa!" Julian said, grabbing his hand. "This is my father. He looks just like me!"

Hans smiled at that comment. He always liked when Julian said that.

"Can he help us with the plants, too?" Julian insisted.

"If he wants to," said Jean. "Yes."

"It is very nice to finally meet you, sir," Hans said, offering out a handshake.

Jean stood there for a few seconds. He wasn't sure what to do. Francine placed her hand on Jean's shoulder.

Jean looked at Hans, holding a Jewish child with his other arm. He slowly walked toward him and finally shook Hans's hand.

"I never thought I would be able to say this," Jean said as his grandson held his other hand. "Welcome to our home, Hans!"

Jean looked at Eugene and shook his hand as well. "Come on in, everyone."

They all entered the house together.

They spent several days in France. Francine had the opportunity to see most of her friends at the hospital and others who had also made it through the war alive.

Hans couldn't go to most places with Francine. Some said it wasn't safe for him to walk around. It was too soon for any of the townspeople to see a German man again. Francine noticed a few of her neighbors and even some old friends were giving her the cold shoulder. She knew it was because she was married to Hans. She only hoped that with time, their hearts and souls would heal.

CHAPTER 52

A few days later, and already back in their house in Switzerland, Hans and Francine started to put their plan into action – a program to help families in need, victims of the war. They bought another house that served as a shelter and information center for anyone who needed help, despite their race, nationality, or background.

Then the days turned into months until an unexpected knock at the door brought them another surprise.

Eugene rushed to the door, curious to see who it was.

"Who is there?" he asked without opening the door. They were still very cautious as Hans still feared that Carson would come to take Abraham away from them one day. But Carson was never found. He was presumed dead until rumors spread about him escaping to Argentina.

"My name is Abraham," a voice politely replied.

Eugene opened the door just enough to take a quick peek.

"I don't recognize him, sir," Eugene told Hans, who was already next to him.

"May I ask who you are looking for?" Hans asked him promptly after opening the door.

"My name is Abraham Cohen, sir. You don't know me, but I was a friend of Denna's, and … I am looking for a man named Hans."

"Abraham?" Hans said, startled. *Did I hear this right? Could he be?* Hans thought.

"Yes, you may have already heard of me," Abraham rushed to explain. "As I mentioned, I was Denna's friend, and after looking for her for a long time, someone directed me to this place."

Hans stood astonished by what he heard. Francine rushed to the door to see who it was.

"Are you all right?" Francine asked Hans, noticing how pale he was.

Hans nodded his head. "I'm all right," Hans said, holding her hand.

Francine stared at that man, who was elegantly dressed but whose eyes emoted a lot of sadness.

"I don't mean to cause you any trouble, Madam. My name is Abraham Cohen," the man said anxiously. "I am looking for Hans Schulze."

"Yes, I am sorry," Hans said, still shocked. "I believe I am the person you are looking for. Did you say the name Denna?"

"Yes, sir …. Denna."

Francine instantly understood who the man was. Hans had told her everything that happened to Denna. She squeezed Hans's hand tighter.

"Well, it is very nice to meet you, Abraham. This is my wife, Francine, and over here, my friend Eugene," Hans finally said.

"It is a pleasure to meet you all," Abraham replied, with tears in his eyes. "I don't know how much you know about me, but Denna and I were to be engaged."

"Please, come in," Francine said as everyone stood still. "This way, please. Eugene, would you be so kind as to ask Victoria to make us some tea?"

Abraham never looked away from Hans. He couldn't believe he had finally found him. It had taken him over a year to be able to track Hans down. But now that he had, he didn't know where to start. "Sir … I …."

"Please, there is no need for formalities between us."

"Thank you … Hans. I have heard so many stories about you and your family. I have come here to thank you, although nothing I can ever say could express my deepest gratitude. What you have done for my Denna, what you …" Abraham began to cry. "I am sorry. It is still so painful."

Hans felt tears fill his eyes as well.

"I tried, but I couldn't …" Hans said, looking down to catch his breath. "I couldn't save her!"

"But, sir, Hans …" Abraham rushed to say. "What you did for her is beyond words. You took care of her."

Victoria entered the room, placing the tray of tea on the coffee table.

"I hope you will stay with us for supper," Francine said, standing up. "I will leave you two alone for a moment and …."

Before Francine could finish her sentence, Julian rushed into the living room, holding little Abraham's hand.

"Abraham," Francine said to the young child. "Why don't you come over here and say hello?"

Abraham robotically got up from his chair and looked at the child. His eyes had the same shape and color as Denna's. He was aware that she died during childbirth.

Hans sat silently, paying close attention to what they were saying.

"Hello," Abraham said, kneeling with tears in his eyes. "My name is Abraham as well."

The small child smiled up at him.

"You look so much like her," Abraham could barely finish his sentence.

Abraham touched the child's tiny hands. A mix of different emotions stirred his soul. He felt as if Denna was right there with him.

Abraham got up, trying to hide the tears coming down his face.

Francine approached their new friend and placed her hands on his shoulders.

"We are very sorry," she said. "Denna was a very special person."

Hans nodded, feeling his heart ache as older memories resurfaced so vividly in his mind.

"I appreciate your kindness, Madam. I was placed in a concentration camp with some of my family members. We were kept there for almost two years. One could never forget …."

"I am so sorry," Hans blurted out. "I wish I could make up for it somehow. I still feel so ashamed of everything that has happened, everything the Nazi Germans did …."

Abraham looked at Hans. "You are not like them. It is not your fault."

Those words had a deep impact on Hans's emotions. He appreciated it even more coming from Abraham.

"I only have to thank you, sir!" repeated Abraham. He turned back around and stood in silence for a few seconds.

"I don't know how to say this … but there is also something else that brought me here," he said, looking again at Denna's son. "I don't know if I have the right, but … what the few members remaining in my family would like to do … well, we would like to request …."

"To take Abraham with you?" Hans asked, already guessing what he wanted to say.

"I am sorry," Abraham rushed to explain. "I don't know how to say it. I have nothing left, sir, besides an aunt and uncle who had escaped earlier in the war. I have lost my parents, siblings, grandparents, cousins … so many of us have died, basically everyone. But worst of all, I have lost the love of my life. And now I look at little Abraham and … I think … I think about her, Denna …."

Hans felt his heart tear apart. He couldn't think about ever being away from the little boy who he considered his own son. But somehow, he knew Denna would want Abraham to take care of the child. She would like him to be raised according to her own beliefs.

Francine walked toward Hans and held his hands. She also wasn't sure what to do or say.

"Why don't you spend a few weeks—or even a few months—with us here," Hans told him. "Take your time, and then we will see what happens. The child needs to get used to you and, well, maybe you can live near us and … we will see …!"

Hans couldn't finish his words. It wouldn't be an easy thing for them to do. But he also knew that was the right thing to do. Hans couldn't see the tears rolling down Abraham's face as well as Francine's.

At that moment, they all felt as if Denna were right there among them, smiling, as a strange force that bound them together. Francine looked at Hans, her children, and their new friend, and she understood it all. Perhaps they all did. Somehow, by managing to survive, they had started to see life in a way that they had never seen before. They felt what only those who had gone through such a long period of pain, loss, and suffering could understand – a feeling so deep, so powerful.

And so, they went on living their lives, cherishing every moment together. They kept the memories of those who were gone surviving within them.

True love resists the uncertainties of time … it resists the temptations of distance, the suffering of wars, and the cruelties born out of hate. True love overcomes everything. It is as infinite as light, shining, moving, and breaking through the darkness.